MOUNTAIN PROTECTORS

LISA JACKSON

B.J. DANIELS

ISBN-13: 978-1-335-01385-9

Mountain Protectors

Copyright © 2018 by Harlequin Books S.A.

The publisher acknowledges the copyright holders of the individual works as follows:

Innocent by Association
Copyright © 1985 by Lisa Jackson

Montana Royalty
Copyright © 2008 by Barbara Heinlein

Recycling programs
for this product may
not exist in your area.

This edition published by arrangement with Harlequin Books S.A.

For questions and comments about the quality of this book, please contact us at CustomerService@Harlequin.com.

® and TM are trademarks of the publisher. Trademarks indicated with ® are registered in the United States Patent and Trademark Office, the Canadian Intellectual Property Office and in other countries.

HARLEQUIN®
www.Harlequin.com

Printed in U.S.A.

CONTENTS

INNOCENT BY ASSOCIATION

Lisa Jackson

1

ANOTHER SCANDAL WOULD surely ruin her.

Megan shuddered, not from the cold, but from the sudden premonition of what was to come.

She could feel her teeth clenching together in determination, and her graceful jaw hardened almost imperceptibly as she realized that everything she had worked so painstakingly to accomplish was about to go down the drain.

The door opened. Megan managed a confident smile as she brushed a wayward wisp of copper-streaked hair out of her eyes and concentrated on the small, wiry man entering the prestigious office of the president of McKearn Investments.

She studied the intense expression on the face of Henry Silvas as the balding accountant rubbed his thin shock of white hair. From the deep furrow on Henry's forehead, Megan sensed trouble. More trouble than she had at first suspected. She had to fight to keep her shoulders from sagging as she met Henry's disturbed gaze.

"Evening," Henry muttered, removing his overcoat and taking a seat on the opposite side of the desk. He settled uncomfortably into the expensive wing chair and smiled tightly. "Where's the rest of the crew?"

"Everyone left at five tonight," Megan explained. "I thought it would be best if I saw you alone."

Silvas nodded and opened his briefcase. "Good idea."

A shiver of dread ran up Megan's spine. She frowned. "I assume that means that you have bad news."

Henry Silvas's small face puckered thoughtfully. "That remains to be seen." He shook his head as if he had encountered the first financial puzzle of his life that he hadn't been able to piece together.

"What do you mean?" Megan crossed her arms over her chest, leaned back in her chair and observed the small man with the reputation for being as sharp as the pencils he used. Henry Silvas was the best accountant Denver had to offer. His fee was stiff, but he was worth every cent. A no-nonsense individual known for his accuracy, Henry left no stone unturned in his audits of financial records. Megan's father had trusted Henry in the past, and Henry had proved himself to be worth his weight in gold.

"I mean that nothing in the internal workings of your office seems out of the ordinary...at least at first look."

"I know that much," Megan stated cautiously as she absently smoothed her sleek auburn hair away from her face. She could feel the hesitancy in the accountant's words.

Henry managed a thin smile and looked appreciatively into Megan's astute gaze. "And that's why you called me," he concluded with a shrewd smile.

Megan nodded, silently encouraging him to continue. Henry withdrew a cigar and rolled it between his thick fingers. "You don't miss much, do you, Meg?"

Her stern lips lifted a little at the corners. Henry Silvas wasn't one to hand out compliments casually. "I hope not," she admitted. "Now, tell me what you found." Before he could respond, she lifted her chin and cautioned him. "And don't pull any punches."

Henry's small dark eyes looked through thick glasses and studied the concern evidenced on Megan's face. Two points of color highlighted her cheekbones, and her smooth forehead was drawn into a concentrated frown. "Something bothers me," he admitted as he struck a match and held it to the end of the cigar.

"I knew it." Inclining her head, she met his worried gaze without any outward sign of the defeat she felt forming in the pit of her stomach. "What did you find?"

"Nothing I could put my finger on," Henry conceded with a shake of his balding head. "All of the books seem to be in perfect order...and the clients' accounts look good..."

"What then?" She had already guessed the answer but wanted his confirmation of the situation.

"It's some of the activity in the accounts," Henry replied with a frown. "It's good...maybe too good." His wise eyes narrowed into shrewd slits.

"I understand." Nervously, she ran her fingers along the gleaming oaken edge of her desk. "I trust you've got the proof to confirm your theory."

"Look at these." Henry extracted computer printouts from his briefcase. Megan recognized the names of the account holders on the September statements. A couple of the accounts were very large. Megan groaned inwardly, though she had expected the worst.

As Megan scanned the thick stack of statements, she noticed red marks with notations of dates on a few of the most lucrative trades. "What are these?" she asked solemnly while reaching for her glasses and studying Henry's notes. Her fingers skipped from one red mark on the paper to the next.

Henry retrieved an envelope of newspaper clippings from his briefcase and without comment handed the yellowed articles to the winsome president of McKearn Investments. Megan's clear gray eyes skimmed the clippings knowledgeably. Across each newspaper article, Henry had scrawled an angry red date. "Date of publication?" Megan asked without lifting her eyes from the incriminating scraps of paper.

"Uh-huh."

Adjusting her reading glasses on her nose, Megan reread each of the clippings before comparing them to the statements of her clients. "All the articles are from the *Denver Financial Times*," she murmured to herself. Henry nodded thoughtfully and puffed on his cigar as the meaning of the evidence became clear to her. "These trades were made two days before the columns appeared in the paper." She took off her glasses, set them on the desk and pinched the bridge of her nose as she thought.

"You expected this, didn't you?"

"Yes," she whispered. "I just hoped that it wasn't true." A headache was beginning to throb at her temples. "Who was the broker?" she asked calmly, reopening her eyes. The look she gave Henry was coldly professional.

"George Samples," Henry supplied.

Megan nodded, having anticipated the accountant's response. "So he was in cahoots with someone at the *Times*, got the information before publication, made his trades and..."

"...made a helluva lot of money for his clients."

"And himself as well, I'd venture to guess." Megan's eyes narrowed speculatively. "This is going to cause an incredible scandal," she predicted. "That's something I'd rather avoid."

"Because of your father's health?"

"That's one reason," Megan allowed. Her intelligent eyes searched the face of the small man sitting uncomfortably across from her. Henry lifted his eyebrows over the wire rims of his glasses.

"This is one helluva mess, Meg."

"You're telling me."

"It won't be long until the SEC gets wind of it."

Megan caught her lower lip between her teeth. Her thoughts were racing wildly through her mind. "I know." She released a disgusted sigh and rose from her chair. "I just need a little time to break the news to Dad."

Henry frowned and shook his graying head. "Impossible. You'll have to take this to the SEC immediately. Your reputation, along with McKearn Investments', is at stake, you know." He considered the ash on the end of his cigar. "As for Samples, you've got no choice but to fire him."

"Gladly," Megan replied. George Samples had been a thorn in her side ever since her father's retirement.

"I'm sorry about all this, Meg."

"So am I."

Henry frowned at the printouts. "I did some checking," he said quietly.

"More?" Her black brows rose inquisitively.

"More than I had to...but I felt that I should because of everything your father did for me."

Megan nodded. The long-standing relationship between her father and Henry Silvas had spanned nearly twenty turbulent years.

"I took the liberty of checking out these accounts—the ones with the illegal trades."

"And what did you find?" For the first time since Henry had entered the room, Megan was uneasy. So far, she had suspected everything his audit confirmed. But the look in his myopic eyes gave her pause. There was more—something that didn't jibe with the rest.

"That's what bothers me," Henry confided. "There are only nine accounts involved, and from what I can gather, eight of the accounts are directly related to Samples—close friends, his fiancée and even a dummy account that I suspect belongs to Samples himself."

"But...?" Megan prodded, sifting through the papers scattered on the desk.

"The ninth one doesn't seem to fit." Henry stubbed out his cigar and retrieved the statement in question from his briefcase. He handed it to Megan.

Megan's breath caught in her throat and her heart seemed to drop to the floor. "Garrett Reaves," she murmured, reading from the front page of the statement. "You think he's involved?" Her gray eyes fastened on the worried face of the accountant, and somehow she managed to hide the fact that her poise was breaking into tiny fragments of the past.

Henry shrugged. "It looks that way."

"But why would Reaves be involved in anything like this? It doesn't make a lot of sense," she muttered, trying to consider the problem from a purely professional point of view and ignore the turbulent storm of emotions raging within her. Megan forced herself to appear indifferent despite the shadowed memories that threatened to distort her objectivity. She had to forget the solitary black weekend filled with raging storms of passion and pain...

"Why not?"

"Reaves Chemical is a very profitable organization," Megan pointed out, though her throat constricted at the memory of his betrayal three long years ago.

Henry seemed skeptical. He tented his fingers as he thought. "But Mr. Reaves doesn't own all of the stock."

"True, but—"

"And his divorce cost him a bundle."

Megan's dignity faltered for a heart-stopping instant. "That's only hearsay," she responded defensively.

Henry squinted and studied the condemning printout. "Maybe," he acknowledged.

"But you don't think so," she prodded, stifling the urge to shudder.

"Let's just say, I think it's highly coincidental." Henry heaved a worried sigh. "The thing of it is that one of the newspaper articles was on Reaves Chemical stock. Mr. Reaves made nearly a hundred thousand dollars on that trade alone."

"That's not unreasonable. He does control a large block of shares. He's a wealthy man." Why was she protecting him? After all of the torture, why would she be so foolish as to try to defend him?

"You think!"

"It's common knowledge," Megan replied, wondering at her uncharacteristic desire to protect his reputation. Garrett Reaves was a bastard, and by all reasonable accounts she should hate him.

In the few months since she had taken over as president of McKearn Investments, Garrett Reaves hadn't made an appearance at the small brokerage. But that was to be expected, considering the circumstances. Garrett didn't want to see her any more than she wanted to confront him. At Jed McKearn's request, when he had retired, George Samples had been given the lucrative Reaves account. And Megan had no reason to think that Garrett Reaves was unhappy with the situation.

Until now.

"Then why did he sell short on his own company's stock?" the feisty accountant demanded. "It just doesn't make much sense...unless maybe he was involved in this scam. It's not common practice for the majority stockholder to speculate on his own company's stock—and some of George's other 'special' accounts have made out on this same trade."

"I can't answer that one," Megan allowed reluctantly.

"And I'm willing to bet that our friend Mr. Reaves can't either."

"He's been out of the country for nearly a year…"

Henry's bushy gray brows quirked. "Not all of the time. From what I understand, the chemical plant in Japan is just about operational." He paused thoughtfully, for dramatic effect. "And it wouldn't be the first time that an executive issued orders for something illegal from foreign soil."

"I suppose you're right," she conceded with a reluctant shrug of her shoulders. Henry's logic was impossible to refute. "But it's hard for me to think of him as a crook."

"I know." Henry's small eyes softened. "Reaves was close to Patrick." At the mention of her brother's name, Megan stiffened and her face paled. The sudden change in her bearing wasn't lost on the accountant. Henry's soft palms turned upward. "Look, Meg, there's a chance that Reaves isn't involved in this mess…but it's a slim one. And you can't afford to wait to find out. Leave that up to the SEC and save your neck, for Pete's sake. If Reaves is innocent, he'll be able to prove it. Right now you have a duty and an obligation to the rest of your clients…as well as to your father."

"Then you think I should call Ted Benson."

Henry nodded at the mention of the attorney's name. "If you can't get through to Benson, talk to one of his partners, but you'd better do it before the SEC comes breathing down your neck. Let the lawyers battle it out."

As Megan saw the situation, she had no choice. If only Garrett weren't involved. From her standing position, she reached for the phone, just barely managing to hide the fact that her hands were beginning to shake. "Thanks, Henry," she said with a tight smile.

"Don't thank me," he replied. "You're in for the fight of your life." Henry noticed the flicker of sadness in her large gray eyes, and he hated himself for being the one who'd had to confirm her suspicions.

"Don't I know it," she whispered as she removed her earring and balanced the phone on her shoulder before dialing the law offices of Benson and Tate. "God, I hate to do this," she murmured, thinking of a thousand reasons, mostly concerning Garrett Reaves, to put off the call.

Henry left the reports on the desk and snapped his briefcase closed. "I'll talk to you later in the week," he said as he rose from the chair and walked out of the room. Megan watched as the heavy wooden door closed silently behind his wiry form.

No one answered at the law firm. Megan replaced the receiver and removed her reading glasses. She shivered as if from a sudden blast of cold air. "Why, Garrett?" she wondered aloud as she stood away from the desk and placed her arms protectively across her breasts.

Darkness had begun to shadow the city as the vivid image of the one man she had vowed to hate raced wantonly through her mind. How long had it been since she'd last seen him—a year?

As the painful memories resurfaced, she pressed her lips together in determination and reached for the phone. Forcing her thoughts away from Garrett, she dialed the offices of Benson and Tate again. After nine rings, a gruff-sounding legal assistant answered the phone and promised to have Ted Benson return Megan's call.

"That's that," Megan whispered to herself as she hung up and stared sightlessly out of the window. Dusk had begun to settle over Denver, and the brilliant lights of the Sixteenth

Street Mall began to illuminate that section of the mile-high city. From her position on the eighth floor of the Jefferson Tower, Megan had a panoramic view of the business district. But neither the city nor the shadowy Rocky Mountains in the distance held any interest for her tonight.

With a weary sigh, she tapped her fingers restlessly on the cool windowpane. "Dear Lord, Garrett, I hope you're not involved in this mess," Megan whispered before turning out the lights and locking the doors of the office.

2

THE BOARD OF directors of McKearn Investments had begrudgingly appointed Megan to fill the vacant position of president of the small brokerage house. At the time, no one had suspected that Jed McKearn's condition would deteriorate, and the stodgy members of the board, along with Megan herself, had believed that Jed would soon return to oversee the operation.

With only a few grumblings and undisguised looks of disapproval, the board members had unanimously accepted Jed's proposal to let Megan sit in her father's prestigious office and helm the course of McKearn Investments. After all, it was only temporary, and Megan had paid her dues. An MBA. from Stanford and three years as Jed's assistant gave her all the credibility she needed, and it didn't hurt that her last name happened to be McKearn.

If she had followed her own instincts and let George Samples go six months ago, she possibly could have avoided the scandal that Henry Silvas had uncovered. She called herself every kind of fool for not striding out of that initial board meeting and resigning on the spot. The presidency had been granted her with a burdensome restriction: Every major decision within the company had to be approved by her father. And now she was paying for it.

As Megan leaned against the cool panes of the office window the morning after her meeting with Henry Silvas, her small hands curled into fists of frustration and she rapped one soundly on the frosted glass. How could she have let this happen? She closed her eyes in disgust. And to think that Garrett Reaves might be involved. Her stomach knotted painfully when she considered the fact that Garrett's name was tied into the scam. Was he part of the swindle—or an innocent victim? Henry's evidence strongly suggested that Garrett had taken a chance—and gotten caught. It wouldn't be the first time.

The news would kill her father.

Last night, after hearing Henry's report, Megan had visited her parents. However, she had been unable to broach the subject of the scam with her father; Jed had suffered a tiring day at the clinic. Megan's mother, after tearfully confiding to her daughter that Jed's condition seemed to worsen with each passing day, had asked Megan not to disturb him. Megan had respected her mother's wishes and had postponed telling Jed about Henry Silvas's audit. All in all, it had been a lousy day that had darkened into a long, sleepless night.

Megan didn't expect this morning to be much of an improvement.

George Samples breezed into the room with his usual swagger, and somehow Megan managed a tight smile for his benefit.

"You wanted to see me?" he asked, nervously rubbing his fingers along his jaw and touching the corners of his thin, clipped moustache as he dropped into one of the side chairs near the window.

Megan took her chair on the opposite side of the desk.

She didn't mince words. "Henry Silvas came to see me last evening."

George looked expectant. Megan could almost hear the *so what?* forming in the young broker's cagey mind.

"He brought these with him." Megan slid the marked copies of the September statements and the faded clippings from the *Denver Financial Times* across the oak surface of the desk.

George retrieved the evidence indifferently before shrugging his shoulders and adjusting the crease in one of the legs of his tailored wool slacks. "What's all this?" His gold eyes slid down the clippings without interest.

"It's proof of a scam, George," Megan began, and then, very patiently, never allowing her white-hot temper to surface, she told him about her meeting with Henry Silvas.

She attempted to give George the benefit of the doubt and allow him to present his side of the story, but George refused to answer her questions rationally. As she spoke, she noticed the flush of anger rise on George's face.

When Megan painstakingly explained the evidence mounting against him, the brash young broker lost the thin thread of control he had over his volatile temper.

"You've been planning this from the first day you took over your old man's job," George accused, his thin lips drawing into an insolent line. His legs were crossed and his right foot was bouncing erratically while his surging rage got the better of him. "This story about a scam is just an excuse to get rid of me!"

Megan's steadfast gray eyes never wavered, not for an instant. What George was suggesting was ridiculous. They both knew it. "You know me better than that, George," she insisted quietly.

"Henry Silvas has a reputation for destroying people,"

George returned with a narrowing gaze. "Boy, have you been conned. I wonder who Silvas is covering up for?"

Megan shook her head slowly, and her round, gray eyes remained clear. "I studied the audit—"

"Sure you did," George scoffed.

A light rap on the door interrupted Megan's response as Jenny, the receptionist, poked her head into the room. "I'm sorry to bother you," the young girl apologized, "but Ted Benson is on line one."

At the mention of the attorney's name, George visibly paled. Until then, he had thought that Megan was bluffing.

Megan noticed George's discomfort. "That's all right, Jenny. I'll take the call," Megan said to the girl, signaling an end to her meeting with George.

Jenny escaped from the strained room, and Megan's hand paused expectantly over the telephone receiver. Her intense gray eyes looked into the wrathful expression of George Samples. The young man's brow was creased with anger and worry. Small beads of perspiration had collected in the thin strands of his reddish moustache. His small gold eyes were shadowed in dark circles and they darted frantically from Megan to the telephone and back again.

"So this is it?" he demanded, using a new tack, hoping to appeal to the kinder side of her nature. "You're really going to fire me? I can't believe it."

"Believe it," Megan replied, and then softened her position slightly. "I'd prefer to think of your departure as a leave of absence until everything is cleared up. And, if I'm wrong about this, you'll have your job back with a sincere apology."

George laughed without any trace of humor. "Wonderful," he muttered sarcastically. "And what will I do in the meantime? God Almighty, I should have known you would fall for a story like this. Well, I just want to be the first to tell you that someone else is behind this scam! Not me! I've worked too many years for this company to throw them away on a lousy swindle the likes of this." His feet dropped noisily to the floor. "You can call it anything you like, but I've been framed!" His eyes narrowed spitefully as he cast Megan one final, vindictive glance before marching out of her office.

Megan waited until George had left the room and then removed her earring before cradling the phone between her shoulder and ear. As she had expected, Ted Benson had grown tired of waiting and had hung up. Megan quickly dialed the number for the legal offices of Benson and Tate.

The rest of the day passed quickly. Megan was caught in the middle of a whirlwind of meetings, telephone conversations and paperwork. The only blessing in an otherwise distressing day was that, as yet, the press hadn't found out about the scam. Unfortunately, it was only a matter of time before the hungry reporters would be collecting within the building. Once the story got out, all hell would break loose. And, no doubt, for the first time in three years, she would come face-to-face with the one man who could cruelly twist her heart until she bled.

The hours flew by. Ted Benson had convinced her that he had the situation well in control. Megan managed to call an emergency board meeting, which was scheduled for the next day. And throughout all of the activity, her thoughts lingered on Garrett. It was as if that single, darkly passionate weekend still bound her mercilessly to him. Patrick's accident might have severed the tangible ties between Megan and Garrett, but it couldn't destroy the intangible emotions that still surrounded her heart. "You're a fool," she chastised herself angrily, and tried to force her concentration back to her notes for tomorrow's board meeting.

George Samples had left her office right after his morning confrontation with Megan, and she was surprised to see him back at his desk later in the day. Megan had assumed that her discussion with George was finished. But she was wrong.

It was nearly closing time when Megan passed by George's desk. Only he and a few other workers were still in the office. A dark frown creased George's face as he slid insolent eyes up Megan's body.

"You've been against me since day one," the brash young broker charged unexpectedly. Megan was forced to pause at his desk and respond to the accusation.

"You know that's not true," Megan replied, keeping her voice down and her composure intact. "I've given you every possible break." Her steely gray eyes withstood his furious attack, and she managed a sincere smile. "If you'd like to discuss this further, let's go into my office—"

"You'd like that, wouldn't you?" George cut in. "We wouldn't want to let the rest of the staff get wind of all of this…would we?"

"George, I think we should talk this over."

"You don't want to discuss anything. You're just looking for an excuse to shut me up." The pompous Yale graduate smiled condescendingly.

"I'm trying to reason with you."

"Ha! You don't know the meaning of the word, Ms. McKearn. Reasoning with you is impossible. It always has been. And I'm tired of taking all of your crap."

Megan realized the situation was irreconcilable. "I'll have the accounting department give you a check for a month's severance pay." She attempted to keep her anger under control. Hoping to prevent speculation by the other employees, who couldn't help but overhear the heated conversation, Megan stepped away from George's desk.

"Just like that, huh?"

"George, I can't keep you on, you know that. I can't even give you a letter of recommendation until this whole business is straightened out."

His sharp eyes accused her of a lie. "Well, what happens when the SEC proves me innocent? What then?"

"I'll be the first person to admit that I was wrong."

"But until then, you're satisfied to kick me out."

"I don't have any other choice."

George placed his fists on his hips. "Isn't that just like a woman!"

Megan's temper flared. "Being a woman has nothing to do with my decision."

"Sure it doesn't," he sneered, while opening his briefcase and stuffing the contents of his desk into it.

"I'm sure my father would do the same thing—"

"Oh, give me a break, will you? You've never been able to hold a candle to the old man! Even that louse of a brother of yours could have run this firm better than you have. Damn, but this company took a nosedive when you took over."

The crack about Patrick hit a sensitive raw nerve. "That's enough," Megan warned, her eyes wide with indignation and authority.

"You're right on that count, Ms. McKearn. It is enough! I've had it with this two-bit operation!" With his final, vindictive comment, George snapped his briefcase closed, jerked it off his desk and marched angrily past the desks of his co-workers. When he pushed open the glass door separating the brokerage firm from the rest of the building, the panes rattled in their frames.

Some of the other brokers who had witnessed the argument turned their confused gazes back to the work on their desks. Though she could feel the muscles in her back stiffen,

Megan forced a confident but tight smile to those employees who caught her eye before she picked up the reports for which she had been searching and carried them back to her office.

"What a day," she murmured to herself as she sat down at her desk. "And it's only going to get worse." Firing George hadn't been easy, but the other tasks she had to face were just as ominous.

She still had to confront her father with Henry's audit and the possible SEC investigation. Despite his illness, Jed McKearn wouldn't want to hear excuses from his daughter, and he would expect Megan to take the proper action to squelch the scandal before it started. The worst part of it was that he wouldn't enjoy hearing what she intended to tell the board members in the meeting tomorrow.

There was also the problem of the clients whose accounts were involved in George's scheme. Pending the legal confrontation between the attorneys and the SEC, the accounts had to be carefully watched. Ted Benson, as attorney for McKearn Investments, had promised to contact each of the account holders. Once again, Megan's wayward thoughts turned to Garrett. Had Ted been able to reach him by phone, or would Garrett receive a crisp letter from the offices of Benson and Tate? Megan knew as well as anyone that Garrett could be merciless in pursuing that which he desired; and yet, she doubted Reaves's participation in the swindle. If he had a reputation for being ruthless in the chemical industry, Megan attributed it to the fact that he had been a poor kid from Seattle who had made his fortune by combining luck with intelligence and pushing his way to the top. Megan had always felt respect whenever she heard the name Garrett Reaves.

Until that one black weekend, nearly three years ago, when her life had been shattered as easily as a crystal goblet.

Megan sighed wearily as she gazed at her cluttered desk.

She picked up the scattered pages of Henry Silvas's audit and tapped them lightly on the polished wood before placing the neatly typed documents into her briefcase. She couldn't put it off any longer. She had to tell her father what was happening.

She felt the intrusion a second before it occurred. The door to her office was thrust open so violently that it thudded against the polished cherry wood paneling and the noise caught Megan off guard. She raised her head questioningly to face the cause of the disruption and found herself staring into the furious hazel eyes of Garrett Reaves.

Megan's throat constricted. Only once before had she seen such indignant wrath storming in a man's glare. The undisguised fury contorted his features and pierced through her composure just as it had in the past.

Reaves stopped in the doorway; he had hoped that there would be someone of authority in Jed McKearn's office, and he was sadly disappointed. The one person he hadn't expected to face was Jed's daughter, Megan, and the sight of her sitting defiantly behind Jed's oak desk made him hesitate—if only for a second.

Though Garrett knew that Megan was running the investment firm, he had understood that her position of president was temporary. George Samples had hinted that Megan was leaving the brokerage house because of some as yet undisclosed scandal, and that Jed was replacing his daughter. Obviously George's information was wrong, or Jed hadn't yet cleaned house.

Whatever the reason, Megan was here, staring accusingly at him with the same wide, dove gray eyes that had touched a dangerous part of him in the past. Her face was still as elegantly sculpted as he remembered, and her flawless skin remained unlined.

Megan slowly rose from the desk and swallowed against

the lump of wounded pride rising in her throat. The moment she had been anticipating and dreading had come.

Garrett's thick black hair was disheveled, as if it had been carelessly blown by the wind. He didn't seem to notice. His angular face and craggy, masculine features were drawn into a frown of angry resentment. Heavy black brows, pulled into an uncompromising scowl, guarded glinting eyes that were more green than brown. Those eyes watched every movement on Megan's even features, accusing her of conspiring against him.

Megan felt the involuntary stiffening of her spine as she straightened to face him, and she noted that his considerable frame in the doorway left little space for Jenny, the petite receptionist, to squeeze through.

"I'm sorry, Ms. McKearn—I couldn't stop him," Jenny announced as she cast Garrett Reaves a perturbed look.

"It's all right, Jenny," Megan replied, not lifting her cool gaze from the famous face of the man standing angrily in the doorway. Three years of her life seemed to melt into the shadowed corners of the room.

Megan had to remind herself that Reaves Chemical was one of Denver's largest industries. Garrett Reaves's face was often photographed to complement stories about the chemical company in the business section of the *Denver Financial Times*.

"Come in, Mr. Reaves, please," Megan said stiffly, and noted that his dark brows quirked at her formality. She motioned toward one of the chairs near her desk. "Take a seat. Can I have Jenny bring you a cup of coffee?" Surprisingly, though her heart was pounding furiously, a modicum of her professional aplomb remained with her.

Garrett eyed Megan suspiciously. His stormy hazel eyes narrowed in thought. "I just want to know what the hell's going on here," he replied, ignoring her polite offer. His voice was low and calm, despite the intensity of his words or his insinuation that something of outlandish proportions was wrong.

Every muscle in his body tensed as he stood in the doorway, and it was evident to Megan that his anger was about to explode.

Meeting his furious glare without giving evidence of any of her own storming emotions, Megan placed her glasses on the bridge of her nose and nodded thoughtfully. The last thing she wanted was a confrontation with the one man who could cut her to the bone. With one malicious word to the press, he could start the first whispers of a scandal that would certainly ruin her professionally. And that didn't begin to touch what he could do to her personally. Once before he had left her life in shambles. No doubt he could do it again.

"I'm sure you do," she agreed softly. "We have a lot to discuss..." Her cool gray eyes left him to rest on the small receptionist. "I can handle this, Jenny. See that Mr. Reaves and I aren't disturbed."

"It's about time to lock up," the pert redhead nervously reminded Megan.

Glancing at the antique clock mounted on the bookcase, Megan confirmed Jenny's remark. The long day was about over. Thank God. "You're right," she murmured. "Would you please lock the doors behind you when you leave? I'll show Mr. Reaves out."

The young girl nodded, and after sliding another ungrateful look in Garrett's direction, Jenny walked out of the room. When the door closed behind the receptionist, Garrett crossed the plush carpet of Megan's office in three swift strides. His condemning gaze swept over the interior of the room before coming to rest on Megan's wary face. The desk was the battle line. It seemed little barrier against Garrett's raging anger.

"I'm waiting," he announced, pulling at his tie before pressing his palms onto the wood, curling his fingers over the edge of the desk and leaning toward Megan. His square jaw was thrust defiantly close to her face.

"For?"

"An explanation," he replied, his eyes blazing with fury. "What's going on, Megan?" he demanded. "Why the hell are you trying to frame me?"

"I'm not," she stated without hesitation. "It seems as if you're doing a good enough job of that on your own."

Withholding the urge to pound his fist on the desk, Garrett pushed his rugged face nearer to hers. She could feel the heat of his breath on her cheeks. His dark eyes scrutinized her with such intensity that she had to force herself to hold her ground and return his unyielding stare.

"If you'll just take a seat—"

"I want answers, lady," he cut in, ignoring her request, "and I want them now!"

"I'll answer anything I can. However, I think it would behoove you to talk to Ted Benson."

"I already have."

"Then you understand my position—"

"Cut the crap, Megan. What're you trying to do? George Samples told me my account's being audited."

"It's only temporary," Megan replied. "Until the SEC—"

"The SEC! What the devil are you talking about?" His anger was replaced by incredulity. Shaking his head as if he didn't understand a word she was saying, he raked his fingers through his ebony hair and let out a disgusted breath of air.

"If you'll just give me a chance to explain, I'll be glad to tell you," she retorted, hiding the pain in her heart at being so near him again.

He looked suddenly weary, as if he hadn't slept in days. Megan sensed that what little patience he held on to was wearing precariously thin. In three years, Garrett had aged. Small lines webbed attractively near the corners of his eyes, softening the hard, angular planes of his face. A few strands of gray stood out against his otherwise dark hair, lending a quiet dignity to his rough features.

"I'm sorry," he said without meaning. "By all means, explain this fiasco to me."

Garrett studied the power and confidence in Megan's eyes. He noticed the regal tilt of defiance in her elegant chin and the refined manner in which her flawless skin stretched softly over her lofty cheekbones. Her inquisitive black brows were arched at him in sophisticated challenge. If she still had any feelings for him whatsoever, she hid them well.

"For starters, let me assure you that there is no fiasco—not so far as McKearn Investments is involved."

He didn't bother to hide his disbelief. "No? Then would you mind telling me exactly why the funds in my account are a part of this mess, whatever the hell it is?"

"I'm attempting to."

"Then let's get on with it." He couldn't conceal the impatience in his voice or the fatigued slump of his shoulders as he settled into one of the chairs near her desk. He leaned his head against the stiff back of the chair, and his eyes roved restlessly around the interior of the room.

The entire office was decorated in deference to her femininity. Though the room still had the air of a business office, the masculine trappings of Jed McKearn had been replaced with Tiffany lamps, royal blue wing chairs and leather-bound editions of classical literature. Gone were the scent of stale cigar smoke and the unspoken invitation of a drink before business was discussed. Now the room held the faint fragrance of freshly cut flowers and a provocative hint of perfume. The same fragrance that had haunted his nights for the last three years...

Garrett pulled his wandering thoughts back into perspective. He was positive that the changes made at McKearn Investments in the last year and a half were not to his advantage. And he didn't like the new atmosphere in this office. It disturbed him and reminded him of a time he would rather forget. He was usually a strong man who made decisions easily, but there was something about Megan McKearn that got to him. There always had been.

It was more than her beauty. It was the fire in her gray eyes and the air of feminine mystique that attracted him and made him cautious. When Garrett first met Megan, he had noticed the regal tilt of her head, the pride in her rigid back and the mystery in her wide gray eyes. Her allure had nearly been his undoing.

Carefully veiled now behind thick glasses and a severe hairstyle, Megan's intriguing femininity was still present. It had beckoned him in the past and still touched him. It was a temptation he had persistently avoided and would continue to avoid. Several years ago he had vowed to stay away from beautiful women. Until this moment, staring face-to-face with Megan, he had never been tempted to break that fateful promise to himself.

He smiled as if at a private irony. "Look, Megan, I've just spent two weeks out of the country. The last twelve hours have been divided between airports and airplanes. I'd like to get this over with so I can go home."

"Then I'll explain it to you as best I can." Peeking over the rims of her glasses, Megan managed what she hoped was a patient smile. She was convinced that the other account holders who had gained from George Samples's scheme had known about the scam from the beginning. Garrett Reaves was another case altogether.

His green-gold eyes clashed with hers, and Megan found it difficult to believe that he was involved in something as unscrupulous as fraud. He was a sensual man, and part of that sensuality came from the honesty in his stare. If she didn't remember her past so vividly, she would be tempted to believe that Garrett was innocent.

"McKearn Investments is currently involved in an investigation by the SEC." Before he might get the wrong idea, she continued, "This is no reflection on the brokerage house itself, you understand, but rather on the actions of one broker, his clients and a financial journal."

"Let me guess," Garrett interjected grimly. "The broker must be George Samples."

"Right—"

"And, therefore, my account is just naturally a part of the investigation." He tented his hands under his chin; his knowing eyes never left her face.

"This isn't just idle conjecture," she insisted.

"Of course not. It's guilt by association. Just because my broker of record is George Samples, you assume that I'm involved." His lips thinned menacingly as if he were appalled at the injustice of the situation.

"Not all of George's accounts were involved—"

"Just mine?" he accused, his voice rising. A small muscle in the corner of his jaw began to work, and his fingertips whitened with the increased pressure as he pushed his hands together.

"There were several," Megan said. "One of them was yours."

"Great!" Disgust was evident in his voice. He shook his dark head as if he couldn't believe what he was hearing. "Just what I need!" He dragged his suspicious eyes away from her face for a moment and sighed, as if to regain some of his diminishing restraint.

"The attorney promised that the SEC will complete the investigation as quickly as possible—"

"How the hell can he speak for the SEC? I don't have time to waste while I wait for a government agency to plow through your records and figure out that I'm not a part of this thing, whatever the hell it is." Once again his dark, knowing eyes assailed her. "I'm going to need most of the funds in my account by late December, and I'm not about to sit idle while McKearn Investments and the Securities and Exchange Commission try to blame me for something I didn't even know about."

"That's your prerogative," Megan stated, sensing that the tight rein on his anger was slipping and knowing intuitively that the full force of his wrath was something she had to avoid at all costs. She had witnessed his rage in the past, and his reputation for being unmerciful in business preceded him. McKearn Investments couldn't afford to have Garrett Reaves as an enemy. Nor could she. The scandal would be vicious enough without the added weight of Garrett's animosity.

"I think that the best way for us to handle this…problem is for you to release the funds in my account," he suggested.

"Certainly. In the morning—"

"Now!" Emphasis was added to his words by the dark shadows of mistrust in his eyes.

"Impossible."

His smile was without humor. "Certainly you've been in business long enough to realize that nothing's impossible." Savage eyes cut into her. He put his hands on the arms of his chair and pushed himself to his full height. "Maybe you don't understand me, Ms. McKearn: I'm closing my account."

"In the morning. After I've talked to Ted Benson."

His fists clenched and relaxed. "It's my money!"

"And right now it could well be under investigation by the SEC!" Megan stood, her face held high to meet the challenge in his intense hazel eyes. "You can't expect me to go against the advice of my attorney." Her hands clenched in frustration. "Look, my hands are tied." Her gray eyes darkened ominously. "Perhaps you should take my suggestion and call Ted Benson." She gestured with her palm toward the phone.

"I'm talking to you, Megan." His palm slapped the desk. "You're the president of this brokerage. It's your responsibility to see that my interests are protected. If an employee of McKearn Investments is involved in anything shady, then your reputation is on the line, not mine! Your father recommended George Samples to me in the first place. Because of Jed's recommendation, I assumed that Samples was a man of integrity."

"We all did," Megan admitted.

"And apparently you were wrong." The hard line of his mouth remained rigid.

Megan was noncommittal. Instinctively she sensed that if she were to be drawn any further into the argument, Garrett might use it against her later. Though he hadn't mentioned the possibility of a lawsuit, she could read the insinuations and warnings in the shadows of his gaze. "We'll see."

Garrett's eyes sparked with fury. "That we will, Ms. McKearn," he threatened dangerously. "That we will."

He strode out of the small office without so much as a glance over his shoulder. Megan waited until the office door swung shut behind him before she lowered herself into her chair.

The poise to which she had been desperately clinging escaped her and she let out a tired sigh. Dear God, how had everything gotten so out of control? And why did Garrett have to be involved? Involuntarily, she shuddered. Closing her eyes, she refused to release the tears of anger burning against her eyelids. Instead, she reached up and removed the pins holding the tight coil of auburn hair tightly in place. The long copper-colored waves tumbled free of the bond to rest in tangled disarray on her slim shoulders. Hoping to relieve some of the tension from the long afternoon, she set her glasses on the desk and ran her fingers through the thick strands surrounding her small, proud face.

Megan knew that she shouldn't let the threat of another scandal unnerve her. And she couldn't afford to let Garrett's presence as a man get to her. She realized that the knots twisting in her stomach weren't so much because of what she was about to face, but because of the past. Memories, fresh with senseless pain, surfaced in her weary mind.

To fight the tears of anguish forming in her eyes, Megan pressed her eyelids shut and swallowed. "I can't think about it…not now," she whispered to herself as she wiped away the tears.

The sound of the door opening once again caught her attention, and she looked up to find Garrett staring at her. For an embarrassing moment, Megan lost control of herself and her battered pride faltered.

The anger on his hard features faded as he witnessed the quiet pain in her large gray eyes. She cleared her throat, and when she spoke her voice was only a whisper. "Is there something I can do for you?" she asked as she recaptured a portion of her fleeing composure.

"Megan… I didn't mean…"

She forced determination into the proud tilt of her chin. The softness in her eyes disappeared. "There's no need to apologize," she assured him, although the sound of her name as he had spoken it caused her elegant brows to lift and her heart to miss a beat.

He took a step toward her, then halted. "Then I'd appreciate it if you would unlock the door."

"The door?" she repeated before realizing what he was talking about. "Oh…of course," she replied, hastily reaching into her purse for her key ring. She chided herself for forgetting that she had asked the receptionist to lock the front door of the office.

As she stood, she picked up her briefcase and tossed her raincoat over her arm. Garrett followed her into the reception area, and though she didn't look in his direction when she unlocked the door, she could feel him standing disturbingly close to her.

"We don't have to be on opposite sides of the issue, you know," he suggested, pondering the curve of her neck and leaning against the tempered glass separating the office from the corridor.

"I don't think we are," she replied. His thick brows cocked dubiously. "As far as I'm concerned, you're still a client of McKearn Investments."

"That's all?"

"That's all," she lied.

"Except that I have no control over the privacy of my account," he pointed out.

"For the time being."

He touched her arm just as she pushed the plate-glass door open. At the intimacy of the gesture, she lifted her eyes and stepped backward. There was something boldly masculine about him that she couldn't define, something powerfully male and overwhelming.

"I don't like the feeling that I'm not in control of what is mine," he said.

"I understand." She had only to remember the past.

"And I won't let it rest," he warned, stepping into the hallway of the building. "Not until everything's settled. Whatever this crime is that you think I committed, you're wrong, Megan, and I intend to do everything in my power to prove it!"

"That's your right," Megan said evenly, wondering just how far he would go with his threats.

"And if I have to, I'll sue McKearn Investments."

"I hope we can avoid a legal dispute." Her voice remained calm, and she managed to hide the desperation beginning to inch up her spine. A lawsuit! The publicity and scandal would destroy everything she had worked for.

"It's all up to you, Megan."

"Then perhaps we can talk it out."

"I tried that already," he stated, his eyes narrowing. "In your office. It didn't work."

"There's nothing I can do…"

Garrett noticed the trace of hopelessness in her voice. When he had walked back into her office he had been stunned at the sight of her, intrigued by the raw vulnerability in the beautiful oval of her face. Three years of his life seemed to have disappeared into the night.

In an instant she had regained her composure, but just for a fleeting moment he had captured a glimpse of the woman he remembered. Quickly she had disguised her feelings. It occurred to him that she might be hiding something else, as well. He decided to gamble.

His face hardened with ruthless determination. "Then I'll call my attorney tonight. No doubt you'll hear from him in the morning."

Megan's throat became tight with dread. "If you think you must—"

"Damn it, lady, you don't give me much of a choice, do you?" he said, looking toward the ceiling as if hoping for divine intervention. "You won't bother to talk this out logically, and then you back me up against the wall. What the hell do you expect from me?"

"Just a little time and patience," she replied, hoping her smile looked more convincing than it felt.

"A little time and patience?" he repeated, the corners of his mouth quirking as if he couldn't believe what he was hearing. "You've got my money, the SEC is probably digging through the records of my account and God only knows what else... in fact, you're acting like I'm some kind of criminal or something, and you expect me to be patient?"

"I guess I forgot that patience isn't exactly your long suit."

Garrett's jaw tightened and he looked pointedly at his watch. "Something tells me that I'm not going to get hold of Ron Thurston now." His dark eyes rose to bore into hers.

"Probably not," Megan agreed. She checked the urge to wince at the prominent attorney's name.

"Unless I bother him at home, I doubt if I can get in touch with him until tomorrow morning."

Megan inclined her head in mute agreement.

"So what are you going to do about it?"

"There's nothing—"

This time his hand reached out and gripped her shoulder. "Look, Megan, I don't want to hear any more canned speeches about the fact that your hands are tied because of the SEC. The reason I'm in this mess in the first place is because of your boy George Samples." The fingers tightened over the soft muscles of her shoulder, and she could feel the warmth of his insistent touch through her jacket. "Now, as I see it, your firm owes me the benefit of the doubt."

Only a small space separated her upturned face from his.

Demanding hazel eyes drilled into hers. "That's probably true," she conceded reluctantly.

"Then give it to me, damn it!"

"What do you suggest I do?"

He released his grip on her shoulder, and he clenched his fists in frustration. "I wish I knew." He raked impatient fingers through his hair as he thought. "Why don't you try telling me exactly what it is I'm up against," he suggested. "I haven't the slightest idea what all of this is about."

Megan calculated the risks and decided that it would be in the best interests of McKearn Investments to help Garrett Reaves. Despite her personal feelings for the man, he was an account holder, and there was the slight chance that he was, as he so vehemently claimed, innocent. If, however, he gave her any indication that he was involved with the scam, she would have no further obligation to him. She couldn't jeopardize the reputation of McKearn Investments. Her tight smile relaxed.

"I'll be glad to go over everything with you," she stated.

"Now?"

"I'd rather have Ted Benson with me."

His dark eyes sparked. "Out of the question. I want answers tonight."

Megan didn't hesitate. "I'll try to get hold of Ted. Perhaps we can meet you later. There are a few things I have to take care of first."

Garrett eyed her suspiciously, as if he thought she might run out on him. But something in her cool gaze convinced him that she would be true to her word. And why not? He held the trump card. He knew how desperate she was to avoid any bad publicity.

"Good." Once again his eyes darted to the watch on his cocked wrist before returning to her face. "Then I'll see you... when? About eight?"

"I'll be here," she assured him, relieved that the confrontation with the president of Reaves Chemical was drawing to a close, if only temporarily. She needed time and distance away from the disturbing man with the piercing hazel eyes.

"Not here," he stated, pushing on the door.

"Pardon me?"

"I'll expect you at my house. You remember the address?"

Megan's heart missed a beat. "I doubt that Mr. Benson will be inclined to drive to Boulder tonight."

Dark eyes sparked with green fire. "Convince him. Or come alone. I really don't give a damn how you arrange it."

"I'd feel more comfortable here, where I have access to all of the records."

"Bring them with you. Believe it or not, I have other things that I'd rather do than run back and forth to this office. I've been out of town for two weeks. Before coming here, I checked in at the office after landing at Stapleton. That's when I found out that all hell had broken lose. Now, I know it might not be convenient for you, but I really don't care. I want to go home, shower, change and answer some rather extensive correspondence that's been stacking up while I was gone. I think, in view of what's happening around here, that's not too much to ask."

She silently weighed the alternatives. There were none. Garrett had control and they both knew it. "I'll see you around eight."

There was a satisfied gleam in his dark eyes, as if he had just won a small victory and was savoring the sweetness of the conquest. Megan had the uneasy feeling that she had fallen very neatly into a well-executed seduction.

As she watched him stride to the elevators, Megan realized that he would stop at nothing to prove himself right—whether he was innocent or not.

3

MEGAN'S FATHER WAS a man of conflicting impulses: strong-willed to the point of ruthlessness in business, but also a man of tender emotions for his family. Megan knew that she had never lived up to his expectations of her. Jed McKearn was from the old school of thought, and he considered Megan's independent streak a character flaw. He had made no bones about the fact that all he wanted from his hot-tempered daughter was a successful son-in-law and several grandchildren he could pamper.

As for the business, Jed had considered his son, Patrick, as the only rightful heir to McKearn Investments. All of his life Jed had worked to see that his son was well groomed for his intended position as president of the investment firm.

In both cases, Jed's ambitions for his children had been thwarted by fate. And now it was Megan's cursed independent streak that had allowed her to run the company.

Megan was sure the irony of the situation escaped her father. It was probably for the best. The less stress for Jed, the better. *Then how can you possibly confront him with the scam?* her conscience nagged. *What will it do to him? Remember Patrick?*

Pressing her full lips together in determination, Megan tried not to think of the unhappy set of circumstances that had led to her succession as president of McKearn Investments. How she'd become president wasn't the issue; what she was going to do about the forthcoming scandal was. Jed had to know what was happening.

As she pulled into the circular drive of her parents' estate, she considered how she was going to break the news to Jed. Sooner or later he would find out about it, and she preferred to tell him about the scandal herself, somehow hoping to soften the blow. No doubt news of the scandal would leak to the press within the next couple of days. George Samples was the kind of man who would make sure his side of the story was told in screaming black and white.

And then there was Garrett Reaves. Megan knew him well enough to read the warnings in his dark, knowing eyes. If things didn't go Garrett's way, he would call his attorney and in a matter of days the story would be in all the local papers...including the *Denver Financial Times*. When the story hit the newsstands, McKearn Investments would be on the defensive.

Garrett's involvement, whether real or not, added an uncomfortable dimension to the problem. True, there was the personal angle; the man got to her, and she had trouble not believing the quiet dignity in his sharp hazel eyes. He set himself apart from the other clients involved in the scam.

But there was more to it than that. At least she hoped so. In all of the other accounts, the issue of involvement in the fraud was cut-and-dried. But with Reaves it was different; Megan hadn't convinced herself that he was a part of the swindle.

Uneasily she wondered if she were confusing her emotions with her business sense. Garrett Reaves still unnerved her—not as a wealthy account holder, but as a man.

With a disgusted sigh, Megan slid out of her Volvo. She attempted to relax as she strode determinedly up the front walk of the contemporary two-storied structure of cedar and glass that Jed and Anna McKearn had called home for the past ten years. Pushing the disturbing thoughts of Garrett out of her mind, Megan assumed an air of responsibility as she knocked once on the door before entering the house.

"I need to talk to Dad," Megan explained, after giving her mother an affectionate hug. Anna's smile faded slightly.

"About the business?"

Megan nodded, the expression on her soft features stern.

"Bad news," her mother guessed, running her fingers nervously along the single strand of pearls at her throat.

"Not the best."

Anna McKearn sighed. "I suppose he has to be told..." She shook her neatly styled red hair. "He's in the living room. You know, it's almost as if he's been expecting you... strange."

Not so odd, Megan thought to herself. Jed McKearn had an uncanny sense of business and he could read his daughter like a book. Megan took a deep breath and strode into the living room to tell her father about Henry Silvas's report and the scam.

Jed McKearn was waiting for his only daughter. He looked out of place in the stark white room filled with bright contemporary furniture and vivid abstract objets d'art. Leaning against the sand-colored rocks of the fireplace, he listened patiently to Megan's story. His only indication of agitation was the nervous drumming of his fingers on the polished wood of his cane.

The stern-faced lecture she had been expecting didn't come. Megan had braced herself for one of Jed McKearn's explosive speeches when she told him about Henry Silvas's report. But Megan's father didn't chastise her or point out her flaws in handling the situation at McKearn Investments. He couldn't. He had hand-picked George Samples as a promising young broker from a competing brokerage.

Jed slowly shook his graying head and pursed his lips together in silent self-admonition. He looked older than his sixty-five years. His once robust appearance had paled, and his full face had hollowed noticeably.

Megan wondered if part of his ill health was directly the result of his concerns about his strong-willed daughter and her management of the business he had put his life into.

"You gave it your best shot, Meg. I can't expect anything more than that," he said, once she had briefly sketched out what had happened.

But he did expect more. Megan could read the undisguised disappointment in his sober expression. And the worst of it was that Jed McKearn blamed himself for what had happened. The guilt-ridden frown on his face gave his thoughts away.

"I should have listened when you came here a couple of months ago," he whispered. "I never thought George would get himself mixed up with something like this. Henry Silvas is sure of this thing, is he?"

"He's convinced that George was involved with someone at the *Times*."

"How many accounts are involved?"

"Just a few. George brought most of them with him when he was hired."

"That's good," Jed remarked. "Those people probably knew what was happening."

Megan wondered how much she could tell her father and decided to make a clean breast of it before the papers distorted the story. "The only account that I'm worried about belongs to Garrett Reaves."

"Reaves was involved in this?" Jed's thin face tightened.

"It looks that way."

Jed nodded mutely. "Then you'd better watch your step."

Megan folded her arms over her chest and eyed her father warily. "You don't trust him?"

"I don't think the man is dishonest, if that's what you mean," Jed said thoughtfully. "But he has a reputation of doing things his own way." Jed's dark eyes clouded in thought. "He got into a little trouble when he first bought out the shareholders of Mountain Chemical eight years ago. Don't you remember?"

"No," Megan whispered. "Eight years ago I was at Stanford and I wasn't too interested in what was going on here."

Jed's bushy gray brows pulled together. "That's right. Patrick was with me then..." His voice faded and he looked away from the pain in Megan's eyes.

"Reaves managed to be part of that, too," he muttered as if to himself. Lowering his gaunt body into a bright plum-colored chair, Jed leaned on the wooden cane and attempted a thin smile. "What do you plan to do now?" he asked quietly. A look of resigned defeat crossed his eyes and he bowed his shoulders. Megan knew that she had let him down—just as she had in the past.

Megan drew in a ragged breath as she settled onto the couch across from him. "Wait until I hear from Ted Benson and see what the SEC plans to do. Tonight I meet with Reaves and tomorrow with the board."

"To tell them about the swindle?"

"For starters." Megan's eyes were kind when they held her father's watery stare.

"Something else?"

"Yes, Dad, there is. I'm going to tender my resignation unless the board agrees that I have full control of what happens in the brokerage. I don't want to have to get your approval before I act. It's time-consuming and awkward. Right now, I'll have to act and react very quickly." She noticed the hint of regret in his eyes. "I hope that you'll back me up on this one."

Jed cracked a sincere smile and winked at her. "You've got it. Should have been that way from the start."

Megan felt as if a ton of bricks had been lifted from her shoulders. "I just hope the SEC doesn't shut me down."

Jed's head snapped upward and a trace of the old fire returned to his tired eyes. "Do you think they will?"

Shaking her head, Megan met her father's hardened gaze. "I don't think so, and both Henry Silvas and Ted Benson agree with me." She leaned back into the soft cushions. "Henry seems to think that they'll continue with the investigation and subpoena records from the company as well as from the newspaper involved."

"We can't afford a scandal."

Megan nodded her agreement. "Fortunately, we caught George before he did too much damage. It could have been worse."

"I suppose so," her father replied as if he didn't believe a word of it.

"Of course it could," Anna McKearn stated as she entered the room, she had heard a portion of the conversation. After setting a tray of iced tea on the small table separating father from daughter, she handed Megan a glass and caught her daughter's eye in a warning glance that begged Megan to be careful. Silently Anna reminded Megan once again of Jed's failing health. "Can't you stay for dinner?" the older woman asked, hoping to change the course of the conversation.

"I'd love to, Mom, but not tonight," Megan replied with a genuine smile.

"Business again?"

Megan took a sip of the cool amber liquid. She nodded at her mother's question. "I was just telling Dad about it. It looks like we have a problem."

"A sizable one, I gather," Anna mused.

"Nothing I can't handle," Megan replied evasively. Anna McKearn had never shown any interest in the business, and she couldn't understand Megan's fascination with the investment world. "I just wanted Dad to be prepared."

"For what?" Anna's blue eyes roved from Megan to Jed and back again before narrowing suspiciously. "What's going on?"

"It looks like one of the brokers is involved in some sort of swindle," Megan explained. "Several accounts are involved."

"And you wanted to tell us before the story got out," Anna surmised with a sad smile.

"McKearn Investments might be in for a little bad press," Megan admitted.

"Well, I guess we'll just have to weather it, won't we?" Megan's mother responded before casting a worried glance at her husband. "We have before."

"But it never gets any easier," Megan thought aloud as she got up from the couch and kissed her mother on the cheek. "I'll call you later," she whispered, cocking her head in the direction of her father. "Take care of him, will you?"

"You're the one who needs looking after," Jed interrupted grimly. "It's not going to be a picnic fighting with the SEC or Garrett Reaves."

"Aren't they both supposed to be on my side?"

"Time will tell," Jed whispered solemnly.

★ ★ ★

The clock chimed the quarter hour as Garrett made a mental wager with himself. What were the odds of Megan McKearn's knocking on his door tonight…after three years? And if she did make it—would she do as she had threatened and drag her attorney along with her? Deciding that the chances of Megan's showing up at all were slim, he scowled into the bottom of his empty glass.

It would be a cold day in hell before Megan returned to the rustic comfort of his mountain retreat. And yet he hoped to see her again. Garrett walked across the room and pulled out an unopened bottle of scotch. He frowned at the label, shrugged and splashed some of the liquor into his glass.

After taking a long swallow of the warm scotch, he kicked off his shoes, bent over the dry wood stacked on the hearth and tossed a couple of pieces of pine onto the fire. The smoldering embers ignited with a crackle against the pitchy wood and scented the air with the warm smell of burning pine.

Garrett's sharp eyes wandered to the window. It was already dark and Megan was a good fifteen minutes late. But that was to be expected, he tried to convince himself. The drive from Denver took over an hour in good weather. Rain pelted the windows and blurred his vision. The temperature was near freezing, and he wondered if the heavy drizzle would turn to snow before morning. Worried thoughts suddenly crowded his weary mind.

Once again he hazarded a glance at the clock. Eight-twenty. Could she have gotten lost—or worse? Weather conditions would make driving difficult. He tried to push away the unwelcome worry by concentrating on the matters at hand. If Megan McKearn didn't show up, he'd call his attorney and blow the story wide open. Either she played by his rules, or he took things into his own hands.

The winsome president of McKearn Investments was between the proverbial rock and a hard place. Garrett promised
himself that he would battle with Megan…this time. The
thought should have given him some glimmer of satisfaction.
Strangely, it didn't.

If the contest between himself and Megan were so simple,
why did he feel a nagging twinge of conscience when he remembered her sitting at the desk, her head in her palms, slim
shoulders slumped in defeat, wild, coppery hair framing a
worried face, tears gathering in her mysterious eyes?

Unable to answer the disturbing question, he lowered himself onto his favorite couch. He groaned when he stretched
his long frame onto the worn leather cushions. The hours
he had spent in a cramped position on the airplane were beginning to take their toll on him. His tired muscles were beginning to ache, and the strain of the long day hadn't been
completely relieved by a hot shower. And now he was concerned for Megan's safety. Where was she?

Carefully balancing his drink on his abdomen, Garrett
stared at the exposed beams of the ceiling. Eerie shadows cast
from the fire shifted silently throughout the room. Just for
a moment, he closed his eyes and tried to relax. He wanted
to think through the dilemma of Megan McKearn and the
problem at hand, but other images assailed him. He remembered lying on this same couch with her, feeling the warm
texture of her skin pressed intimately against him, tasting the
salt of her sweat trickling seductively between her gorgeous
breasts… Just at the thought of her, he groaned and forced his
thoughts away from the subtle allure in her intelligent eyes.

The woman aroused feelings within him that he had hoped
were buried far too deep to resurface, and he wondered if insisting she come here had been an incredible miscalculation.
There was still something seductive and enticing about her,

something he couldn't name and didn't like to consider. He knew instinctively that he should avoid the sensual promises of her dove gray eyes.

Yet he was the one who had demanded that she come here, to the remote seclusion of the mountains. "You're a damn fool," he softly swore before stretching his fingers and pushing them recklessly through his dark hair. "Even if she tried, she'd have a hell of a time remembering how to find this place."

His home was located northeast of Boulder in the rugged foothills of the Rocky Mountains. Sometimes the commute to Denver was tedious, but he had decided long ago that his privacy was well worth the price of an extra hour or two on the road.

After draining the remainder of his scotch, he refocused his eyes to stare through the window and into the night. In the distance he noticed pale beams from the headlights of a car winding through the thick stands of pine trees surrounding his estate. He heaved a sigh of relief.

Then his square jaw hardened and a gleam of satisfaction flickered triumphantly in his eyes. Hoisting his empty glass toward the window, he saluted her with a mock toast.

"Congratulations, Ms. McKearn. You've got more guts than I gave you credit for."

Megan squinted into the darkness and her fingers tightened over the cold steering wheel. She was already late, and the narrow road with its sharp curves was difficult to follow. Rain ran down the windshield despite the tireless effort of the wipers to slap it aside.

A newscast from the radio reminded her of the time, and she grimaced as she turned the radio off and rounded the final bend in the road.

He was expecting her. Half a dozen floodlights illumi-

nated the immense house hidden in the stately pines. Warm
lamp glow from the interior of the house spilled through the
windows to diffuse into the dark night.

She stopped the car and killed the engine as she reached the
garage. Hiking her raincoat around her neck, Megan grabbed
her briefcase and, after only a moment's hesitation, opened
the car door. The rain had softened to a gentle mist. With renewed determination Megan hurried up the walk toward the
gracious Tudor manor. Hardly a mountain cabin. The house
was constructed of gray stone and heavy dark timbers. It rose
three stories from the knoll on which it stood, and the deep
pitch of the roof was angled with several intricate dormers.
Megan remembered it all too well.

After rapping soundly on the solid oak door, Megan waited
and forced her wandering thoughts away from the troubling
past. Within moments the door was opened and she was staring into the intense hazel eyes of Garrett Reaves. The scrutiny of his gaze was as seductive as it had been on the night
she first met him.

Tonight Garrett was dressed casually in gray cords and an
ivory sweater. The sleeves were pushed over his forearms, re-
vealing tanned skin stretched over taut, corded muscles. An
expectant smile played on his lips.

"You made it." He sounded relieved.

"I said I would. Sorry I'm late... I forgot that you lived
halfway to Wyoming," she responded, her cheeks coloring
slightly under his studious inspection.

"Not quite that far." His smile broadened into an appre-
ciative grin that tempered the harsh angles of his face. He
stepped out of the doorway, allowing enough room for her
to pass. "Please come in." And then he added, "I take it Benson couldn't join you?"

"A little short notice, wouldn't you say? Most attorneys

have busy schedules and better things to do than bow down to the demands of the opposition."

Instead of becoming incensed, Garrett smiled—a deadly smile that could play havoc with her rational thought.

Brushing past him, she ignored the warmth of his grin and the familiarity it engendered. Megan reminded herself of the past and the pain and the fact that he was most likely involved in the current scam of the investment company.

She stood in the expansive foyer and eyed the opulent warmth of the interior. Soft light from a suspended brass fixture bathed the entry in a warm glow that reflected in the patina of the oak floors and the rosewood paneling on the walls. A staircase, complete with a hand-hewn wooden banister, climbed up the far wall before disappearing into the floor above. Tapestries in vibrant hues of royal blue and burgundy adorned the walls, and handwoven Persian rugs in the same rich colors were carefully placed on the floor.

Megan studied the expensive furnishings as she absently unbuttoned her coat. Nothing much had changed. When she returned her eyes to the man in the doorway, she discovered that he was staring at her, watching intently as she slowly slid the final button through the hole to remove the mauve raincoat.

Their gazes locked. For an instant, Megan's throat constricted. His knowing hazel eyes searched hers and made a silent promise that touched a feminine part of her soul. Megan was forced to look away from the unspoken invitation. *He's doing it to you again,* she warned, swallowing against the tightness in her chest.

"Let me take your coat," he suggested as she pulled her arms out of the sleeves. When he helped her remove the garment, his fingers brushed against the back of her neck. She tried to ignore the delicacy of his touch and the faint tremor of anticipation his fingers had inspired.

After hanging the coat over one of the curved spokes of an antique hall tree, Garrett turned toward a hallway branching from the foyer toward the rear of the house. "Would you like a drink?" he asked, leading her into the library she remembered all too well. Bookcases with glass doors filled the wall between the fireplace and the bay window.

"Some wine, if you have it," she replied, taking a seat in one of the chairs near the stone fireplace. She opened her briefcase to withdraw the documents concerning his account at McKearn Investments, then adjusted her reading glasses on her face. She was thankful to discuss business.

"Why don't you level with me, Megan, and tell me just exactly what's going on." He handed her a glass of chilled Chablis and leaned against the warm stones of the fireplace. Eyeing her speculatively over the rim of his glass, Garrett took a sip of his scotch.

She smiled faintly and set her wineglass on the small table near her chair. "I've known that something was wrong for quite a while," she replied.

"With my account?"

She shook her head, and the firelight caught in the raindrops still lingering in her hair. "No, I had no idea your account was involved. I just knew...had a feeling that something wasn't right."

"A feeling? This is all based on a feeling?" The warmth on his face faded. The intimacy between them dissolved into the night.

"Of course not," Megan replied, her eyes meeting his frosty gaze steadily. "It started out as a feeling—something I really couldn't define—so I called an accountant for an unscheduled audit of all the books. Every account was studied."

"Including mine."

"Right."

"And how many accounts turned out to be…suspect?"

"There were several. Nine altogether."

"And the broker of record for all of the accounts just happened to be George Samples," Garrett surmised, frowning darkly into his drink. When she nodded, he let out a disgusted breath of air. "Okay, so what happened, exactly, to cause all of this commotion?"

Megan extracted photocopies of the clippings from the *Denver Financial Times* from her briefcase. She handed him the articles, along with a copy of his latest statement. He surveyed the documents warily, scanning the trades circled in red. The furrow on his forehead deepened. "I don't understand…" he murmured, but his voice trailed off as he raised his eyes to meet hers. "The trades were made before the articles were printed," he guessed, checking the dates on the clippings against the statement.

"And you didn't know about it?" Her eyebrows lifted dubiously over the frames of her glasses.

"No."

"But you have control over your account. All of those trades were authorized by you."

"Of course they were." His fingers rubbed the tension gathering in the back of his neck as he tried to come up with a logical explanation.

"How do you explain that?"

"It's simple. Samples would call me with an investment suggestion. If I agreed with his line of thinking, I'd tell him to go ahead with the trade."

"But you didn't know where his foresight in the market was coming from?"

Hazel eyes drilled into hers, and the features on his face

became stern. "Did you?" When she didn't immediately respond, he crossed the small space separating them and leaned over her chair, boldly pushing his face near hers. "I assumed that George Samples was a sharp broker. Your father seemed to think that he was, and everything he did for me worked to my advantage."

He was so close to her that his warm breath, laced with the scent of scotch, touched her face. "It seems to me, Megan, that I should be the one asking the questions here, not you. If my account was inappropriately used, it was because I trusted you—or at least your father—and the integrity of McKearn Investments. Jed was always as good as his word, and his advice had been sound in the past. Why would I question his judgment? As for George Samples, the bastard proved himself to me."

"By making money for you illegally."

"I didn't know that." His thick brows blunted. "You see, I was under the impression that anyone working for McKearn Investments was honest and hardworking. You know, full of good old American integrity."

Megan shifted uneasily in the chair and took a sip of the cool Chablis to wet her suddenly dry throat. All of Garrett's insinuations were vocalizations of her own fears. Pensively twirling the long stem of the glass, she thought aloud, "Generally, they are—"

"Except for Samples," he viciously reminded her. "If anyone should have known what he was doing, it was you. You're running the investment company. George Samples worked for you." Garrett seemed to be warming to his subject. His eyes narrowed menacingly. "And as far as profiting from his trades, how about McKearn Investments? Certainly its reputation wasn't hurt by Samples's underhanded deals. He made you look good—damn good." Garrett straightened, putting some distance between his lean frame and hers. His dark eyes never left her face and continued to drive his point home.

"Until now," she retorted. "McKearn Investments is left holding the bag because of one man and his greed."

"You should have been on top of this, Ms. McKearn," Garrett charged. "From day one."

She couldn't argue with him, nor would she admit that part of her problem stemmed from listening to her father's advice. Any excuse would sound as flimsy as it was. The bottom line was that Megan McKearn was responsible for what had transpired while she was calling the shots. "Arguing about it won't solve the problem."

"But you can, at least as far as I'm concerned." He placed a foot on the raised hearth and leaned his elbow on his bent knee. His sweater stretched across the broad muscles of his back.

She was instantly wary. "How?"

"By removing my account and my name from suspicion. Come on, Megan, you know me well enough to realize that I had no part in this. What George Samples did has no reflection on me."

"Except for the trade involving Reaves Chemical," Megan replied, her gray eyes never wavering.

"What trade?"

"Look on your April statement." He shuffled the papers until he came to the page in question. His eyes scanned the figures as Megan continued to speak. "On April tenth, you asked George to sell short on your own company's stock. Was that his idea?"

"There shouldn't have been any problem. He suggested it. I filed all the appropriate papers—" A muscle tightened in the corner of his jaw, and his eyes took on a deadly gleam.

Megan's heart was pounding erratically. What she was

about to suggest was difficult, and her throat became dry with dread. "Of course you did, but that doesn't matter. What's important is the fact that you made nearly a hundred thousand dollars on that trade alone."

"Is that a crime, Ms. McKearn?" he asked, his voice dangerously low, his hazel eyes threatening.

"I don't know," she admitted. "That's for the SEC to determine..." Her voice trailed off, and she wondered if she'd given too much of herself away.

"There's more, isn't there?" he guessed, inexplicably reading the hesitation in her gaze. "It's more than that one trade."

"You profited from several of the transactions."

"Of course I did!" he snapped back, throwing his arms up in disgust. "I haven't a clue why Samples decided to use my account—it doesn't make any sense. Why involve me?" His bewilderment appeared sincere, and every muscle in his whip-lean body tensed.

Megan watched his sure movements. Were they well rehearsed, or was he really as disgusted as he seemed? Her wide eyes scrutinized his chiseled features, searching for the smallest trace of emotion that might give his thoughts away.

Garrett frowned darkly as he tossed another piece of wood onto the fire and jabbed at it with a piece of kindling. His cords stretched over his tightly muscled thighs and buttocks, and Megan forced her attention back to the harsh planes of his masculine face.

Dusting his hands on his pants, Garrett straightened before turning to face her again.

"You have no idea why George would involve you?" she asked, running a tense finger over the rim of her wineglass.

"No. Unless it wasn't George at all, but his boss." His lips drew into a thin, tight line and his dark gaze pierced into hers.

"Meaning me?"

"Right—a personal vendetta."

Megan's gray eyes flared with indignation. "No matter what happened between us, Garrett," she whispered with ironclad determination, "I would never sabotage your account."

"Revenge is supposed to be sweet," he ventured, purposely goading her.

"You would know."

He grimaced. "You swore that you hated me," he reminded her, and visions of that wild night filled with heated passion and dark despair raced through her head.

"Why would I have waited so long?"

"Maybe because you never had the opportunity before."

"I don't think there's a reason to dignify your insinuations with an answer! If you'll excuse me..." She stood and straightened her shoulders, intent on leaving him to his ridiculous hypotheses.

Garrett studied her a moment and seemed convinced by her outburst. "Relax, Megan... I'm sorry. I just had to be sure that this wasn't your way of getting even."

"It isn't," she replied coldly.

"Then my guess is that good old George did it for protection."

"Protection?" Megan's interest was piqued. She set her unfinished glass of wine on the table and removed her reading glasses. "What do you mean?"

"It's just a guess, Megan, but the only plausible explanation is that George was hedging his bets. He must have known that he might get caught, and he was hoping that I might be able to bail him out."

"How?" Megan settled back into her chair, her eyes never leaving the rigid contours of Garrett's face.

Garrett shrugged indifferently. "I've got the best lawyers in town working for me. I also have some influence in Denver—which George must have known wouldn't hurt his cause. Samples is shrewd. He must have figured that I'd fight this thing with everything I've got." He read the disbelief in her eyes. The corner of his mouth twisted downward. "I said it was only a guess."

"There might be another reason," she ventured.

His eyebrows lifted, silently inviting her to continue.

"Maybe the profitable trades were a way of repaying a favor."

"A favor? To me? What are you getting at?" The anger he had restrained started to simmer as he began to understand her convoluted line of reasoning. In the long seconds that followed, only the crackle of the fire disturbed the silence.

"I just wondered if you knew that you weren't the only one who made money selling short on Reaves Chemical. Some of George's other accounts earned a substantial amount of cash by following your example." Her voice was controlled but her stomach was twisting in painful knots. She had come a hairsbreadth from accusing Garrett of leaking confidential information about Reaves Chemical for profit.

The insinuation hit its mark. Garrett's skin tightened over his cheekbones, and he had to force himself to maintain a modicum of control over his seething anger. "You're grasping at straws, Megan. You and that investment company of yours are in a tight spot and you're looking for a scapegoat."

"We don't need one," she interjected with more authority than she felt. "George Samples took care of that."

"And you're willing to hang me along with him?"

"I think you've hung yourself."

"This is a frame-up, isn't it?" He shook his dark head and snorted disdainfully. "God, Megan, I would have expected more from you than some cheap swindle—"

"Look, I'm not about to hang anyone. Not you—or George Samples, for that matter," Megan interjected. Why was it suddenly so important that he understand her? "I'm just trying to clear all this up so that I can talk to Ted Benson or the SEC and give them some answers."

"So that you don't look like a fool!"

Megan sighed and shook her head. "So that I can prevent these mistakes from being repeated. And, if you'll remember, I came here because you asked me to."

He stared into the honesty in her wide gray eyes. The same vulnerability that he had witnessed so many times in the past was present in her gaze. He had seen it fleetingly this afternoon, and it was evident now, as well. It was a softness she tried to hide, but it wouldn't leave him alone.

Absurdly, he wondered what it would be like to kiss her eyelids and try to erase the pain she quietly bore. The pain he had inadvertently caused years ago.

"So where does that leave us, Megan?" he asked.

"With a problem. A very big problem."

4

LEANING HIS SHOULDER against the mantel, Garrett thoughtfully ran his thumb along his jaw as he stared at Megan with undisguised interest.

"What you meant to say was that McKearn Investments has a problem," he speculated. Moving his eyes from the gentle contours of her face, he looked through the window and squinted into the darkness. Before she could reply, he continued. "And you don't really know how to handle it."

Megan bristled. "I think I've done all right so far—"

"But the going hasn't got tough yet. Just wait till the press gets ahold of this. They're going to have a field day," he predicted. "And all at the expense of McKearn Investments."

"Your name will come up."

He lifted his shoulders and returned his intense gaze to her worried face. Her gray eyes had clouded with uncertainty, and he pressed his point home. "I'm used to it. Chemical companies are always under the gun because of new products. No matter how many times you test a new drug, and despite approval from the FDA, there's always a chance that somewhere, with the right combination of other stimuli, something might go wrong. But with you it's different," he guessed, noting the nervous manner in which her fingers slid back and forth on the loosely woven fabric of the chair.

"A scandal is never easy," she replied, meeting his discomforting stare.

"Especially when it falls so quickly on the heels of another one."

Her spine stiffened and the color drained from her face. Her eyes, when they returned to his, were wide and shadowed in silent agony. "You should know," she whispered, hiding a trace of bitterness.

Unforgiving eyes drilled into hers. "You still blame me for Patrick's death, don't you?" he charged.

"What happened to my brother has nothing to do with the reason I came here."

"The hell it doesn't."

Her fingers were trembling, and she was forced to press them into her palms to quiet the storm of emotions raging silently within her. Tears, hot with betrayal, stung her eyes.

"But that's what this is all about," he insisted. "The scandal involving your brother taught you a lesson. You're trying to find a way to take the heat off of yourself and your family." Dark eyes challenged her to disagree as he crossed the small distance separating them.

Megan rose from the chair. Her chin inched upward in silent defiance. "I came here tonight to reason with you."

"You came because you didn't have much of a choice."

"I was hoping that we could talk this out—"

"You were looking for someone to blame."

Her face paled under his vicious accusations, but she stood her ground. "I think I should leave," she said, reaching for her glasses and quickly putting them into her purse. Indicating the loose stack of papers lying on the table with a tired wave of her hand, she turned toward the door. "You can keep those. I have other copies."

She reached for her briefcase, but Garrett's hand restrained her. Warm fingers closed over the bend in her arm. "This is always your answer, isn't it? Running from the truth."

"I'm not running from anything—"

His fingers tightened. "Knock it off, Megan. I know you. Remember? I was there the night Patrick was killed. You ran that night, too. Who was it you couldn't face? Me? Or yourself?"

The lump in her throat made it difficult to speak. She closed her eyes against the haunting memories of the dark night Patrick was killed. Guilt, like a heavy black shroud, settled on her slim shoulders. They sagged from the burden. "This…this isn't getting us anywhere." She straightened her spine, aware of his fingers still pressing warmly through the silken fabric of her blouse.

"I don't know about that."

She looked down disdainfully at the hand on her arm. "If you think you can goad me into saying something I'll regret later, you'd better forget it. And bringing up the past won't help. Ted Benson—"

"Leave him out of this. What's happening here is between you and me. Period. We don't need lawyers, accountants or the SEC to clutter things up."

"I think I'd better go…"

The grip on her arm tightened. "I'm only trying to uncover the truth."

Her lips curved into a disbelieving smile. "And that's why I came here—"

"Is it?" His eyes threw dark challenge in her face. Erotically, they probed into the most secret part of her mind.

"I thought I owed you the benefit of the doubt. I'm sorry I wasted your time."

"You don't owe me anything, lady. You came here because you thought you might be able to talk me out of a potential lawsuit."

"I hoped that you would be reasonable." The arch of her brow indicated she now realized the folly of such a hope.

"Damn it, woman, I'm trying..." With his free hand he rubbed the back of his neck, as if in that single action he could relieve the tension of the long day. He closed his eyes for a fraction of a second and squeezed them tight.

The fingers coiled possessively over her elbow didn't relax. She tried to withdraw her arm. "I think I'd better go..."

"Megan," he whispered gently as his eyes opened. Her name lingered in the warmth of the room and brought back the memories of yesterday. Firelight and shadows made his face appear strained, and the regret in his eyes seemed sincere. "Let's not argue." Silently his eyebrows lifted as if to encourage an intimacy she had hoped to avoid.

Megan swallowed against the dryness settling in the back of her throat as his fingers moved seductively up her arm. "Wait. Look, I think we should stick to the issue at hand. Bringing up what happened to my brother is beside the point." She felt his quiet fury in the grip on her arm.

"But that's why you're here, Megan. Face it. You and I both know that you came here tonight because I threatened you with a lawsuit. That coupled with the scandal could cripple McKearn Investments. You're afraid that McKearn Investments can't weather another scandal. Not after all the rumors and speculation about Patrick's death."

"Do you really think you have that much influence—?"

"I know I do." His dark eyes hardened.

Megan moistened her lips and shook her head. "I think the corporation can stand the adverse publicity—"

"But can you—or your family?" he demanded, roughly shaking her imprisoned arm. "How do you think your father is going to react to another public disgrace? How do you think it will affect his health?"

The anger that had been simmering quietly within her suddenly exploded. Her voice shook. "You really can be a bastard, can't you?"

"Only when I have to be." His hard features softened as he gazed into her furious gaze. "You've pushed me into a corner, Megan, and I'm trying to claw my way out. This is nothing personal—"

"Nothing personal!" She couldn't mask her disbelief. "How can you stand there and say that your repeated attacks against my family aren't personal, for God's sake! First you bring up my brother's death, and now my dad's health. What are you trying to do—browbeat me into submission? Do you expect me to cower from all your vague threats?" Her gray eyes moved upward in cool appraisal. "I'm not as weak as I used to be."

"I think you're a lot of things, Megan. But weak? Never. I'm just trying to make you understand my position."

"Which is?"

"That I'm innocent, damn it!"

"Then why the scare tactics?" She tried to step away from him, to put some distance between his anger and hers, to separate the intimacy of their bodies. He placed his free hand on her shoulder, as if by physically touching her he could communicate his feelings.

"I think you should know what you're up against," he whispered ominously. His eyes darkened seductively as he stared down at her upturned face.

"Meaning you—your money, your lawyers, your power." Her breath caught in her throat as she watched his anger disappear, to be replaced by something infinitely more dangerous.

"I won't let my name be dragged through the mud. Nor will I sit idle while your auditor and the SEC set out to destroy me. I had no part in George Samples's scheme, and I'll do everything in my power to prove it!"

"Then you are threatening me—"

"No. I'm just telling you what's going to happen so that you can be prepared." He hesitated a moment, as if unsure of his words. "You have to believe one thing, Megan," he whispered, gazing deeply into her eyes.

Her pulse was racing wildly at the intimacy of his tone, but she managed to raise one eyebrow to encourage him to continue.

"I would never...never do anything to hurt you."

He seemed so honest, and yet all she had to do was remember the past to see through his lies. "Unless you were forced into it."

He winced as if she had stabbed him. His grip on her shoulders tightened. Slowly, he drew her body to his until she could feel the hard contour of his chest pressed against her breasts. His breath, laced with the scent of scotch, fanned her cheeks. She felt the heat of his desire in his touch and noticed the smoldering passion in his searching gaze.

Her heart was pounding erratically in her chest, and the blood rushed through her veins in unwanted, betraying desire.

I can't want this man, she told herself vainly; *not after what he did to me!* His head lowered and his lips hovered expectantly over hers.

Garrett isn't trustworthy, she cautioned herself. *He would do anything to make me believe him.* She knew it in her heart, and yet she couldn't resist the bittersweet temptation of his caress.

His lips touched hers lightly…softly enticing a response from her with his gentle kiss. She tried not to respond; her arms reached upward in defense and her hands pressed against his chest to push away from him, but her efforts were futile. Her fingers, instead of forestalling the attack, moved gently against the knit of his sweater and felt the lean, rock-hard muscles of his chest. Memories, long silent and aching with torment, filled her mind. It seemed like only yesterday when he had last held her.

He groaned and his strong fingers splayed against the small of her back, silently urging her to press against him. Hard, unyielding thighs touched hers. His breathing was as rough as her own. His lips continued to mold against hers, becoming more bold with each bittersweet second that passed. His tongue touched her lips, daring to part her mouth and slide against the polish of her teeth before insistently slipping into the warm invitation of her mouth.

Megan was aware that her knees were weakening and that her arms had wound around Garrett's neck. She knew that she was playing the part of the fool, but she couldn't resist the seductive magic of his touch. Closing her eyes against the painful thought, she sighed and gave in to the intimacy of the night. They were alone, separated from the world, and all she could consider was the warmth of his embrace.

Strong arms secured her against him, catching her protectively as the weight of his body pressed her urgently but gently to the carpeted floor.

The hands that held her moved slowly up her back to the tight knot of hair at the base of her head. Gently cradling her head as he kissed her, Garrett let his fingers twine in the thickly coiled braid before slowly withdrawing the pins holding the sleek knot in place. Her hair tumbled in soft curls to rest in seductive disarray at her shoulders. Amber light from the fire caught in the burnished strands, gilding her hair with fiery highlights.

"You're beautiful," he murmured against the gentle curve of her throat. His hands loosened the first button of her blouse and the soft silken fabric parted. He kissed the exposed white skin, and Megan shuddered as a chill of reality ran through her.

It would be so easy to fall in love with him again.

"No," she whispered faintly, her protest feeble.

Another button came free of its bond.

"Please... Garrett."

His head dipped lower and his wet lips made a dewy impression against the delicate curve of her collarbone.

The third button slid out of its restraint.

Megan tried to clear her mind, attempted to cool her body from the warm inspiration of his touch. The cool night air caressed her skin, and his lips brushed gently in the hollow between her breasts.

"I can't," she whispered. "Garrett, please, this is wrong."

His hands stopped their gentle exploration and he looked up to stare into her eyes. "It's never been wrong with you," he persisted, his voice rough.

"I don't love you, Garrett," she said, her tongue nearly tripping on the lie. "Maybe I never did." A challenge, bright with frustration, burned in his gaze. "I... I should never have let this happen," she admitted, trying to soothe the pain of rejection. Shaking her head, she fought against the unwanted tears burning in her throat. "I had no intention..."

"Neither did I." She watched him will back the rising tide of passion that had washed over him.

"I'm sorry..."

"Megan..." he whispered, reaching upward and softly touching her hair. "There's no need to apologize."

Her voice caught at the tenderness of the gesture, and the tears began to pool in her eyes. "I didn't mean to let things go so far."

"Shhh…it's okay." He took her into his arms and softly kissed her forehead.

"I've got to go." Quickly she began to rebutton her blouse. How had she let things get so out of hand? Was she really still so susceptible to him? Why was it so easy to forget the pain of the past? Garrett's betrayal? She extracted herself from his embrace and reached for her purse.

"You don't believe me," he guessed as his lips pulled into an incredulous frown. "After everything we've been through, you still think I had something to do with this scam."

She shook her head and the firelight played in the coppery strands of her hair. "I hope you didn't," she whispered fervently. "I hope to God you're innocent."

His dark eyes pierced her soul. "Trust me."

"Oh, Garrett, if it were only that easy," she whispered, holding his gaze.

He reached forward and traced her chin with his finger. "It's as easy as you make it. Stay with me tonight…"

She smiled wistfully. His offer was more tempting than she would like to admit. "I can't. You know that. It would only make things more difficult."

"You've never forgiven me, have you?"

"Do you blame me? You lied to me." She forced back the uncomfortable lump in her throat, and her eyes narrowed to glinting slits of silvery suspicion. "You were engaged to Lana. All the time that we were together."

"That's not the way it was," he protested, his dark brows blunting.

"I'm not used to being 'the other woman.' It's a role I try to avoid." She pulled herself to her feet, but he was beside her in an instant, his hazel eyes glowering with indignation. As she attempted to walk out of the room, he placed his hands possessively on her shoulders and forced her to turn and face him.

"Believe me, Megan, I never thought of you as anything but the only woman in my life."

For a moment she was tempted to believe the pain in his eyes. It would be so easy to trust him and fall victim to his seduction all over again.

But the truth came back to her in a blinding flash. All too vividly, Megan remembered the yellowed article that Patrick had silently handed to her only hours before his death. A picture of Garrett, with his arms draped lovingly over Lana Tremaine's shoulders, had accompanied the announcement of Garrett's engagement to the attractive blonde heiress.

She closed her eyes and stepped away from him. "It doesn't matter...not anymore. I've said what I had to say to you. Anything else should be handled through my attorney." She whirled on her heel and headed for the door.

"Megan."

She hesitated only slightly but kept walking. In the foyer, she reached for her coat but didn't bother to put it on. She had to get away. Away from the house. Away from the lies. Away from Garrett.

She heard his footsteps as he pursued her. He caught up with her just as she reached for the handle of the door. She turned the knob and tugged. The door opened a crack before Garrett's flat hand pressed against the smooth wood and pushed it shut.

"You've got to believe that I had no part in this, Meg."

Her slim shoulders sagged. "Why?"

"Because I'm innocent, damn it!"

"So you've been saying."

"I thought that, in this country, one was still innocent until proven guilty."

"The evidence—"

"Circumstantial."

"But convincing."

His muscles tensed and he let his hand fall away from the door. "I'm going to fight this thing with whatever it takes."

"Good night, Garrett." Without a backward glance, she pulled open the door and disappeared into the night.

Garrett waited until the car engine started, the headlights illuminated the rain-drenched night and Megan drove quickly away from his home. As he heard her tires squeal against the wet pavement, his concern for her resurfaced. "Be careful," he whispered in the direction of the disappearing vehicle.

A few moments later, he closed the door and strode back into the den, silently leveling an oath at the disturbing set of circumstances that had brought her so decidedly back into his life.

He grabbed the receiver of the phone and punched out the private number of Ron Thurston. One of Thurston's teen-aged kids answered the phone, and Garrett had to wait. He scowled into the fire while his fingers drummed restlessly on the scarred maple desk.

"Hello?"

"Ron? Garrett Reaves."

"What the devil?" the surprised attorney asked. "For heaven's sake, Reaves, why are you calling me at this hour?"

"I didn't mean to call you so late—"

"Don't worry about it. Jason was beating the pants off me at one of those damned video games." Ron Thurston chuck-led at the thought of his son whipping him. "What's up?"

"It looks like I might be in a little trouble."

Instantly the attorney sobered. "The McKearn Investment

scam," Thurston guessed. This wasn't the first of Garrett's calls. Nor would it be the last.

"That's right."

"You still think you're being framed?"

Garrett rubbed the tension from the back of his neck with his free hand. "Sure of it."

"By whom?"

Megan's name hovered on the tip of his tongue. She was the logical choice. The woman with the means and the motive. By all rights, she should hate anything associated with Garrett Reaves. But her response tonight had surprised him. More than once he had caught a trace of longing in her silvery eyes. "I'm not sure," Garrett hedged, realizing that he had created a lag in the conversation. "But I'd start with George Samples."

"Did he have it in for you?"

"I don't think so—anyway, I couldn't begin to guess why."

There was a pause on the other end of the line. Garrett suspected that Ron, whose interest was aroused, was taking quick notes on his ever-present legal pad. "Anyone else?"

Garrett hedged. "I doubt it. But you might check into all the members of the McKearn family."

"Jed and his daughter?"

Taking in a sharp breath of air, Garrett replied. "Yes."

"Okay. Got it. You planning to file against McKearn Investments?"

"You tell me."

"I will. After I do some checking—tomorrow."

"Thanks, Ron."

"Later."

When Garrett hung up, the warm sense of vengeful satisfaction he had hoped to find was sadly missing. He walked over to the bar, contemplating another drink, and kicked at an imaginary adversary before splashing three fingers of scotch into his glass.

As he sat on the hearth, cradling the warm liquor in both of his hands, his thoughts centered on Megan. It had been a mistake to get involved with her three years ago. He had known it at the time. And it was an even bigger mistake to get involved with her now, when there was so much at stake. But he couldn't help himself. Whenever he thought about her, his head began to throb and the desire in his loins caught fire. It had never been that way with any other woman. Even Lana. At the thought of his ex-wife, Garrett frowned in disgust and swallowed the remainder of his drink.

Megan shuddered as if with a sudden chill, but her hands were sweaty where she gripped the steering wheel. "Don't let him get to you," she warned herself as she took a corner too quickly and the tires slid on the wet pavement.

Thoughts of Garrett and his erotic touch wouldn't leave her alone. She could still taste the hint of scotch on her lips where he had kissed her. "Don't be a fool," she whispered scathingly. "He only wants something from you—just like he did in the past."

5

THE BOARD MEETING the following day went reasonably well. Despite a poor night's sleep filled with dreams of making love to Garrett, Megan managed to pull herself together and face the curious members of the board with the news of the investment scam and potential scandal.

After the initial shock had worn off, each of the members had studied the photocopied statements and the evidence against George Samples. Megan explained her position, and with only a few minor grumbles, the board backed her up.

When she gave her ultimatum requesting complete authority without having to seek approval of her decisions from Jed, there was some dissent. However, Gordon Wells, a personal friend of Jed's, came to her defense and convinced the other board members that Megan's temporary position should be considered permanent.

"You can't expect her to operate with her hands tied, Marian," the rotund ex-banker had responded to Mrs. Chatwick's objections.

"But what about Jed?"

Gordon Wells's eyes were kind. "We all expected Jed to

return, but...well, we have to face facts. Jed's health has been deteriorating for quite a while. We have an obligation to the stockholders to run this company as well as can be expected—with or without Jed."

"I explained everything to my father last night. He supports me in my decision," Megan stated, her gray eyes calm but determined. "Now I think we should concentrate on the problem at hand and how we're going to deal with it."

From that point on, there were no further objections. Ted Benson pointed out the legalities of the situation and explained that he had been in contact with the local office of the Securities and Exchange Commission.

After the board meeting, Megan had lunch with Ted Benson in a small bistro on the Sixteenth Street Mall. The restaurant was intimate and quiet. Business could be discussed without too much fear of being overheard.

The tables near the windows offered an interesting view of the pedestrians hurrying along the flagstone mall and rushing into the various shops, boutiques and eating establishments. Slow-moving shuttle buses ambled down the length of the mall, past white metal chairs and wood benches located on the flagstones.

Megan's lunch consisted of fresh shrimp salad, hot tea with lemon and a tense discussion with the attorney for McKearn Investments.

"I mentioned at the board meeting that I've been in contact with the SEC," Ted announced, his piercing blue eyes stone cold as he pushed aside his plate.

Megan felt her muscles tighten defensively. Had Ted or the SEC found incriminating evidence proving that Garrett had been involved? She sipped her tea and met Ted's cold gaze without hesitation. "And?"

"They were onto the scam. Had it monitored by one of their computer systems."

Megan nodded. She had expected as much. George Samples was a fool to think that he could get away with so obvious a swindle. "What did they say?"

"Not much. Obviously, the investigation is still in progress."

"Do they want to talk to me?"

Ted shook his head of thick white hair and frowned before taking a long swallow of his tea. Bushy dark brows guarded his intense eyes. "So far, they haven't wanted to speak to anyone."

"Isn't that odd?"

"I don't think so. They're probably just getting all the facts."

"What about the accounts involved?"

Ted shrugged his broad shoulders, withdrew a cigarette and lit it. "We'll just have to sit tight and see what the SEC comes up with. So will the account holders," he decided as he inhaled deeply on the cigarette. "We don't have much choice in the matter. For now, it's business as usual."

"Easy for you to say," Megan observed with a wry smile.

"Take it easy, Meg. You haven't done anything illegal."

"Tell that to the SEC."

"I did."

Megan couldn't help thinking about Garrett. Was he involved in the swindle up to his seductive hazel eyes, or was he an innocent victim of George Samples's scam?

"Something wrong?" Ted asked, assuming a concern that was far from fatherly.

Megan managed a tight smile. "You mean something else?"

"You're a million miles away." He stubbed out his cigarette as a waiter discreetly left the bill on the table.

"I was just wondering how many of George's accounts were in this with him."

"All of them," the attorney said without equivocation. "That is, all of the accounts that Henry Silvas dug up." The attorney smiled broadly. "Are you sure I can't get you a drink?"

Megan shook her head and refused to be deterred from the subject. "Even Garrett Reaves's account?" Megan questioned, watching Ted's reaction.

Ted sighed audibly. For two years he'd been interested in Megan, but he could never lure their conversation away from business. "Even Reaves. He has a reputation for stepping on anyone he has to in order to make a buck. Seems to me that this sort of thing would be right up his alley." He left some bills on the table, stood and thereby dismissed the subject.

Megan wasn't put off. "But why? Why would a man of his stature take such a risk?"

"Money."

"Reaves has money."

"Okay then, more money. No one ever has enough." He carefully retrieved Megan's raincoat and helped her on with it. "That's what keeps lawyers like me in Porsches. Greed."

"You think Garrett Reaves is greedy?"

Ted held the door open for her and smiled. "No, I think people in general are greedy. Reaves is no different."

"Wanting to make some money and going about it illegally are two different things."

Ted Benson shrugged. "Maybe." They walked, heads bent against an icy wind, toward the Jefferson Tower and the offices of McKearn Investments. "But men have gone to almost any lengths to make money or keep their business afloat."

"Reaves Chemical seems to be solid," Megan countered.

"But he's expanding—maybe more rapidly than he should. There's the plant in Japan—another under consideration in Brazil. All that takes money." He noticed the look of wariness in Megan's eyes and changed tactics. "Look, in all fairness to Reaves, I suppose it's possible that he's not involved in the swindle."

"But unlikely?"

Ted squinted his steely blue eyes over his hawkish nose. "Seems that way to me. I think the opportunity presented itself and he grabbed it." He paused at the door of the office building. "It's happened before... Hey, why all the interest in Reaves? What's he to you?"

Megan pursed her lips thoughtfully and sidestepped the personal aspects of Ted's pointed question. "An account holder who just might be innocent."

"And might not."

"I'll keep that in mind."

Megan walked into the modern building and stopped to purchase a copy of the *Denver Financial Times* in the lobby. Ted's dark brows quirked. "Don't you subscribe?"

Megan smiled wryly and clutched the paper in a death grip. "This one's for me. Sometimes, after the brokers get through with it, the newspaper is literally torn to pieces."

She and Ted parted at the elevators. Megan stepped into a waiting car and pressed the button for the eighth floor. Ted Benson grabbed a descending elevator that would take him directly to the parking lot and his sleek black Porsche.

The weekend slipped by with no word from Garrett. Not that Megan had expected to hear from him. She hadn't left him Thursday night on the friendliest of terms. And yet, a small, very vital and feminine part of her had hoped that he would call.

She told herself that no news was good news. Hadn't he all but threatened her with a lawsuit? She half expected to hear from Garrett's attorney.

Megan kept herself busy by visiting her father and telling

him about the board meeting. He didn't look well, but seemed pleased that she had taken a stand and demanded control of the investment house. Perhaps he was mellowing in what he expected of his daughter. Megan hoped so.

The rest of the weekend she spent studying records for the brokerage firm and worrying about the impending scandal. She was determined in her efforts to forestall any unnecessary rumors.

No account escaped her scrutiny. She worked until two in the morning, reading statements and fortifying herself with hot cups of strong, black coffee. When at last her eyes burned from the strain, she took off her reading glasses and begrudgingly headed for bed.

There, between the cold percale sheets, she desperately tried not to think about Garrett or wonder what she could have shared with him if Patrick's tragic accident and the ensuing scandal hadn't driven them apart.

"Don't torture yourself," she mumbled as she lay restlessly in bed. *Garrett lied to you,* she reminded herself, *and married another woman.* All those hours alone with him were stolen from Lana Tremaine, the woman Garrett intended to marry all along. Patrick had nothing to do with that.

Sleep was fitful and broken with violent nightmares of a red Jaguar skidding out of control on an icy stretch of road in the middle of the night. The car fishtailed down the mountain highway before ripping through a guardrail and turning end over end down a snow-covered embankment.

Megan's own scream awoke her. She was shaking from the ordeal of the recurring dream. She glanced at the clock. Five in the morning. It was still as dark as the middle of the night. With clammy hands, she grabbed hold of the covers and pulled them more tightly around her neck. Maybe if she concentrated she could fall back to sleep.

After an hour of tossing and turning, she reluctantly pushed the blankets aside and headed for the shower. The hot spray woke her up and relaxed the knots of muscle strain at the base of her neck. She slipped on her robe, made coffee and drank heartily of the black liquid while her eyes scanned the morning edition of the *Denver Herald*.

Nothing on the front page. Even the financial section didn't mention George Samples's scam. Megan breathed a long sigh of relief, settled back in one of the kitchen chairs and sipped her coffee. News of the swindle was sure to break, but the longer it could be put off, the better. It gave her more time to get the facts together and hope that she could determine the extent of George's crime and the identity of his accomplice. Also, it would give her a chance to discover how deeply Garrett was embroiled in the scam.

Though it had been hours since she had eaten, she wasn't hungry. All she could handle for breakfast was a piece of buttered toast. She set the dishes in the dishwasher before returning to the bedroom to get ready for what promised to be a grueling day at the office. Megan expected the story of George's scam to break at any minute, and she wanted to be prepared.

She dressed in a French blue wool suit accented by an ivory silk blouse that tied sedately at her throat. Her coppery hair was twisted into a soft chignon at the base of her neck. The only jewelry she wore were understated Cartier earrings, which added just the right touch of elegance to her otherwise professional attire. When she left the apartment, she was confident that she looked the part of the smart young executive. She had a feeling that today, Monday, the second of November, would be remembered as the day that the solid timbers of McKearn Investments were shaken.

And she was right.

A throng of reporters greeted Megan in the lobby of the office building, much to the aggravation of a security guard who was desperately trying to disperse the uneasy crowd.

"Ms. McKearn," a loud reporter wielding a microphone called to her while ignoring the attempts of the security guard to regain control of the crowd. Megan recognized the faces of some of the wealthy clients of the investment company interspersed with the cameramen, newscasters and newspaper reporters. She had to get hold of the situation.

"I'm sorry about this, Ms. McKearn," the security guard apologized. He was a large man with a winning smile, but today he wasn't smiling and anger snapped in his dark eyes. Megan had known him for years and understood his frustration with the crowd.

"It's all right, Alex," she assured him, and turned with poise to the anxious reporter advancing upon her.

"Ms. McKearn, please, could you answer a few questions for me?"

Megan smiled confidently. She had to control the growing crowd and create as little of a disturbance as possible. With the clients of McKearn Investments hanging on her every word, it was necessary to handle everyone as politely and efficiently as possible. "Of course I will, but I would prefer to do it upstairs, in my office, where there's a little more privacy—if it's convenient for you."

"It doesn't matter where. As long as I get the story." The reporter with the thick moustache waved to a cameraman shouldering a portable unit.

"The eighth floor," Megan said to the crowd before her throat suddenly constricted. On the outskirts of the noisy mass of bodies stood Garrett. His arrogant eyes and slightly amused smile never left Megan's face. Her heart missed a beat at the sight of him lounging against one of the interior columns supporting the high, brightly tiled ceiling of the lobby of the Jefferson Tower. It was almost as if he were enjoying the spectacle of excitement and confusion.

Was Garrett the cause of this uncomfortable scene? Had he taken it upon himself to inform the press about the investment scam—taking his revenge against her? She felt his eyes searing into her back when she turned abruptly and walked into a waiting elevator car.

The elevator ride was the longest of Megan's life. The tension in the small cubicle as it raced toward the eighth floor was thick and uncomfortable. She felt nervous beads of perspiration between her shoulder blades.

Once she was in her office, however, she fielded the questions hurled at her as if she had done it all her life.

"Ms. McKearn," the reporter with the thick brown moustache shouted. "George Samples is saying that he was framed in some kind of investment scam that originated here at McKearn Investments. Could you comment on his statement?"

Megan was thoughtful for a moment. She was aware of Garrett the moment he sauntered into the room, his sharp hazel eyes missing nothing of the strained confrontation. Megan had to be careful. Anything she might say could be used against her later in court if George Samples, Garrett Reaves and God only knew who else decided to sue. "It's true that Mr. Samples is no longer with McKearn Investments," she replied evasively. "However, I don't think it would be prudent to discuss the reasons for his departure."

"Wait a minute!" one of the clients objected. "Samples was my broker. What's going on here?"

"Nothing's going on, Mr. Sinclair. Mr. Samples left and Ms. Barnes is taking over his accounts. Unless you would prefer someone else." She hazarded a glance at the television camera and realized that the eyes of the press were still capturing everything she said on film. "I'd like to speak with you later," she suggested with a confident smile, and fortunately Mr. Sinclair said nothing more.

When she turned back toward the bulk of the crowd, Megan noticed that Garrett had quietly maneuvered himself closer to her. He leaned arrogantly against the bookcase, his angular jaw tense, his strong arms crossed lazily over his chest as he silently observed everything about the unscheduled press conference. Megan looked for a fleeting moment into his incredible, mocking hazel eyes before her attention was forced back to the anxious reporters.

"Ms. McKearn." Another reporter caught Megan's attention. This time it was a short blond woman with suspicious brown eyes. "Mr. Samples indicated that there is in fact an investment swindle that originated here—in McKearn Investments. Is there any truth to that rumor?"

A few more reporters began to hurl questions in her direction. Megan held up her palms to the crowd and looked directly into one of the television cameras. "Absolutely none." Megan smiled with feigned equanimity. "Let me take this opportunity to say that no account holder has lost any money on any of the transactions that are currently being investigated—"

"Then there was a scam," the blonde surmised with a triumphant gleam in her eye.

"There was an indiscretion or two," Megan allowed. "But our auditors discovered the situation before it got out of hand, and I have personally reviewed all of the accounts to assure our clients of the highest security for their investments."

"Is that meant to let the account holders know that their money is still safe with you?" the blonde reporter asked with obvious disbelief. Uncovering a story of this nature could become her springboard into the big time, and she wasn't about to let it slip through her fingers.

"Of course it is." Megan held the young woman's suspicious stare. "I will personally assure it."

"You're reasonably new at running this company, aren't you, Ms. McKearn?" the moustached man interjected.

"I've worked with the investment company for several years—"

"But not as president. And when you took over, you were hired as a temporary replacement for your father, weren't you?"

"My position as president is no longer temporary."

The man didn't listen to her reply. "Well, tell me, do you think that if your father were still running the company, this situation would have occurred?"

Megan glanced nervously at Garrett before answering the question. All trace of amusement had faded from Garrett's angular face. The gleam in his eyes was deadly.

Megan turned her attention back to the reporters. Though seething inside, she managed a tight smile. "I couldn't venture a guess. That situation is purely hypothetical. Now, if you'll excuse me—" she smiled at the hungry members of the press "—I have work to do."

"Well, can you give us any insight on what exactly was going down?" the man persisted.

"Not until the investigation is complete." She turned away from the camera, as if to dismiss the crowd. "Mr. Sinclair?" The thin man nodded. "I'll be right with you."

Begrudgingly, the reporters filed out of Megan's office, and she was left with the task of straightening ruffled feathers and consoling some of McKearn Investments' most prestigious clients. Hazarding a sidelong glance toward the bookcase, she noted that Garrett had exited her office with the last stragglers of the departing press. He must have felt satisfied that he had thrown her day into utter chaos.

Ignoring the renewed sense of betrayal overtaking her, Megan concentrated all of her energy on putting her clients' minds at ease. Marlin Sinclair was easily placated, but Taffeta Peake took more cajoling. The small, eightyish widow sported curly blue-gray hair, brightly colored knit dresses, and had a suspicious mind that was still sharp as a tack. Fortunately, the elderly woman was a loyal person by nature and a close friend of Megan's aunt Jessica. After nearly an hour of conferring with Megan, Mrs. Peake decided to leave her investments as they were…at least for the time being.

The hours hurried by. Megan barely had time to breathe. One after another the company's anxious clients came to call. Just when Megan thought she had finally convinced the last of her worried investors that their money was safe and secure, Garrett strode, unannounced, into her office.

Megan wondered if he'd been waiting for her all day. "You, too?" she asked. Just at the sight of him, with his charismatic smile and dark knowing eyes, her hostility began to melt and a slow smile spread across her lips. She read the concern in his warm gaze.

"Wouldn't want you to feel neglected."

Her smile turned into a frown. "No need to worry about that. Not today." The friendly conversation was comforting, and she leaned back in her chair, relaxing slightly from the tension that had been her constant companion ever since waking.

"You haven't been lacking for company?"

"Not for a minute." Her eyes grew serious and she ran her fingers along the edge of the desk. "Tell me something—did you leak what was happening to the press?"

"No." His clear hazel eyes were honest.

Despite her earlier doubts, she knew at once that he was telling the truth. "I didn't think so," she lied.

"Well, at least that's some progress. Now, if you'd just listen to what I've been telling you all along, we could straighten everything out." Her pulse jumped at the double meaning.

She hesitated and nervously toyed with a pencil. "I don't think so."

"Why not?"

She shrugged. "Conflict of interest, for starters."

His lips thinned into a dangerous line and he pinched his lower lip pensively between his thumb and forefinger. Dark eyes impaled her. "I don't suppose you've located Samples's accomplice."

She shook her head. A few dark wisps of coppery hair fell out of her coiled chignon. She tucked the wayward strands neatly in place. "I expect that the SEC will find the culprit soon."

"I hope so," Garrett admitted, flopping into a side chair near the desk and running his gaze appreciatively up the curve of her calf.

"Why's that?"

He smiled the same smile that had touched her in the past. Decidedly lopsided, showing just the hint of strong, white teeth, it was nearly boyish in its charm. That smile could be a devastating weapon when used to Garrett's advantage. "I think it would be best if we got this whole stinking scandal behind us."

"That will take time."

"Not for us, it won't."

Her elegant brow quirked. "What do you mean, us?"

The smile fell from his face, and for a moment, the only sound in the room was the quiet ticking of the antique clock perched on a polished shelf of the bookcase.

"We've meant too much to each other to have this kind of

a misunderstanding," Garrett said softly, and Megan's breath caught in her throat.

"Let me get this straight," she whispered. "You mean that because we were lovers in the past, I should ignore the fact that your account is under suspicion?" Her heart was beating a breathless cadence as what he was suggesting became blindingly clear. "You want me to cover up for you?"

Garrett's jaw tensed. His eyes looked boldly into hers. "There's nothing to cover up, damn it. I'm only asking for your trust."

She took in a deep breath and lifted her chin. "You asked for that once before, and I was naive enough to believe you," she murmured, knowing for certain that he was using her again, twisting her feelings for him like a knife in her heart.

He pinched the bridge of his nose as if trying to forestall a headache. "Megan, listen," he began, just as a rap on the door announced Ted Benson's arrival. The attorney stepped into the middle of what very obviously was a personal confrontation. His steely eyes took in the scene before him, glanced at the clock and then returned to Megan's angry gaze.

"I'm sorry," Ted apologized stiffly. "Jenny's not at her desk, and I thought we had a meeting scheduled—"

"We do, Ted." Megan turned stone-cold eyes on Garrett. "My business with Mr. Reaves is over."

"I could wait a couple of minutes," Ted suggested without moving toward the door.

"No need." Garrett rose from the chair. "As Ms. McKearn stated, our business is finished—for now." Then, with a possessive swing of his head back toward Megan, he continued. "I'll talk to you later."

Megan didn't bother to respond, but turned all of her attention to the attorney, who was settling in the seat Garrett had just vacated. She didn't watch Garrett's retreat, but she heard the door slam behind him as he exited the tension-filled room.

The sound echoed hollowly in her heart.

6

GARRETT HADN'T MISREAD the look on Ted Benson's face when the attorney walked into Megan's office. It was obvious to Garrett that Ted Benson considered himself more than just the lawyer for McKearn Investments. Benson was interested in Megan as a woman, and just the thought of the stuffy attorney laying a hand on Megan made Garrett's blood boil savagely. Garrett didn't doubt for a minute that the feeling was mutual.

Cursing under his breath, Garrett jammed his hands into the back pockets of his slacks and paced along the short hallway between the investment firm and the elevators. He didn't have to wait long. Within ten minutes, the fiftyish attorney swung out of Megan's office wearing a pained expression on his Ivy League face—an expression he managed to shift to bored nonchalance at the sight of Garrett leaning against the wall near the elevators.

"Still here?" Benson asked, with only the slightest edge to his well-modulated voice.

Garrett nodded stiffly. The less said to the wily attorney, the better.

Ted reached for the elevator call button and hesitated. "I wouldn't press my luck, if I were you."

A slightly crooked and obviously amused smile touched Garrett's lips. His hazel eyes glittered dangerously. "Luck has nothing to do with it, Benson. If I'm pressing anything, it's my advantage."

It was the lawyer's turn to smile. "Have it your way."

"I will."

The elevator doors opened, and with a daring look that silently warned of further, more deadly battles, Ted Benson strode into the waiting car.

Garrett grimaced to himself as the elevator descended. Something about Ted Benson didn't sit well with him. The lawyer's reputation was impeccable, and yet there was something about the emptiness in Benson's stone-cold eyes that bothered Garrett. It was as if the man were out to get him; Garrett had read it in Benson's glare.

He rubbed his chin and chastised himself for his paranoia. Face it, Reaves, he cautioned himself, the man is interested in Megan, and that's what gets to you. The thought of another man touching Megan did dangerous things to Garrett's mind.

The jingle of keys on a ring caught his attention, and he looked up to see Megan locking the doors of the investment company. She was bent over the door, and the elegant weave of her skirt stretched becomingly over her backside. Garrett eyed the provocative hint of lace that peeked from beneath her skirt, and the gentle curve of her calves. He gritted his teeth together in frustration. What was it about that woman that wouldn't leave him alone? The more he saw of her, the more he wanted. His desire for Megan was becoming an uncontrollable hunger that he suspected would prove to be insatiable.

Megan finished locking the office and turned to face the

elevators. She was confronted by Garrett's uncompromising stare.

"I… I thought you left," she said, walking toward him, her fingers clenching her briefcase in a death grip. Her raincoat was tossed casually over her arm, and she paused at the elevator to put it on.

"We're not through talking."

Megan sighed. The long day had left her feeling tired and wrung out. "I don't think we really have anything more to discuss." She couldn't hide the worry in her voice. Ted had advised her that the SEC would most likely file a civil suit against all the participants in the scam. Including Garrett.

"Lady, we haven't begun," he assured her as he took her arm and escorted her into the elevator. The twin doors closed and the small car started with a jolt. "I want you to come to the house in Boulder. There are a few things we need to get straight between us."

"We've tried talking before. It didn't work."

"Maybe we just didn't try hard enough."

She shook her head wearily.

"Or maybe the timing was wrong." The elevator shuddered to a stop.

"Timing?"

"You and I should have worked things out three years ago."

Megan strode out of the elevator, conscious of the steely fingers wrapped protectively over her arm. Her pulse was racing dangerously, and she could see by the determined gleam in Garrett's eye and the slant of his jaw that he meant business. "They say that hindsight is twenty-twenty," she observed.

"And they also say that love is better the second time around."

Her steps faltered slightly. "Shows you just how foolish old wives' tales can be…"

"Megan. Stop it." He pulled her up short. His dark eyes smoldered. "I don't like playing games. I want you to come home with me."

Outrage flashed in her eyes. "Just like that?"

"Just like that."

"After three years?"

"We need to pick up where we left off."

If only she could believe him. He seemed so honest and so sincere, but the threat of his involvement in the swindle along with his bitter rejection of the past made her cautious. "I'm sorry, Garrett." Slowly she withdrew her arm from the welcome manacle of his grip.

"So am I."

She shook her head at the absurdity of the situation. "I... I just can't." When she lifted her eyes they were shadowed in pain. "The house has too many memories that I'd rather not think about."

He smiled sadly and swore a silent oath at himself for his own impetuosity. "Then how about dinner—here, in town? Diablo's?"

"I don't know." What if someone saw them together? The scandal was about to blow wide open. Being caught with one of the suspected participants could ruin her. "I'm not sure that being seen in public would be wise."

"We're just going to dinner, for God's sake. Don't tell me that's suddenly become a crime, too."

Megan had to laugh in spite of herself. "Not that I know of. At least, not yet."

"Come on. I'll walk you."

"It must be eight blocks—"

"Give or take a few." He winked broadly, charmingly. The way she remembered him. "The exercise will do you good."

"This is madness, you know," she protested weakly, already caught up in the daring of it.

"This is probably the sanest thing I've done in the last three years." Without much ceremony, he took her briefcase in one hand, her arm in the other, before pushing the glass doors of the building open with his body.

The autumn air was crisp with the promise of snow, and Garrett slipped his arm around her shoulders to warm her. He whispered to her as they walked to the mall and followed it until reaching Larimer Square.

Diablo's was located in a Victorian building flanked by authentic gas lanterns and decorated ornately with gleaming gingerbread. Long ebony shutters flanked paned windows, and a broad front porch welcomed the visitors. Inside, rich wainscoting and muted wallpaper gave a nineteenth-century charm to the renovated building.

Megan and Garrett were led by a liveried waiter to a private room on the second story. The bowed window near the table overlooked one of Denver's oldest—and at one time wildest—streets.

"Why wouldn't you come back to my house?" Garrett asked, once the waiter had delivered the white Burgundy and Garrett had given it his approval.

"I think we'd better keep our relationship strictly professional."

"Why?"

The question startled her. The answer seemed so obvious. She picked up the stemmed wineglass and rotated the cut crystal in her fingers. "What we had was based on a lie, Garrett. The time you and I spent together shouldn't have happened. I can't go back to that house. Too many ghosts from the past live there."

He placed his elbows on the table and rested his chin in his hands to stare at her. His thick brows were pulled together in confusion. "You came last Thursday."

She shook her head and the soft light from the lantern shimmered in the red streaks of her hair. "I was coerced."

"By me?"

She nodded. "And it didn't accomplish anything."

He seemed about to protest just as the waiter came into the room and silently placed a steaming platter laden with broiled trout and wild rice onto the table. Only after the dark-haired waiter disappeared did the tense conversation resume.

"We need some time together," he said.

"Because you're in trouble."

"Because I want to be with you." The rueful slant of his mouth suggested that he was telling the truth.

"Why, Garrett? Why now? After three years?"

"Because I'm tired of paying for my mistakes."

Like the mistake you made when you joined forces with George Samples, Megan thought, and her suspicion must have shown on her face.

"This has nothing to do with the situation at the investment company," he said quietly.

Her gray eyes glinted like newly forged steel. Just how gullible did he think she was? "Don't lie to me, Garrett," she whispered. "I may have believed everything you told me once, but I'm not that stupid anymore. If George's scam hadn't come to light, we wouldn't be here tonight."

"Maybe not tonight. But that doesn't alter the fact that I want to be with you."

"It only embellishes it."

"Oh, Megan, can't you make the effort to trust me—just for a little while?"

I did once, she reminded herself, *and it ended in disaster.* "It's not that easy, not now."

"Too many ghosts, is that it?"

She nodded mutely and pretended interest in her meal. Looking at Garrett was only making it harder to say no. The honesty in his hazel eyes was nearly her undoing. The hard, familiar angle of his jaw and the easy manner in which he stared into her eyes was a sensual invitation—a difficult one for Megan to resist.

He leaned back in his chair, tossed his napkin aside and studied her. "I think you're making excuses, Megan. The truth of the matter is that you're afraid of being alone with me."

"I just don't think it would be wise."

"That didn't stop you before."

"I guess I'm a little more careful now."

"Jaded, you mean."

She lifted her shoulders and wrapped her trembling fingers around the stem of her wineglass. He was getting to her. The intimate meal, the heady wine and the persistence in his bold eyes were beginning to touch a part of her she would have preferred to keep hidden. Reason and composure were escaping in the seductive atmosphere of the room.

When the meal was finished and the check was paid, both she and Garrett lingered at the table, as if they were afraid to go any further with the night. Where could it lead? What would happen if she gave in to the persistent questions in his eyes?

Reluctantly Megan followed Garrett down the sweeping staircase of the old manor. Her fingers slid easily along the polished oak rail as she descended. She was on the last step, when her eyes met those of a moustached man standing near the bar. Recognition flashed across the young man's face.

"Ms. McKearn?" he asked, stepping away from an attractive brunette and a frothy mug of beer.

Megan paused, trying to place the face. Garrett stopped and

watched the young man with suspicious eyes. Megan could feel her pulse beginning to quicken.

"I'm Harold Dansen from KRCY news." He seemed disappointed that she didn't remember him. "I interviewed you this morning."

Megan's heart hit the floor, but the brash young man ignored her obvious discomfiture. "I'd like a private interview with you." When she didn't immediately respond, he pressed his point home. "You know what I mean: a more personal story about you, your family, how you got to be president of the company, what McKearn Investments' position on this investment scam really is. That sort of thing."

"I'll let you know," Megan replied vaguely, just as Garrett stepped closer to her side and cut off any more of the anxious reporter's questions.

Flinty eyes moved from Megan to Garrett and back again, and the reporter smiled in obvious satisfaction. "Hey, you're Garrett Reaves."

The McKearn Investments story had just become a lot more interesting to Harold Dansen. Garrett Reaves was a man who valued his privacy. A very wealthy man who scorned public attention. And Reaves was here, with the president of McKearn Investments, a company whose credibility was dropping faster than a stone in water. To top matters off, Megan McKearn looked very disturbed that she had been recognized with Reaves. The story made for interesting copy—very interesting copy indeed. Harold Dansen noticed the angry gleam in Reaves's eyes and warned himself to be careful.

Discreetly, Garrett took Megan's arm and propelled her toward the door. An interview with the likes of Dansen now would be a disaster.

"Wait a minute," Dansen demanded.

Megan couldn't afford to anger the press, and yet she knew that she had to sidestep Dansen and his pointed questions. She looked over her shoulder and graced him with her most winning smile. "I'll call you," she promised. "Harold Dansen, KRCY, right?"

Harold nodded, struck for a moment by her intriguing beauty. Megan McKearn was a woman who could turn heads with only the flash of her delicate smile. He watched her walk out of Diablo's and noticed Garrett's proprietary hand on her arm.

Harold Dansen smelled the hottest story to hit Denver in over a year.

"You're a liar," Garrett accused as he drove through the dark streets of Denver. He had walked Megan back to the Jefferson Tower and then had insisted that he drive Megan home. She had reluctantly agreed, and they were now seated in his silver BMW. The first snowflakes of winter were falling from the black sky, and the interior of the car was cold.

"What do you mean?"

"You have no intention of calling that Dansen character. At least I hope you have more brains than that."

"I didn't lie." Megan laughed. "I will call him. I'm just not sure when."

"After all the publicity has died down, unless I miss my guess. When that happens, KRCY won't be interested in McKearn Investments." Garrett smiled and let out a low laugh. "And you used to tell me I equivocated."

"It's not quite the same thing as lying."

"Just a fancier word."

Garrett drove directly to the town house where she had lived for the past five years, one of several tall, nineteenth-century-looking row houses joined by common walls. After finding a parking place on the sloped street, Garrett helped Megan out of the car.

The snow had begun in earnest, and powdery flakes were giving an eerie illumination to the dark night as they fell past the glowing streetlamps. Megan's breath caught in her throat before condensing in the cold night air.

"Would you like to come in for a minute?" she asked, and felt an embarrassed tinge color her cheeks. "I could get you a drink...or a cup of coffee..."

Garrett's smile was wistful. He watched her struggle with the words. "I've been waiting for an invitation like that all night."

Ignoring the huskiness of his voice and the deeper meaning in his words, Megan unlocked the door, stepped into the hallway and flipped on the lights. She tossed her coat onto a chair near the closet and walked into the kitchen.

Garrett followed her at a slower pace, his eyes looking into the rooms, which were only vaguely familiar. He had only been to her home once before, and that was nearly three years ago. He remembered the polish of the gleaming hardwood floors, the Italian marble on the fireplace, the bright patina of the antique brass bed...

By the time he passed by the staircase and entered the kitchen, Megan had poured two cups of coffee laced with brandy. Garrett noticed that the snowflakes that had clung to her hair were melting. Her cheeks were flushed from the cold, and silvery anticipation sparked in her eyes.

Garrett took off his coat and accepted the warm mug she offered before following her into the living room. The room was small, decorated with an eclectic blend of solid wooden antiques and several overstuffed pieces in rich tones of dusty rose and ivory.

Megan took a seat on the padded couch and tucked her

feet under her. She took an experimental sip of the brandied coffee and observed Garrett as he set his drink on a small table, took off his jacket, loosened his tie and set to the task of building a fire from the kindling and paper sitting in a basket on the hearth.

"You don't have to—" Megan began to protest, but stilled her tongue. For a strange reason, she was pleased by the thought of Garrett building a fire in her home. It made him seem as if he belonged here, and she found the idea comforting, if slightly dangerous.

It took a few minutes, but soon the room was filled with the scent of burning pitch and the crackle of flames as they consumed the dry wood. Garrett dusted his hands and sat on the edge of the hearth, letting the warmth of his efforts heat his back. "It should be a law that you have to build a fire during the first snowfall," he decided as he reached for his drink. He took a long, satisfying swallow of the blend of brandy and coffee and watched the snowflakes begin to mound on the window ledge.

"Garrett?" The tone of her voice brought his eyes crashing back to meet the uneasiness in hers. "Why don't we quit stalling and get right down to the reason you're here?"

His friendly smile slowly disappeared. "I wanted to see you again."

She took a sip from her mug and shook her head before leaning wearily against the plump cushions of the rose-colored couch. "Why?"

A muscle worked in the corner of his jaw. "Because it's obvious that you don't trust me, and I think I can understand why," he stated with a sigh. "But you'd better face facts, lady. You're in this as deeply as I am."

"So we'd better form some sort of alliance, is that it?"

His dark eyes flashed with angry gold sparks and the brackets surrounding his mouth deepened cynically. "I think I owe you an explanation."

"About how you got involved with Samples?"

He pondered the black liquid swirling in the bottom of his cup. "About how I got involved with Lana Tremaine."

Megan's throat went dry. The old pain of betrayal cut into her heart. "Maybe we shouldn't bring up the past," she suggested. What would it accomplish? Old wounds would only be reopened. "It's over and done with."

"I don't think so." He finished his drink in one swallow, straightened and strode over to the couch. "There's a lot you don't understand," he stated, touching the curve of her jaw with a sensitive finger.

She held up her palm to forestall the attack on her senses. The conversation was becoming too personal and dangerous. All at once she wanted to crawl back into the safe cocoon of her life and forget about the past. Garrett read the regret in her wide gray eyes.

"I handled everything wrong."

"And now you want to atone for your mistakes?" Megan couldn't hide the bitter sound of disbelief that had entered her voice.

"Let me say what I have to, Megan." He shook his head at the wonder of her. "You never were very good at listening."

"Maybe that was because you weren't very good at confiding in me."

"It wasn't intentional—"

"Not intentional?" she echoed with tears beginning to well in her eyes. "How could you forget the fact that you were engaged to another woman while conducting an...an affair with me?"

"Lana and I had called it off—"

"You never even mentioned her," Megan protested, tears of anguish starting to burn in her throat.

"It wasn't something I wanted to dwell on. I assumed you knew about her."

"No one saw fit to tell me." Gray, condemning eyes studied the rugged planes of his handsome face. "Until—"

"Until it was too late," he finished for her, following the path of her thoughts. "Is that what you thought it was between us...a mistake?"

"Yes."

"Oh, lady," he murmured, edging closer to her on the couch. His hand reached upward and slowly removed the pins from her hair. At the intimacy of the gesture her lower lip trembled and she closed her eyes. "Knowing you was never a mistake."

"Don't—"

"Shhh. It's time you listened to me." She felt the whisper-soft touch of his fingers against the curve of her jaw. Tears burned her eyelids in wistful remembrance. How could anything once so beautiful turn so painful in the course of a few short hours?

His fingers toyed with the ruffle of her blouse, lingering over the pulsing hollow of her throat. And his eyes, vibrant green streaked with brilliant gold, touched the most intimate part of her.

Despite the pain, despite the lonely years, despite Garrett's betrayal, Megan wasn't immune to the seductiveness of his touch. The feel of his fingers toying with the collar of her blouse made her pulse quicken and her heart begin to pound. Thoughts of a younger, more innocent time, before the tragic night of Patrick's death, began to flirt with her mind.

His fingers caught in the fiery strands of her hair and felt for the nape of her neck. "You're a very beautiful woman,

Megan," he whispered as his eyes caressed the refined contours of her face. "Even more beautiful than I remembered."

He was touching her, disturbing rational thought, and a small but very vital part of her was exhilarated by the knowledge that he still wanted her. Her voice, a throaty whisper, was filled with the ache of raw emotions. "I don't think it would be wise to get involved again."

"Too late," he murmured, moving nearer to her. His breath whispered across her hair. "I'm already involved."

She intended to push him away, but the fingers pressed urgently against his chest were little barrier against his weight as he slowly let his body cover hers.

His lips brushed gingerly against the column of her throat before moving upward against the silken texture of her skin. He groaned as the familiar scent of her perfume invaded his nostrils and his fingers twined in the soft waves of her auburn hair. When his lips found hers, the passion of his kiss bridged the black abyss of three forgotten years.

Megan's breathing was irregular, and the weight of Garrett's body, crushing against her rising and falling breasts, was the sweetest aphrodisiac she had ever known. The familiarity of his scent, the seduction in his hazel eyes, the sensual quirk of his dark brows made her ache for him as wantonly as she had in the past.

She welcomed the urgent pressure of his tongue against her teeth, and without hesitation she parted her mouth to accept his warm invasion. Savoring the taste of him, Megan sighed expectantly when his fingers reached for the buttons on her blouse.

Slowly, applying the most excruciatingly sweet torture possible, he slid the pearl buttons from their bonds to part the silken fabric and touch the delicate flesh near her collarbone. The creamy blouse slid off her shoulders and onto the floor while his fingers surrounded the swell of one lace-covered breast. The cool night air coupled with the warmth of his touch made her breasts ache and her nipples tighten under the tender persuasion of his gentle fingers.

"Garrett, please," Megan whispered as the sweet agony enveloped her. The silk and lace of her camisole slid seductively over her breasts, and the thin strap holding the frail garment fell off her shoulder, exposing more of the velvet softness of her skin to him. He kissed the rounded swell of her breast before letting his lips hover over one expectant nipple.

She sighed and wound her fingers in the coarse strands of his heavy hair as she felt the wet impression of his tongue against her skin. Cradling the back of his head and holding him tightly against her breast, she moaned as he suckled her gently through the moistened fabric. Her breathing was raspy, and she couldn't find the strength to stop him when he unbuttoned the waistband of her skirt and slid it over her hips to let it fall, unnoticed, to the floor.

Sweat beaded on Garrett's brow as he surveyed the woman lying seductively beneath him on the couch. Megan's eyes were glazed with a passion only he could spark, and the rapid whisper of her breath through her parted lips invited him to take all of her.

The lacy cream camisole clung erotically to her body, conforming to the rounded contours of her figure. Auburn hair streaked with jets of flaming red surrounded a perfect oval face that was flushed with the heat of intimate passion. Shadowy lashes lowered seductively over silvery eyes. Dark nipples, hard with desire, peaked through the scanty lace, beckoning with rosy invitation.

He groaned as his head lowered to touch them with the tip of his tongue. Megan closed her eyes and abandoned herself to him. Gone with the day were all of the doubts that had plagued her, replaced by the night and the need for his gentle touch. Her body arched intimately against his, aching for the familiar feel of his skin pressed urgently against hers.

Her fingers found the buttons of his shirt, and they trembled as she slowly parted the soft cotton fabric. The shirt fell open, exposing the muscles, rock-hard and lean, that moved fluidly over one another as he raised his body from hers, unbuttoned his cuffs and tossed the unwanted shirt over the back of the couch.

Tentatively her fingers touched his chest. He pulled her hand away and pressed his tongue into her palm. Dark eyes held hers fast, and her blood ran in heated waves throughout her body when his tongue flickered between her fingers.

"I want you," he murmured, his voice thick with the promise of unleashed passion. Those same words echoed from the past, and touched a dangerous part of her mind.

"I… I don't know if that's enough," she gasped, trying to reach for rational thought.

"Let me love you." He leaned over her again and she felt the pressure of his hard torso crushing her breasts. His breath caressed her face, and his eyes, bright with unleashed desire, drove steadily into hers. She felt as if he were reading her darkest secrets. "Let it happen, Megan."

The palm of his hand slid beneath the satiny fabric of her camisole and cupped her breast. Megan gasped as his fingers toyed with her nipple, creating a whirlpool of hot desire deep within the most feminine part of her soul.

His lips touched hers, and his tongue outlined her parted mouth before his head lowered and he placed the warmth of his mouth over the exposed breast. Megan took in a shuddering breath and didn't object when she felt him shift off the couch to encircle her body with his arms.

In one sure movement he stood and carried her out of the

living room and up the graceful staircase to the second floor. First one shoe and then the other dangled from her toes to drop unheeded on the staircase.

Garrett stared steadily into her eyes, silently demanding answers to the unasked questions of the past.

It would be so easy to fall in love with this man again, she thought. So easy and so dangerous. Why hadn't she learned her lesson? How could she contemplate letting him into her life again when so many painful years stood between them?

He carried her into the shadowy bedroom and didn't bother with the lights. She felt the hardness of his mouth as he kissed her again, and desire ripped through her body in white-hot spasms. His tongue probed into her mouth forcefully, touching each intimate part of her with renewed determination and mastery.

She felt the cool polish of the satin comforter against her back when he placed her firmly on the bed. As his dark eyes held hers, he deftly removed the rest of her clothes and tossed them carelessly onto the floor.

His eyes never left her face as he unclasped his belt buckle and slowly removed his pants. Within seconds, he had stripped himself of his clothes and walked boldly back to the bed.

As he lowered himself onto the antique brass bed, Megan felt the sag of the mattress and the welcome warmth of his body covering hers. Her fingers splayed around his back and gently traced the supple curve of each muscle.

The lips he pressed against hers were hard and demanding. No longer was he asking her for her compliance; he was taking what he felt was rightfully his. And she didn't deny him.

Megan felt the exquisite wonder of his hands as they molded against her body, and she realized that her need of him had become white-hot with desire. He touched her legs, letting his fingers slide erotically up her calf and thigh until she moaned from the torment of the hot void aching within her.

His weight, when he pressed against her, was a pleasant burden. His hands offered both torment and solace to her anxious body, and his tongue—God, his tongue!—danced deliciously over her skin until she writhed with the passion flooding her mind and washing over the most intimate parts of her.

"Garrett, please," she moaned against his shoulder. She tasted the salt of his sweat when her mouth touched his skin, and she sighed in grateful relief when at last, she felt his knee part her legs and the firm gift of his manhood joined with her.

The coupling was strong and heated. Words of love, lost in the wonder of the night, sprang unbidden from her lips. And when the final moment of climactic surrender bound them, Megan knew that she was a woman powerless against her love for this man.

7

PALE MORNING LIGHT filtered through the sheer curtains and partially illuminated the quaint room with the silvery iridescence of dawn. Memories, filled visual images of passion and satiation, sifted through Garrett's mind. He squeezed his eyes tightly shut and smiled as thoughts of last night invaded his senses. He felt younger than he had in years. Megan's body was pressed against his back. Garrett stretched before rolling onto his side to watch her cuddle against him without waking.

A pale green sheet was seductively draped across her breasts, and the satin comforter had slipped from the bed to the floor. One of her arms rested comfortably across Garrett's chest. Garrett grinned to himself and brushed aside a lock of auburn hair that had fallen over her cheek. Her dark lashes fluttered open and her eyes, heady with sleep, opened slowly.

"Garrett?" she whispered, her elegant brows drawing together in confusion before she remembered the events of the evening. She smiled up at him lazily, thinking that she was alone in bed with the only man she had ever loved.

"You're beautiful," he said, his eyes holding hers. "I could get used to this."

Megan was running her fingers through her tousled hair when reality struck her like a bolt of lightning. "My God, what time is it?" Bracing herself on one elbow, she peered over his body to the antique sewing machine that served as a nightstand.

Garrett grinned broadly as she held her hair out of her face and squinted at the alarm clock. A dark frown creased her forehead when she read the digital display.

"I've got to get up…"

"You're not going anywhere," he protested, his hands wrapping possessively over her wrists.

"It's nearly eight!"

"And I can't think of a better place to start the morning than here."

Megan's eyes were earnest. "Neither can I," she admitted, trying to withdraw her hands from his grasp. "But I should be at the office in ten minutes."

"You'll never make it."

"Not unless you let go of me." She saw the teasing light in his eyes and tried to defuse it. "Look, Garrett, the New York Stock Exchange is already up and running. And, with all the bad press the investment house is getting, I can't afford to be late—"

"You already are."

"Not for long." She attempted to pull free of his embrace, but he pulled on her arms and her torso followed. Soon she was lying atop him and all she had succeeded in accomplishing was to be drawn closer to him. Her dark hair tumbled in disheveled curls around her face, and she looked at him with mock consternation. "Don't you have somewhere you're supposed to be?" she asked, changing tactics and appealing to his sense of responsibility.

"Uh-huh." His lips touched hers provocatively. "Right here."

"What about your company?"

"They can get along without me for a few hours." His hands rubbed suggestively up her spine, and she knew she was losing the battle.

"You're impossible," she said with a sigh.

"And you love it."

"Garrett, be serious."

"I am."

"I have to get to work."

"What you have to do, lady, is talk to me."

"There's no time." She lifted her finger and touched his beard-roughened cheek.

"Make time," he suggested, kissing the finger that had caressed his cheek.

"Can't we talk later?" She slid a glance of seductive speculation in his direction. "Or was this just a one-night stand?"

He stiffened beneath her. "You know better than that."

"Then it can wait."

Garrett hesitated. "I want to explain about Lana—and for once, I want you to listen."

A painful shadow crossed her eyes and her frail smile turned wistful. She closed her eyes for a moment and fought against the tears that always threatened whenever she thought about Garrett's betrayal. "Maybe we should avoid that topic."

Something in his eyes turned cold. "I just want you to understand that I never loved Lana. The marriage was a mistake from the beginning."

"Then why, Garrett?" Megan asked suddenly, the question she had asked herself for nearly three years springing from her lips.

He rolled his eyes heavenward. "I wish I knew," he admitted. "At the time, I thought it was the right move. You never wanted to see me again." A quick shake of his head stilled the protests forming on her lips. "And I really couldn't blame you." He closed his eyes as if against a sudden stab of pain. "I should have told you that I had been engaged to her, but…" He let out a disgusted breath. "The timing never seemed right. I guess I took the coward's way out. You know the old adage, what she doesn't know won't hurt her. The more involved I was with you, the less my relationship with Lana mattered."

"But you still married her," Megan whispered, her eyes bright with unshed tears.

His jaw hardened and defeat saddened his gaze. "She was waiting for me. When you shoved me out of your life, she was there." He cradled the back of his dark head and stared at the ceiling. "It doesn't make it right," he admitted, his voice rough, "but that's the way it happened."

"I thought we meant so much to each other," Megan whispered.

"So did I." His voice was cold. "But after Patrick's accident, you wouldn't return my calls. You wouldn't have anything to do with me." His voice lowered and he was forced to clear his throat. "It seemed obvious to me that you wanted me out of your life—for good," he added, turning his head to look at her.

"It was a difficult time for me," she hedged, averting her eyes from his penetrating gaze. There were so many things she wanted to tell him—so many things he couldn't begin to understand.

Garrett shifted on the bed, sensing that Megan was shutting him out. "Megan, talk to me."

"I will," she promised huskily, silently hoping for a little time to put her scattered thoughts in order. Last night she had been swept away in the heated tides of passion. This morning she was forced back to reality. The bitter pain of the past and the suspicions of today. Not once had Garrett mentioned the investment swindle, but Megan couldn't forget that he might very well be involved in the scam. "But I don't want to rush it," she insisted. "Right now I've got to get ready for work." She swallowed back the tears and managed a tight smile before laying a comforting hand on his shoulder. "I didn't mean to push you away back then, Garrett. It's just that there were so many things I didn't understand... Patrick's death was very confusing." Slipping off the bed, she reached for her robe and wrapped it tightly around her body despite the protesting sound from Garrett.

Before he could say anything else, she hurried into the bathroom, where she showered, applied a little makeup and pinned her hair in place. Her thoughts lingered on the man she loved. The night had been an intriguing blend of romance, mystery and seduction.

As she stared sightlessly into the steamy mirror, she wondered if it were possible that he loved her—just a little. He obviously cared; she could read that in the stormy depths of his dark, brooding gaze. At the thought of his erotic eyes, her pulse began to quiver and she had to force herself not to run back into the bedroom and into his waiting arms. There were too many barriers standing between them. Not only the past separated them, but also Garrett's involvement in the investment scam. Though he still protested his innocence, he had threatened to sue McKearn Investments. Her teeth sunk into her lower lip. She doubted that he would use her to his advantage, but she had only to consider the past to realize what he could do if he felt cornered.

She set down the hairbrush. Perhaps he was right. Maybe they should talk things over and clear the air. If she lost him now it would hurt, but she could pull herself together again. If her involvement with him deepened, the pain would only be worse.

With new resolve, she stepped into the creamy robe and decided to face the truth. Garrett was right. Before she could begin to trust him completely, they would have to discuss his brief marriage to Lana Tremaine as well as the potential lawsuit. The story he had just told her didn't quite jibe with Lana's version.

Her heart was hammering when she opened the door to the bedroom. "I think it would be best if we talked," Megan announced—to the empty room. Her hand was still poised on the bathroom door and her eyes scanned the small bedroom. Garrett's clothes were missing. Hers had been neatly folded and placed on the freshly made bed. With a lump in her throat, she realized that Garrett might have left her...again.

She turned when she heard a noise behind her, and then smiled when she realized that Garrett was still in the house. He was mounting the stairs two at a time. When he dashed into the room, he was wearing only his slacks and unbuttoned shirt. The exposed muscles of his chest were taut. Tucked under his arm he carried the morning edition of the *Denver Herald*.

"I think you'd better get dressed," he said tersely as he handed her the folded newspaper."

"Why...what's happened?" she asked, noting the wariness in his dark gaze, the strain of his muscles as he began buttoning his shirt.

"Page one," was the clipped reply.

Megan opened the newspaper with trembling fingers and

her throat became suddenly arid. In bold, angry letters, the headlines read:

MCKEARN INVESTMENTS TIED TO SWINDLE
Broker Claims He Was Framed

George Samples, an investment counselor for McKearn Investments, stated yesterday that he was framed in an investment scam originating at the Denver-based brokerage. Samples declared that he is an innocent party to the swindle, which includes several of his accounts. When asked about Samples's allegations, the president of McKearn Investments, Megan McKearn, declined comment. Ms. McKearn inherited the position of president of the eighty-year-old investment company from her father, Jedediah McKearn, who successfully ran the business for nearly forty years. Mr. McKearn, who is semiretired, was unavailable for comment concerning the alleged framing and subsequent dismissal of Samples. According to Samples, the Securities and Exchange Commission is investigating the situation.

"Oh, no," Megan whispered, her eyes scanning the column. Along with the biased text were two pictures. One was of a stern-faced George Samples and another fellow, captioned as George's attorney. The second picture was a snapshot of Jed, taken several years ago when he was still running the company.

Without reading any further, Megan tossed the offensive paper onto the bed and called her parents. The line was busy. She tried again. The monotonous signal beeped in her ear. "Dear God, why won't they leave him alone?" she whispered as she replaced the receiver and shuddered as if from a sudden chill.

Garrett came over to the edge of the bed and placed a strong arm over her shoulders. "You knew it would come to this," he said, trying to calm her.

"Damn!" Megan's small fist crashed forcefully on the sewing machine before she picked up the receiver again and angrily punched out the number for McKearn Investments.

After several rings, a ragged-sounding Jenny answered the phone.

Megan identified herself, and she could hear the relief in the receptionist's voice. "The press has been calling all morning, but I wouldn't give them your number," Jenny stated with a sigh.

Silently Megan cursed her private listing. No wonder the reporters were hounding her father. "That's good, Jenny," Megan said, despite inner fears. "Tell the reporters that I'll be in later in the day and I'll make a statement at that time. Then please call Ted Benson and tell him I'll stop by his office if he's free—I'll check back with you to get the time. Right now, I'm going over to visit my father. If you need me, you can reach me there."

"What about the clients?" Jenny asked hesitantly.

"Each broker should deal with his own. I will personally speak with any of George's clients when I get to the office. I'll call you in a couple of hours."

With her final statement, Megan hung up the phone and tried to call her parents one last time. The line was still busy. "Great," she muttered under her breath, only partially aware that Garrett was watching her.

"Let me drive you," Garrett suggested as he saw the concern etched in Megan's face.

She shook her head. "I don't think that would be wise— Oh, damn!"

"What?"

"I left my car at the office."

Garrett stood and tucked the tails of his shirt into his slacks. "Look, Megan, I'll take you to Jed's house. But I think we'd better hurry. No doubt the reporters are knocking on his door this morning."

Without further argument, Megan reached for a heather-colored wool skirt and matching sweater. She tugged on gray boots and slung a tweed jacket over her shoulders before racing down the stairs and out into the bright, snow-covered morning.

It took nearly twenty minutes for Garrett to maneuver the BMW across town. Most of the streets were passable, but the overnight accumulation of the first snow of winter made driving more difficult than it had been since early spring. Though the day was clear and a brilliant sun radiated from a blue sky, Megan shivered with dread. The newspaper was tucked under her arm, the condemning article hidden by the folds of newsprint.

Megan's fingers tapped anxiously on the armrest of the car, and her face was strained as she stared out the window. How would her father react to the article? Would a bevy of reporters be camped on Jed's doorstep? If it weren't for his failing health… Megan swallowed back the rising dread in her throat.

The wheels of Garrett's car spun for a minute as he turned into the long drive of the McKearn estate. Megan noticed the fresh tracks in the snow. At least one reporter was already there. Through the pine trees, brilliant flashes of red and white light caught her attention. Megan's heart felt as if it had stopped beating.

"Oh, my God," she whispered when she first set eyes on the ambulance parked near the garage. It was facing the street, its lights reflecting ominously in the pristine stillness of the snowfall. "Dad…" A few other cars were parked near the house, and people, mostly from the press, had collected near the doorway. Megan didn't notice them.

Garrett drove toward the ambulance, and Megan reached for the handle of the door before the car had completely stopped. A strong hand over her arm arrested her. "Megan, brace yourself," Garrett advised. She stared for a moment into his concerned eyes and then opened the car door and hurried toward the house. She heard Garrett's footsteps behind her.

Questions were tossed in her direction.

"Ms. McKearn, what's going on?"

"Is there something wrong with your father? Rumor has it that he collapsed this morning."

"Did he know about the investment swindle?"

"Ms. McKearn?"

Muffled voices. Obscured whispers. Pieces of a conversation drifted to her ears over the sound of her boots crunching in the snow.

"Hey—who's she with?" a husky voice inquired. "Doesn't that guy look like—"

"Garrett Reaves. Wasn't she involved with him a few years back?" was the higher-pitched response.

"Don't know. That's about the time her brother was killed."

"Oh, yeah, now I remember—and a girl, too, right?"

"And Reaves was involved then, too? Hey—this is looking better all the time." Then louder, "Ms. McKearn. If I could have just a few minutes…?"

But she was already near the back door. She hadn't heard most of the questions, and those that had met her ears she ignored. Her father's life was on the line. Nothing else mattered. The same sick feeling that had overtaken her the night Patrick was killed had returned.

Megan's gray eyes were deadly when she turned them on

the curious reporters. "Just leave me and my family alone," Megan cast over her shoulder as she jerked open the door. For a moment she thought she caught a glimpse of Harold Dansen, but she quickly forgot the reporter for KRCY as her worry and dread mounted.

Inside, the house was mayhem. Two attendants were wheeling a stretcher toward the door. On it was Jed, his face ashen, the lines of age wrinkling his once robust skin.

"What's happening here?" Megan demanded of one attendant. "I'm Jed's daughter."

Anna McKearn, her red hair unkempt around her swollen face, intervened. "They think he's had another attack," Megan's mother choked out. "Thank God you're here."

"We're taking him to Mercy," the attendant stated as Jed was wheeled out of the house. "You can ride with us."

Anna nodded.

"Wait, Mom. I'll come with you."

"Sorry, lady. No room," the larger attendant said. He turned to his partner. "Let's move."

Megan hugged her mother quickly before Anna followed the attendants out. She stood in the doorway and watched the ambulance roar out of the driveway, siren screaming and lights flashing.

Most of the reporters had taken Megan's angry advice. The more persistent journalists had lingered, only to be told by Garrett that there would be no comment on anything until Jed's condition had stabilized.

Garrett was leaning against his car when Megan emerged from the house some ten minutes later with a few of Jed's belongings, packed into an overnight case. "Dad might need these," she explained feebly, fearing that Jed might never have the opportunity to use the shaving kit and pajamas.

She slid into the car and fought against the tears of despair filling her eyes. Garrett placed his hand over hers, then turned the car around and headed for Mercy Hospital.

"Heart attack?" Garrett asked, softly.

Megan nodded mutely and stared out the window at the snow-covered city. She felt suddenly empty and completely helpless.

The next few minutes seemed like hours until the stark concrete hospital building came into view. Garrett parked near the emergency entrance and helped Megan out of the car. The snow had been shoveled from the parking lot, and Megan walked briskly toward the building. Garrett walked with her, his face set in a grim mask of determination.

Anna McKearn met her daughter in the waiting area. Her face was pale, and for the first time in her life she looked her fifty-six years.

"How bad is it?" Megan wanted to know.

Anna's blue eyes held her daughter's for a second and then slid anxiously away from Megan's probing stare. But in that silent, chilling moment when their eyes collided, Megan knew that her father wasn't expected to live. Tears formed in her eyes, but she forced them back, hoping to find courage against the grim situation.

"What happened?" she finally asked.

Anna tried to speak, couldn't, and just shook her head. Megan gripped her mother's hand firmly, and silently wondered if Jed's heart attack had been triggered by the series of events exploding around the investment company. Jed was under doctor's orders to avoid stress, and the events of the last few days must have put pressure on his frail condition.

The wait was tedious. After about an hour, a young doctor with thick glasses took a chair near Megan's mother. From the defeated expression on the doctor's boyish face, Megan realized that her father was gone.

A strangled cry erupted from Anna's throat before she managed to pull herself together and listen to Dr. Walker. He explained that the resuscitation attempts on Jed had failed. He had never regained consciousness, and his heart had given out completely shortly after he arrived at the hospital.

Megan was stricken and felt a burning nausea rise in her stomach. Though she had known her father's condition was weak, she had never really considered how empty her life would be without him. A cold, black void of loneliness loomed before her.

After holding her mother for a few minutes, Megan found her voice. "I think we should go home... I'll stay with you."

"I'll... I'll be fine," Anna sniffed, squaring her shoulders, but beneath the show of bravado in Anna's blue eyes, Megan recognized disbelief and despair.

"Come on. We have a lot to do." Somehow, despite her own loss, Megan was able to lend her mother a strong arm on which to lean.

Garrett had witnessed the painful scene from a distance. When Anna was on her feet, he offered her a cup of coffee.

"I don't think so," she said with a weary frown.

"Then let me drive you and Megan home."

"I don't want to inconvenience you," Anna replied. "Megan can call a cab."

"Please," Garrett insisted, and Anna McKearn accepted his offer quietly.

Once back at the house, it took Megan several hours to convince her mother to rest. In the meantime, Megan had called the office twice, arranging to have her car driven to her mother's home and promising that she would be in no later than tomorrow morning.

Jenny assured her that, under the circumstances, the staff could work one day without Megan's presence.

Garrett stayed just long enough to convince himself that both Megan and her mother were able to care for themselves.

"You'll call me if you need me?" he said softly as he was leaving.

"I'll be fine," Megan assured him. She was dog tired, but tried to hide that fact from Garrett. He, too, looked as if he could sleep for two solid days.

"And your mother?"

"She's stronger than you might think. I've already called Aunt Jessica. She'll be here in the morning to help with the funeral arrangements and take care of Mom. I'll stay here for a couple of days—until I know that Mom's okay." Megan leaned against the bookcase near the entry, but she had to look away from a framed photograph of her father and brother, which was sitting at eye level on a nearby shelf. The snapshot had been taken when Patrick was only fifteen.

Garrett's hand reached out and touched her chin, forcing her to look directly into his eyes. "And how about you—are you okay?"

She couldn't lie. Instead, she shook her head regretfully, and the tears she had silently kept at bay filled her eyes. "I will be—in a few days."

"You're sure?"

She forced the tears back and smiled sadly. "Of course I will. It just takes a little time."

His eyes lingered on her worried face. "Would you like me to stay?"

She couldn't answer at once. Too many feelings were storming within her, and the loss of her father ached deeply in her heart. First Patrick. Now her father. All of the men who mattered in her life were gone…except for Garrett. And she couldn't stay with him. Not until some of the angry pain had subsided. "Not tonight, Garrett," she whispered, praying that he would understand.

He smiled sadly before bending over to place a tender kiss on her lips. "I'll call," he promised before walking out of the house.

When the door closed behind him, Megan slumped against the cold wood and released the quiet tears of grief that had been burning against her eyelids for the better part of the day.

8

THE WEEK SPED crazily by. Between the turmoil at the office, the continued onslaught of reporters interested in unraveling all of the sordid details of the swindle, the SEC investigation and care for her grieving mother, Megan didn't have a moment's peace. From the minute she woke up each morning until she dropped wearily into bed late at night, Megan had no time to herself. It was as if her entire world were beginning to crumble and fall, piece by piece.

She didn't see Garrett again until the funeral. The crowd of mourners attending the service was larger than Megan had expected, probably because of Jed's reputation in the investment community. Megan also suspected that some of the sympathizers dressed in somber black suits were no more than curious sightseers who knew Jed slightly and had suddenly become very interested in the rumors surrounding Jed McKearn and McKearn Investments. The thought was a bitter pill, and behind the protection of her dark veil, Megan's eyes narrowed with indignation.

With the passage of time, Anna McKearn was beginning to accept the death of her husband. Aided by her daughter's support and the kindness offered by her widowed sister, Jessica, Anna was able to compose herself during the brief ceremony at the funeral parlor. However, standing now in the chill air, staring down at the grave site, Anna's composure started to slip and she had to lean heavily upon her sister's arm.

Megan whispered a silent prayer of thanks for Aunt Jessica. She was a heavyset woman with taffy-colored hair and her feet planted firmly on the ground. She accepted everything life dealt her and made the most of it. Common sense and a dry humor had gotten her through several personal crises of her own and were now helping Anna with the trauma of widowhood.

Dry snowflakes had begun to fall from the heavens, and a cold blast of wind blowing east from the Rocky Mountains chilled the late-afternoon air with the promise of winter. Brittle leaves swirled in the gray skies before settling to earth and becoming covered with a frigid mantle of white snow. The somber wreaths collected powdery snow on their fragile petals.

As Megan stood over the grave site, she let her eyes wander past the family members to scan the interested faces in the crowd huddled nearby. How many people had come to pay their respects to Jedediah McKearn and how many were merely curious onlookers?

She forced her attention back to the preacher and berated herself for her cynicism. Too many days at the office fighting off reporters, dealing with worried account holders and fending off members of the board had given her a jaded outlook, she decided. Just as Garrett had suggested.

The fourth estate hadn't neglected Jed's funeral. The press was represented in full force, including reporters taking copious notes and photographers with their wide-angle lenses trained on the mourners. Megan recognized the hungry faces of the reporters who had been in her office on the day the story about the investment scam was given to the press by George Samples. Like vultures circling carrion, the reporters hovered near the crowd. Megan was bone tired, and it was all she could do to hold her tongue when Harold Dansen cast a baleful look in her direction.

Garrett stood on the fringes of the crowd, keeping his distance from Megan, just as he had on the day the story broke about the investment swindle. Though he was detached, his dark, probing eyes never left her face. Beneath the seclusion of her black veil, she could feel the intensity of his smoldering gaze. He stood slightly apart from the crowd, and though he was dressed only in a dark business suit, he didn't seem to notice the cold wind biting at his face and ruffling his thick, ebony hair. He looked as tired as she felt, and Megan had to force her gaze away from the weary angles of his face.

The funeral had been tiring. Megan was glad when the final prayer had been whispered and the coffin was lowered slowly into the brown earth. Her mother looked tired and pale when Megan took hold of her arm and maneuvered both Anna and Jessica toward the waiting limousine.

Megan managed to avoid members of the press as well as Garrett. Though she longed to be with him, she knew that she couldn't risk it. When her gaze locked silently with his for a heart-stopping instant, Megan was able to communicate to him without speaking, and he appeared to accept her unspoken request for privacy. He understood as well as she did the need for discretion. Already there was speculation that Megan and Garrett were romantically linked, and until the SEC investigation was complete, neither Megan nor Garrett could afford the adverse publicity their romance might engender.

As she reached the car, a heavy hand wrapped possessively around her forearm. Megan looked up, expecting to see Garrett. Instead, she was staring into the cold blue eyes of Ted Benson.

Megan forced a polite smile, which the lawyer returned. "I think we should talk," he suggested. "About Jed's will."

"Can it wait? Mom's tired and we expect a few guests to show up at the house."

Ted didn't expect that response. Nor did he like it. His thin lips pursed together tightly. "I suppose so. I could drop by in a few hours, after the crowd has thinned a little. We could talk then. Since you inherited Jed's share of the stock in McKearn Investments, we have a lot to discuss."

Megan hesitated. The day had already taken its toll on her mother. "I don't know. Tomorrow might be better—"

Ted frowned darkly. "I'm planning to go out of town tomorrow. Business. I'd like to start this ball rolling as soon as possible. Probate could be complicated."

"I'm not sure Mother's up to it," Megan hedged, casting a worried look at Anna, who had climbed into the limousine. Her head rested between the cushions and the shaded window, and her eyes were closed. Little lines of strain were visible on her otherwise flawless skin.

Ted sensed Megan's concern. "Then let me talk to you. Alone. We'll include your mother when I get back into town—the first part of next week." He paused dramatically. "There are a few other things we should discuss, as well. Things that don't have anything to do with the will."

"The SEC investigation?"

"To start with."

Megan hazarded one last look at her mother. Aunt Jessica had slid into the car beside her sister and was patting Anna's hand affectionately. Anna managed a smile.

"What about now?" Ted suggested.

"I can't. I've got to go back to the house—"

"Let me drive you. We can talk on the way."

It seemed like the only solution to the problem. "Just a minute." She explained what was happening to her mother and Aunt Jessica, then reluctantly followed Ted Benson to his car.

Ted held the door open for her, and as she slid onto the plush leather seat, her eyes collided for a minute with the angry glare of Garrett Reaves. He was standing near his car and had watched the entire sequence of events between Ted Benson and Megan. The chilling look he sent her took Megan's breath away.

It was late by the time Megan convinced Ted to take her home. The afternoon at her mother's had been nearly as draining as the funeral itself. Ted Benson hadn't left her alone for a minute, and his insinuations about Garrett worried her. Ted seemed convinced that Garrett was involved in the scam and Megan found herself staunchly defending him. The thought of Garrett being linked to the scandal made her stomach turn, and she couldn't help but wonder if she'd been kidding herself about Garrett's innocence all along. She wanted so desperately to believe him.

Megan had expected Garrett to make an appearance at her mother's house. He hadn't. As each new guest had arrived to express condolences to the family, Megan had secretly hoped that Garrett would be the next. She had been disappointed.

Ted Benson had finished several drinks in the early evening and it became clear during the drive to Megan's apartment that he wanted to discuss more than her father's will. The digital clock on the dashboard of his Porsche quietly announced that it was nearly ten when he parked the car near the curb in front of her town house.

"Thanks for bringing me home," Megan whispered as she

reached for the handle of the door. Ted wasn't deterred. He put a staying hand on Megan's sleeve.

"There are still things we should go over," he suggested, and his fingers crept up the soft leather of her coat.

"They'll keep," Megan replied.

"I'll be out of town."

"Then we'll discuss them when you get back. Maybe by then the investigation will be complete and everything will have calmed down a little."

"Don't kid yourself."

She opened the door.

The throbbing engine of the Porsche stopped as Ted extracted the key from the ignition. "Megan—"

The sound of her name as it sprang from Ted's lips was too familiar. His flirtations had gone much too far. She turned cold eyes toward him.

"Don't you think you should invite me in?" he asked suggestively, his thick white hair gleaming silver in the darkness.

"What I think, Ted, is that you should go home to your wife and children," she stated pointedly. Indignation sparked in her gray eyes.

"My children are grown and Eleanor and I have separated—"

"Not good enough, Ted." He looked as if she had slapped him. "In my book, married is married."

"Eleanor is going to file for divorce in a couple of weeks. We're just working out the details. You understand."

But of course, she did. "Look, Ted, I don't think we should confuse our professional relationship."

"Who's confused?"

"You are," she said firmly. "Because that's all there is. You're the attorney for McKearn Investments. I'm the client. It's simple." Her words sounded cruel, but the last thing Megan wanted to do was lead the man on. He had earned both his reputations: as an excellent lawyer, and as a womanizer. Megan didn't want to give him even the slightest encouragement that she was interested in anything other than his professional services.

"So where do you get off—acting so pure?" he asked suddenly as he fumbled in the inner pocket of his jacket for his cigarettes. He shook one from the crumpled pack, and lit it with his gold lighter. The red ash glowed brightly in the dark interior of the car.

"I'm just telling you that I'm not interested—"

"These are the eighties. You're a free woman. You run the investment company, you're independently wealthy—or will be when Jed's estate is probated—"

"And I don't get involved with married men."

"Unless his name happens to be Garrett Reaves," Ted suggested. Megan stiffened. "I remember what happened between you and Reaves, Megan. You were seeing him when he was engaged to Lana Tremaine. At least, that's what your brother insisted." Ted took a long drag on the cigarette. "So don't act so damned virginal with me."

"Look, Ted, you're getting way out of line," Megan shot back. "I'll talk to you when you get back…about business!"

"You'd just better be careful," Ted warned, slurring his words slightly. "Reaves isn't the god you make him out to be."

"I don't—"

Ted waved off her protests. "Save it, Megan. You've defended him from the minute you found out about the scam."

"I'm just not sure that he's involved."

"Because you're too blind to see the truth. If Reaves were as innocent as you seem to think, why would he have Ron Thurston and his associates poking around, trying to find out everything there is to know about George Samples, McKearn Investments and you?"

Megan had begun to slide out of the car, but she stopped. What was Ted insinuating? Dread, like a clammy hand, began to climb up her spine. "What are you talking about?"

Ted smiled in satisfaction. "It seems Mr. Reaves is covering his bases. I wouldn't be surprised if he slapped you with a lawsuit for defamation of character or some such nonsense, just as a legal ploy."

"To put me on the defensive?" she whispered.

"To save his ass."

Megan tried to rise above the attorney's speculations. "How do you know all of this?"

Ted laughed and stubbed out his cigarette. "The legal community is pretty tight, or didn't you know that? Not much happens in this town that I don't know about. That's what your company pays me for. Remember?" Carelessly he reached for her hand. "Come on, Meg, lighten up. Ask me in and I'll let you buy me a drink—"

"Go home, Ted," she said firmly, extracting her hand. Then realizing how inebriated he had become she changed her mind. "Look, maybe you'd better not drive. I'll call a cab."

"I could just stay here."

"Out of the question."

With her final rebuff, she shut the car door and marched up the steps of her porch, intent on calling a cab to retrieve him. It was too late. She heard Ted swear loudly and start the engine of the flashy car. Then the wide tires squealed and the engine roared noisily into the night.

"Some men never grow up," she muttered to herself as she unlocked the door and entered her homey town house. Angrily she mounted the stairs; she was still seething when she hung up her clothes and slipped into her warm robe. Knowing she was too restless to sleep, she went back downstairs and made herself a warm cup of cocoa. She sipped the creamy hot drink and smiled grimly. The hell with calories. The hell with reporters. And the hell with men like Ted Benson who thought they could charm any woman into their bed.

Maybe that's my problem, she thought. *Maybe I can't deal with the new morality.* Sleeping with a man without commitment, quick one-night stands for pure physical pleasure, weren't her style and never had been. Sex was more than just a physical need; it was an expression of mental attraction and companionship, as well.

Then what about Garrett? He's never been committed to you! You're a hypocrite, Megan McKearn—saving yourself for the one man who has never done anything but use you. Ted Benson seemed to think Garrett was just using her again. She tried to ignore the lawyer's thoughts, dismissing them as idle conjecture from a tongue loosened by alcohol, but she couldn't. There was a thread of truth to Ted's convictions nagging at the back of her conscience.

The phone rang sharply. Megan nearly spilled the remainder of her hot chocolate at the sound. Despite the lingering suspicions in her mind, Megan prayed that Garrett would be on the other end of the line.

"Ms. McKearn?"

Megan's mouth turned into a frown of disappointment. "Yes."

"Harold Dansen. KRCY news." Though it was after ten at night, the tenacious reporter still had the audacity to call.

"Sorry to bother you…" he apologized.

Then why did you? she thought angrily.

He was just getting to that. "…but I haven't been able to connect with you. Remember the other night at Diablo's? You promised me an interview," he wheedled.

"I haven't forgotten," Megan stated, biting her tongue to

keep from giving him a piece of her tired mind. "It's just that I've been extremely busy."

"I know, and my condolences," Dansen interjected. "What about later in the week?"

"I don't know. My schedule is pretty full, and I don't have my appointment book with me. Could you call the office Monday morning and talk to my secretary, Jenny Hughs? Or better yet, I'll have her call you."

"I was hoping we could get together some time this weekend," he suggested.

Megan's voice was cool put polite. "I'm sorry, Mr. Dansen. My weekend is booked. If you could call the office Monday—"

"I tried that already." Megan could almost hear the smirk in his voice. Without words he was accusing her of avoiding him.

"Then let me call you next week after I've checked my schedule."

Knowing that he'd pushed as hard as he dared, Harold Dansen hung up the phone, determined to get to the bottom of the McKearn Investment fraud story and whatever other secrets Megan McKearn kept hidden.

When Megan placed the receiver back on the cradle of the phone, she let her hand linger on the cool, ivory-colored instrument. For a moment she considered calling Garrett, and then, realizing how late it was, decided against it. Besides which, she couldn't afford to be seen with him again. Since her father's death, Megan had been under more scrutiny than she ever would have imagined.

The press had refused to leave her alone. The phone hadn't stopped ringing since the day Jed passed away. Even though her number was unlisted, the press had gotten hold of it. Megan suspected that George Samples had eagerly provided the news media with her personal number and address.

Changing telephone numbers hadn't been difficult, but she didn't relish the idea of moving. At least not yet. She didn't have the time or the energy. Megan took another sip of her now cool cocoa and frowned.

Somehow, Harold Dansen had gotten hold of her new phone number. It wouldn't be long before the rest of the media would have it, as well. With a sigh, she drained her hot chocolate, licked her lips and walked into the kitchen. After setting her empty cup in the sink, she started up the stairs. When she was on the third step, the doorbell chimed and Megan bristled.

Who would be calling on her at this hour of night? The most probable person was Ted Benson. No doubt he had stopped at a local bar for a nightcap on the way home and with renewed fortification was approaching her once again. This time she would make her position undeniably clear, even if it meant she would have to hire another lawyer to handle the legal work for McKearn Investments.

When Garrett watched Megan leave the cemetery with Ted Benson, his jaw hardened and his back teeth pressed together uncomfortably. Jealousy swept over him in a hot wave. He was able to hide his anger by pushing his fists deep into his pockets and avoiding eye contact with any of the lingering mourners. But the sense of vengeful jealousy overtaking him made his dark eyes glower ominously.

Common sense told him he couldn't cause a scene, but a primal urge akin to possession clouded his judgment. Only after several minutes of wrathful deliberation did he decide to bide his time...until he was certain to corner Megan alone.

And now, many hours later, the waiting was over. He'd given Megan more than enough time to return to her apartment. It was nearly eleven when he finally called and the monotonous beep of a busy signal told him Megan was home.

It took him less than ten minutes to drive from the bar to her apartment. After hours of quietly sipping a beer and disinterestedly watching cable sports, he was anxious to reach her. He parked the car less than a block from her building and strode meaningfully to her door.

Tonight he had a plan. After three years of excuses and lies, he was done with all the indirect messages and vague insinuations, the usual crap that happened between a man and a woman. Tonight he was interested only in the truth and one woman. And he intended to have both.

He rang the bell impatiently. Within seconds Megan peeked through the window, recognized him and opened the door. Her smile was tight and there was a new wariness in her stance as she leaned against the door and watched him through eyes narrowed in undisguised suspicion.

Garrett heard the door close softly behind him. He stood in the hallway, his hands thrust into the pockets of the same suit pants he had worn all day. When he turned to face her, he noticed that she hadn't moved. Her arms were folded beneath her breasts, and one shoulder was pressed against the wooden door for support.

"Pack an overnight bag. You're coming with me," he announced without any trace of a smile.

Megan stood stock-still. It was evident that Garrett was angry, but he was shouting orders to her as if he'd lost his mind.

"Wait a minute…"

"I said, get some clothes together," Garrett instructed, his voice low and commanding.

"Why?"

"I told you. I want you to spend the weekend with me."

Her elegant eyebrows arched expressively. "Did it ever occur to you to ask?"

"Look, Megan, I'm tired of all the double-talk. I want you to come to Boulder for the weekend. I've waited all day for you, and I'm sick of worrying about your reputation, the lawsuit, the past and all the other ridiculous excuses we've used to avoid the real issue!" he exclaimed, his voice rising with the intensity of his words.

"And I'm tired of men trying to manipulate me." A thin smile curved her lips, and she shook her head as if she couldn't believe what she was hearing. Her coppery hair glinted in golden streaks as it swept against the plush velour of her robe. For a moment, Garrett was tempted to forget everything but making love to her long into the night. Angry color gave her cheeks a rosy hue, and her round eyes seemed silvery in the dim light of the room.

"The only people who are manipulated are those who let someone else run their lives."

"Then you'll understand why I think we should forget about spending the weekend together."

"Don't do it, Megan," he warned, the skin tightening over the angular planes of his face. He pointed an unsteady finger at her face. "What I understand is that there is only one real issue here."

"And that is?"

"That either we care for each other, or everything we've shared isn't worth a plug nickel. Do we have something special, or is this whole...relationship built on lies? Is it real or is it a lot of bull?" He flipped his wrist upward in an impatient gesture of annoyance and then slapped the wall near the door with his rigid hand. "Damn it, Megan, just what the hell are we doing to each other?" he asked in a lower, more cautious voice. His broad shoulders sagged, as if the burden were suddenly too much to bear.

Garrett was leaning against the wall, only a few feet from her, and yet she felt that the wide abyss separating them could never be bridged. Could she ever learn to trust him? Could she take the chance? Was the prize worth the risk?

The emotional day had taken its toll on her, and she felt an uncomfortable lump forming in her throat. Garrett straightened his shoulders and pulled angrily at the knot in his tie. The lines near his eyes were deep, evidence of the strain robbing him of slumber.

Despite her earlier doubts, Megan felt her heart bleed for this man. She touched him gently on the cheek, and the tips of her fingers encountered the rough hairs of his beard. Garrett closed his eyes and groaned as if in physical pain.

"Why don't you stay here," she suggested. "We've both been through a lot. You're tired…"

"Of people who don't know what they want." His eyes opened quickly, and he pushed aside the seduction of her hand. "If I stay here tonight, nothing really will change. It's too convenient. When I'm in the city, I spend the night." He shook his dark head and scowled. His eyes pierced into her soul. "I want more."

"I don't understand—"

"You're not trying." His hazel eyes flashed savagely. "Casual nights aren't enough."

"And you think a weekend in Boulder will be?"

His dark gaze slid downward from her mysterious eyes, past her parted lips, the column of her throat, the curve of her breasts to linger on the sash holding her bathrobe closed. He wanted her as desperately as he ever had, and the heat in his loins throbbed mercilessly. He shifted uncomfortably.

"I don't know if there is enough," he admitted in a hoarse whisper, and forced his gaze back to her face.

Megan's lips pulled into a wistful frown. "You really have no right, you know," she said calmly. "No right to come barging in here and making demands on me."

"Are you coming with me or not?"

It was an ultimatum—pure and simple. She had no doubt that if he left tonight he would never be back. But there was more to it than that. In his own way, he was reaching out to her... The decision was easy.

"It will only take me a minute to pack."

9

SILENCE AND DARKNESS.

The interior of the car was shadowed, and the only sound to disturb the stillness of the night was the whine of the engine as the sporty vehicle headed toward Garrett's remote mountain home. Headlights pierced through the darkness and reflected on the large snowflakes falling from the dark sky and beginning to cover the little-used country road.

The tension inside the BMW was so charged that Megan's stomach had tightened into painful knots. Her fingers drummed restlessly on the armrest. Garrett was near enough that she could have touched him with the slightest of movements. She didn't. When she chanced a secretive glance in his direction, she noticed that the square angle of his jaw was set in a hard line of determination. He looked like a man hell-bent to get accomplished whatever task he set for himself.

Disturbing thoughts flitted through Megan's tired mind, creating a small, dull headache behind her eyes. Had Ted Benson been right after all? Was Garrett setting Megan up just to watch her fall? She closed her eyes against the thought that, just possibly, Garrett was desperate and ruthless enough to use her fragile relationship with him as a weapon in the courtroom battle he had promised. Ted Benson had assured her that Garrett planned to sue McKearn Investments. According to Benson, it was only a matter of time before Garrett played his trump card and sought revenge against McKearn Investments.

As he drove, Garrett's eyes never left the slick pavement winding through the foothills. He concentrated on holding the sporty car on the road. Several times the tires of the BMW spun wildly against the snow-covered pavement and he silently cursed himself for not bringing the Bronco. The accumulation of snow made driving more hazardous than he had predicted, and his hands grasped the steering wheel in a death grip. He attempted to keep his mind on driving and off the gentle curve of Megan's knee, which his fingers sometimes brushed when he shifted gears. Even though she was wearing heavy winter clothes, she was the most damnably seductive woman he had ever met.

Megan sat nervously in the passenger seat. Occasionally she would let her gaze wander surreptitiously to the tense features on Garrett's face, but for the most part she, too, stared out of the window and waited to see what the night, and the enigmatic man sitting next to her, would bring.

The strain of the forced silence finally got to her. She had expected an explanation from Garrett, but when, after nearly a half hour, he hadn't spoken, she decided to take the bull by the horns and get to the bottom of his unspoken hostility.

"Why was it so important that I come with you tonight?" she finally asked, tilting her head to face him.

"I told you, I'm tired of playing games."

"Is that what we were doing?"

"You were avoiding me."

"Oh, Garrett." Her words were expelled in a weary sigh.

"I was only being cautious." For the first time she realized just how tired he looked. His hair was unruly, his face nearly gaunt with lines of worry. How many sleepless nights had he spent recently, and why?

"Tonight, lady, we're going to work this out," he promised as a tiny muscle worked angrily in his jaw. The car slid on an upgrade, and with a curse, Garrett downshifted. His fingers grazed her knee, causing Megan's heart to trip.

She lifted her shoulders in a dismissive gesture that belied her turmoil of inner emotions and concern for him, then turned to stare out the window once again.

The rest of the drive was accomplished in silence, and Megan was relieved to see the dark silhouette of Garrett's house when the car slid around the final curve in the road.

Once Garrett had parked the car, he opened the door for Megan and hoisted her small valise from the back seat. The stone manor, tucked sedately in the snow-laden pines, seemed slightly forbidding. The windows were dark and the panes covered with a thin layer of ice. Snow piled on the flatter surfaces of the roof, to glisten in the ethereal illumination of the security lights near the garage.

Frigid air brushed over Megan's face and snowflakes clung tenaciously to her hair. Involuntarily, she shivered as Garrett unlocked the heavy wooden door and stepped aside to let her enter.

The interior of the Tudor home was as cold as the night. When Garrett flipped on the lights and adjusted the thermostat, Megan tried not to stare at the disheveled state of the rustic old house. Very obviously something was wrong here.

The carpets were rolled and bound. The warm wood floors were covered with a thin layer of dust and most of the furniture had been draped with heavy sheets. Clothes, books and various memorabilia were scattered haphazardly around the rooms branching from the foyer.

Only the den looked as if anyone had cared enough to keep it clean and comfortable.

Garrett noticed Megan's confused look as she stared at the disarray in the beautiful old house. "Maid's day off," he joked bitterly.

"Not funny, Garrett. What happened?"

"I'm living in the apartment in Denver," he responded with a disinterested lift of his broad shoulders. He kneeled before the stone fireplace and began arranging kindling as if to start a fire. His actions said more clearly than words, end of discussion.

Megan wouldn't be put off. After all, he was the one who had dragged her here. "But I don't understand," she whispered, her eyes roving restlessly over the pine walls. Distractedly she ran a finger along the bookcase and then brushed the dust on her jeans. "I thought you liked living here."

"I did." The fire ignited and began to crackle against the pitchy wood. Garrett stared into the golden flames.

"Then why?"

"It was something you said," he stated, rising from his kneeling position on the hearth and dusting his hands together. "Something about too many ghosts from the past." His hazel eyes touched hers for a moment, and then, obviously uncomfortable, he dismissed the difficult subject. "You look like you could use a cup of hot coffee," he decided. "I'll be right back." After flashing her what was intended to be his most charming smile, he walked out of the room.

He looks older than he should, Megan decided. Had guilt over the investment scam and worry about being found out aged him?

Megan tightened the ribbon holding her hair and shook

off the uneasy thoughts. She considered offering to help him with the coffee, but decided to wait and see what the evening had in store for her. This was Garrett's idea; let him show his hand. For someone who wasn't interested in playing games, he was doing a damned good job of keeping Megan in the dark.

In the short time that Garrett was gone, Megan fidgeted and studied the interior of the home he had so dearly loved. Why would he move?

Memories of the fateful night three years ago assailed her senses and crowded her mind. A wistful smile caressed her lips as she remembered the touch of his fingers as they'd softly caressed her skin, the taste of his lips as they'd whispered softly over hers, the feel of his muscles, strident and lean, as they'd pressed urgently against her body. The powerful images, as fresh as if they had happened yesterday, reawakened feelings for Garrett she had hoped would die.

Even though she had been with him once since that tragic night, Megan wasn't sure of herself. Nor did she know where her feelings of love might lead. The future appeared as stormy as the past.

Tears threatened to spill, but she valiantly held them at bay. Perhaps it was better to forget what she and Garrett had shared...

Megan gritted her teeth against the familiar feelings of love that began to fill her mind. She shivered from the cold, and though the fire took hold and the hungry orange flames began to give off a little warmth, she still sat huddled on the hearth, dressed only in the faded pair of jeans, bulky ski sweater, thick parka and boots she had hurriedly donned when Garrett insisted that she come with him.

"It'll warm up soon," Garrett solemnly predicted as he walked back into the room and noticed her chattering teeth. He was carrying two steaming mugs. The welcome fragrance of coffee scented the air. Garrett hesitated at the bar. He reached for a bottle of scotch, read the label, frowned and replaced it. "Can I get you anything else?"

Eyeing the liquor dubiously, she shook her head. "I don't think so." The heat from the fire was beginning to touch her back, and for the first time since leaving her apartment she was beginning to feel warm. "The only thing I want from you tonight is an explanation."

"For?"

"Cut it out, Garrett. You're the one who doesn't want to play games. Remember?" She pushed her palms on her thighs, rose to her full height, picked up her cup and walked toward the window. "Why don't you explain to me why, all of a sudden, in the middle of the night, it was so bloody important to shanghai me here."

His thick brows lifted expressively. "You came of your own volition," he pointed out. Her mouth quirked downward but she refrained from protesting. "That, at least, is encouraging," he muttered under his breath.

Forgetting his earlier decision to abstain, he grabbed a bottle of brandy and splashed some of the amber liquor into his mug before lifting the bottle in a gesture of offering. Megan frowned and shook her head. Tonight she didn't want any alcohol to cloud her judgment. She couldn't afford to replay the tragic scene from her past.

"Why did you bring me here?"

"I want to talk to you."

"About the SEC investigation," she guessed.

"Among other things."

"You and half the population of Colorado—"

"What's that supposed to mean?"

"Only that my phone hasn't stopped ringing for the past

two weeks." She stared into the knowing eyes of the only man she had ever loved. When would it end?

He smiled mysteriously. "Then maybe it's a good thing that you came here tonight. At least you won't be subjected to the phone for the rest of the weekend...and you and I won't be interrupted." A gleam of smoky satisfaction lighted his eyes as he took a long swallow of the scalding liquid and observed her over the rim of his cup. His thick, black hair curled in unruly waves over his ears. Had it not been for the lines of worry on his face and the cynicism tainting his charming smile, he would have been as ruggedly handsome as he had ever been.

The hard angle of his jaw relaxed slightly, and Megan felt all her earlier hostilities dissipating into the cold mountain night. The hint of a bemused smile tugged at the corners of his mouth.

"I talked to Ted Benson today," she said, and took a sip of her coffee. It burned the back of her throat.

"I noticed." The smile faded. Garrett was suddenly wary.

"He seems to think that you plan on dropping a lawsuit in my lap."

Garret studied the delicate contours of her face. "Why?"

She shrugged. "Rumor, I guess. He insinuated that you asked your attorney to find all the skeletons in my family closet."

"That doesn't make too much sense, does it?" he scoffed, but despite his feigned nonchalance there was an involuntary tensing of his muscles.

"Why not?"

"Because I already know about them all—I was there the night Patrick died."

A suffocating silence settled in the room. Megan stared into the black depths of her coffee before taking a seat near the fire. "What's that supposed to mean?"

"The only skeletons I'm concerned with are those that keep pushing you away from me. That night, three years ago, started all the trouble between us. And if we're ever...going to rise above what happened, we'll have to understand it first."

"I don't see any reason to dredge up the past." She looked away from his probing stare.

"I do." His voice was cold and determined. "You still blame me for Patrick's death...and I want to know why." The frustrations of three painful years contorted his face. "For God's sake, Megan, I barely knew your brother."

"You've got it all wrong," she whispered, forcing herself to meet his dark, uncompromising gaze. "It's not you I blame." She closed her eyes against the torture of the truth.

"But I thought—"

She silenced him by raising a trembling palm. "If anyone's to blame... I am." Her voice was barely audible.

He was stunned. "Why?"

She set her cup on the flagstone hearth and wrapped her arms around her knees. The secret she had hidden from Garrett in the past came reluctantly to her lips. "Patrick told me that you were engaged." Garrett frowned, but didn't interrupt. "Earlier that day he had shown me the proof—an article torn out of a paper—the engagement announcement. He thought you were using me."

"And you believed him." Garrett's face had twisted into a mask of disgust.

"Of course not!" Megan sighed wearily and fought against the tears that always threatened when she thought of that one painful night. Images of Patrick's boyish face, contorted in condemnation and self-righteousness, flashed through her mind. He had tried to help her—hoped to warn her about Garrett—and she, in her own stubborn, prideful way, hadn't listened. "I told him that you wouldn't use me, and to prove it to myself I came back here...to meet you..." Her voice faded, and a shiver as cold as the winter snow ran down her spine. Garrett sat down next to her and silently brushed a tear from her eye.

"Oh, Megan," he moaned, remembering her innocence and vulnerability. It was his fault, he told himself. He had pushed her into something she wasn't able to accept. He had known that Megan had been distracted earlier that evening, but he hadn't been able to guess the reason for her unease. And he hadn't been able to coerce her into telling him what was bothering her. He had tried to comfort her, and Megan had responded willingly. Her surrender had been complete, and he had thought that the tears in her eyes as his body had claimed hers were tears of selfless love. He had trusted her completely for those few intimate hours—until the morning newspaper had callously announced to the world that Patrick McKearn, only son of a wealthy Denver businessman, had been killed in a single-car accident. The other passenger in the car was dead, as well. Garrett closed his eyes against the memory of Megan's tortured face when she had read the article and flung the offensive paper across the room.

"No!" she had screamed, refusing to believe that her only brother was dead.

"I didn't believe Patrick," Megan said, swallowing against the dryness that had settled in her throat. Her gray eyes beseeched him. "I was so convinced that you weren't involved with anyone else that I didn't mention my argument with Patrick to you. I thought if I brought it up it would seem as if I doubted you."

"And you did." After three years, he finally understood the wariness in her eyes when he had first made love to her.

"No!" she nearly shouted, before lowering her quavering voice. "At least not then."

"But later?"

"Garrett, you married Lana."

"On the rebound, Megan. You wouldn't see me," he reminded her.

"Because of the guilt, damn it!" she said in an explosive burst of anger. "While you and I were here, in this very room, drinking imported champagne and making love, Patrick was trying to reach me!" The tears began in earnest, flowing down her cheeks in hot rivulets of grief and frustration.

"What does that have to do with anything?" Garrett asked, placing a comforting hand on her shoulder. Quickly Megan stood, breaking the physical contact between them.

"Patrick was in trouble that night. He knew it and he tried to reach me—"

"Didn't he know you were with me?"

She shook her head, and her hair, still damp from the melting snowflakes, glistened in the fireglow. "He thought we'd broken up. He assumed that, after I cooled off, I would come to my senses and believe the newspaper article he'd given me."

Garrett wasn't convinced. "He could have guessed that you were here."

Her gray eyes pierced into his. "Don't you remember, Garrett? We took the phone off the hook so as not to be disturbed." Megan rubbed her temple with her fingers, trying to relieve the pressure building behind her eyes. "He was probably looking for me when the accident occurred."

"You don't know that."

"But I have to live with it. Every day of my life."

"You can't blame yourself."

She smiled grimly. "Funny. That's what I've told myself, over and over. I guess I'm just not very convincing."

Garrett was trying to make some sense out of what she

was saying. "You said that Patrick was in trouble. What kind of trouble?"

Megan hesitated, sure that she had divulged too much already. Garrett seemed sincere, and in her heart she felt she could trust him with her most intimate secret... And yet, he had betrayed her in the past and had reason to lie to her now.

Garrett read the doubts clouding her normally clear gaze. He ran tense fingers through his hair and tried to think straight. How much of what she was saying was true, and how much was the result of three burdened years of guilt? He damned himself for the brandy clouding his mind.

But was it the liquor or the woman? He didn't seem to think clearly whenever she was near him, and he had vowed that tonight he would have all the answers to the questions that had been plaguing him for three long years. It was his move.

"I had been engaged to Lana," Garrett admitted. He finished his coffee and tossed the dregs into the fire. The flames sputtered noisily as he collected his ragged thoughts. "But I thought it was over. Honestly, Megan, you have to believe that. I just hadn't gotten around to making an official announcement. I wanted to give Lana the time to handle it her own way."

"It doesn't matter," she lied.

"Of course it does." When he stood, he reached for her, and this time she didn't pull away from him. "As long as there is anything or anyone standing between us, it matters." He folded her into the strength of his arms, holding her in an unwavering embrace. "Now, tell me, when Patrick tried to get hold of you...what happened?"

Her face contorted with pain. "Don't you remember?"

"What I remember is that I spent the night here, right in

front of this fireplace, with the most beautiful woman I've ever had the misfortune to meet."

Megan managed a thin smile, and he touched her chin with his finger. When she looked into his eyes, she felt as if she could die in their warm, hazel depths.

"It was a wonderful night, Megan…" he murmured against her hair. Her pulse jumped and her heart throbbed painfully in her chest.

Garrett kissed her softly on the forehead, his lips warm and familiar against her skin.

"It was the night Patrick was killed," she said dully, all her beautiful memories shattered by that one last, tragic fact. She slipped away from the tenderness of his embrace and wrapped her arms around herself as if experiencing a sudden chill. It was so like the last time she was here. The cold promise of winter, the inviting crackle of the fire, the warmth of Garrett's arms. She stared sightlessly out the window.

"Megan." His voice was low and filled with pain. "I want to hear the rest of what happened that night."

"I'm sure you read about it—"

"The press may have exaggerated, or been paid to cover up some of the facts."

"By whom?"

"Who do you think? Your father was a pretty influential man. If he wanted to, he could have bought any of the reporters—"

"If he'd wanted to, and if he'd found someone dishonest enough to distort the facts."

"Everybody has a price."

"Do they, Garrett?" she asked with a glance in his direction. "And what's yours? What would you pay to keep your name out of the mud?" Then, when he didn't immediately respond, she turned her back to him and thought aloud, "Just how far would you go? For example, would you be willing to leak a little inside information on your company to a broker, so that he could let some other investors make money on a few well-placed trades?"

"Of course not!"

She turned to face him, disguising the fact that her heart was beating with dread. Tense lines of strain webbed from his eyes and bracketed his mouth. "But that's exactly what happened last April."

His eyes glittered dangerously. "If anyone—other than myself—made money selling short on Reaves Chemical stock, it was because of George Samples. It had nothing to do with me, Megan."

She wanted to believe him, but a trace of doubt still remained. "Then why would George take the chance and let your account become involved with his scam?"

Garrett shook his head. "I don't know."

"It just doesn't make much sense," she whispered as her secret fears mounted. With a sigh, she dropped into the corner of the couch, pulled off her boots, tucked her feet beneath her and rested her head against the leather cushions. It had been a long, grueling day, and she was exhausted.

Garrett shook his head in bewilderment and swore softly. He had been studying this same puzzle for weeks. He felt sure the answer was within his grasp—if only he could find it. "I was hoping that by now this entire mess would be behind us. I thought the SEC would have nailed the culprits and exposed whoever it was over at the newspaper who helped George with his scam."

"It takes time."

"Maybe not." Garrett's eyes suddenly sparked. "If I know Samples, he'll talk. He's not about to take the rap himself.

Right now he's got a few of his friends involved with him, and so far, no one is rocking the boat."

"Except you."

"Exactly. So who's he covering for? Someone who works at the newspaper."

"Or...someone who does research for the *Denver Financial Times*," Megan surmised. "It could be anyone attached to the paper, not necessarily a reporter."

"What about the columns? Were they written by the same person?" He placed his hands on his thighs and sat next to her on the couch.

Megan shook her head. "I don't know, but I don't think so. If only one reporter were involved, it would be too obvious and the SEC would have already found him out."

"Maybe they have," Garrett said cryptically. "Maybe the government is just waiting until all the evidence is compiled before they act."

"It could take months. Anyone could have been working with George. A reporter, a delivery boy, a secretary, even a janitor—anyone who had access to the offices and knew where to look could have called George before the stories were printed." Garrett was listening to her intently, and he tugged thoughtfully on his lower lip.

Megan saw a glimmer of secret knowledge flicker in his eyes. "Wait a minute—you've figured something out, haven't you?"

"I'm not really sure," he evaded, stretching his arms and clasping them behind his head. "But, dear lady, I think that I'm about to be cleared in this swindle."

"You think you know who George's accomplice is," Megan surmised with a quick intake of breath. Was it possible that Garrett really wasn't involved in the scam and that he was just as desperate as she to find the culprits responsible for the scandal? Her heart missed a beat in anticipation.

"A theory."

"Which you have no intention of sharing with me."

Garrett's easy smile slanted across his face. "Not yet. As I said, it's only a theory."

"No proof to back it up." Megan's fingers tapped nervously on the arm of the couch as her mind worked in crazy circles. Who? Who would be involved with George, worked for the *Denver Financial Times* and was clever enough to avoid suspicion? It was obvious from the satisfied smile on Garrett's face that he thought he knew the answer. His eyes had taken on a ruthless, vengeful gleam.

A comfortable silence settled between them, and Garrett placed his arm around her shoulders. "I've missed you," he admitted raggedly.

She laughed at the irony of the situation. "I've missed you, too."

The arm across her shoulders tightened and drew her close to him. "We've been through a lot, you and I, together and apart. I'd like to think that we can face whatever happens in the future together."

She swallowed with difficulty. Anticipation mingled with dread. "Together?"

"I've done a lot of thinking, Megan. After your father died and it was nearly impossible to see you, I decided that it would be best if we made a clean break. You go your way and I go mine. I even went so far as to move out of this house and talk to a real estate broker about selling it."

Megan closed her eyes. A clean break from Garrett. Now that she had been with him again, would she be able to survive without him? She braced herself against his brutal rejection. Not only was he pushing her aside, but this beautiful old house, as well. "But you haven't…put the house on the market?"

"I couldn't."

"Why not?" she whispered, barely able to breathe.

"The ghosts are here for me, too," he conceded. "But I'm not afraid of them. In fact—" he placed a strong finger under her chin and tipped her face upward to meet the conviction of his gaze "—I like the memories we shared here. Selling this place would be like cutting out a very important part of my life—a part I would rather keep."

Her lips trembled as they parted. Slowly he lowered his face and covered her mouth with his. Strong fingers twined in her hair and cradled her head against his. Her pulse began to race wildly as hot, insatiable urges uncoiled within her. Her fears fled as he slowly untied the ribbon holding her hair away from her face. The auburn curls tumbled free of their bond in tangled disarray.

"Garrett, please," she whispered, surrendering herself to the heat of his passion. His tongue slid between her teeth to savor the sweet moistness of her mouth and flick with lightning swiftness against its mate. Megan responded with a compliant moan.

He unzipped her parka, slid it off her shoulders and tossed it onto the floor. His warm fingers found the hem of her sweater and slowly discovered the supple muscles of her back. His hand splayed possessively over her spine to inch slowly upward, tracing each of her ribs with an exploring finger.

Megan's hands released the buttons of his shirt and touched the rock-hard muscles of his chest. With an impatient movement he jerked off the cotton garment and tossed it recklessly onto the floor near her parka.

His eyes glittered savagely as she moved first one hand and then the other against the soft mat of black hair covering his bronzed skin. The muscles of his chest flexed when one of her fingers toyed with his nipple; he was forced to close his eyes against the sweet agony.

"You're wanton," he whispered as his mouth brushed her eyelids.

"Only with you."

His entire body became rigid, and his eyes drilled into hers. "Don't lie to me, Megan," he warned. His hand moved upward, and he felt the weight of her breast in his palm.

She moaned softly as his fingers moved in slow, delicious circles near her nipple and she began to ache with the want of him. "I've...never lied to you, Garrett," she murmured, disappointment crossing her face when he removed his hands.

"Maybe not," he decided, lifting his body away from her and capturing her wrists between the steel-like fingers of one hand. "But you've certainly evaded the truth."

Her chin inched defiantly upward. "I can't say that I've never been interested in another man," she admitted, filled with fierce pride and outrage. "And I really don't care if you believe me or not. But the fact of the matter is that I've never had the urge to become intimate with anyone."

He snorted his disbelief. "You've never slept with another man?"

"It's none of your business, Garrett. That was your decision."

His jaw tensed in frustration. "You can't expect me to believe you were faithful to me."

"I don't give a damn what you believe!" she lied, and smiled cynically. "I don't subscribe to the double standard, you know. And as far as being faithful, I didn't intend to be. You were married, for God's sake! I didn't feel I owed you any fidelity whatsoever."

He cocked an interested eyebrow, begging her to continue.

"But…it just didn't happen," she said slowly.

She expected him to be relieved, but the expression on his rugged features was one of torment and self-disgust as he gazed down on her. Slowly he released her wrists. "I never meant to hurt you, Megan," he insisted, wrapping his arms around her shoulders and pushing a wayward strand of hair from her eyes. "I've always loved you." It was a reluctant admission, and Megan would have willingly given her soul to believe him. If it hadn't been for his brief marriage, she might have trusted the honesty in his eyes and the pain in the tight corners of his mouth. As it was, she accepted what he said as an easy excuse brought on by the heat of the moment.

Her fingers ran through his wavy dark hair, and her eyes filled with the love she had always felt for him. "Just love me tonight, darling," she whispered, forcing his head down and touching the tip of his nose with her lips.

He responded by pressing his lips ruthlessly against hers and plundering her mouth with the supple grace of his tongue. She tasted the sweet maleness of him and returned his passion with all of the heat welling in her body. Her heart pounded wildly within the prison of her chest.

He slid her sweater over her head and watched in satisfaction when she shook her hair free and it tumbled in coppery splendor against the soft white skin of her shoulders. The ivory-colored bra hid nothing from his knowing eyes. Her breasts heaved against the lacy fabric, and the dark nipples formed shadowy peaks that invited his touch. He outlined first one and then the other of the nipples with his tongue, moistening the sheer fabric before removing the soft barrier between his mouth and the aching sweetness.

When he captured one taut nipple in his mouth, his hands gripped Megan's shoulders and he reversed their positions. She was atop him, her hair falling forward and whispering against his chest in featherlight strokes. He groaned as he pushed against Megan's back, forcing her rosy nipple once again into the warm cavern of his mouth. Megan felt his teeth against her, nibbling and teasing her with expert prowess. She sighed convulsively when he began to suckle.

"Dear God," she whispered, her blood pounding dizzyingly against her temples.

One of his hands slipped between her jeans and the soft skin of her abdomen. Involuntarily, she sucked in her breath, allowing him the freedom to touch all of her. She felt the zipper slide and the pants being pushed down until the chill of the night touched her skin.

Garrett moved out from under her and stood next to the couch. Bereft of his touch, she watched through the veil of thick lashes while he slowly, sensuously, unbuckled his belt. It slid through the loops to fall to the floor. Her eyes caught his for an instant, then dropped once again to his hips, watching while he lazily stepped out of his pants.

He stood naked before her, his lean, corded muscles flexed with the restraint he was demanding of his body. Beads of frustrated sweat clung to his forehead. He bent to turn off the one lamp that remained, and she caught a glimpse of the fluid muscles of his shoulders sliding against each other before the room was suddenly dark, illuminated only by the scarlet shadows of a dying fire.

"I want you," he said, still keeping the few inches of space between them. "But more than that, I want to know what we share won't be just for one night."

She smiled mysteriously, reached for his hand and pulled on his arm, forcing his body closer to hers. "I've wanted to hear those words for a long time," she admitted as he leaned over and kissed her cheeks. "Love me, Garrett."

"I always have." With his final vow, he gently pressed his

weight against her and covered her lips with his. The heat within him became unbound, and desire, molten hot, surged through his veins.

She felt his rippling muscles straining against hers, moving in the gentle rhythm of love. One knee parted her legs and she willingly arched against him, anxious to have the burning ache within her salved by his gentle movements.

Her breathing was shallow and rapid, and a thin sheen of perspiration covered her body. Her fingers dug into the firm muscles of his shoulders until, persuaded that she needed him as desperately as he wanted her, Garrett kissed her fiercely at the moment his body found hers.

He pushed her into a faster tempo of love, pulsating with the liquid fire running in his veins, until they exploded as one, coming together in a union of flesh that was as savage as it was tender. The stillness of the mountain night was shattered by Megan's impassioned cry of love. Her breathing was ragged, and for a moment she thought her heart would burst with the passionate love she harbored for this one man.

Tenderly he pushed her hair out of her eyes, letting his fingers linger against her wet skin. "Sweet lady," Garrett whispered lovingly, "I need you."

Megan swallowed against the lump forming in her throat. Firelight reflected in his intense gaze. "And I need you, love," she murmured, blinking back the tears of happiness pooling in her eyes.

10

"GET UP, LAZYBONES."

Garrett's familiar voice pierced into her subconscious and slowly dragged Megan out of her dream-filled sleep. As consciousness returned she realized that she had spent the final few hours of the night making passionate love to the man she loved. A happy smile tugged at the corners of her mouth as she stretched.

After opening an experimental eyelid, she curled into a ball and hiked the bedcovers around her neck. "Wake me when it's morning," she grumbled good-naturedly, and rolled over intending to get a few more hours of desperately needed sleep.

"That will be a while." Garrett made a dramatic show of checking his watch. "About twenty hours, as a matter of fact. It's nearly noon now."

"Just a few more minutes—"

"Not on your life." He gave her rump a sound pat, and she groaned as she rolled over to face him, clutching the pale blue sheet over her naked breasts. The look she sent him could have melted stone.

He laughed at her consternation. "I didn't bring you up here just so you could spend the day in bed."

She cocked a disbelieving eyebrow. "You could have fooled me," she teased, a seductive light glinting in her gray eyes. Her dark hair tumbled freely around her face and she licked her lips provocatively as she stared up at him.

Garrett's eyes flicked over her body with obvious interest. "If you don't get up now, you may never again get the chance," he warned with a cynical smile.

"Promises…promises." With a petulant frown, she started to rise, but Garrett was beside her in an instant, stripping off his clothes in disgust.

"You seductive little witch," he muttered. "You're making me crazy."

"And you love it," she laughed, raising the sheet as he slid into the bed next to her. His fingers caught in her thick, unruly auburn curls.

"What I love, lady, is to spend time with you." He shifted his weight over her and pressed anxious, hungry lips to hers. "You're a tease…a beautiful, wanton, wicked tease."

His hard, lean body rubbed sensuously against the silkiness of her skin, and his eyes darkened with the desire only she could inflame. Never had Megan looked more beautiful. Never had Garrett wanted her more. His body ached with the need of her, and he wondered, as his lips found the hollow of her throat, if he would ever get enough of her.

After a hearty breakfast, Garrett insisted that Megan follow him to the stables. Despite her teasing protests, he saddled two of his three horses and helped a laughing Megan into the saddle.

The remainder of the afternoon was spent horseback riding through the thick stands of pine and aspen surrounding the estate. A wintry afternoon sun glistened against the snow covering the ground.

The horses' breaths misted in the cold mountain air as the animals followed an overgrown path through the woods. Garrett explained that when he stayed in the city, a neighbor, Sam Jordan, took care of the animals and had offered to buy all of them if Garrett decided to go through with his plan to sell the mountain retreat.

Just the thought of Garrett giving up the house that he so obviously loved saddened Megan. "You can't sell the horses," she complained, bending forward in the saddle and patting Mariah's thick, dark neck. The horse snorted her agreement and tossed her black head in the air, jingling the bridle.

Garrett sat astride Cody, a large buckskin gelding who swished his black tail impatiently and flattened his ears against his head as if he knew he was the center of attention. "I don't want to," Garrett admitted, casting Megan a rueful glance. "But it's not that easy commuting to Denver in the winter."

"You've got the four-wheel drive and an apartment in the city in case you get stranded or have to stay overnight." Megan frowned and bit on her lower lip. "Looks to me like you have the best of both worlds…besides which, you love it here. You could never sell it to a stranger."

Garrett let out his breath and didn't immediately respond. He guided Cody along the seldom-used path that twisted through the leafless trees. A sad smile pulled at the hard corners of his mouth. "That's what I thought, too," he said at length, his hazel eyes reaching for hers. "But things changed." With an expressive lift of his broad shoulders, he leaned forward and prodded the horse into a slow gallop just as the path gave way to an open field bordering the stables.

Megan urged Mariah forward, and the quarter horse responded eagerly. The black mare raced through the snow with a quick burst of speed that closed the gap and brought her alongside the longer-strided Cody. "Race you," Megan called to Garrett with a laugh as Mariah sensed the thrill of a contest and spurted ahead of the big buckskin.

Megan heard the sound of Garrett's laughter as she leaned forward over Mariah's neck and the stout black mare sprinted toward the stables. The cold wind rushed at her face and caught in the auburn strands of her hair, but Megan didn't care. She felt younger, happier than she had in years. The race was exhilarating!

The sound of Cody's thundering hoofbeats warned Megan of Garrett's approach, but the tough-spirited Mariah wasn't easily beaten. The little mare dug in and managed to make it back to the stables a few seconds ahead of the gelding.

Garrett's eyes were dancing with laughter and admiration when he reined Cody to a halt and dismounted. "Well, ma'am," he drawled in an affected Western accent, "you done a right smart bit of ridin' back there."

Megan winked broadly and swung to the ground. "I think some of the credit should go to Mariah," she said fondly as she patted the mare's glistening rump. Mariah tossed her head menacingly into the air as if to give credence to Megan's words.

Garrett took the reins of both horses in one hand and grabbed Megan's shoulders with the other. They walked to the stables with their arms entwined and Megan smiled comfortably. Never had she been happier than these last few, fleeting hours with Garrett. Away from the pressures of the city and the office, she had rediscovered that special feeling they had shared three years ago. It was easy to think that she and Garrett were falling in love, all over again...

"I'll take care of these fellas," Sam Jordan announced. He had been repairing some of the equipment in the toolshed, but had come toward the stables when he heard all the noise. He was a grizzled man of about seventy-five. Though he walked with a slight limp and his skin was weathered, his bright blue eyes sparked with youthful mischief.

"Who won?" he asked with a devilish grin as he took the reins from Garrett. Mariah nuzzled the old man affectionately and Sam produced a carrot from his pocket for each of the horses, including Winthrop, a twenty-year-old roan who spent most of his days inside his stall.

"It was a victory for women's lib," Garrett replied as he removed the saddle from Cody's broad back.

"Was it, now?" Sam chuckled. He turned his attention to Megan. "I'm not surprised. That little lady—" he nodded in the direction of Mariah "—she's full of fire. Doesn't like to be beaten."

"None of us do," Megan responded with a merry laugh.

"And Cody." Sam shook his head, removed his hat and rubbed his fingers over his scalp. "He's got the speed, but he's just plain lazy—aren't you, boy?" Sam ran his palm fondly down the sleek tan coat of the horse in question. "It's all right. You'll beat her yet."

"Not likely," Garrett interjected with a playful frown.

"Maybe all he needs is a decent jockey," Sam suggested with a laugh.

"Good idea. Next time, you ride him."

"That I will," Sam mumbled, leading the horses into the stable. "That I will."

When Sam was out of earshot, Megan linked her hand through the bend in Garrett's elbow. "You're fond of him, aren't you?"

"Who, Sam?" Garrett's grin was slightly sheepish. "He and his wife, Molly, have been good to me for as long as I can remember." He pulled Megan toward the house. "Sam and

Molly Jordan never change. Salt of the earth. The kind of people who would never let you down. People like that are hard to find."

That night, sitting with their backs propped against the couch, Megan and Garrett watched the dying embers of the fire. Garrett had pushed the couch forward, and Megan was able to lean her head against the soft leather cushions with her stockinged feet up against the warm flagstones of the hearth.

She balanced a chilled glass of Chablis in her hands, staring at the reflection of the red embers in the cut crystal and twirling the stem of her glass in her fingers. Not too long ago she had sat in this very room, nervously drinking wine and telling Garrett about the swindle. So much had happened since then, it seemed like ages ago. Now, huddled before the scarlet coals, even the silence was comfortable.

"I'm glad you came for me last night," Megan said, her eyes still studying the glass.

"I had to."

Her features drew into a pensive frown. "You didn't have to, but I have to admit that you were right."

"That's a first," he snorted. "About what?"

"You said that I needed to get away for a while." She paused as if she couldn't quite find the right words to convey all the feelings within her. "This time with you, Garrett, it's...well, it's been very special for me."

He set aside his glass and took her hand. "That's what I meant when I said that things have changed." His thumb moved sensuously against her wrist. "I've lived here a long time, maybe too long."

Reluctantly he released her hand and drew his knees up to rest his chin against them. "A lot has happened to me under this roof." He frowned into the fire. "And when you left me—the first time, when Patrick was killed—it was difficult to stay here. I forced myself, and after a while I got used to the fact that you weren't coming back. Lana called me, we got together, and I decided that I needed to settle down. For good. I was bound and determined, dear lady, to get you out of my system once and for all."

"By substituting another woman?" Megan was incredulous.

"By any means possible." His eyes had narrowed with the painful memories. "Anyway, it didn't work, and maybe that was my problem. Maybe Lana knew how I felt. I don't know and I don't suppose it matters—not a whole hell of a lot." He ran his thumb along the edge of his jaw as he considered the succession of events that ended with the divorce. "The marriage was a mistake."

Megan swallowed with difficulty and her voice grew hoarse. "Are you trying to convince me that you didn't love her?"

"I didn't." When he noticed her surprise, Garrett added, "I tried to convince myself that I loved her; certainly I had feelings for her. Anyway, she told me that breaking off the engagement had been a mistake—mine, mind you—and we should give it another shot. Since you made it pretty clear that you didn't want to see me again, I capitulated. One thing led to another and we decided to get married."

"Just like that?"

His lips thinned angrily. "Sorry if I offended you. I don't remember my marriage to Lana as any big romance."

"It's just hard for me to understand."

"We all make mistakes, Megan. I shouldn't have to remind you of that."

The point hit home. Megan remained silent while Garrett kneeled before the fire and stoked the charred logs.

"I was stupid enough to think that a wife and family were what I wanted."

Megan felt something die within her. "But they weren't?"

"Are you kidding? The marriage was over almost before it began." He shook his head at his own folly. "I'll grant you that it wasn't all Lana's fault. We wanted different things in life. Lana wanted a career. I thought I wanted children. The two didn't mix, and I guess I wasn't very patient.

"I tried to understand when her work would take her to New York or Chicago. She was a freelance journalist. She was an economics major in college and so most of her articles were on economics—from a woman's point of view. She became quite popular, what with the women's movement and all, and it didn't take her long to decide that she could support herself and shed the man who was hounding her for a family." He sat down beside Megan once again. "Seems that I'm attracted to the independent, career-oriented type, doesn't it?" He didn't wait for a response. He saw the shadows in her eyes. "So you can see why I thought about getting rid of the house."

"Not really," she muttered.

"When Lana and I were separated, it seemed to me that the only solid thing in my life was this house." He paused and looked up at the ceiling as if by staring at the weathered timbers he could make some sense out of his life.

Megan felt her throat constricting. Her voice was barely a whisper. "So what made you change your mind?"

"You."

The single word sent a shiver down her spine.

"When you walked back into my life, I thought that, despite the impending scandal, regardless of the past, we could work things out. I thought that if you just came back here and stayed with me, we could find what we gave up."

Megan tucked a wayward strand of hair behind her ear. "But you're considering moving."

He turned his darkened eyes upon her. "I was. The first

night you were here, when you brought me the statements, didn't go as I had hoped. You left before we could really talk."

"You can't expect me to believe that you wanted to work things out between us," she said with a small laugh. "If I remember correctly, you were furious about the scam and the investigation. In fact, you threatened to sue me."

He couldn't deny the truth. He heaved a weary sigh and shook his head. "I said some things I shouldn't have."

"Does that mean there won't be a lawsuit?"

"What it means is simply that we, you and I, just can't help hurting each other."

"You mean that the lawsuit was an idle threat?"

"No. Just that you keep confusing what's happening to us professionally with what we feel on a personal level. One thing has nothing to do with the other."

She turned intelligent eyes on the rigid planes of his face. "So what are you telling me—what's all this leading up to?"

"Just that after your father's death, when we couldn't see each other for professional reasons, I decided that enough was enough and that I would find a way to get you out of my system. Once and for all. By selling the house, and purging any tangible evidence of what we had shared together, I thought I could forget you."

"But?" she prodded, her heart beating irregularly.

"But I made a costly mistake and went to your father's funeral. And there you were—with Ted Benson, no less."

"I wasn't with him."

"It looked like it from where I stood."

"He drove me home. Said he wanted to talk about Dad's will…"

"Did he?"

Megan smiled ruefully when she remembered the scene in Ted's car. "At the very least—"

His eyes drilled into hers. "What's that supposed to mean?"

Megan frowned pensively. "That Ted made a pass at me, but I was able to dodge it."

Every muscle in Garrett's face tensed and his hands clenched into tight fists of fury. "That miserable lowlife! It would serve the bastard right if I did decide to take this thing to court!"

Megan attempted to change the course of the conversation. "Relax, would you? I handled it." Megan's voice was calm, but her eyes glittered with pleased amusement. The last emotion she had expected Garrett to display was jealousy.

"You're very sophisticated and cool about a married man trying to seduce you, for God's sake!"

"Garrett, look. I'm thirty years old. I'm used to fending off unwanted attacks on my virtue." She laughed at the frustration on his face. "Forget it. It won't happen again."

"How can you be sure?"

"I know Ted Benson. He's too smart an attorney to blow it with me. Ted's partial to his lifestyle, and McKearn Investments is one of his most lucrative clients. I doubt that he'll jeopardize his yearly retainer for the sake of a good-night kiss."

"I'm sure he had more than a kiss in mind," Garrett growled.

"Doesn't matter. I'm only interested in one man."

The consternation on Garrett's face slowly dissipated and his eyes darkened seductively. "You know just what to say, don't you?"

"Only with you," she promised as she felt his lips brush against hers. "Only with you."

Sunday afternoon came much too quickly, and the relaxed atmosphere in Garrett's house began to melt with the snow. They had made love deep into the night, and the taste of passion was still on Megan's lips when she opened her eyes.

Once again, after a hearty breakfast, Garrett had taken her

on a horseback ride. This one was much slower paced, and Megan had to fight Mariah to keep the spirited horse from bolting once she eyed the field where the race had taken place just the day before.

Garrett broiled steaks for dinner and served them on a platter laden with fresh parsley and buttered noodles. The meal was excellent, but conversation lagged as the time to return to the city drew near.

"I want you to come back, Megan," Garrett stated, once the table was cleared and Megan had mumbled something about having to get back to Denver.

"I'll think about it."

Garrett wasn't easily put off. He placed a comfortable arm around her shoulders and she leaned her head familiarly against his chest. "I'm not talking about a night, or a weekend, or even a temporary arrangement. I want you to move in permanently."

The words she had been waiting to hear for three years took her by surprise. Megan shifted away from him uneasily. He was offering what she wanted most in life, and yet she couldn't accept. "I'd like to," she whispered, "but I can't. Not yet."

"Why not?" The muscles in Garrett's back stiffened with suspicion.

"There's more to consider than just what I want to do. I have to think about the business—"

"To hell with the business."

"—and my mother."

"Isn't your aunt living with her?"

"For the time being, but I can't throw any more problems in her direction."

"Living with me wouldn't be a problem, and certainly not hers!"

Megan was tempted, sorely tempted. The life she had imagined was at her fingertips. All she had to do was say the word. Her smile was wistful, and unshed tears of love glistened in her round eyes.

"I just need a little time," she whispered, hoping that she wasn't throwing away her one chance at happiness. "There are so many things you and I have to work out."

"How much time, Megan?"

"I... I don't know."

He studied the honesty in her eyes. Strong fingers wrapped around her forearms, and his hazel eyes reached into hers. "As long as I know that you're not stalling and that you want to live with me..."

"Oh, Garrett, of course I do. You know that. More than anything—"

"Except the business."

"I just want to get the scam behind us."

"Because you don't trust me."

"Because I don't want to start off on the wrong foot."

"Like three years ago?"

"Exactly."

His dark brows blunted for a moment as he regarded her, but the fact that she returned his unwavering stare and managed a sad smile convinced him that she was being sincere.

"All right, Megan. We'll play it your way—for a little while."

Her teeth sank into her lower lip as Garrett pulled her into his strong embrace and his lips lingered against her hair. "I love you, you know," he murmured, "but I'm not a patient man."

11

MEGAN HAD NEVER gotten over Patrick's death. Not completely. And the guilt she silently bore hadn't lessened despite all of Garrett's arguments. She couldn't forget that it was she who had let Patrick down when he needed her most. Even now, as busy as her days were at the office, when she got home at night her thoughts would involuntarily shift to Garrett and the night three years ago when her brother was killed. The brief happiness she had shared with Garrett couldn't displace her sense of guilt.

Tonight was no different from any of the other nights. She sat alone in her apartment, huddled beneath a patchwork quilt while staring listlessly at the television. Though she tried to push thoughts of Garrett and Patrick aside, they continued to nag at her subconscious, disturbing her concentration. With a pointed remark aimed at herself, Megan pressed the buttons on the remote control for the television, but each detective program or sitcom looked like the last and failed to capture her attention.

"You're a damned fool," she scolded. With a self-mocking smile, she clicked off the set, put down the remote control and picked up a magazine from the untidy stack on the coffee table.

It had been over a week since she had seen Garrett. He had called several times, but the conversations had been short and stilted, leaving Megan to second-guess herself and wonder if she had made the wrong decision. Maybe Garrett was right. Perhaps she should just ignore the problems at the business, the investigation, everything except her love for him. It was a pleasant thought and it brought tears of yearning to her eyes. If only things were so simple. In disgust, she tossed the magazine back onto the table.

What was she waiting for? An engraved invitation? She eyed the telephone and even went so far as to pick up the receiver before casting aside all thoughts of calling Garrett. It was ten o'clock at night and what could she say? *I just wanted to hear your voice? I miss you? I love you?*

She shook her head and set the receiver back in the cradle. The timing wasn't right. It might be weeks before the investigation would be complete, and she wanted to start her new relationship with Garrett on a positive note, with no doubts to cloud their future...

After pouring herself a cup of tea, Megan leaned against the counter and stared out of the kitchen window into the night. Patrick. Why couldn't she forget about the tragic set of circumstances surrounding her brother's death? Frowning into her tea leaves, Megan sighed and swirled the hot, spicy liquid in her cup.

Patrick had been the apple of his father's eye. Even though by nature Patrick had been reckless and carefree, Jed McKearn had made no bones about the fact that he expected Patrick to settle down someday and take over the helm of McKearn Investments. Patrick considered it his birthright, but somewhat of a joke. An amused twinkle would lighten his clear green eyes whenever Jed would introduce the subject of running the company.

For his daughter, Jed had chosen the perfect mate, a single man who was a successful engineer. Bob Kendrick was also Patrick's best friend.

The sparks Jed had anticipated between Bob and Megan had never ignited. Megan and Bob Kendrick had remained only good friends, neither person interested in deepening the relationship. Bob was more interested in running around with Patrick than spending time with Megan, which was just as well. When Megan met Garrett, all of her time and thoughts were spent on him. She had little to spare for Bob...or Patrick.

Megan closed her eyes as the truth hit her with the force of an arctic gale. Patrick had needed her, and she had abandoned him. The result was that he had died senselessly. Her hands were trembling as she wrapped her fingers around the cup, as if for comforting warmth.

The trouble with her brother had started when Patrick had come to Jed and admitted that he was involved with a girl who was barely seventeen. The involvement included an unwanted pregnancy. The girl, Felicia Sterns, was due to have Patrick's baby in the early summer.

Anna McKearn had been crushed. Megan could still remember how her mother's face had washed of color and the pain that had darkened her eyes as she leaned heavily against her husband for support. But Jed had stoically accepted the news. Felicia's parents forced the issue, insisting that Patrick take responsibility for his unborn child and marry their daughter. Though Jed didn't approve of the hasty marriage, it was his hope that Patrick would finally settle down and become interested in working at McKearn Investment Company. As a new husband and father-to-be, Jed had reasoned, Patrick's reckless days were over.

It hadn't happened. According to Bob Kendrick, Patrick balked at the last minute. He didn't want to be strapped with a baby or a wife. He wasn't yet ready to shoulder that kind of responsibility—not for Felicia or anyone else.

Patrick had confided to Bob that he was tired of being pushed by Jed into a role he couldn't accept. To add insult to injury, Patrick had found out that Megan was seeing Garrett Reaves, a man Patrick had known through a mutual acquaintance, Lana Tremaine.

Patrick was livid when he confronted Megan with the condemning newspaper clipping, and when Megan ignored Patrick's warnings and ran off to meet her lover, Patrick started drinking and didn't stop. Then he set out to find Megan. Felicia was with him, and though Bob Kendrick tried to stop his friend, Patrick pushed Bob out of the way, climbed into the car with Felicia and roared off into the night.

The Jaguar slid off the road less than ten miles from Garrett's home and both Patrick and Felicia were killed instantly. Felicia's parents sued the estate of Patrick McKearn, and the scandal hit the papers with the force of a bolt of lightning. No one was left unscathed. Even Garrett's name was mentioned.

From that point on, Jedediah McKearn's health deteriorated and Anna McKearn became a shell of her former self. When Jed suffered his first heart attack, Megan took over the business on a temporary basis, but she had always hoped that Jed would resume his rightful place as the president of McKearn Investments. Now he was dead.

The sharp ring of the telephone startled Megan out of her unpleasant reverie. She jumped at the sound and put down her empty teacup as she reached for the phone.

"Hello?" Her voice sounded shaky. She clutched the ivory-colored receiver in a death grip.

"Glad I caught you at home." The warm sound of Garrett's

voice forced a smile to her lips despite her morbid thoughts of the past. "How would you like to go to Rio?"

"Rio de Janeiro?" Megan asked, caught off guard.

"Do you know of any other?" he answered, the laugh in his deep-timbred voice infectious.

If only she could. "When?"

"Monday."

Megan closed her eyes as grim reality settled on her shoulders. "Garrett, I can't. Not now. I thought maybe you were talking about six months from now—"

"It can't wait," he interjected. Megan could hear the irritation in his voice. "I've got to look at a site for another plant. I thought it would be a chance for us to get away—together, alone—without worrying about the investigation."

"It sounds wonderful…"

"But?" he challenged. Megan could imagine the glint of anger in his eyes.

"I just can't get away. At least not for another month or so."

"Sorry. It's now or never." His voice was clipped, as if he were impatient to get off the phone.

Now or never. The words sounded so final. Desperation clutched at her throat and her knuckles whitened as she gripped the phone. "You know that I want to be with you," she whispered.

The only response was a ragged sigh.

"Garrett?"

"Forget it, Megan. And just for the record, I don't know anything about how you feel. Not one damned thing. Not anymore. Sometimes I think I'm dealing with a stranger." There was a short pause before he added, "Maybe it's better that way."

Without a word of goodbye, he hung up and Megan was left with a haunting fear that she might not ever hear from him again.

★ ★ ★

Garrett had been out of the country for nearly two weeks, and though Megan's work at the office was more than enough to fill her hours, she felt incredibly alone. She had only heard from Garrett once, late at night, and the telephone conversation had been more than uncomfortable. The connection from Rio was bad, the conversation interrupted by frequent crackling noises and the phone lines had seemed to hum with unspoken accusation.

The short, tense talk had left Megan aching for him. Had it only been a few weeks since those passion-filled nights and happy days at his home near Boulder? How, in such a short period of time, had things gone downhill so rapidly? And how much of it was her fault for not accepting Garrett's proposal to live with him? What more could she want?

Each day that passed without Garrett became more tedious than the last, and Megan was left with the uneasy feeling that something was wrong...terribly wrong.

Ted Benson stretched his long legs in front of him. He didn't seem particularly pleased with the news he had brought, but Megan was ecstatic.

"You have to realize that this is very preliminary," Ted warned, his watery blue eyes squinting as he lit a cigarette and waved the match in the air. Since the incident in his car on the day of Jed's funeral, the attorney had been less arrogant than usual and had kept his meetings with Megan on a strictly professional level. He sat slumped in one of the wing chairs near her desk and inhaled deeply on the cigarette before blowing a stream of pale blue smoke toward the ceiling.

"But it looks as if the SEC might not name Garrett in the suit." Megan's heart was beating triumphantly. Soon, Garrett would be proved innocent of any part in the scam.

"If there is a suit at all. You know, at this point, nothing's written in stone."

"But it looks good, right?" Megan slid her reading glasses up her nose and tapped her pencil on the desk. Why did she sense that Ted was warning her of something?

"It looks like Reaves won't be named—if that's what you consider good. You have to remember, Megan, McKearn Investments hasn't been cleared of any wrongdoing, at least not yet. And as for Reaves, well, anything can happen."

"What does that mean?" Megan's exhilaration slowly melted into dread. She let the pencil fall onto the desk and quietly clasped her hands together as she stared boldly into the attorney's cold eyes.

"Just because it seems the SEC might not go after Reaves, that doesn't mean it won't happen—especially if some new evidence is discovered linking Reaves to the scam. And then there's the question of criminality."

"Whether the swindle is a civil suit or a—"

"Felony." The word cut through the air like a knife and Megan paled slightly.

"George Samples may be up on criminal charges?"

"A very concrete possibility," Ted allowed, flicking the ashes of his cigarette into the tray. "Only the SEC knows what course of action it will recommend, and then the courts will decide what will happen. So," Ted said, pleased that he finally had all of Megan's attention, "you see that we're not out of the woods yet." As an afterthought he added, "And neither is Reaves." With a confident smile, Ted ground out his cigarette and slipped his arms through the sleeves of his imported raincoat.

"But it could be just a matter of time," Megan thought aloud, hoping she didn't sound as desperate as she suddenly felt.

Ted shrugged his shoulders in a dismissive gesture. "Could

is relative, Megan. You might remember that. Too many people go around living their lives wondering what could have been instead of concentrating on the here and now." He grabbed his notes, stuffed them into his briefcase and headed for the door of her office. "I wouldn't go out celebrating tonight. You still have a tough row to hoe ahead of you."

"I'll remember that," Megan said, her eyes growing stern. "It's just that I'd like a little more good news for a change."

"Wouldn't we all," Ted muttered as he let himself out of the office.

Once the sober attorney had left, Megan picked up the phone and dialed the number of the airport. In a brief conversation she was told that Garrett's plane had been delayed for several hours because of a bomb scare at the airport earlier in the afternoon.

Regardless of Ted Benson's vague warnings or the tense situation at the airport, Megan smiled to herself as she grabbed her purse and coat. With or without Ted's news concerning Garrett's innocence, Megan had finally come to the decision that, despite everything, she wanted to live with Garrett Reaves.

Ted Benson had been wrong about one thing, Megan decided as she walked to the elevator and into the waiting car: Tonight she was going to celebrate until dawn with the only man she had ever loved.

Stapleton International was a madhouse. Cars, buses and taxicabs jammed the parking lot. Angry horns blasted, and tires slid on the slick streets.

"Hey, lady, watch out!"

Megan heard the shout and an explicit oath as she pushed her way into the building. Not bothering to see if the warning were meant for her, she plowed her way through the confused mass of people milling in the terminal.

Between poor weather conditions and the bomb scare, the concourses were filled with anxious relatives, more anxious security guards and interested members of the press. Busy travelers who had waited all afternoon to catch delayed flights bustled through the terminal as they tried to claim baggage, connect with late incoming flights or just leave the airport. Shouts, angry grunts and muttered oaths were issued at random.

Pieces of conversations reached her ears, but she paid little attention to anything other than locating Garrett. She found the gate where Garrett's plane was to disembark and she waited nervously for the jet to land.

Oblivious to the commotion going on around her, she paced from one end of the windows to the other, alternately hiking her coat around her neck and checking her watch. A determined smile curved her lips and her eyes pierced the darkness as she waited impatiently for Garrett's return.

Her heart was hammering in her throat as she watched the 747 land and heard the roar of the engines fade.

Garrett was one of the first passengers to disembark. Though he strode rapidly up the ramp, he looked haggard and tired. A garment bag was slung haphazardly over one of his shoulders, and he carried his briefcase with his free hand. Dark circles shadowed his eyes, his mouth was compressed into a thin, hard line and his dark hair was rumpled.

He didn't notice her until an elderly gentleman who was blocking his path stepped aside. At that moment, Megan's eyes collided with his and for a heart-stopping instant a smile tugged at the corners of his mouth.

"You're a sight for sore eyes," he said, setting his bag and case on the ground.

It was all the encouragement she needed. Heedless of the crowd of onlookers, Megan threw herself into Garrett's arms. "I've missed you," she whispered hoarsely against his ear as his arms wrapped protectively around her. Tears of love filled her eyes. The arms holding her tightened and she heard him sigh wearily against the auburn strands of her hair.

"You don't know how long I've waited to hear you say that," he admitted, kissing her on the head.

Megan smiled through her tears, opened her eyes for just a moment and thought she recognized a face...a young, moustached man with dark eyes and a satisfied smirk who blended in with the crowd.

Garrett stiffened. "What's going on here?" he asked suddenly.

"What do you mean?"

"What's with all the photographers?" His hazel eyes scanned the crowd as he lifted his luggage in one hand, placed his other arm securely over Megan's waist and started toward the door.

Megan shrugged and tried to dismiss his unease. "There was a bomb scare earlier..."

"I know. I thought all the commotion had died down."

"The photographers are probably still hanging around, hoping for something to happen."

"Humph." Garrett didn't seem convinced. "Let's get out of here." His voice had become wary and his restless gaze never left the ever-moving crowd. Suddenly his jaw hardened and his eyes narrowed.

"Garrett, what's wrong?" Megan asked, as he quickened his strides toward the doors leading out of the building. "What about your bags?"

"Got 'em." The cold air hit Megan in the face when the doors to the terminal opened. "Do you have your car here?"

"Yes—but wait a minute—"

"Where is it?" Garrett demanded.

"Over there, near the lamp…" Megan pointed a cold finger toward her car.

"Let's go." Garrett was already walking and Megan had to run to keep up with him. The darkness of the parking lot was lessened by the eerie light from the security lamps.

"Ms. McKearn!" a male voice shouted from somewhere near the doors of the terminal building. Megan stopped midstride.

"Ignore him, Meg," Garrett insisted, wrapping possessive fingers over her arm and nearly dragging her after him.

"Wait a minute. Who is it? And why are you acting so paranoid all of a sudden?"

"It's that damned reporter from KRCY news. If you want to stand around here and give him an impromptu interview, go right ahead. I'm not in the mood. Besides, I think one of those photographers back in the building snapped a picture of us together. In light of George Samples's accusations, I'm not all that crazy about the idea."

The cold night made Megan shiver. Garrett was the one who hadn't cared about the adverse publicity—or so he had claimed. Suddenly reporters made him uneasy. "Garrett, what's happening?" she asked.

"You tell me." Garrett's voice was harsh, his face an angry mask of determination. Dansen's rapid footsteps approached.

Garrett and Megan made it to the car just as Harold Dansen caught up with them. "Ms. McKearn, if you don't mind, I'd like to ask you a few questions."

"The lady does mind," Garrett interjected as Megan rifled through her purse looking for her keys. Her fingers were nearly numb from the cold.

"I'm asking her," Dansen remarked, and turned his dark eyes on Megan. "You've never given me that interview."

Megan managed a frozen smile. "My oversight."

"I would have thought McKearn Investments would want to tell its side of the story to the press. We've already had George Samples on the air."

"I can't do that. Not until the investigation is complete," Megan replied as she read the warning signs in Garrett's angry glare. "But once it is—"

"You'll call me, right?" Harold guessed with an I've-heard-it-all-before look that cut Megan to the core.

"Exactly," she stated with more authority than she felt.

"It's your funeral," Dansen returned.

Megan had opened the car door, but she stopped at the un-professional remark. "Pardon me?"

"Nothing," Dansen replied with a condemning smirk. "Just remember, I gave you the chance to set the record straight."

"Which I will."

"Yeah, when the story's cold. Old news." He shrugged his shoulders indifferently. "Your choice." With his final words he turned on his heel and headed back to the terminal.

"Why do I have the feeling that I made the wrong deci-sion?" Megan wondered aloud as Garrett slid into the driver's seat and turned on the ignition.

"Because that's the way he wants you to feel. The guy knows how to manipulate people. I'll give him credit for that." Garrett maneuvered the car through the parking lot, paid the cashier and headed toward the heart of the city.

"You think it's an admirable quality?"

"What?"

"To manipulate people."

"Of course not. Just necessary sometimes." Megan was left with a cold feeling settling between her shoulder blades.

An uneasy silence settled over the black interior of the car.

Tense minutes passed before Megan said, "Ted Benson was in to see me today."

All of the tired features on Garrett's face hardened. His eyes stayed on the road ahead of him. He shifted gears and the little car lurched forward. "What did he want?"

"To talk about the investigation."

"Is that all?" A hint of mockery edged his words. He turned the car onto the side street near Megan's town house.

"Yes. Damn it, Garrett, don't you trust anyone's motives?"

"Not when we're talking about Harold Dansen or that attorney of yours."

As Garrett parked the car, Megan turned to him and arched an elegant eyebrow. "This time you might be grateful to Ted."

"I doubt that."

"He seems to think you might be cleared of any charges." Megan smiled, but Garrett's eyes sparked in the dark interior of the car.

"He knows someone at the SEC?"

"A few people."

"And these sources have told him as much."

Megan was taken aback by Garrett's reaction. She had expected Garrett to be elated. Instead he seemed irritated. "To quote Ted, 'Nothing's written in stone.'"

"I'll bet." Garrett let out a long, ragged sigh and dropped his forehead onto the steering wheel. The frigid night seemed to seep through the windows.

"I think it's a positive sign," Megan whispered, her eyes fastened on the fatigued slump of Garrett's shoulders. She reached forward and, with hesitant fingers, quietly touched his temple.

"We're not out of the woods yet," he said quietly.

"It's a start, Garrett," she murmured, caressing his cheek. "And that's all we need."

He lifted his head, cocked it in her direction and studied the beautiful lines of her face. The searching look in his eyes begged her to explain herself.

"I've been doing some thinking since you've been gone," she stated, her gray eyes shining in the night.

"Go on."

"I was wrong about what would be best for us." Every muscle in his body froze. His eyes were stone cold, as if he were bracing himself for the worst. "I would love to come and live with you in Boulder," she whispered. "That is, if the offer is still open."

His hand softly touched her hair and his gaze wouldn't release her. "You're sure about this?" he asked with obvious reservation.

"More sure than I've been about anything in a long, long time." She placed her palms on either side of his face and slowly brushed her lips over his. "I love you, Garrett."

"Dear Lord, woman, why didn't you say so?" His arms captured her in an embrace as strong as it was gentle. Lips, suddenly swollen with desire, closed over hers and persuaded the kiss to deepen passionately. Her blood began to heat and pulse wildly in her veins.

Megan's eyes closed and she twined her arms around his neck. Her senses reeled with the thought that at last they were together…forever.

"Let's go inside," Garrett suggested, when he finally drew away from her. His hands were shaking as he rammed tense fingers through his hair in frustration.

They stood on the doorstep together, and Garrett leaned against the doorframe as Megan unlocked the door. He had expected several possible scenarios to develop once he re-turned from Rio, but never had he envisioned Megan's acceptance of his offer to live together. It didn't make a lot of sense, considering the tense phone calls they had shared.

Hating himself for his lingering doubts, he watched as Megan pushed the door open and turned her incredible eyes upon him. The smile on her face was irresistible, beckoning. He took one step toward her, then hesitated, giving her one last chance to change her mind.

As Megan stepped into the hallway, Garrett's hand reached out and captured her arm. She was in the house; he was still on the porch. Their eyes met. "You're sure about this?" he asked, solemnly studying the emotions on her face.

Her response was a gentle laugh that touched the darkest corner of his soul. "I've never been more sure of anything in my life."

Throwing aside his inner doubts, Garrett walked into the hallway, gathered Megan into his arms and kicked the door shut with his heel.

12

MEGAN FELT THE mattress shift as Garrett rolled to the side of the bed. He didn't move for a minute, as if contemplating the sanity of waking so early, and then he stood and pulled on his pants. The belt buckle jingled slightly, breaking the stillness of the early-morning hours.

"What're you doing?" Megan mumbled into the pillow, then turned to face him. The room was still dark, and a glance at the luminous face of the clock confirmed what she had guessed: It was barely dawn.

"Sad as it is," Garrett replied with honest regret heavy in his voice, "I've got to shower and change at my apartment before I go to the office." Garrett reached for his shirt, which had been slung over the high back of a chair near the vanity.

"Now?"

He chuckled softly. "Now."

She could barely make out his figure in the darkness—a black silhouette of a lean, well-muscled man against the soft illumination of the streetlamps filtering through the sheer curtains. "I'll get you breakfast…"

"Don't bother. I'll get something at work." He leaned over

the bed and smoothed back her hair before placing a warm kiss against her forehead. "Go back to sleep."

Disregarding his suggestion, she pulled herself into a sitting position, held the satin comforter over her breasts and watched with obvious pleasure as he slipped into his dress shirt, fumbled with the buttons and carefully straightened his cuffs.

"Goodbye, Megan," he whispered, and the sound of his steps on the stairs echoed hollowly in Megan's mind. The bed seemed suddenly empty and cold.

I've got to get up anyway, she decided as she rolled to her side and grabbed the robe lying on the foot of the bed. When she got to the landing, she was cinching the tie around her waist.

Garrett was in the foyer. A small table lamp gave a warm illumination to the hallway. He had already retrieved his garment bag and coat, and he looked up at the sound of her footsteps on the stairs.

"I'll call you later," he promised.

Megan stood three steps above him, watching as Garrett shrugged into his raincoat. She fingered the belt of her robe, then, yawning, pushed her tousled hair out of her eyes.

"You could stay longer..." she invited, wondering at her sudden need of him. She didn't want to let go of the few precious hours they had shared. The love, the passion, the honesty of the night—she couldn't release them. Not yet.

Garrett shook his head but smiled broadly. His hand was poised over the doorknob, and he hesitated for a moment. "Don't tempt me," he cautioned, his lips compressed pensively. "I just might take you up on it."

"Then why not?" Megan observed him through the silky curve of black lashes still heavy from recent slumber.

"Something you'll understand very well, I think. It's called responsibility."

"Business before pleasure?"

"In this case, I think we've already had pleasure before business," he pointed out. "I'll see you later." Garrett opened the door and a cold rush of morning air blew into the house. "Here." He picked up the rolled newspaper from the doorstep and tossed it to Megan. Then he was gone.

The door shut with a thud and Megan was left with only the cold newspaper in her hands and an emptiness deep within her soul. She shuddered from the cold air and the feeling of loneliness stealing over her. "Dear Lord, Megan," she chided, mounting the stairs, "you've lived without him for over three years. Certainly a few hours won't make a difference."

After scanning the newspaper and placing it on a small table, she went into the bathroom to shower and change for work.

Before she left for the office, Megan made herself a light breakfast and decided to call her mother. It had been several days since she had seen Anna, and Megan wanted to make sure that her mother's spirits hadn't flagged.

It wasn't quite seven. Although it was early, Aunt Jessica was usually up and about before dawn. Jessica complained of insomnia, but Megan suspected that her aunt was just one of those people who thrived on only a few hours of sleep.

"Good morning," Megan called into the phone, once Jessica has answered.

"Megan. I was wondering when we would hear from you."

"I called yesterday. No answer."

"Must've been when we were out shopping." Jessica chuckled.

"Did Mom go with you?" Megan asked, concern sharpening her voice.

Aunt Jessica understood. "Did she ever. Nearly bought out the stores." And then, on a more somber note, "She's doing okay, considering."

"I thought I'd drop by after work."

"Wonderful!" Aunt Jessica was once again her lively self. "It's been nearly a week since you've shown your face around here."

"You're right," Megan admitted, feeling a twinge of guilt.

"Don't worry about it. Anna and I have kept ourselves busy," Jessica assured her. Megan believed it. Aunt Jessica never seemed to run out of energy.

"Then I won't be interrupting your plans if I come over?"

"Never, child. Oh, by the way, I'm trying to talk your mother into taking a trip to the islands. You know, either before or after Christmas. I think she'd enjoy the sunshine for a change. Do her a world of good," Jessica predicted with authority.

"I'm sure it would," Megan agreed. Her mother had always wanted to visit Hawaii, but Jed's attention to his business had always interfered with the trip. And then, when he did retire, his health had declined to the point that Anna wasn't interested in anything other than caring for her ailing husband.

"Then you'll give her that extra nudge?" Jessica asked.

Megan laughed. "Count on it. Listen, I've got to get ready for work. See you two later."

It was nearly eight when she finally got into her car and braved the inclement weather conditions. The snow had fallen throughout the night, but for the most part, traffic flowed smoothly. Megan wheeled the little car into the parking lot of the Jefferson Tower just a little later than usual.

Nothing seemed out of the ordinary until she stepped out of the elevator on the eighth floor and realized that the reporters were back. A hodgepodge of anxious journalists crowded around the door to the investment company, and Megan guessed that there were more media people pacing uncomfortably just inside the glass doors. And they were waiting for her.

Megan forced a polite smile on her face as she pulled off her gloves and observed the reporters. A few had noticed her arrival and were heading her way. Fortunately, there weren't as many journalists today as there had been on the day George Samples's story hit the papers. However, there were enough inquisitive faces, note pads and photographers to test Megan's resolve. She strode purposefully toward the small crowd. Interested eyes turned in her direction.

"Here she is," someone whispered to his peers.

"Ms. McKearn," a young, well-dressed woman with intelligent blue eyes accosted her. "Is it true that you're seeing Garrett Reaves?"

"Pardon me?" Megan was taken aback. Her patient smile faltered slightly.

The blonde smiled. "Rumor has it that you're romantically involved with Mr. Reaves. True?"

Megan managed to pull her crumpled poise into place and forced a thin, professional smile for the woman and the rest of the members of the press. "Mr. Reaves and I are friends." A noncommittal lift of her shoulders accompanied the statement, as if anything else that might be implied by the question were totally out of line.

"Despite the investment swindle?" the young woman persevered, undaunted by Megan's nonchalance. The blonde was writing furiously in a notebook.

Megan eased her way to the door of the investment firm. "I've known Garrett Reaves for over three years."

"Then you knew him when he was married to Lana Tremaine," Harold Dansen stated, his black eyes focusing on Megan.

Though she felt herself withering inside, Megan met the

reporter's suspicious gaze squarely. A thousand questions raced through her mind. Why were the reporters here this morning? What had happened? And why did the mention of Garrett's ex-wife cause a feeling of cold dread to chill her from the inside out?

"I knew him then," Megan responded without batting an eye. Though her palms were sweating, she maintained the image of a confident executive. "If you'll excuse me, I have work to do."

"Were you lovers?" the blonde asked, and though Megan's complexion paled slightly, she moved her eyes away from the presumptuous young woman.

"One more question, Ms. McKearn," Dansen persisted, fingering the thick strands of his moustache. "Did you know that Lana Tremaine was George Samples's accomplice?"

"What?" Megan whispered before she recovered herself. The accusation hit her like a bolt of lightning and she had to force herself to face the anxious eyes of the press.

"I asked if you knew that Lana Tremaine, Garrett Reaves's ex-wife, was involved in Samples's swindle?"

Megan's heart was beating so rapidly she was sure everyone could hear it. All eyes were on her. Lana Tremaine! A part of the investment scam! Maybe it was a mistake. She hadn't read about it in the paper this morning. She heard herself speaking while crazy thoughts, filled with suspicions and doubts, flitted through her mind.

"As you know, Mr. Dansen, I'm not at liberty to discuss Mr. Samples or the alleged scam. Excuse me." Not waiting for any further questions to be thrust in her direction, Megan pushed her way past the reporters. When she got into the office she told the receptionist that she wouldn't meet with any newspaper people until late in the afternoon.

Megan felt strangled, and when she read a later edition of

the paper alleging that Lana Tremaine had, in fact, been a part of the scam, her stomach knotted so painfully that she had to sit down.

Don't go off the deep end, she warned herself. *Maybe this is all a mistake. And, even if it's not, it doesn't mean that Garrett's involved.*

Forcing a calm facade over her elegant features, Megan asked Jenny for a cup of coffee and instructed the receptionist to call Henry Silvas and Ted Benson immediately.

When she got each of the men on the phone, she arranged for them to meet with her in her office.

The coffee did little to calm her nerves, and she was pacing back and forth in front of her desk when Jenny buzzed the intercom to announce that Henry Silvas had arrived.

"Please, send him in," Megan suggested, her voice strained.

Henry entered the office, rubbing his thinning hair frantically.

"Good morning," Megan said.

"Morning."

Megan stopped her pacing long enough to level a searching glance at the accountant. "Can you tell me what the devil is going on?" she asked. "The press have been camping out near the elevators for hours."

"Just heard about it myself—from Ted Benson. He should be here soon. He said he tried to call you but couldn't get through."

"I know. I got through to his secretary a few minutes ago." Megan sighed and dropped into her chair. "He must have called me at the apartment while I was talking to Aunt Jessica."

"Doesn't matter. Here's the story." Henry fumbled in the inside pocket of his suit jacket, withdrew a cigar and began puffing furiously on the imported blend of tobaccos. "It seems that the SEC has found George's accomplice."

Henry's dark eyes, magnified by his wire-rimmed glasses, were troubled.

Megan's fingers tapped restlessly on the edge of her desk as she waited for him to continue.

"Ever heard of Derrick Van Weiss?"

Megan shook her head and rubbed her temples. The name was unfamiliar.

"Didn't think so. He's only written a couple of columns for the *Denver Financial Times*. A freelancer. Works out of New York."

"No, never heard of him."

"He's not very well-known, but once in a while a few of the papers run his stuff."

"I still don't understand—"

"Van Weiss was only one of Samples's partners."

"So who else was involved?" Dread took a stranglehold on her heart. She knew the answer.

"Lana Tremaine Reaves."

Megan's face lost all its color. "How?" she whispered. The newspaper article had been sketchy, obviously added after the first edition had been printed.

Henry sighed and set his cigar in the ashtray. "It's not as complicated as it sounds, but it appears that Van Weiss is the brains behind the operation. It might involve more than one paper. Anyway, Van Weiss and Lana Reaves know each other. One of them—probably Lana because she's from here and knew George Samples in the beginning—approached Samples with the idea. He took to it—"

The door to the office whispered open and Ted Benson strode into the room. "That George did," Ted agreed with a shake of his head. "Created a damned mess." Ted slid into a chair near Henry and his stony blue eyes impaled Megan.

"The hell of it is that I think the SEC will find that others are involved."

Megan felt as if the bottom had dropped out of her world. Without saying it aloud, Ted Benson was implying that suspicion had once again reverted to Garrett. Her stomach lurched and she had to swallow against the dryness in her throat. "So we're not out of the woods yet," she said, inadvertently quoting Garrett.

"Not by a long shot," Ted said with a frown. He tugged at his tie in a gesture of self-importance. "And, I'm afraid, the press will demand that you make some sort of statement. Don't do it. Not yet. I'll handle that part. It's going to look bad for McKearn Investments, no doubt about it. Not only did the broker work here, but several accounts were involved, including that of Garrett Reaves—Lana Tremaine's husband."

"Ex-husband," Megan pointed out.

"Could get sticky," Henry thought aloud.

"It already has," Megan said with a weary sigh. No wonder the reporters were questioning her relationship with Garrett. Her stomach began to knot painfully, and she nervously ran her fingers through her neatly coiled hair.

"You'll have to be careful, Megan," Ted warned. "Anything you say or do will be under scrutiny from the press."

"I know."

"Especially concerning Garrett Reaves."

"That's right," Henry agreed, puffing thoughtfully on his cigar. "Your mother told me you were seeing him. You'll have to be discreet."

"Or end the relationship," Ted offered. "At least temporarily. No reason to add fuel to the fire."

"You think Garrett's involved, don't you?" Megan asked, eyeing the two men boldly but already knowing the answer. A sinking feeling of betrayal settled on her slim shoulders.

"It's conceivable that Reaves worked with his ex-wife. At least it looks that way to me," Henry answered honestly, and he noticed the pain in Megan's eyes. "I'm sorry, Meg, but I call 'em as I see 'em."

"Agreed," Benson interrupted. "Reaves apparently used information from his ex-wife to make money in the market, via George Samples."

"So now you've decided he's guilty." Megan's voice was low and sounded tired. "Just yesterday you were suggesting that the SEC might drop the investigation—as far as Garrett Reaves was concerned."

"A man is innocent until proven guilty," Ted assured her, "but you can't refute the evidence stacking up against Reaves. As for what I thought yesterday, it's of no consequence. It happened before the SEC collared Van Weiss and linked him to Lana Reaves."

"That still doesn't mean—"

"Look, Megan," Henry interrupted. "I told you in the beginning that Reaves might be involved. His account was one of the nine that made money off George's inside information." The accountant shifted uneasily in his chair. The last thing he wanted to do was make it more difficult for Megan, but he had no choice. He dealt in dollars and cents and the truth.

"True, but—"

"And, he did sell short on Reaves Chemical stock."

"After filing the necessary papers."

Ted Benson frowned. "Other people made money on that trade—George Samples's special clients."

"Probably because George advised them to." Megan couldn't control her urge to defend Garrett.

"Any way around it, Megan," Henry stated. "McKearn Investments is on the hook. No matter what actually happened, it looks as if George interpreted the selling short as a signal from Reaves and he passed the information along. In return, Reaves became one of George's special clients and was awarded favors."

"In the form of big profits on trades made based on the inside information gained from Lana Tremaine Reaves and Derrick Van Weiss," Megan surmised.

"Exactly." Ted Benson lit a cigarette and pondered Megan's quiet composure. She was in a state of shock, that much was obvious, but there was still a defiant lift to her chin and a promise of steel-hard determination in her soft gray eyes. The woman had more grit than Ted ever would have guessed. "That's why you've got to be careful. Until the investigation is complete, anything you do will be under scrutiny by the SEC as well as the press."

Courageously, Megan met the concerned eyes of the two men sitting opposite her. She knew in her heart that what they were suggesting was for the good of the firm—and herself as well—and yet she couldn't believe that Garrett was caught in the intricate web of intrigue and scandal Derrick Van Weiss, Lana Tremaine and George Samples had woven.

She turned her attention to the attorney. "Speaking strictly as legal counsel for McKearn Investments, what course of action would you advise?"

"Low profile for you," Ted answered as he ground his cigarette into the ashtray. "As for the investment firm, it's business as usual. Investor confidence is imperative."

Henry Silvas pursed his lips together, clasped his hands, and nodded his head in mute agreement.

"But you don't think I should assure the press that we're operating as if nothing has happened?"

Ted shook his head. "I'll take care of it. You can issue a statement in a couple of days, once all the furor has died down.

Right now your main concern is angry clients who may read
the paper and misunderstand the facts."

"And if it doesn't die down—the furor, that is?" Megan
wondered aloud.

"We'll cross that bridge when we come to it." Ted cocked
his wrist, checked his watch and grabbed his briefcase. "I'll
handle the press for now—but remember, they're gunning
for you."

"Don't I know it," Megan muttered, remembering the
look of cruel satisfaction in Harold Dansen's eyes this morning. What had he said last night at the airport? Something
about its being her funeral? Well, he hadn't exaggerated. At
least not much.

Henry Silvas and Ted Benson left the room, and after a
few moments of hesitation, Megan lifted the receiver of the
phone and dialed the offices of Reaves Chemical.

"I'm sorry," Megan was informed politely when she had
asked to speak to Garrett, "Mr. Reaves hasn't come in this
morning and I doubt that he'll be in all day."

"But I was under the impression that I could reach him
there," Megan replied, her heart missing a beat.

"Not today. Mr. Reaves has been out of the country for a
couple of weeks, you know. If you'd like to leave your name
and number, I'll have him return the call."

"No, thank you," Megan whispered, her eyes blurring as
she replaced the phone. The secretary acted as if she hadn't
expected to see Garrett. Had he lied to Megan this morning?
It just didn't seem possible. After a night of honest confessions
of love, why would he lie? Megan shook her head as if to
clear out the cobwebs of confusion. Nothing made any sense.

After a moment's hesitation, she called Garrett's apartment
in the city. No answer.

Without realizing the desperation of her actions, she
grabbed the phone again and dialed the number of Garrett's

home near Boulder. Perhaps he had changed his mind and decided to go back to his home. Megan's teeth sank into her lower lip as she counted the rings.

"Pick it up," she whispered. "For God's sake, Garrett, be there."

After ten rings, she replaced the receiver. She walked slowly to the window and stared out sightlessly, unaware of the snowflakes falling from a leaden sky or of the scattered pedestrians milling on the sidewalks far below her. She leaned her forehead against the cool glass and wondered, if only fleetingly, if Garrett had ever stopped loving Lana Tremaine.

Once before he had used Megan as an idle flirtation. Could he be doing it again? But why? One part of Megan, fiercely loyal to the man she loved, screamed that even the thought of Garrett's caring for his ex-wife was preposterous.

Hadn't Megan seen the look of love in his eyes last night when he held her in his arms and made slow, wonderful love to her? He did it before. Remember the night of Patrick's death?

Hadn't Garrett himself stated that Lana meant nothing to him, that the marriage was the result of Megan's rejection? But that could have been a lie as well—a cover-up of the truth to avoid arousing Megan's suspicions.

Then why had Garrett bothered to rekindle their affair after three long years? Because he needed her protection. He was banking on her vulnerability to him, and he had used it as a weapon against her.

A silent tear slid down her face. Whether she wanted to or not, Megan was forced to consider the facts. The facts that Ted Benson, Henry Silvas, the Securities and Exchange Commission and the rest of the world would use to condemn Garrett Reaves.

Face it, Megan, the rational side of her nature admonished, *Garrett used you...again.*

★ ★ ★

Somehow, despite what seemed overwhelming odds, Megan got through the rest of the day. The phone hadn't stopped ringing, but Megan's secretary had fielded the calls from the press.

The one telephone call she had hoped to receive hadn't come through, and each time Megan had phoned Garrett's apartment or home, no one had answered.

She had tried to keep her mind away from thoughts of Garrett. At work it had been difficult, but dinner at her mother's house had helped a little. Even though Megan's spirits were depressed, seeing that her mother was adjusting to widowhood was comforting.

"I've just about convinced her," Aunt Jessica was teasing while she served thick wedges of deep-dish apple pie. The three women were sitting around the massive dining room table sipping coffee.

"Convinced me of what?" Anna asked.

"Why, of coming to Hawaii with me, of course." Jessica smiled slyly in Megan's direction. "What do you think?"

"A good idea," Megan stated, hoping she sounded more enthusiastic than she felt. "Perfect time of the year."

"I don't know if I can get used to Christmas lights on palm trees…"

"Oh, go on." Jessica laughed, tossing her shiny blond hair. "For your information, they ship fir trees to Hawaii, just like any other state. Besides, the sun will do you good."

"Humph. To listen to her, you'd think I needed a keeper," Anna said to her daughter, and all three women laughed.

Later, when Jessica was fussing over the dishes, Anna McKearn pulled her daughter aside. "What's going on, Megan?" she inquired, looking past the pretense of calm in Megan's eyes. "Trouble at the company?"

Megan lifted her shoulders and put on her coat. "A little."

"Or a lot?"

"Really, Mom, it's not that serious."

"Isn't it?" Anna patted her daughter's arm. "You're a lot like your father, you know. And I could read him like a book. This swindle business has got you down, hasn't it?"

Megan smiled wanly. "I'd be a liar if I didn't admit that I'll be glad when it's over."

"Amen," Anna breathed before kissing Megan on the cheek. Anna paused for a minute, and her expression became more sober. "I see that Garrett Reaves's name has come up."

Megan nodded, and Anna caught the small wince of rejection on her daughter's face.

"Are you seeing him again? He was with you at the hospital—"

"I'm not exactly sure...just what Garrett's feelings are right now. We're both busy."

"Of course you are." At that moment Aunt Jessica marched down the hall.

"Leaving, Meg?"

Megan nodded. "I'm a working woman, you know."

Jessica waved off her niece's excuses. "Next time don't make yourself so scarce."

"I won't."

After saying a hasty goodbye, Megan walked through the snow to her car and drove to her apartment—to face the long, cold night alone.

13

WHAT TO DO?

Megan paced the living room floor of her apartment like a caged animal. Her phone calls trying to locate Garrett had been fruitless, and at this point, mindful of Ted Benson's and Henry Silvas's warnings against talking to Garrett again, Megan decided she would stop her attempts at tracking him down. Garrett knew where she was, and he had to know that she was waiting to hear from him.

After all, it was he who had promised to call. Last night, while lying in the security of Garrett's strong arms, Megan had put her heart on the line. Garrett had apparently decided to walk all over it.

Anger and fear colored her thoughts. Where was Garrett? What was he doing? With whom? Though her love for him was as strong as it ever had been, the questions rattling in her head made her faith waver. There had been too many lies in her relationship with him to trust him blindly.

The evening edition of the paper was lying on the coffee table. Almost as a reminder to Megan of how foolish she had been to trust Garrett, the headlines, bold and black, stated: LANA REAVES SOUGHT IN SEC INVESTIGATION.

The article outlined the basic story, but as an added aside, it noted that Lana Reaves's ex-husband, Garrett Reaves, had an account with McKearn Investments and that he was romantically linked with the president of the investment firm, Megan McKearn. Next to the lengthy article was a slightly blurred photo of Garrett and Megan embracing in the crowded concourse of Stapleton International Airport, only last night.

Megan groaned when she glanced at the photograph one last time. Her small fists clenched and she stamped one foot in frustration. "You're a fool," she chastised herself with a grimace. After all the agony in the past, how could she have let herself fall into the very same trap?

Because I love him, she thought painfully, and realized that she would never stop caring for Garrett. No matter how dirty the scandal became, despite all the malicious gossip and snide innuendos, she still loved him. Just as desperately as she had the first night she had been with him, three years ago. But though she would probably always love him, she couldn't allow herself to be entangled with him. Not now. Not ever. It was painfully clear that whatever blissful moments she had shared with Garrett were the last. She tried to convince herself that it was over—there was just no other way out of this mess.

Damning herself for her weakness, she turned on the television and sank onto the couch. The last half hour of the prime-time drama did nothing to catch her attention, and she shifted uneasily on the comfortable cushions while thumbing disinterestedly through a financial magazine.

When the phone rang, she started. Telling herself that it was probably just another reporter, Megan risked answering and silently prayed that it would be Garrett's voice on the other end of the line. Not only did she need to hear from him, but she had to tell him that she couldn't see him again. Not that he cared...

"Hello?"

Disappointment clouded Megan's features, and the small headache at her temple began to throb mercilessly. "Megan. Didn't wake you, did I?" Ted Benson's voice had an unsettling effect on Megan, and exasperation weighed heavily upon her.

"No—I'm still up." She managed to hold her voice steady while her foot tapped restlessly.

"Good. I thought I'd keep you abreast of the latest."

"I saw it in the evening papers." Once again Megan eyed the slanted article.

"It's not as bad as it looks."

Megan sighed. "Hard to believe, Ted, because it looks bad—damned bad,"

The attorney's voice was firm. "Look, Lana Reaves has been found. She was in New York. The legal grapevine has it that Ron Thurston has agreed to defend her, should she be prosecuted."

"Oh, my God," Megan whispered, a chill as cold as the wintry night piercing her heart. "But he's a local attorney..."

"I know. Works for her husband. I suppose that's why Thurston's taking the case."

"But they're divorced," Megan protested weakly. Even to her it sounded like a frail defense.

"Megan, look, you'd better face facts. Lana Tremaine and Garrett Reaves were married. She's in trouble. So is he. Looks as if they're in this mess together." His voice had become softer, more consoling. "I know you don't like the sound of it, but I think Reaves used you to protect his ex-wife."

No! her heart screamed. Megan's head dropped into her hands. She twisted an auburn strand of hair nervously in her fingers and tried to remain calm. "Why are you telling me all of this, Ted?" she asked, feeling suddenly defeated.

"Because you've got to pull yourself together. If you thought today was tough, wait until tomorrow. The press will be standing at your doorstep."

"Ready to eat me alive?"

"Close enough."

"Dear God," she whispered.

"Whatever happens, Megan, just stay cool. The reputation of McKearn Investments is on the line. Now that Jed's gone, you're it; the man in charge, so to speak. Everyone will be watching you—the press, the members of the board, the investors, the works. You're in the spotlight, whether you want to be or not. I'll help you any way I can, but in the end it's up to you to present the professional, full-of-integrity attitude that will convince the public that McKearn Investments is just as solid today as it was when Jed was running the corporation." He paused for a moment and then added, "You can do it, Megan, if anyone can."

"Thanks for the vote of confidence," she murmured before saying goodbye and hanging up.

Great! Things seemed to be going from bad to worse.

She went into the kitchen, made herself a pot of cinnamon tea and returned to the couch, settling in the corner and placing the steaming cup on the overstuffed arm. Memories of Garrett wouldn't leave her weary mind alone.

As she stirred the amber tea, images invaded and tormented her mind: sipping wine before the quiet flames of a dying fire; riding horseback through snow-laden pine trees. "Oh, Garrett," she moaned to herself. "Why couldn't it be easy for us?"

On the television, the eleven o'clock news was just going on. The local anchorwoman, a petite redhead with a winning smile, was sober tonight as she gave a quick rundown of the featured stories.

The first story made Megan's pulse jump. She nearly spilled the hot tea, and her eyes never wavered from the small television set. The petite redhead was talking rapidly.

"Garrett Reaves, local businessman and president of Reaves Chemical, stood by his ex-wife's side while she was interviewed by reporters concerning her involvement in the alleged investment scam that broke at the *Denver Financial Times* and McKearn Investments last month.

"Mrs. Reaves's involvement in the scam was undisclosed until late this afternoon, when she made a brief statement to the press."

The television screen switched from the anchorwoman to what was obviously a prerecorded tape. The scene was Stapleton International, and the man and woman dominating the screen were Mr. and Mrs. Garrett Reaves. Photographers and journalists crowded the couple, and the noise in the busy airport interfered slightly with the audio.

Megan felt her throat constrict as she saw the weariness of Garrett's features. He was holding on to Lana's elbow possessively as they shoved their way through the throng of reporters and interested travelers.

"Mr. Reaves," a reporter called, and Megan recognized the voice of Harold Dansen. She felt herself shrivel inside. Dansen, whose face now appeared on the screen, asked, "Could you or Mrs. Reaves comment on her involvement in the scam?"

"No comment," Garrett stated, looking squarely into the camera and attempting to break through the barrier of reporters blocking his path.

"Just a minute." Lana Reaves, a slender woman with a thick mane of glossy blond hair, placed a restraining hand on Garrett's coat sleeve. It was an intimate gesture, and it ripped

Megan to the bone. The noise from the crowd seemed to hush as Lana boldly stared into the camera.

Her eyes were an intriguing shade of blue accented by thick brown lashes. Lana Tremaine Reaves was one of the most beautiful women Megan had ever seen. No wonder Garrett, or any man for that matter, couldn't resist her. Megan nearly burned her fingers by clenching the cup of tea so tightly.

"I have nothing to say at the moment," Lana stated calmly, her eyes looking steadily into the camera, "other than that I've made a full statement to the SEC. Any other questions can be answered by my attorney." With an arrogant toss of her head, she once again began moving, and Garrett was at her side, helping her out of the building and into a waiting car. The camera followed Garrett's movements until the car had been driven out of sight.

Megan sank into the cushions. She felt drained and hoped that the story was complete. It wasn't. Before the feature was finished, a snapshot of Megan was flashed onto the screen while the anchorwoman gave a brief history of Megan's career, along with her alleged involvement with Garrett Reaves.

Also included in the story was a photograph of her father, and a mention of Patrick's tragic death.

"Not again," Megan murmured, witnessing with horror as personal shots of Jed and Patrick were flashed onto the screen.

Megan was shaking with indignation by the time the story was finished and the news had turned to the political scene.

Megan snapped off the set. She felt dead inside. Ted and Henry had been right. Garrett had used her, and she had been fool enough to let him. With a sigh, she turned out the lights and went upstairs.

It looked as if the cards were stacked against her, but Megan was determined to pull herself together and face whatever the press had in store for her tomorrow. No matter how shattered she felt inside, she would manage to show a strong image to the press, the investment clients, the members of the board and, most especially, to Garrett Reaves. Tears pooled in her eyes, but she forced them back. There was no room in her life for tears over a mismanaged love affair.

As she pulled on her nightgown and surveyed the bed in which she and Garrett had made love only the night before, a small cry broke from her lips. "Why must I love you?" she wondered aloud before sliding into the bed and holding on to her pillow as if for dear life.

A strange, loud noise throbbed in Megan's ears. She awoke with her heart in her throat. Her dream had been vivid and painful. Images of Patrick's car, a twisted red mass of metal against the stark white snow, had been dispersed and replaced by the cold, angry lines of Garrett's face.

The incessant pounding, which had brought her so rudely out of slumber, resumed, and Megan's tired mind suddenly registered. Someone was at the door, though it was four in the morning.

She was down the stairs in a flash, throwing her robe over her shoulders and slipping her arms through the sleeves as she raced to the window and flipped the light switch to illuminate the porch. She peeked through the window. There, standing on her step, his face just as angry as it had been in her dreams, was Garrett. Her heart turned over at the sight of him.

Opening the door just a crack, she let her gray eyes clash with his. He looked as if he hadn't slept since she had last seen him. He probably hadn't. The tiny lines near the corners of his eyes had deepened, and the set of his jaw showed that he was furious. The cold, damp morning air seeped through the small space between the door and the wall.

"Are you going to let me in?" he asked.

Megan was tempted, but reason tempered her response. "I don't think so."

He placed his hand against the door and rested his forehead wearily against his arm. "Why not?"

"Things have changed since last night."

"You're telling me," he admitted. "I think we need to talk."

"And I think it might be too late for it." Her voice shook, and her eyes, which she hoped would seem determined, were a misty gray and decidedly vulnerable.

His fist balled and pounded against the door. Megan felt the reverberations through the cold oak panels. "Damn it, woman, it's freezing out here and my patience is gone. Let me in and let's straighten this mess out."

Her fingers tightened over the doorknob. If she would just unhook the chain, he would be with her. Inside. Warm. Away from the rest of the world. She could pretend that what had happened yesterday was just a bad dream… But it wasn't. She shook her head, and the blue light from the porch lamp caught in the coppery tangles of her hair. "We've been trying for weeks and weeks, and it seems like the more we try, the worse it gets."

"Maybe that's because we didn't have all the facts," he said wearily. "I'm too damned tired for games tonight, Megan. I think you should have the decency to listen to my side of the story. No doubt you've heard everyone else's."

Megan hesitated only slightly before releasing the chain. Silently the door swung inward and Megan stepped out of Garrett's path, mutely inviting him into her home.

Garrett strode into the foyer and clasped both hands over his head, stretching his tired back muscles. Tossing his down jacket over an oak hook on the hall tree, he turned to face Megan just as she closed the door.

They were alone.

Together.

It should have been enough, but the aloneness and the to-getherness didn't begin to bridge the black, gaping abyss of misunderstanding that separated them.

"It's four in the morning," Megan admonished with a shake of her head.

"And I'm beat."

'You look it," Megan allowed. A dark shadow of beard covered the lower half of his face, and the spark that usually lighted his hazel eyes was missing. The corners of his mouth were hard and turned down, and deep marks furrowed his brow. His black hair was windblown, and he was wearing the same corduroy slacks and dress shirt he had been wearing when he left her house nearly twenty-four hours ago. "What happened to the shower and change before going to the office?" she asked.

"Didn't happen."

"Obviously."

"Look, if it wouldn't bother you too much, do you think you could be hospitable for a few minutes?"

She crossed her arms over her chest and leaned against the arch separating the foyer from the living room. "I don't know, Garrett," she admitted with a sad smile. "You see, I'm not crazy about being used over and over again by the same man. In fact, I don't like it at all."

Pain and anger flared in his intense gaze. "Good Lord, Megan, I've never meant to hurt you. Everything I did today, I did for you."

"Tell me another one—"

"Damn it, Megan, cut it out! You're not the only one whose reputation has been dragged through the mud, you know."

"But the difference is, I know who did the dragging."

Garrett raked tense fingers through his windblown hair. "There are so many things you couldn't possibly understand."

"And maybe I don't want to."

His eyes impaled hers, looking past the pretense of righteous indignation and into the pain beyond her fragile facade. "Oh, God, Megan," he whispered, and his hands dropped to his sides. "I've lost you, haven't I?"

A lump was forming in her throat and her words were choked with the emotion of the last few days. "I think…that lost is the wrong word. In my opinion, Garrett, you threw me away." Her shoulders slumped and tears pooled in her eyes. "Along with everything we shared."

"You're wrong—"

She put up her palm to interrupt him. "And I always have been, at least when it comes to you." She was shaking by this time, and her slim shoulders moved convulsively as she wrapped her arms around herself. "Don't you understand what I'm trying to say? I'm tired of being used, tired of being a fool for a man who doesn't care for me, tired of being manipulated like some little pawn. It's over, Garrett—if it ever began."

Garrett's jaw worked and his eyes narrowed as he watched her proud display and wondered how much of what she said was from her heart. Without thinking, he crossed the short distance that separated them, took hold of her arm and pulled her into the living room. Once there, he pushed her into the soft cushions of the couch. "I'm tired and cross—"

"Cross? Tired? You're being incredibly kind to yourself," she snapped, her temper beginning to ignite.

The silent warning in his eyes halted any further interruptions she might have voiced, so she contented herself with staring up at him and soundlessly accusing him of betraying her…again.

"I've been on airplanes and in airports for more days than

I'd like to count, so it would be wise not to test my patience any further."

Gathering all of her pride, she slowly turned her palm out in his direction. "I'm all ears."

His jaw hardened and he looked as if he wanted to grip her shoulders and shake some sense into her. Instead he walked to the other side of the room and stared for a moment out of the window into the black, cloud-covered morning. "When I left you, I did go back to the apartment," he stated, watching to see if she were bothering to listen. Satisfied that he had her complete attention, he continued. "When I got there, Ron Thurston was there."

Megan nodded, wanting to believe him. The honesty and pain in his stare was beginning to work on her, and all her earlier convictions began to fade.

Garrett continued. "I'd asked Ron to do some digging... look into the scam, try to find anything on the swindle, George Samples and you."

Megan stiffened. Ted Benson had warned her that Garrett was looking for skeletons in her closet. She nodded, encouraging him to continue.

Garrett realized that she had known about his private investigation for some time.

"Between what Ron dug up, and what I could piece together myself, I thought that Lana might be involved with the Samples scam."

"But why?" Megan wanted so desperately to believe him, to trust blindly in anything he might say, but she couldn't, not yet. Too many times she had fallen victim to just that trap.

"Because I know my ex-wife and what she's capable of—and because she's done freelance articles for the *Denver Financial Times* on occasion. I figured George Samples's accomplice had to be someone who wasn't in the office on a day-to-day basis, otherwise, the SEC would have been onto the scam the minute it started. Knowing Lana, I put two and two together..."

"But your ex-wife—"

"Is not the pillar of virtue she would like everyone to believe." Garrett's eyes darkened dangerously. "There was a time, before we split up, that she lost a very expensive diamond ring. She claimed it was stolen. The insurance paid off to the tune of nearly fifty thousand dollars, and then I found the ring, hidden very neatly in the chandelier. It was a fluke that I found it at all." Garrett's eyebrows had blunted in disgust, and his lips had compressed into a thin, uncompromising line.

Megan felt strangely calm. Listening to Garrett speak of some incident with his ex-wife seemed surprisingly natural. If only she could believe what he was saying.

Garrett walked slowly to the fireplace, propped one foot on the hearth, bent over his knee and stared into Megan's distrustful eyes. "Anyway, to make a long story short, I paid back the insurance money—which by that time Lana had managed to spend. They were satisfied and didn't press charges. So, when I finally got to thinking about this scam, it wasn't too difficult to put two and two together. Ron Thurston hired a private investigator and talked with the SEC. It took a couple of weeks to get the documentation together and prove that Lana was involved, along with this Van Weiss character, whoever the hell he is."

"You don't know?"

"And I don't want to." Garrett pinched the bridge of his nose between his fingers. "If I had to hazard a guess, I'd bet that Van Weiss is the latest in Lana's string of lovers."

Megan wasn't entirely convinced, though her heart screamed at her to believe him. There were too many unanswered questions. She toyed with the lapel of her robe. "What about today? I saw the paper." She tossed it to him for his perusal, but he set it on the hearth without even the slightest glance at the condemning pages.

"I read the article."

"I think we're still in a lot of trouble. The press is having a field day."

"Let them. Tomorrow—I mean, later today—we'll handle it." Seeing that she was beginning to believe him, if only a little, Garrett sat down on the hearth and held his face in his hands. A low sigh escaped from his lips as he rubbed his forehead.

His bent figure, burdened with sleepless nights and—perhaps—unfair guilt, got to Megan. No matter what had happened, she still loved him, and she couldn't bear to see him suffer.

Casting aside all rational thought, she went to him and placed a comforting hand on the back of his neck. When he looked up, she managed a thin smile. "Don't get me wrong," she whispered, "you still have a lot of explaining to do, but I think you should rest..."

"All I need is a shower and a cup of black coffee," he argued.

"And about forty-eight hours' worth of sleep."

His eyes sought hers. "In time."

"Shhh... I'll start on the coffee. You work on the shower." Tenderly, she placed a kiss on his forehead and was surprised when he reached for her and buried his head in the curve of her neck.

"Thank God you're here," he whispered, his voice thick with unspoken emotions. Then, just as quickly as he had captured her, he let her go.

While Garrett went outside to retrieve the garment bag from his Bronco, Megan started the coffee. She heard him trudge up the stairs, and she listened intently while the water ran in the bathroom.

When he came back downstairs, Garrett looked slightly refreshed. A smile tugged at the corners of his mouth as he surveyed the hearty breakfast she had prepared for him. His shirt gaped open, displaying the hard muscles of his chest. Beads of water still glistened in his ebony hair. His sleeves were rolled over his forearms, and he looked as if he belonged in her home.

"My favorite," he said, nodding at the food. "Thanks." As he sat in one of the cane-backed chairs in the nook, he took a long swallow of the hot coffee. "Aren't you joining me?"

Megan shook her head. "Too early. I'll eat later."

"You'll need some strength to fend off the reporters today."

"And you're going to give it to me—in the form of the truth."

Garrett smiled cryptically and speared a piece of sausage. Within minutes the entire breakfast of sausage, eggs and toast was demolished. Garrett leaned back in his chair, his shirt still open, and set his empty cup on the table.

"You were on the news last night," Megan challenged.

"With Lana." Garrett nodded thoughtfully.

"I don't understand."

"I went to New York. To her town house. And guess who else was there?"

"I couldn't," Megan retorted, her words sounding crisp and dry.

"An investigator from the SEC."

Megan's heart skipped a beat. She took a long, steadying swallow of her coffee as Garrett continued. "I'll admit it was poor timing on my part. Lana practically fell to pieces when she saw me. I stood by her—because she needed my support, not because of any love between us."

Garrett's dark eyes drilled into Megan's and she had to look away. "I told you before that Lana and I never had anything in common. That marriage was the second largest mistake of my life."

"And...and the first?"

"Letting you go."

The words echoed in the small room, and Megan felt the sting of tears burning behind her eyelids. How could she love this one man so hopelessly?

Garrett cleared his throat. "Lana made a full confession yesterday, once we got back here and she had talked to Ron Thurston."

"I saw the interview on television. Lana didn't impress me as the type of woman who would fall to pieces."

"She had her act together by the time of the interview, because she knew that if she didn't, it would be all over. Maybe it is anyway. Who knows if this will be a civil suit or a criminal case? I doubt that Ron will be able to protect her much."

"Oh, God, Garrett, this whole business is just such a mess." Megan rubbed her arms as if to ward off a sudden chill. "Why did they have to pick McKearn Investments in the first place?"

"Simple. George Samples worked for McKearn. Basically, it was nothing against you. You just got in the way."

Megan's eyebrow lifted in doubt. "Is that so? Well, since you seem to be the man with all of the answers today, why don't you tell me how George got involved and why you were one of the clients singled out to be part of the scam? Why your account? No matter what your story is, you'll probably have to convince the SEC that your ex-wife didn't give you the inside information before the articles hit the papers."

"I already have."

"What? When?"

"Lana may be a lot of things, but she wouldn't let me take

the fall for this. Not now. Oh, she might have if Van Weiss and Samples had pressured her, but I was there when the SEC came down on her, and she assured them that I wasn't a part of the plan."

"Do they believe her?"

Dark eyes glinted. "Do you?"

Megan paused. The clock ticked off the silent seconds as her eyes reached into his. "I've never wanted to believe anything more in my life."

"But you don't…"

Megan shook her head. "I know it's illogical and crazy and absolutely ridiculous, but I do believe you, Garrett. Why, I don't know."

"Because it's the truth." He pushed the chair away from the table. It scraped against the hardwood floor as he stood. "Megan, everything I've done was to insure that you and I will be able to start again—without the yoke of past or present scandals to burden our relationship."

He reached for her, and the gentle touch of his fingers against her face made her knees grow weak.

"Just trust me."

She didn't pull away from the pleasure of his touch. Instead, she looked into his eyes. "But what about George? Why did he involve you? It doesn't make any sense."

"Remember what I told you before—about George protecting himself and hedging his bets?"

Megan nodded, encouraging him to explain himself. Garrett smiled, and his finger slowly slid down her throat until her heart began to beat in a faster cadence.

"That was only part of his plan. According to Lana, he wanted to make a lot of money for my account because he was hoping to be in my good graces. He was planning to take a job at a rival brokerage house and steal accounts away from

McKearn Investments. You see, my darling, George Samples had reconciled himself to the fact that he couldn't work with you. He knew that either he would be fired or he would quit, whichever came first. When you stumbled onto his scam, he wasn't left with much of a choice.

"My guess is that he would have involved other large accounts in the swindle in hopes of taking them with him when he left, but he didn't get the chance."

Garrett's arms encircled her and Megan didn't pull away. She rested her head against his chest and listened to the rhythmic hammering of his heart. It was so warm in the protection of his arms. It felt so right. As if she belonged.

"So what do we do now?" she asked as her arms fitted around his waist.

He placed both of his hands on her chin and forced her to look into the wisdom of his eyes. "What we should have done long ago."

"Which is?"

"I love you, Megan," he whispered. "I want you to marry me." He reached into his pocket and extracted a gold ring with a solitary diamond. "Will you be my wife?"

Megan swallowed back her tears of joy. "Don't you think we should wait—"

"We have." Garrett gently nudged her neck. "Three years is long enough. And don't give me any business-before-pleasure garbage, because I won't buy it. You and I both know that we'll be able to face the press, come what may. My guess is that the Securities and Exchange Commission will have this case wrapped up by the end of the week, and that you and I, lady, will be off scot-free."

"You think so?"

He placed a kiss of promise on her parted lips. "I guarantee it."

"A few hours ago I was ready to purge you from my life."

His lips brushed seductively over hers. "I would have convinced you otherwise—"

"Sure of yourself, aren't you?"

"I just know that I love you and that you, dear one, whether you admit it or not, feel the same about me. So—" his finger slid between the lapels of her robe "—what do you say?"

Megan smiled through the shimmer of her tears. All of her doubts had disappeared into the mists of the past. "Of course I'll marry you," she whispered hoarsely.

With a glint of satisfaction lighting his eyes, Garrett slipped the ring on her finger. He bent and caught her knees with the crook of his arm, lifting her off her feet. "It's still early," he explained, "and you and I have a lot of catching up to do."

"I'm all yours…"

"Thank God," he whispered fervently. "This time it's forever."

★ ★ ★ ★ ★

MONTANA ROYALTY

B.J. Daniels

1

THE NARROW SLIT of light between the partially closed bedroom curtains drew him through the shadowed pines.

He moved stealthily, the moonless darkness heavy as a cloak. The moment he'd seen the light, realized it came from her bedroom window, the curtains not quite closed, he'd been helpless to stop himself.

He'd always liked watching people when they didn't know he was there. He saw things they didn't want seen. He knew their dirty secrets.

Their secrets became *his* dirty little secrets.

But this was different.

The woman behind the curtains was Rory Buchanan.

He began to sweat as he neared the window even though the fall night was cold here in the mountains. The narrow shaft of light from between the curtains spilled out onto the ground. Teasing glimpses of her lured him on.

As he grew closer, he stuck the wire cutters he carried into his jacket pocket. His heart beat so hard he could barely steal a breath as he slowly stepped toward the forbidden.

The window was the perfect height. He closed his left eye, his right eye focusing on the room, on the woman.

Inside the bedroom, Rory folded a pair of jeans into one of the dresser drawers and closed the drawer, turning back toward the bed and the T-shirt she'd left lying on it.

He didn't move, didn't breathe—didn't blink as she began to disrobe.

He couldn't have moved even at gunpoint as he watched her pull the band from her ponytail, letting her chestnut hair fall to her shoulders.

She sighed, rubbing her neck with both hands, eyes closed. Wide green eyes fringed in dark lashes. He watched breathlessly as she dropped her hands to unbutton her jeans and let them drop to the floor.

Next, the Western shirt. Like her other shirts and the jackets she wore, it was too large for her, hid her body.

Anticipation had him breathing too hard. He tried to rein it in, afraid she would hear him and look toward the window. It scared him what he might do if she suddenly closed the curtains then. Or worse, saw him.

One shirt button, then another and another and the shirt fell back, dropping over her shoulders to the floor at her feet. She reached down to retrieve both items of clothing and hang them on the hook by the door before turning back in his direction.

He sucked in a breath and held it to keep from crying out. Her breasts were full and practically spilling out of the pretty pink lacy bra. The way she dressed, no one could have known.

She slid one bra strap from her shoulder, then the other. He could hear her humming now, but didn't recognize the tune. She was totally distracted. He felt himself grow hard as stone as she unhooked the bra and her breasts were suddenly freed.

A moan escaped his throat. A low keening sound filled with

lust and longing. He *wanted* her, had wanted her for years, would do anything to have her...

Instinctively, he took a step toward the back of the ranch house. Rory was alone. Her house miles from any others. Her door wouldn't be locked. No one locked their doors in this part of Montana.

The sound of a vehicle engine froze him to the spot. He dropped to the ground behind the shrubs at the corner of the house as headlights bobbed through the pines. The vehicle came into view, slowed and turned around in the yard. Someone lost?

He couldn't be caught here. He hesitated only a moment before he broke for the pines behind the house and ran through the woods to where he'd hidden his car.

As he slid behind the wheel, his adrenaline waned. He'd never done more than looked. Never even contemplated more than that.

But the others hadn't been Rory Buchanan.

If that pickup hadn't come down the road when it did...

The sick odor of fear and excitement filled the car. He rolled down his window, feeling weak and powerless and angry. Tonight, he could have had her—and on his terms. *But at what cost?* he thought as he reached for the key he'd left in the ignition of the patrol car, anxious to get back to Whitehorse.

He froze. The wire cutters. He didn't feel their weight in his jacket pocket. His hand flew to the opening only to find the pocket empty.

2

RORY BUCHANAN HUNKERED down in the dark beside the stables as six royal guards trooped past, all toting semiautomatic rifles.

To say she was in deep doo was an understatement. Not only was it now completely dark, but a storm had blown in. She felt the chill on the wind only moments before the first stinging drops of rain began to fall.

Shivering, she checked her watch. Earlier, she'd left her ranch with only a lightweight jacket, planning to return long before dark. The sky had been clear and blue, not a cloud in sight. But this was Montana, where it could snow—and did—in any month of the year.

According to her calculations the next set of guards wouldn't come past for another three minutes. Fortunately, most of the grooms and trainers had left the stables, but she could still hear someone inside with the horses.

Rory waited until the guards disappeared into the dark before she made a run for the woods.

She'd never done anything like this in her life and hated to think what her parents would have said had they still been alive. But Rory doubted her new neighbors would be trying to take her ranch if her father were around.

A duke and duchess or prince and princess—she didn't know or care which and wouldn't know a duke from a drug lord and doubted anyone else in Montana would either—had bought up all the ranches around hers.

An emissary for the royals had been trying to buy her ranch, putting pressure on her to sell. Clearly they were rich and powerful and had built a palace with all its trapping just miles from her ranch.

Rory had turned down the first few offers, saying her ranch wasn't for sale at any price. But the offers had kept coming, and just that morning she'd seen tracks again where someone had been snooping around her place.

The footprints in the dust definitely weren't hers, and since she hadn't had any male visitors for so long she couldn't remember...

She didn't even want to think about that.

Her mare was where she'd left her, hidden in the ponderosas. Retrieving her horse, Rory swung up into the saddle thinking maybe she would try to outrun the worst of the storm.

But she hadn't gone fifty yards when the sky above the pines splintered in a blinding flash of lightning followed in a heartbeat by a boom of thunder. From over by the stables, she thought for a moment she saw a dark figure standing in the shadows watching her.

Her horse shied and she had to rein in the mare to keep her seat and the mare from taking off for home. When Rory looked toward the stables again, the figure was gone. Had the person gone back inside to call the guards?

With a shudder of both cold and fear, she pulled down her

cowboy hat to the storm and took off at a gallop, praying she hadn't been seen—and could get away.

Rain ran off the brim of her hat as she spurred her horse, racing toward her ranch. She regretted that she hadn't even had the sense to grab a slicker earlier. It had been one of those beautiful fall Montana days, the stands of aspens glowing red-gold in the sunlight and the air smelling of the fallen leaves, while over the tops of the ponderosa pines, clouds floated in a sea of blue.

Lightning lit the western horizon ahead of her. She tightened the reins as thunder exploded so close it made the hair on her neck stand up. Glancing back, she could see the lights of Stanwood, a blur in the pouring rain, disappear. If she was being followed, she couldn't tell.

Suddenly being caught by armed foreign soldiers didn't seem as dangerous as trying to get to the ranch in this storm.

Better Safe Than Sorry had never been Rory Buchanan's motto. But in this case, trying to get home in the storm and darkness was crazier than even she was normally. Especially when there was an old line shack just up the mountain in a grove of aspens.

The fact that the line shack was on royal property gave her a little pause. But she valued her neck and her horse's more than she feared her neighbors at the moment. Not only was the line shack much closer than her ranch house, but also there was an old lean-to that would provide some shelter for her horse and get her out of the weather, as well.

She doubted the royal owners even knew the shack was there given the enormous amount of property they'd bought up around her. Just the thought forced a curse from her as she rode through the drowning rain and darkness to the shack.

Rory's head was still swimming with the excessiveness she'd seen only miles from her century-old ranch house. The new owners had built a palace that would rival Montana's capital. Behind it was a private airstrip, stables with an arena and a colony of small cottages and a dormitory that could house a small army—and apparently did given the number of armed soldiers she'd seen on the grounds.

Of course what had caught her eye were the horses. She'd watched a dozen grooms at least exercising the most beautiful horses she'd ever seen. She hated to think what even one of those horses might cost.

All that wealth and all these armed soldiers had her even more worried that her royal neighbors wouldn't stop until they forced her off her ranch. That and the fact that someone had definitely been snooping around her place.

She'd always felt safe on the ranch.

Until recently.

Another burst of lightning splintered the dark horizon. Thunder ricocheted through the pines. A blinding flash of lightning exposed the line shack in eerie two-dimensional relief. Rory braced herself for the thunderous boom that wasn't far behind. She hated storms worse than even the idea of spending a cold rainy night in a line shack. Her baby sister, Brittany, had disappeared on a night like this and just four years ago Rory's parents had been killed in a blizzard on their way back to the ranch. It had come right after she'd graduated from college and had left her with no family and a ranch to run alone.

Dismounting, she hurriedly unsaddled her horse, hobbling the mare under the lean-to and out of the downpour.

Soaked to the skin, she carried her saddle and blanket into the shack, stomping her feet on the tiny wooden porch to make sure any critters living inside would know she was coming and hopefully evacuate the premises.

The shack was about ten feet by twelve and smelled musty,

but as she stepped in out of the rain, she was glad to see that there didn't seem to be anything else sharing the space with her.

It was warmer and drier inside, and she was thankful for both as she put down her saddle and slipped the still-dry horse blanket from under her arm to drop it on a worn spot on the floor next to the wall that appeared to have the least amount of dust.

Chilled, she had just started to strip off her soaked jean jacket when a flash of lightning shot through a crack in the chinking between several of the logs of the line shack, making her jump.

Outside, her horse whinnied as thunder rumbled across the mountaintop. She froze at the sound of an answering whinny from another horse nearby.

Drawing her wet jacket around her, she opened the door a crack and peered out.

A beautiful white horse with leopard spots stood in the trees below the shack. Rory caught the flash of silver from the expensive tack and saddle as lightning sliced through the darkened sky. The horse started, then bolted, taking off into the trees back the way Rory knew it had come.

She recognized the horse from earlier. A Knabstrup. She'd only read about the horses before she'd seen the groomers working with them at her royal neighbors'. Not surprising since the horses were originally from Germany—the Knabstrup breed having always been a symbol of the decadence of the aristocracy in Europe.

But where was the rider?

Rory swore as she turned back inside the shack to button her jacket and grab her hat, knowing even before she stepped into the pounding rain that the rider of the horse had been thrown and was probably lying in a puddle on the ground with his fool neck broken.

As much as she disliked storms—and the kind of neighbors who'd bought up half the county to build a palace in the middle of good pasture land that they wouldn't live in for more than a few weeks a year, if that—Rory couldn't let another human die just outside her door.

The temperature had dropped at an alarming rate, signaling an early snowstorm. Anyone left out in it was sure to freeze to death before morning.

"It would serve the danged fool right," she muttered to herself as she stomped down the mountainside to where she'd seen the horse. "Who with any common sense would go out in this kind of weather?" Unless they were trespassing on their royal neighbors' property, of course.

In a flash of lightning, she spotted the man lying in an open spot between the trees, surrounded by a bed of soft brown pine needles and a thick clump of huckleberry bushes, both of which, she hoped, had broken his fall.

She heard a groan as she neared, relieved he was alive. As he tried to sit up, she saw the blood on his forehead before the rain washed it down onto the white shirt and riding britches that he wore. He saw her and tried to struggle to his feet and failed.

"Easy," she said as she dropped down next to him on the ground.

A lock of wet black hair had tumbled over his forehead. She brushed it back to check the source of the blood and found a small cut over his left eye. There was also a goose egg rising on his temple.

Neither looked fatal.

He turned his face up to her and blinked into the driving rain. His dark hair fell back and she saw the dazed look in his very dark blue eyes. His lips turned up in a ridiculous grin as those eyes locked with hers.

"A beautiful forest sprite has come to save me?"

A forest sprite?

Clearly he was either drunk or delirious. Maybe he'd hit his head harder than she thought. He had that odd accent like the others she'd seen at her royal neighbors'. As she leaned down to gaze into his eyes, lightning flashed around them and she was able to rule out a concussion.

"It is my lucky day, is it not?" From the smell of brandy on his warm breath and that goofy grin on his face, she'd say the man was tipsy.

Now that she saw he wasn't badly hurt and was apparently intoxicated, she took some satisfaction in the fact that he'd been thrown from his fancy mount and immediately felt guilty for the uncharitable thought.

Her teeth chattered as she glanced around for his horse, wanting nothing more than to get out of the cold and rain. His horse had apparently hightailed it back to its expensive heated stables. She couldn't blame it. She would have loved a heated stable herself just then.

A horse whinnied nearby, startling her. Not his horse. She'd seen the way it had bolted, and she doubted the horse had doubled back for the groom. Was it possible he hadn't been out riding alone? More than possible, she realized. One of the other grooms must have been with him.

"Hello?" she called through the rain and the thick darkness of the pines and descending nightfall. "You've got a groom down over here."

No answer.

She looked at the groom at her feet. He was still grinning up at her. She might have found him cute and charming and this whole incident humorous under other circumstances. Or not.

Her horse whinnied from the lean-to. This time the answering whinny was farther away. If he had been riding with someone else, they had turned back toward home, leaving him to fend for himself.

She was almost tempted to do the same thing given that the man was clearly inebriated and would now have to share her shack.

"Come on," she said cursing under her breath as she bent down to help him up. "Let's get you on your feet."

Like her, he was underdressed for this type of storm, soaking wet and shivering. She had no choice. Given his condition, he would never be able to find his way back.

"Take me to your palace, beautiful forest sprite," he said and attempted a bow.

"Palace, indeed," she muttered.

Unsteady on his feet he plainly wasn't going far under his own power. He slung an arm over her shoulder. As they started up the mountainside, she wondered if he had any idea of how much trouble he was in.

He was bound to get fired for taking such an expensive horse out while drunk. He'd better hope that horse made it back to the barn safely. She'd bet that animal was worth more than this groom made in a year.

Lucky for him that he would be able to sleep it off before he had to face his boss—the duke or prince or whatever. As long as the horse returned unharmed, he might be spared being returned to his country to face a firing squad.

He shifted against her. "You are too kind, fair forest sprite."

"Aren't I, though," she grumbled. Lucky for him she couldn't let him die of hypothermia or wander off a cliff in the dark.

Lightning illuminated the landscape, the line shack appearing for an instant out of the rain and darkness. She stumbled toward the structure, staggering under the man's drunken weight as thunder boomed overhead.

"I owe you a great debt," he said as she shoved open the line shack door. "How shall I ever repay you?"

3

RAIN POUNDED THE tin roof overhead as Rory closed the line shack door behind them. It was pitch-black in the small room except for the occasional flashes of lightning that shot through the holes in the chinking. Earsplitting booms of thunder reverberated through the shack.

Teeth chattering, Rory untangled herself from the groom and eased him to the floor beside the horse blanket. He slumped against the wall, shuddering from the cold, his eyes half-closed, making her aware of his long dark lashes—and the fact that he looked as if he was about to pass out.

Thunder rumbled overhead again, and she shivered from the cold—and her aversion to storms. She could feel the damp seeping into her bones. She was going to have to get out of her wet clothes, and quickly. So was he. And they had only the one blanket.

Fortunately, the groom looked harmless enough.

"You need to take off your wet clothing," she informed him over the pounding rain.

No response. She kicked off her boots, then started to unbutton her jeans in the dark of the cabin. She heard a thump and in a flash of lightning saw the groom had fallen over onto his side. He was curled up, shaking from the cold and apparently out like a light.

"Great." She cursed and knelt down to shake him lightly. The lashes parted, the blue behind them clearly fighting to focus on her as another shaft of light from the storm penetrated the slits between the logs. "Your clothes. They're wet," she said enunciating each syllable.

He grinned, pushed himself up and attempted to unbutton his shirt, but she saw in the flickering light from the storm that he was shivering too hard to do the job.

"Here, let me help you," she said, pushing his ice-cold fingers away to work at the buttons.

"I'm afraid my life is in your hands, my fair forest sprite." His eyelids drooped again, and she had to catch him to keep him upright.

"You *should* be afraid," she said, her own fingers trembling from the cold as she unbuttoned the dozens of tiny buttons on his fancy shirt.

As the storm raged over their heads, she pulled him forward to slip the fabric off one broad shoulder, then the other. His muscles rippled across his chest and stomach, a trail of dark curly hair dipping in a V to the waist of his riding britches.

She half turned away as she removed his britches. He slid down the wall to the floor, eyes fluttering open for a moment. Britches off, he drew the horse blanket to him, curled up and closed those blue eyes again.

Two seconds later he was snoring softly.

"Just like a man," she muttered as she stripped down to her underwear. She was chilled to the core and *he* had the horse blanket.

She stared down at the man for a moment. He had passed out, obviously having consumed more than his share of alcohol. Outside, the storm wasn't letting up. There was little chance it would before morning. She was stuck there, and while she didn't mind sharing what little she had—the shack and her only dry horse blanket—she was piqued by the groom.

As drunk as he was, he'd had no business riding a horse, and she intended to tell him so first thing in the morning.

In the meantime... She knelt down next to him, gave him a nudge. He didn't budge. Nor did he quit snoring. Sliding under the edge of the blanket with her back to him, she shoved him over.

"Blanket hog," she muttered.

He let out a soft, unintelligible murmur, his warm breath teasing the tender skin at the back of her neck as he snuggled against her. She started to pull away, but his body felt fairly warm and definitely very solid, even the soft sound of his snoring reassuring. At least the man was good for something.

As much as she had grumbled and complained, the truth was she didn't mind having company tonight. As she began to warm up, she almost forgot about the storm raging around them as she closed her eyes and snuggled against him, drifting off to sleep.

Rory woke to the sound of her horse's whinny. Aware of being wonderfully warm, as if wrapped in a cocoon, the last thing she wanted to do was open her eyes.

Her horse whinnied again close by. Confused, since her horse should have been out by the barn some distance from her ranch house, she opened her eyes a slit.

Three things hit her at once.

She wasn't in her bed at the ranch.

There was an arm around her, a body snuggled behind her. *And* she was *naked*.

Rory froze, listening to the man's soft, steady breathing

as the events of the previous night came back in a rush. The storm, the shack, the groom she'd taken in out of the goodness of her heart.

But she was absolutely certain she had been wearing her undergarments, as skimpy as they were, when she'd lain down next to him last night. She recalled snuggling against him under the blanket to get warm…

She let out a silent curse as she recalled drowsily coming, half-awake, during the night to what she'd first thought was an erotic dream.

He stirred behind her, his warm breath tickling her bare shoulder, his arm tightening around her, one large hand cupping her left breast.

With a silent groan, it all came back, every pleasurable dreamlike moment of it, up until she'd awakened to the shock of her life.

She wasn't in the habit of waking with a stranger in her bed, let alone with a stranger on the floor of a shack under a horse blanket after having wild wanton sex.

This was all Bryce's fault. After breaking off her engagement with him four years ago, she'd been gun-shy of men. But then, who could blame her?

Blaming Bryce for this made her feel a little better. And of course there were other factors to blame: the storm, her fear of storms, the intimacy of the dark shack, the closeness of their near-naked bodies, the need for warmth to survive, Bryce again and that other need she'd ignored for obviously too long.

Not to mention trying to run the ranch single-handedly. She hadn't had time to date even though she'd had a few offers. Shoot, she'd bet everyone in the county was laying odds that she would end up a spinster. After all, she *was* nearly thirty.

Not that any of that was an excuse. She had her principles. And sleeping with a royal groom, whose name she didn't even know, didn't meet any of them.

As his breathing slowed again, signaling he'd fallen back into a deep sedated sleep, Rory slowly lifted his arm and slipped out from under it and the horse blanket. He stirred. She froze.

Then he rolled over, pulling the blanket with him, but not before she'd seen his naked backside.

She closed her eyes as she was assaulted with images of the two of them in the throes of lovemaking. A groan escaped her lips. She clamped a hand over her mouth, her eyes flying open, fearing she'd awakened him.

With relief, she saw that he was still sleeping soundly.

Her clothing was on a nail, where she'd hung it the night before. Her underwear was at the end of the horse blanket next to the groom's bare feet.

She gingerly extracted the lingerie and pulled it on. From the nail, she retrieved her shirt, which was almost dry, as were her socks. Her jeans and jean jacket were still cold and wet.

But she hardly noticed as she dressed and tried her best to ignore the hot flush of her skin or the slight whisker burn on certain parts of her body.

Don't think about it.

She wished it were that simple. She was appalled that she'd made love to a perfect stranger—and that she'd enjoyed it more than she should have.

Completely dressed, she stood for a moment telling herself maybe it *had* just been a dream. *Right.* She wasn't letting herself off that easily. Last night had been reckless, scandalous and…and…amazing. At least according to her limited experience.

As she turned to stare at the man curled in her horse blanket, she felt almost guilty about just leaving him there to meet his fate. When she'd found him lying in the pine needles drunk and confused, she'd thought he deserved whatever punishment his royal boss would give him for riding, in an inebriated state, such a beautiful horse.

But this morning she worried that he really might be sent home to face a firing squad. She hoped that wasn't the case, but there was nothing she could do about it. In fact, since she'd refused to sell her property to his employer, it was good that no one would ever know where the groom had spent the night—or with whom.

She was grateful that he didn't know who she was. With luck, she would never see him again since the man obviously was a bad influence on her.

It dawned on her that the only two men she'd ever slept with she now had to avoid.

Not a great track record, she told herself as she picked up her saddle, eased open the door and slipped out.

Devlin Barrow woke with the worst hangover of his life. He opened his eyes to find himself wrapped in a horse blanket.

Sitting up with a start, he looked around in confusion— and alarm. He spotted his clothing draped over nails on the log walls of what appeared to be a very small cabin. But he didn't recall hanging his clothing there any more than he could remember this place or the previous night.

The sun was up and a slight breeze blew through several cracks between the logs, chilling what he realized was his very bare skin.

"What the devil?" He rubbed his stubbled jaw and desperately tried to remember how he'd gotten there.

He had not the faintest idea. Not as to how he'd come to be there nor where he even was. Nor could he explain his massive headache or the cut over his left eye or the tender bump he felt on his temple.

Getting shakily to his feet, he retrieved his clothing and dressed. Since he'd been wearing his riding britches and boots, he could only assume he'd gone for a ride. So where was his horse? Where was *he*?

His riding britches were cold and damp to the touch. He frowned as he remembered something. He quickly searched his pockets, only to find the first empty. In the other, he discovered a slip of paper.

The note that had been slipped under his door yesterday afternoon.

The ink had run on the paper, but he could still make out the words: *I must see you. Meet me in the aspen woods a mile to the east of Stanwood tonight after dark.*

If he'd met someone in the woods last night, he couldn't remember it.

The bump on the head, the hangover from alcohol he couldn't remember drinking and the feeling that something important had happened last night made him fear that he'd been tricked into coming to this isolated spot not to receive the news he so desperately sought, but to be…what? Killed?

He stuffed the note into his shirt pocket and, fighting a wave of nausea, opened the door and stumbled out into the sunlight. To his growing concern, he saw no sign of his horse. Nor had the horse blanket he'd been wrapped in been one from Stanwood stables.

He was becoming more concerned about the consequences of finding himself in such a predicament. He licked his lips, his mouth dry and tasting of stale brandy. Another taste teased his memory.

He shook his head as if to clear away the cobwebs and shuddered at the pain. Why was it he could remember having only one drink since he must have imbibed more than that to be feeling this awful?

Common sense told him he wouldn't have gotten drunk before his meeting in the woods. So how did he explain this headache, his lack of memory?

The thick pines outside at least told him he was in Montana, but nothing looked familiar. Not that he'd been there long enough to know his way around. Yesterday had been his first day at Stanwood.

That seemed to jar a memory. He saw himself standing in the main parlor, having a brandy with several of the nobility visiting Stanwood. He'd been called up from the stables and complimented on his riding abilities. After that, he recalled nothing.

His riding abilities? How ironic since it appeared he'd not only lost his memory—but his horse, as well.

The ground, he noted, was still wet, the pine boughs dripping bejeweled drops that caught the sunlight in blinding prisms. When had it rained? He recalled being cold, then warm.

An image flirted with his memory, but didn't stick around any longer than to make him anxious. He had to get back to Stanwood.

Taking a moment, Devlin studied the angle of the sun and started walking down the mountainside, hoping to find a road or fence or someone who could tell him where he was.

As he rubbed the knot on his temple, he chastised himself for being a fool. He'd wager he'd been tricked into riding into the storm and woods last night. As terrible as he felt, he had a feeling he was lucky to be alive.

He'd gone on a fool's errand and now he would have to pay the price. He feared it would mean his job and being sent back to his home country. He couldn't let that happen.

He'd come too far, had already taken too many chances to get at the truth.

Stumbling through the woods, he headed due west. He wasn't sure how far he'd gone when he heard the thunder of hooves pounding toward him, and he looked up to see a half dozen of the royal police bearing down on him.

All Rory wanted was to get back to the ranch, take a hot shower and put the storm and the groom out of her mind.

If only she could exorcize the images of the groom as easily. His lips on her skin, his strong arms around her, his hard body pressing into—

She swore as she rode out of the pines and saw the car parked in front of her ranch house.

Deputy Griffin Crowley stood against his patrol car, arms crossed over his chest, a frown on his face. He glanced at his watch as she approached, then back up at her with obvious irritation.

Rory had completely forgotten about her call to the sheriff's department yesterday morning when she'd discovered the tracks in her ranch yard. The sheriff had been unavailable. The dispatcher had promised to give someone the message though.

And here was Deputy Crowley. He'd certainly taken his sweet time getting there.

But that didn't bother her as much as the fact that she was going to have to put off the shower and dry clothing awhile longer.

"Rory," Griff said with a nod as she swung down from her saddle. He was a big man, with a head of dark blond hair and a thick mustache that curled around his thin lips. He looked like the boy next door, more boyish than handsome.

"I heard you called. The sheriff's off to some lawman's seminar in San Francisco. I got here as soon as I could. I was getting worried." He studied her openly. Almost as if he knew that she'd spent the night in the line shack with a fancy-dressed foreign groom.

She and Bryce Jones had double-dated with Griff and his girlfriend back in high school when the boys had been football stars, taking the team to state all four years. The two men had been close friends. She'd always suspected that Griff hadn't forgiven her for breaking her engagement to Bryce any more than Bryce had.

But Griff and Bryce weren't such close friends that the deputy hadn't asked her out soon after the breakup and after Bryce's leaving town. She'd turned Griff down all four times he'd asked her out since. To her relief, he'd finally quit asking.

Unfair or not, Griff reminded her of Bryce, which was the kiss of death as far as she was concerned, not to mention she couldn't forget the way Griff had tormented her when they were kids.

"Sorry. Let me put my horse up." Needing a moment, she led her horse into the barn, slipped off the saddle and tack and hung everything in the tack room.

On the ride back to the ranch, Rory had told herself that she'd put last night behind her. It was over and done. No reason to beat herself up over it. And no one had to know about her lapse in judgment. Or whatever it had been in the middle of the night during the storm. The groom had no doubt been fired by now and was probably on his way back to whatever country he'd come from.

She filled the mare's bucket with oats before turning to find Griffin standing in the doorway watching her.

"Early morning ride?" he asked.

She knew her hair was a mess as well as her clothing, and saw no reason to lie. "Got caught in that storm last night. I had to spend the night in an old line shack."

He raised an eyebrow. "I didn't know you had a line shack on your property."

"I don't. The one to the west was closer than trying to make it back to the ranch," she said avoiding his gaze.

Fortunately, he let it drop. "Well, at least that explains why I couldn't reach you when I called last night and again this morning," he said. "I was worried about you out here all alone after you called the department. That was a pretty bad storm last night. Temperature dropped quite a bit. I'm surprised you didn't freeze to death."

She'd always been a lousy poker player, every emotion showing in her face. "It wasn't bad in the line shack," she said, turning her whisker-burned face away.

Out of the corner of her eye, she saw him frown. "Isn't that line shack on the old Miller place? I thought that land was bought by—"

"That's the reason I called you," she cut in. "Someone has been hanging around the ranch. I think it's my new neighbors, that duke—"

"Prince. He's a prince."

"Whatever." She just wanted to cut this short and get a hot shower and into some dry clothes. "He's been trying to buy my property and since I've made it clear I'm not selling—"

"You're telling me that the prince has been sneaking around your ranch? Come on, Rory, that's the craziest thing I've ever heard."

This was exactly why she hadn't wanted Griff responding to her call. "What are those people doing in Montana anyway? Do you even know? They could be infiltrating our country to attack us."

Griff shook his head as if he couldn't believe this. "A *prince and princess*?"

"How do you know that? Have you checked their identification? What do you actually know about these people?" She could see that he didn't know any more than she did. Maybe less since she doubted he'd been over there, while she had.

"Shouldn't someone try to find out exactly what these people are up to given they have soldiers over there carrying semiautomatic weapons?"

"How do you know what kind of weapons they carry?" he demanded.

She said nothing, not about to incriminate herself further.

Griff let out a long sigh. "First off, because they are royalty of course they are going to have armed guards. Second, you don't have to sell your land to them. Just ignore the offers."

"What about whoever's been on my property snooping around?" Rory saw his expression. "You're not going to do a thing, are you? Why am I not surprised?" She started to turn away from him, too angry to have this discussion with the pig-headed, son of a...

"Hold on, now," Griff said grabbing her arm and turning her back to face him. "I'll have a look around, okay?"

She jammed her fists on her hips and said nothing.

Apparently he seemed to think it best to follow her example and stepped past her to circle the house.

She thought about going into the house and letting him do his job, but she knew Griff. Tailing after him, she watched him wander around her ranch yard, looking bored and annoyed. He glanced back once to see if she was watching him. She was.

After a few minutes, he stopped his pretense of investigating and came back to where she was standing, her arms crossed over her chest.

"There's some tracks where someone has been hanging around, all right," he said.

"I believe I'm the one who told you that," she said, trying

to contain her temper. She was cold and tired and couldn't wait for him to leave. It would be a cold day in hell before she called him out there again. Maybe when the sheriff got back...

The deputy sighed. "Look, I've been meaning to talk to you about this very thing. I don't like you living out here alone. I'm worried about you, Rory."

She shot an eyebrow upward. "Why? Since you're so sure I have nothing to worry about with my new royal neighbors..." She couldn't help the sarcasm. His concern apparently only went so far.

"Damn it, Rory, you have no business trying to run this ranch alone and this proves it. By your own admission, you got caught in that storm last night. What if you hadn't been able to get to the line shack? Or worse—what if you'd gotten bucked off your horse and hurt?"

She bristled. "I'm *fine*."

Griffin was shaking his head. "I'm not sure you can trust your judgment on this. You aren't behaving rationally, and you know it."

If he only knew. "If you're going to tell me you think I should sell the ranch—"

"You know you're doing this out of sheer stubbornness. It would be different if you had a man around—"

"I'm in no mood for this."

"I can see that you didn't get much sleep last night," he said. "Maybe this isn't the best time to bring this up."

"There is no good time if this is about me getting rid of the ranch," she said with heat although she knew others in town had speculated on the same thing—if not bet on how long before she ran the place into the ground. What Griffin and everyone else didn't seem to understand was that she loved the ranch and couldn't bear to part with it.

Just this year, she'd sold off the cattle and leased the land, telling herself it was only temporary, just until she could get the ranch back in business.

"I'm not selling." With that she turned and stomped toward the house.

"I wasn't offering to *buy* the place," Griff called after her. "I was asking you to *marry* me."

Rory stumbled to a halt, his words pelting her like stones. Slowly she turned to look back at him.

"What?" she asked, telling herself she must have heard wrong. She'd turned him down for even a date. What would make him think she would marry him?

"We should get married." He walked to her, kneading the brim of his hat in his fingers nervously as he approached. "I'd planned to ask you a lot better than this, but when you weren't around this morning… I'm asking you to marry me."

Her first indication was to laugh, but the deputy looked so serious… "Griff, I don't know what to say." That was putting it mildly.

"I know this is probably a little unexpected."

You think?

"But I've been considering it for some time," he continued, clearly nervous. "You need a man out here. You can't run the place by yourself."

She bristled at that. "Even if that were true, it's no reason to get married," she said, still stunned by his proposal.

"Hell, Rory, people get married every day with a whole lot less in common than the two of us. You and I have known each other all our lives. There shouldn't be any surprises."

Yeah, who'd want any surprises in a marriage? Or mystery? Or excitement? Or, say…love?

"Griff, I appreciate the offer, but I believe people should be in love when they get married. I don't love you." She hardly liked him after the way he used to tease and taunt her when they were kids.

"Love?" He snorted. "Like you're one of those silly romantic types."

"I beg your pardon?"

"Come on, Rory. Look at you. The way you dress. The way you act. Hell, if someone saw you out in the pasture they'd take you for a cowhand rather than a woman." He sounded angry with her.

For a moment, she was too shocked to speak. She might be a tomboy, but that didn't mean she wasn't a woman under these clothes. She had a right to romance, love, passion. A red-hot memory of last night in the shack leaped into her thoughts against her will. Talk about passion…

"You know what I mean," he said, softening his words. "You've never acted like a woman."

"If there is a compliment in there, I'm afraid I missed it," she said, fire in her eyes.

"What are you getting all riled about?" Griff demanded. "I was just saying that you could do a whole lot worse than me."

"I think you've said enough, Griff."

"I didn't mean to offend you."

"I'm not offended." She was. Not that everything he'd said wasn't the truth. Obviously, she didn't dress or act much like his idea of a woman. But under her damp dirty clothes, there was a woman's body and a beating heart.

Her thoughts flashed to the groom she'd shared her horse blanket—and a lot more—with last night. He'd found her desirable, hadn't he? True, he'd been drunk as a skunk and thought she was a forest sprite.

"Well, at least consider my offer," Griff said irritably. "I'll give you some time to think about it. But I could be the answer to your problems."

"I don't have any problems," she snapped. Except Griff right then. "You and I are *friends*." A lie. "Let's leave it at that."

"*Friends* isn't a bad place to begin a marriage."

"My answer is no," she said more forcefully.

"You are one mule-headed woman, you know that?"

"Thank you. That's the nicest thing you've said to me this morning." She turned again and headed for the house, calling over her shoulder, "Let me know about what you find out about my new neighbors."

Once inside the house, the front door locked behind her, Rory waited until Griff drove away before she stripped off her damp clothing and stepped into the shower, hopping mad. Griff had caught her off guard with his ridiculous marriage proposal. But it was his description of her that had her fuming because she feared it was too close to the truth.

She'd been so involved in saving the ranch that maybe she had forgotten how to be a woman.

Until last night.

4

WITH DREAD, DEVLIN watched the horsemen approach. Jules Armitage, the head of royal security, rode in the lead, his back ramrod straight.

Devlin heard Armitage referred to as "Little Napoleon" behind his back. Small in stature but with an air of importance because of his long-standing position with the royal family, Jules was a man easily ridiculed.

But Devlin knew Jules Armitage was also a man to be feared. Jules had been in the service of the royal family for thirty years. His loyalties were never questioned, his harsh dealings with those under him legendary.

Devlin had seen Jules take a horse whip to one groom. Another groom had simply disappeared. The head of security had free rein here in Montana. Anything could fall under the protecting of the only daughter of the king, including murder.

Devlin could see even from a distance that the head of security was furious. It showed in the set of his shoulders, in the way he forced his horse's head up. Jules would report this incident—if he hadn't already.

This was the worst thing that could happen. Devlin couldn't

be sent home now, and yet he knew the princess could do whatever she wanted with him. He was at her whim. As were the rest of those under her rule here at Stanwood.

With a wave of his hand, the head of security ordered the other riders to hold back. Jules rode on alone, bringing his horse to an abrupt halt within a few feet of Devlin.

His horse danced to one side as Jules dismounted with a curse that could have been directed at the horse—or at the groom.

Back still stiff, his reproach barely contained, Jules turned to face him. "Lord Ashford requests your presence in the stables at once," he said, voice taut with fury.

Devlin expected a tongue-lashing at the very least. This reaction was all wrong. "Lord Ashford?" he repeated, his aching head adding to his confusion.

Jules's complexion darkened. "I suggest you ride directly to the Stanwood stables. His lordship is *waiting*." The little man held out his reins with a stiff arm, and Devlin realized Jules was furious at being sent on such an errand let alone being forced to give up his horse in doing so.

While Jules could do little about Lord Ashford, he could definitely make Devlin's life hell—and his look promised as much.

Without a word, Devlin took the reins and swung up into the saddle. His head swam and he had to steady himself for a moment before he spurred the horse and took off at a gallop toward the stables.

As Stanwood came into view, Devlin thought, as he had the first time he'd seen it yesterday, it was amazing what too much wealth and self-indulgence could do when let loose.

Stanwood, a miniature of the royal palace in their homeland, rose out of the pines, a massive palace of quarried stone.

One second-floor wing housed the princess and her prince, while the other wing was for royal guests.

Behind the palace were the stables, corrals and arena. Tucked back into the mountainside in the trees were a dozen small cottages that had been built for the grooms and horse trainers. Servants quarters had been erected in the opposite direction for those who saw to the princess and her entourage's daily needs as well as those of visiting nobility.

As he stepped into the stables, Devlin found Lord Nicholas Ashford, one such guest, leaning against a stall door. One glance around told him that the building was empty except for Lord Ashford. This, he knew, was no accident.

Lord Nicholas Ashford was tall, slim and immaculately groomed as any in his social stratosphere. Like the other nobles Devlin had come in contact with, Ashford had an air of privilege about him and an underlying impatience; he was easily bored. And he was a man who didn't like being kept waiting.

Nicholas frowned when he saw him. "You look like hell."

"I feel worse," Devlin said. He glanced around. Even though the stables appeared empty, he always feared that someone was close by, listening. Royal gossip was a hot commodity.

"We're alone. I cleared everyone out." Nicholas smiled. He'd never made it a secret that he enjoyed the privileges that came with wealth and power. His smile waned, though, as he studied Devlin.

"I feared something had happened when I heard your horse returned last night without you. Apparently there was cause for concern," he said, eyeing the knot on Devlin's temple. "What the devil happened?"

"It seems I was unseated from my horse."

Nicholas scoffed. "You? Not likely."

Devlin had practically grown up on the back of a horse.

The last time he recalled being thrown was when he was five. "I have no memory of it."

"The head wound doesn't appear that serious," Nicholas noted.

"It's not. I fear it was the brandy I had before I left Stanwood. I suspect it was drugged." How else could he explain ending up in that cabin with the unfamiliar horse blanket and no memory of what had happened the entire night?

"Drugged, you say?" Nicholas didn't seem surprised. "There's something you might want to see."

Nicholas, he realized, had been waiting for him at the stall containing the horse Devlin had ridden out into the woods last night. The horse that had returned without him.

"Take a look at his right hind quarter," Nicholas said as Devlin opened the stall door. The mount shied away from him, eyes wild, nostrils flaring.

Devlin felt his senses go on alert. The horse hadn't behaved in this manner when he'd ridden him away from Stanwood last night. Even when the storm had come in, the horse hadn't reacted to the thunder and lightning because it had been trained to be ridden by hunters, who would be shooting while riding.

Speaking in a low soothing voice, Devlin cautiously entered the stall. The horse relaxed some as Devlin continued to gentle it with his words and slow, measured movements. Gingerly, he ran his hand the length of the animal and felt something. The gelding shied away from him again.

"Easy, boy." He found the spot Nicholas had mentioned. Something had penetrated the hide, leaving a small hole. It wasn't deep, hadn't come from a bullet.

He glanced at Nicholas, who nodded. "Shot with, if I had to guess, a pellet gun. You do recall that old pellet gun we used to get in trouble with?"

Devlin did indeed. Their friendship had been a secret. The son of a stables owner and the son of a noble. Nicholas, who'd been skinny and pale, had been sent to the stables to learn to ride. They'd been close in age, Devlin strong and fearless, Nicholas puny and timid.

The friendship had been good for both of them. Nicholas had learned to ride a horse, as well as take part in rough-and-tumble adventures with Devlin. And in turn, Devlin had learned the speech and manners of a noble.

"I think we can assume that someone knows why you're here," Nicholas said, concern in his tone.

"It would appear so." Devlin took out the note that had been slipped under his door at his cottage. "You didn't send this, then?"

Nicholas took the piece of paper, squinting in the poor light at the water-blurred writing.

"I don't recognize the handwriting, but whoever sent it either appeared to be in a hurry or purposely scrawled the note so as to remain anonymous," he said, handing it back.

"I thought it might have been from you. Or Anna," he added quietly. His mother's housemaid and friend had been an excellent horsewoman.

"Dev, I was as fond of your mother as my own, but even if you find out who murdered her, it won't bring her back and will only succeed in getting you killed, as well. I was opposed to this from the beginning, but now that someone knows why you're here…" Nicholas stopped as he must have realized he was wasting his breath.

They'd had this conversation before and always with the same outcome. Devlin had to know not only who had murdered his mother but also why. It made no sense. His only lead was the woman who'd found his mother's body—his mother's housemaid and friend. Anna Pickering had been in the house.

She would know if the rumor he'd heard was true—that a royal soldier had been seen leaving the house that night shortly before his mother's body was discovered.

It made no sense to kill a woman who owned a stable, who wasn't politically motivated and who had always catered to royalty.

"If you're right about Anna seeing the murderer that night, she won't want to see you," Nicholas said.

Devlin didn't blame the woman. She had disappeared right after the murder. Nicholas had helped Devlin trace her to the princess's new palace in Montana—and had helped Devlin get hired as a groom there.

"Do you remember who handled your drink last night?" Nicholas asked. "I'm afraid I didn't notice."

Devlin had replayed the scene in his mind. He'd been given a brandy in the main parlor of Stanwood, surrounded by the noble class.

Nicholas had instigated the whole thing as a way to get Devlin into Stanwood so he could check out the layout of the place. He'd introduced him as a master horseman, touted his skills at training horses and riders alike, himself included, and made sure everyone understood his kinship with the groom and respected it.

Of course, that wouldn't save Devlin if the princess found out what he was really up to.

"The longer you stay here, the more dangerous it will become," Nicholas said now. "Perhaps I should try to speak with this woman, Anna Pickering. You say she is a handmaid for the princess?"

"You have done enough." Nicholas had already stuck his neck out far enough just helping him get the groom job—and getting him access to Stanwood last night.

"If anyone can persuade her to meet you, it's me," Nicholas said with a grin.

"And should she tell Princess Evangeline what you have done?"

"I shall deny it, of course." Nicholas laughed. "Just as I shall deny any knowledge of your deception when you get caught."

"Of course," Devlin said, but knew better. He feared Nicholas would put himself in danger to save his friend.

That was why he had to protect Nicholas—and Anna—at all costs.

"Watch your back around Jules Armitage," Devlin warned his friend.

"Don't worry about the Little Napoleon. I can handle him."

Devlin didn't doubt it, but he'd seen how upset Jules had been. The head of security didn't like being treated like an errand boy. He wouldn't forget this slight. Nor who had caused it.

After saddling a horse for Nicholas, as if that had been why Lord Ashford had ordered him to the stables, Devlin headed for his cottage to shower and change.

Last night was still a black hole. Worse, he couldn't shake the feeling that it was imperative that he remember. There was little doubt that he'd been lured into the woods, drugged and meant to lose his horse, but for what purpose?

Had his attacker hoped the fall from the horse would kill him? Or had his attacker planned to finish him off but hadn't for some reason?

He was almost to his cottage when he had a sudden vision. Hot skin, silken and flushed with heat, full rounded breasts, nipples erect and thighs as creamy as... He stumbled in surprise.

Being drugged and thrown from his horse had done more

than left him with a raging headache. It had apparently played hell with his dreams last night.

Restless after chores, Rory stormed into the house and went straight to her bedroom and the antique full-length mirror that had belonged to her grandmother.

Her face was flushed from the cold morning, tendrils of her chestnut hair curled around her face from where they'd escaped from her ponytail. Her Western jacket and flannel Western shirt had been her father's. She hadn't been able to part with either of them. The jacket was worn and too big for her, but like the shirt, it was soft and comfortable and one of her favorites.

Her jeans were boot-cut, slim-fit but the large shirt and jacket she wore over them pretty much hid her figure.

She cocked her head, shoved back her Western straw hat and studied her face in the mirror. No makeup. She'd bought some lip gloss recently, but she didn't know where she'd put it. As for mascara, well, she hadn't worn any since...her high school prom? Had it really been over ten years ago?

Rory groaned. Griff was right. She looked like a cowhand. She'd always preferred working outside with her father rather than being in the kitchen cooking with her mother.

Even now, if she wasn't on a horse, then she'd just as soon be out mending fences. Because of that, she was a mediocre cook, could bake if forced to, and her sewing abilities extended to reinforcing a button.

She much preferred jeans and boots to dresses and had never owned a pair of high heels. She'd borrowed a pair of her mother's for the high school prom—and had kicked them off the moment she'd gotten to the dance.

Damn Griffin Crowley. Tears smarted her eyes. She brushed angrily at them. It made it all the worse that Griff of all people was right, she thought as she stalked into the kitchen and dug out her mother's recipe book.

Damn if she wouldn't cook something.

It would keep her mind off last night and the groom who'd awakened something in her that she realized had been asleep. Or in a coma.

Head of security Jules Armitage watched the small jet taxi to a stop on the airstrip behind Stanwood. Lord Charles Langston emerged from the craft.

A steady flow of guests had been arriving for several days, no doubt to attend the masquerade ball the princess had planned for this coming Saturday.

But still, it seemed odd that the royal family barrister would be invited to the ball. More than likely, Princess Evangeline had sent for him on a legal matter.

Jules knew the princess felt slighted because being born female exempted her from the throne in their home country. Nor could her husband, merely a lord before he married the princess, take the throne upon her father's death.

But Prince Broderick would be elevated to a high position within the country should the king die. That was part of the reason for the unrest in their home country. Few people wanted to see Prince Broderick Windham having anything to do with the running of their country.

It was one reason Jules suspected that the princess and her husband had been sent to Montana. While the princess had overseen the construction of Stanwood since the first shovel of dirt had been turned over, she clearly hadn't been happy about her apparent exile.

Her husband, Prince Broderick, had been in charge of buying up as many ranches as possible for their new home.

Jules questioned this entire move. While he could understand the king's reasoning, since both Princess Evangeline and Prince Broderick were definite liabilities in their homeland, Jules had to wonder, why the US—let alone Montana?

If the king hoped that Montana would change his son-in-law and perhaps keep him at home long enough to produce an heir, His Royal Highness would have been sorely disappointed had he known the truth.

Jules swore as a second person stepped from the plane onto the tarmac. Lady Monique Gray, a recent widow. Black widow, that was.

What was *she* doing here? As if Jules had to ask. The princess's husband. Broderick had been anything but discreet about his scandalous affair with the woman. If the king hadn't controlled the media, it would have been all over the news. Princess Evangeline had to have heard about it, even though her father had worked so hard to keep it from her.

What the king didn't know was that his precious princess was a lot less fragile than he thought. She could squash a black widow like Lady Monique Gray—and would if given half a mind to. Lady Gray might not realize it yet, but she'd made a mistake coming here. Here in Montana, Princess Evangeline ruled like her father. If there wasn't blood shed within a fortnight, Jules would be surprised.

"Royals," he muttered under his breath, then quickly turned to make sure no one had overheard. In Stanwood, the walls had ears and unless he wanted to lose his, he'd best watch himself. The king had personally put him in charge of the princess's safety. Not that she needed it. Instead, he would probably find himself trying to protect the others from her.

He found the whole lot of them tiresome. Especially the lords and ladies who hung around the princess like flies to spoiled meat. Lord Nicholas Ashford came to mind. Jules hated beginning the day by being sent like a messenger boy to find a missing groom.

Especially this particular groom.

Princess Evangeline had asked him to keep an eye on Devlin Barrow and make sure he had everything he needed, including a cottage of his own near the stables and the run of the place. Jules suspected she planned to take him as a lover. What other reason could she have for singling out the groom?

Jules had done as ordered, but there'd been a breach in security just before dark last evening and he'd lost track of the groom. Someone had been seen on the property, sneaking around. That had taken his attention and the next thing he'd known Devlin Barrow had disappeared, last seen riding off into the rain and darkness.

It wasn't until that morning that Jules had been informed that a horse had returned without a rider—and that not all of the hired help had been accounted for. Devlin Barrow hadn't returned.

Jules had barely gotten that news when Lord Nicholas Ashford had demanded that the head of security not only find Devlin, but bring him at once to the stables.

Given no choice, since he was subordinate to every guest of the princess's, Jules had done as ordered.

But it had stuck in his craw. Why had the groom ridden off so late last night and in a storm? And where had he spent the night after losing his horse?

If Lord Ashford hadn't ordered his favorite groom be found for his morning ride, Jules would have given the groom more than the tongue-lashing he deserved. Within reason, he thought, as he reminded himself that Devlin Barrow was to receive special treatment. Wasn't it always the troublemakers who curried the nobles' favor?

But why this particular groom?

Jules knew he should just let it go. Who cared what had happened to the groom last night? The princess hadn't found out. Better it be forgotten.

But Jules couldn't let it go. As head of security, he was going to find out not only what Devlin Barrow had been up to last night, but also why the son of a stables owner was suddenly being afforded such special treatment.

Picking up the phone, Jules called down to the stables. "Ready me a horse. No, I'll be going alone."

Princess Evangeline Stanwood Wycliffe Windham studied herself in the full-length mirror. Behind her back, she knew people tsk-tsked about how sad it was that she'd taken after her mother's side of the family instead of her father's. The king was quite good-looking, while her mother, rest her soul, had been average.

Evangeline herself was below average. While she was average height, slim enough, blessed with her father's dark hair and dark blue eyes, her facial features would have been more attractive on a horse than a woman.

She knew she was being too critical. She had what once would have been called *handsome* features. Strong, striking bone structure. And she carried it off with a regal air that had definitely made some men turn their heads.

But then again, she was *the* princess. She knew that was why Broderick had pursued her. He'd wanted the title, the wealth, the prominence. He'd been so handsome, so charming and so attentive that she'd overlooked his less favorable qualities and married him because she thought they'd produce beautiful heirs to the throne.

Evangeline snorted and spun away from the mirror to stare out the window. "Bastard," she spat out at the thought of her philandering husband. She could overlook his infidelities and had. But his latest offense was unforgivable.

The bastard hadn't given her an heir and now he wasn't even sharing her bed. Maybe he thought he'd outlive her and have a chance to rule. Once her father was dead.

Her father. Just the thought of him made her a little ill. She knew he found her a scheming wench. He had no idea, she thought, then warned herself to tread carefully. She had taken too many liberties as it was. She'd disappointed her father too many times.

Her failure to produce a male heir, any heir at all, had angered him. He blamed her even though Lord Broderick Windham had given her little choice. Broderick, it seemed, was her punishment for her sins.

And sins, she had many. Her latest, though, was the most dangerous. She knew if she crossed her father that she risked not only being exiled from her homeland indefinitely, but also losing her freedom, possibly even her life.

Not that she didn't have everything under control. She reminded herself how clever she'd been when Lord Nicholas Ashford had come to her with his request that she hire Devlin Barrow as a groom at her new home in Montana.

It was clear to her that while Devlin had gone into hiding and no one had been able to find him after his mother's murder, Lord Nicholas was in contact with him.

Evangeline had provided the bait—Anna Pickering—by bringing the woman to Montana on the pretense of protecting her. Everything had worked just as she'd planned it.

So far.

But Evangeline could feel time slipping through her fingers like the finest sand. It was a two-edged sword, keeping both Anna Pickering and Devlin Barrow safe while at the same time planning their destruction.

Evangeline let out an un-princesslike curse as she focused on the scene below her window.

"What is Monique doing here?" her companion Laurencia cried as she joined the princess at the window.

Evangeline spun away from the window as the Black Widow entered Stanwood.

"You don't think *Broderick* invited her, do you?" Laurencia asked, wide-eyed.

"Of course not," Evangeline snapped sarcastically. It was so like her friend to say the obvious. Who else could have invited her? Lady Monique was relentless once she set her sights on a man. And now apparently she'd set her sights on the prince. And vice versa.

This was the last straw. Evangeline had put up with her husband's philandering for the last time. The fool was going to produce a bastard who would try to overthrow the crown one day. Evangeline had to get pregnant, and soon, to put an end to the talk of her being barren.

But that would mean getting her husband into their marital bed. That, she knew, would take more than fortitude on her part, due to his complete lack of interest—and her own.

It would take a miracle.

Or something Princess Evangeline was better equipped for: deception.

"You should have Lady Monique sent from the grounds at once," Laurencia was saying. "She is only here to rub your face in her affair with your husband."

Thank you, Laurencia, Evangeline thought. That was the problem with having a stupid companion—while she could be useful, she was annoyingly clueless.

"We will welcome Monique," Evangeline said as she suddenly saw Lady Monique's arrival as a possible godsend.

"But I thought—"

"Best let me do the thinking," she told her. Laurencia had always been the perfect companion—meek and slow-witted and completely loyal. In short, Evangeline could wrap her around her little finger.

"I want you to be nice to Monique," the princess said. "She has arrived just in time for the masquerade ball. In fact, I want you to make sure she wears the costume *you* were planning to wear. I shall have the seamstress make you something more suitable."

Laurencia looked disappointed but nodded.

Evangeline smiled. Her original plan had been to use her companion to lure in Lord Prince Broderick by offering Laurencia on a silver platter. But this new plan would work much better since she had been dangling Laurencia in front of her husband for weeks and he hadn't gone for the bait.

With Monique, the Black Widow, there would be no need to dangle her. Instead, Evangeline would have to make sure Broderick was kept so busy he wouldn't have the time to catch Monique—until the night of the masquerade ball.

With everyone masked, it would be the time to spring her trap and produce an heir to the throne. Broderick, without realizing it, would do his part. Once she was pregnant with a legitimate heir…well, then she wouldn't need Broderick anymore, would she?

Montana was such a wild, isolated country. Anything could happen to a man as adventurous as Prince Broderick Windham. Most certainly a very painful death.

Evangeline glanced at her watch. "Off with you now to make sure Lady Monique is comfortable in the large suite on the east wing." Laurencia, who as always did as she was told, scampered off to do the princess's bidding.

The princess stepped to the window again, pleased with herself. A lone rider galloped across the meadow.

Jules? Riding off alone? Odd, she thought, but quickly returned her thoughts to a more important task. Tying up one last loose end.

At the sound of a knock on her suite door, Princess Evangeline glanced at her watch. The man was prompt, she thought as she opened the door to her second cousin by marriage, Lord Charles Langston, the family barrister from a noble but poor family.

"Your Royal Highness," Lord Charles said with a bow. He looked scared out of his wits. She considered that a very good sign as she ushered him into the room, closed the door and demanded to see what he'd brought her.

Holding her breath, she watched him reach into his briefcase and draw out a large manila envelope. What Charles carried was of such high security that if caught with the papers, he would have been put to death.

Her fingers shook as she took the envelope and drew out the papers, noting not only the royal seal, but the thick, pale green paper used only for important government documents in her country.

"These are the originals?" she asked.

Charles nodded.

"So it is true," she said, feeling sick to her stomach. There would be no turning back now. She put the documents back into the manila envelope, willing her fingers not to tremble at even the thought of what she'd done.

Finally, she looked to the family barrister. She feigned surprise, then anger. "Where is this bastard?"

"In your employ, your Royal Highness. He's one of your grooms."

Jules rode to the spot where he'd encountered Devlin Barrow that morning. The day was cold and clear, the sun slicing through the tall, dense pines. Plenty of light to track Devlin's footprints in the still-wet ground.

Determined to find out where the groom had spent the night, he followed the trail, glad for last night's rain, which made tracking easier.

A hawk squawked as it circled over the treetops. Closer, a squirrel chattered at him as he worked his way through the pines.

Jules lost the tracks at one point in the thick, dried pine needles but picked them up again as he led his horse up the mountainside, surprised the groom had ridden this far from the ranch. He could make out the old county road—all that stood between the princess's property and the one ranch that was still privately owned.

The owner had refused to sell. He'd heard Evangeline discussing the problem with her husband, Prince Broderick. The Buchanan Ranch was now all that stood between the prince's holdings and the river.

The owner would *have* to sell. It was only a matter of time since the princess wanted it—and Broderick was responsible for acquiring the property for her.

Jules turned his attention back to the mountainside and the boot tracks he'd been following. As he walked through a stand of aspens, the leaves golden, he saw the small log structure ahead.

The groom's boot tracks led right up to the front door. Was it possible this was where Devlin Barrow had spent the night?

Ground-tying his horse, Jules walked toward the shack, noting the shed roof off to one side. A horse had been kept under the overhang recently. He could still smell it.

Not the groom's horse since it had returned to the stables without him. Had Devlin been thrown? That would explain his odd behavior that morning as well as the wound on his temple.

Except that Devlin Barrow was extolled as being an extraordinary horseman.

To Jules's surprise, the door to the structure wasn't locked. Cautiously he peered inside, not sure what he expected to find.

That was just it. He hadn't expected to find *anything*. It took a moment for his eyes to adjust to the darkness—and see the horse blanket lying on the shack's worn wood floor.

Frowning, he stepped in for a closer look. The horse blanket wasn't one of Stanwood's, which were monogrammed with the royal crest.

He caught a scent in the stale air of the small room and smiled knowingly. A man who knew about the baser desires, Jules was familiar with the aroma of sex.

He stared down at the blanket, wondering who had shared that blanket with the groom last night and how he could use that knowledge to his advantage.

Obviously, the woman wasn't from the Stanwood household or she would have been riding one of the royal horses with the monogrammed blanket and tack.

So who was she?

He started to turn to leave when he saw something that stopped him. Crouching down, he lifted the edge of the horse blanket. It had appeared to be nothing more than cheap material like most blankets used under a Western saddle in this part of the world.

But this blanket had leather trim. It was what had been stamped into the leather that caught his eye. Whitehorse Days.

Jules frowned as he read the date and the words: All-around Best Cowgirl.

He dropped the blanket back to where he'd found it and

rose. All-around Best Cowgirl. She shouldn't be that hard to find given that he now had the event date.

If Devlin Barrow—or even the princess—thought either of them could keep secrets from him, they were both mistaken.

5

"WHAT IS THAT?" Georgia Michaels asked as she answered the door to find her best friend standing on her step.

Rory held out the dish as an offering. "Pie. Apple. I baked it."

Georgia looked suspiciously from Rory to the pie and back but didn't take it. "You're kidding."

"No. Take the damned thing. Why is everyone giving me such a hard time about this?" Rory said, shoving the pie at her friend.

Georgia took the pie, eyeing her warily, before leading the way into the house. "Who's giving you a hard time about this pie?" she asked on the way to her warm, sunny kitchen.

"Deputy Griffin Crowley. And not about the pie," Rory said with a groan as she climbed onto a stool at the breakfast bar. "He asked me to marry him."

"Get out of here." Georgia laughed as she found a knife, cut the pie and dished them up each a slice, still eyeing the pie with suspicion.

"He called his proposal an *offer* and made it sound like a business proposition."

"Romantic." Georgia took a tentative bite of the pie, her expression turning to one of surprise. "Hey, this is *good*."

Rory cut her eyes to her. "Don't sound so shocked. I can bake. If I want to."

"Did Griff say you couldn't bake? Is that what this is about?"

"He insinuated that I wasn't a real woman."

Georgia raised an eyebrow.

"He actually made fun of me when I told him I didn't want to marry anyone I didn't love, then he pointed out that I wasn't much of a *girl*."

Her friend laughed. "I remember when you punched Joey Franklin in the mouth in third grade because he called you a girl. You can't have it both ways."

Rory had to laugh, as well. "I know."

"So what did you tell him?" she asked and took another bite of the pie.

"I told him no, of course. He said he only suggested it because I need help with the ranch. I think I hurt his feelings. He got pretty angry."

Georgia kept her gaze on the pie in front of her. "You do need help out there. What are you going to do?"

"I don't know." Rory didn't have money to hire hands and the place was getting run down without an infusion of cash. She couldn't afford to ranch. And she couldn't afford not to since ranching was her life.

"Have you given any more thought to my offer?" Georgia asked cautiously. Her friend wanted her to come into the knitting shop as a business partner even though attempts to teach Rory to knit had failed miserably.

"I'd die without the ranch," Rory said dramatically. "Or at least I'd want to. And as for selling out to royalty..." She shook her head. "I hate that they bought up so many working ranches to build some monstrosity. You know they'll tire of it and go back to wherever they came from. Or just visit here a few months a year after ruining all that range land."

"Nice to see you getting along so well with your new neighbors. Can I assume you didn't take *them* a pie?"

Rory let out a curse that made her friend laugh. "But I did meet one of the grooms from the place."

"Oh?" Georgia's head came up, eyes gleaming. She knew Rory too well.

"We both got caught in that big storm that blew through last night," Rory said, picking up her fork and poking at her piece of pie. She still hadn't taken a bite.

"And?"

Rory wished she hadn't mentioned it. But Georgia was her best friend and had been since they were knee-high to a squirrel. And Rory couldn't just bake a pie and show up on her best friend's doorstep and not confide all.

"And...we might have made love," she blurted.

"Might have? You don't *know*?"

Rory felt her face grow warm. "I'm pretty sure we did."

"It couldn't have been very memorable."

"Actually..." She looked away, her face now flaming.

"Rory!" Georgia laughed. "Does this mean you aren't joining the nunnery like everyone in town has been saying since your breakup with Bryce?"

"Not funny."

"So when are you seeing him again?"

"I'm not."

"What?" Georgia didn't even bother to hide her disappointment.

"Even if he didn't work for my royal-pain-in-the-behind neighbors, I'm pretty sure he got fired after last night." She wasn't about to admit that she'd been thinking of riding back over there that afternoon, get close enough that she could see the grooms exercising the horses to see if he was all right.

She doubted he remembered last night as out of it as he'd been. But it would be nice to know he hadn't been sent back to his country to be executed for risking one of the horses.

"You haven't touched your pie," her friend noted suspiciously again.

"I haven't been hungry all day. I feel like I'm coming down with something."

"Nothing kills my hunger," Georgia said proudly and finished her piece of pie. "Except love." Her eyes shone as she grinned at Rory. "Maybe you're in love."

"Please. I don't even know the man's name and I can assure you what happened last night wasn't love. It was more like lust. A lot like lust."

"Or fate. Apparently this royal *groom* thought you were a woman," Georgia said, hiking up one eyebrow. "You should have told Griffin Crowley that!"

Rory laughed, glad she'd come to see her friend, glad she'd confided in her. Georgia always made her feel better. "Thank you. Talking about last night, well, I feel better."

"I suppose this means no more pies, then," Georgia joked.

Talking about last night, though… Rory let out a curse and jumped to her feet. "My horse blanket."

"What?" Georgia looked alarmed.

"I left my horse blanket in the line shack. The groom was still sleeping on it so I left it."

"So it's probably still there," her friend said reasonably. "Or you can replace it, right?"

"You don't understand. I just remembered. It was the horse blanket I won at Whitehorse Days in high school."

"That old thing?"

"Georgia, the date of the event, Whitehorse Days and All-around Best Cowgirl were imprinted on the leather trim."

Her friend's eyes widened. "So he'll find you. What's wrong with that?"

"I told you, he is probably on his way back to his country right now." Rory had to get the blanket back. She was sure it was still in the shack. The blanket was old and certainly not a keepsake since Rory had won her share of horse blankets over the years. But she didn't want anyone else to find it and trace it back to her.

The last thing she needed was for her royal neighbors to find out she'd been trespassing on their property.

Devlin had gotten called back to the stables to saddle more horses for the royal guests.

Hours later, he finally reached his cottage. Now, standing under the spray of the shower, he closed his eyes. His head still ached, but he felt a little stronger. He'd tried to remember who'd poured him the brandy last night. It could have been anyone, one of the servants or one of the aristocrats who'd been in the room.

He'd tried to picture where everyone had been as he'd entered. Princess Evangeline Windham had been sitting on the couch. Her husband, Prince Broderick, had been standing before the fireplace, a drink already in his hand.

Nicholas had been talking to Lady Laurencia Hurst, a mousy-looking woman with timid brown eyes. Lord Alexis Kent had been behind Evangeline. A pretty boy, Alexis had been the lover of a variety of royal women, including Evangeline herself, at least according to Nicholas, and Nicholas did love royal gossip.

None of them had looked as if they were a crack shot with

a pellet gun, but looks could be deceiving, Devlin knew only too well.

He had been introduced by Nicholas as his favorite groom from the famous Barrow Stables.

"He comes highly recommended," Nicholas had said.

"Here, here," said Prince Broderick. "Your mother trained some of our horses. A fine, talented woman." Some of King Wycliffe's horses, not the Windhams', Devlin had thought. Broderick's family had been at the low end of nobility.

"Devlin's mother is recently deceased," Nicholas had added.

"Oh?" Broderick had seemed genuinely surprised to hear that. "My condolences. Get the man a drink," he'd said to the servant at the bar.

Then Princess Evangeline had insisted Devlin have a seat in front of the fire next to her and tell her how she could improve her riding skills.

All Devlin remembered was someone thrusting a glass into his hand. As darkness had descended, he'd excused himself and hurried to the stables, anxious to reach the stand of aspens and his appointment.

Had someone left the group in the main parlor and followed him through the rain and darkness? Or was the person who'd sent him on the wild goose chase not of royal class? And the person who shot his horse, an accomplice? Perhaps a servant? Or a royal soldier?

Devlin closed his eyes and concentrated on the feel of the hot water pelting his body. The images came in a rush, hitting him harder than the water, bombarding him with visions of a woman with green eyes, long legs and—

His eyes flew open, the images were so real he'd half expected to find the woman in his arms. Disappointment and confusion made his head swim.

He leaned against the shower wall for a moment, wondering if he was losing his mind or if it had just been the drug he'd been given. But the images were so vivid, so defined, so powerful...

How was it possible that he could remember the feel of the woman's skin beneath his fingertips, the weight of her breasts cupped in his palms, the sound of her quickened breathing if it had only been a dream?

Because it *hadn't* been a dream.

He shut off the water, his head clearing a little. What if he hadn't been alone last night?

It was the only explanation for the taunting images of this illusive green-eyed mystery woman. She was branded on his skin and still raging in his blood.

But who was she? And what had she been doing in that old cabin last night?

He'd been sent to that clearing, drugged, his horse shot and thrown from his mount to be injured. How had he ended up in the arms of a woman?

His every instinct told him that all of it—including the woman—was part of something much larger. But what? How could any of this tie in with his mother's murder thousands of miles across the sea in another country?

Even with his screaming headache, it was clear what he had to do.

Find the woman.

And get the truth out of her.

On returning to the ranch, Rory stopped only long enough at the mailbox on the county road to pick up her mail.

Another official-looking letter from her royal neighbors. She cursed under her breath, then reminded herself cursing wasn't very ladylike and only proved that what Griff had said about her was true.

She cursed at the thought—and Griff—as she drove to the ranch house. She didn't bother to open the letter, knowing it was just another offer on her ranch from her new royal neighbors.

She tossed the offer into the fireplace. How many times did she have to say it? No amount of money could make her change her mind about selling her ranch.

They'd thrown serious amounts of money at her already, as if convinced she could be bought—the price just hadn't been agreed on yet. She'd written them numerous times and even called twice, both times being told she should leave a message since it was impossible for her to speak to Her Highness.

Maybe in the princess's country she could force Rory to sell, but they were in America now.

More to the point, they were in *Montana*. Montanans didn't take kindly to being pressured into anything, especially when it came to their livelihood.

In Montana people like her felt that not only did they have the right to protect their land, they were also capable of doing so. It was one reason there were more shotguns over the fireplaces in this state than in any other. There was still a little of the Old West alive and well up here, and her royal neighbors were going to find that out if they didn't leave her alone.

The woman with the green eyes haunted Devlin throughout the rest of the day as he worked in the stables with the other grooms. Several more guests had arrived.

But the guest who had the grooms gossiping when no nobles were around was Lady Monique Gray.

"They call her the Black Widow," one groom confided. "All her husbands die."

"Which makes her richer than the king," one said.

"Not the king," another argued. "But richer than us, that's for sure."

They all laughed.

"She just buried the last one, so you know what that means. She's here looking for her next prey."

"Maybe back to even the score with her former lover, Lord Alexis. I heard she threatened to kill him if she ever saw him again."

The servants of the court did love the drama that always surrounded royalty.

"I say the Black Widow has her eye on the prince himself," interjected one groom.

The others exchanged nods.

"If that be the case, then I'd wager the king sent her so he could finally get Broderick out of the family," the groom said quietly, afraid of being overheard. It was one thing to speak of lords and ladies. Another to be heard disparaging the royal family.

Devlin only half listened to the gossip. He'd heard enough about Princess Evangeline that he doubted she would allow anyone to steal her husband.

He left the group to see if he could find Nicholas as he was returning from his ride.

"I'm sorry, Dev. I can't say who left the main parlor after you last night. I had to make a phone call before dinner. All I can tell you was that everyone was in the dining hall when I arrived for dinner."

"But someone could have followed me and gotten back in time to dress for dinner?" Devlin asked.

"I suppose they could have. You're that convinced it was one of the guests?"

"I'm just trying to consider all the possibilities." He thought about mentioning the green-eyed woman. She hadn't been one of the royal guests staying at Stanwood. If she was one of the servants, Nicholas wouldn't know. Maybe when Devlin had more information about her, he'd ask for Nicholas's help. But for the time being, he would keep the woman to himself.

It wasn't until later, his work done for the day, that Devlin saddled a horse on the pretext of exercising it. He planned to take a circuitous route to the cabin he'd awakened in that morning. Just in case he was being followed.

He couldn't wait to find a clue to the green-eyed woman haunting his every waking thought.

That was probably why he didn't notice someone standing in the shadows of the stables as he left.

Only one set of eyes seemed to follow his departure with interest. The dark blue eyes of Princess Evangeline.

Rory told herself she had no choice but to return to the line shack and retrieve her horse blanket. But this time, she felt even more nervous about trespassing—let alone getting caught.

What if the groom had told someone about her?

As she neared the line shack, Rory slowed her horse. A magpie cawed from a pine as she dismounted in the trees several dozen yards from the shack. The sky overhead was blue and cloudless after the storm last night, the peaks lightly dusted with fresh snow.

A slight breeze stirred the heavy boughs of the pines, emitting a soft sigh, as Rory walked toward the shack, her senses on alert. She half expected to hear the sound of hooves pounding in her direction. Light and dark played in the thick stand of aspens as she glanced in the direction of the royal palace, but she saw no spotted horses, no fancy dressed grooms, nothing but sunlight and shadow.

At the shack door she hesitated, listening for any sound

within before she pushed it open. The hinges groaned loudly, the door giving only a few inches, the noise making her jump. She let out an embarrassed, nervous chuckle and started to enter when she heard a familiar sound that stopped her cold.

The jingle of a bridle. She'd know that sound anywhere. Leaving the door ajar, she hurriedly stepped to the side of the shack, flattening herself against the outer wall as she heard a horse snort. The snort was followed by the sound of horse's hooves in the fallen leaves of the aspen grove on the far side of the shack.

Rory glanced toward her own horse, only partially visible through the pines, and prayed the mare didn't make a sound. Fortunately her horse seemed more interested in munching the tall grass.

The creak of leather made her freeze as she heard the rider dismount. The horse let out a shudder and pawed at the ground, taking a few steps closer to where she was hidden.

The door of the shack groaned all the way open. Silence. Then the heavy tread of boots on the worn wooden shack floor as the rider entered the building.

Rory didn't dare breathe. What could someone be doing in there?

More footfalls on the wood floor. The line shack door groaned closed. She heard him swing up into the saddle, the leather creaking again, the sound of the horse moving, and feared for a moment he might ride in her direction and see her.

Silence.

She hadn't heard him leave. Was he just sitting there?

Unable to stand it a second longer, Rory edged to the corner of the shack and peered around it.

Her heart jumped.

It was the groom from last night.

A gasp caught in her throat.

He had her horse blanket in his hands and was studying the lettering in the leather.

She ducked back, cursing silently. To hell with the horse blanket. It was too late anyway.

With relief, she heard him ride away from her, back in the direction he'd come, back toward the royal kingdom he must still be employed by. So he hadn't gotten fired and sent back to his country.

Rory would have been relieved—if he hadn't taken her horse blanket.

Her pulse thrummed in her ears.

Was it possible he was looking for her?

Why else return to the line shack? Why else take her horse blanket with him?

He was trying to find her.

But why?

6

IT HAD COME back to him, standing in the shack over the horse blanket. The images of the green-eyed woman in the throes of lovemaking had almost dropped Devlin to his knees.

He felt confused by the images, worse by the emotions the images evoked. The woman had touched him in a way that surprised and angered him. Clearly, she'd done her job well. But to what end, other than to lure him to the woods so she could seduce him?

He ground his teeth at the thought that he'd let himself be deceived in such a manner.

Well, the woman would answer for it when he found her. And he would find her—and her accomplice. Someone at Stanwood knew the truth and he was bound and determined to find them.

Devlin rode the horse a few yards into the trees, then circled back. He'd seen the fresh tracks around the old shack. His instincts told him that whoever had been there, hadn't left. He feared that after last night, he couldn't trust his instincts.

But he'd been right about the green-eyed woman. She *did*

exist. All-around Best Cowgirl. Oh, yeah, she existed all right and he had a feeling he was about to find her.

He eased through the pines until he could see the back side of the shack. Just as he'd thought, a figure moved from the shadows along the side and headed into the trees.

He frowned. It didn't appear to be a woman. Western hat pulled low, large old worn jean jacket, jeans and boots. A horse whinnied in the distance. Whoever it was had ridden there.

Just as he'd feared, his horse let out an answering whinny. He spurred his mount as he heard the pounding of horse hooves as the person took off.

Devlin caught sight of the rider racing through the pines and went after him. He loved nothing better than the chase. The wind in his face. The powerful horse beneath him. The knowledge that no one could outrun him. Not on a horse. Especially the one he was riding.

But the rider in front of him was giving him a damned good run. Devlin pushed his horse, gaining on the horse in front of him. The pines parted in a wide open meadow rimmed in aspens. Devlin drew alongside, both horses running flat out, neck and neck.

That's when he saw not only that the rider was female— but very familiar. Fear flashed in a set of beautiful green eyes. The same beautiful green eyes that had been haunting him since last night.

Reaching over, he grabbed her reins, drawing both horses up. His horse danced to a stop under him as hers bucked.

Devlin bailed off his horse, grabbed her by the waist and swung her down to the ground, surprised how well she'd managed to stay on the bucking horse.

"What are you doing?" the woman demanded. "You could have gotten us both killed!"

Her hair had come loose of the Western hat. She jerked the

hat off and slammed it on her pant leg. Chestnut curls tumbled around her shoulders. Devlin remembered the feel of her hair beneath his fingertips. Remembered those eyes firing with passion in a flash of lightning. Remembered the body hidden beneath the oversized worn jean jacket she now wore.

"It's you," he said, sounding as breathless as he felt. His gaze lit on her mouth and he was struck by the memory of the taste of her. For a moment, he forgot that this woman was part of a plot against him.

"Who hired you to lure me to that shack last night and seduce me?" he demanded, towering over her as that memory came back to him.

Those green eyes flashed with fury. "*Excuse* me? You're the one who seduced *me*."

"That's not the way I remember it."

"I'm surprised you remember anything given the shape you were in," she snapped.

"I remember," he said, his gaze locking with hers. "I have flashes of you naked in my arms."

Her cheeks flamed, but she didn't break eye contact. "From that, you decided I was part of some kind of diabolical plot against you?"

He grinned. "I have to admit that part of the plot did make me wonder."

"If you remember as you say, then you'd know that I saved your life," she said with a shake of her head.

"You saved my life?" He let out a humorous laugh. "You were in on the plot to get me to that shack. Don't deny it. I found your horse blanket."

"I don't know what you're talking about, but I want my blanket back," she said reaching for it.

He stepped between her and his horse, where her horse blanket was still thrown over his saddle. They were so close he could feel her warm breath brush his cheek. "If you didn't lure me to the cabin, then how was it you just happened to be there?"

"Luck. *Good* luck for you. If I'd left you out in that storm after you got thrown from that beautiful horse you were riding, I doubt we'd be having this conversation right now. But then again, as drunk as you were, maybe the alcohol in your system would have kept you alive."

"I wasn't drunk. Someone drugged me."

She raised an eyebrow. *"Drugged?"*

He nodded, scowling at her. "And that beautiful horse I was riding? Someone shot it with a pellet gun to unseat me."

Her horrified expression surprised him because it appeared to be genuine. "Who would do such a thing?"

"Why don't *you* tell me?"

"If you think I would be involved in anything that injured a horse…" The ferocity of her words made him take a step back to study her.

"Okay," he said, finding himself at least wanting to believe her. The fall air smelled of pine and fallen aspen leaves. He breathed it in, picking up the fresh scent of the woman, as well. The last of the day's sunlight caught in her hair, turning it to spun gold.

"So you're trying to convince me that what happened wasn't planned?"

She snorted under her breath. "Not on *my* part."

The breeze rustled the aspens. A moment later, they were showered with dried leaves that danced around them like snowflakes.

He watched her shake off the leaves that caught in her hair.

"You never said what you were doing there last night, if not waiting for me." He couldn't help being suspicious.

"Actually, I suspected you were following me." She sighed

again and he could see her making up her mind whether to tell him something as she settled her hat back on her head. "I was checking out the royalty and got caught in the storm."

He wouldn't have taken her for one of those people impressed by royalty.

"I knew where the line shack was so I headed for it. When I heard your horse and looked out to see you on the ground, I braved the storm to bring you into the line shack, where you hogged my horse blanket. You were so drunk—"

"Drugged."

She sighed. "Fine. Drugged. You called me a forest sprite and asked how you would ever be able to repay me for my kindness. Right before you passed out."

Her words had such a ring of truth to them… He cringed at how he'd repaid her. "If you're telling the truth—"

"Of course I'm telling the truth."

"Then someone didn't expect you to be there and take me into the line shack."

She brushed her hair back from her face as another gust scattered leaves around them. "I did hear a horse nearby and thought you might not have been riding alone, but the other mount went back the way it had come."

So there had been someone out there. Maybe the plan *had* been to finish him off if being drugged and thrown from his horse didn't do the job.

As he looked at the woman, he realized she very well may have saved his life. *If* she was telling the truth.

He pulled her to him, his mouth dropping to hers. She tasted familiar. He felt desire shoot through him as their lips touched. He'd definitely made love to this woman. The experience was burned in his soul.

The kiss brought back the memory of her warm and willing in his arms and left an ache when she pulled back to glare angrily at him.

But the kiss was impulsive and dangerous. What *had* he been thinking? That from one kiss he could tell whether she was lying or not....

"That might have worked once," she said, sounding as breathless as he felt. "But this time we're not sharing a horse blanket."

"I had to know the truth." The truth was he'd been dying to kiss her from the moment he'd pulled her down from her horse and seen it was the same woman from last night.

She cocked her head at him. "That was a *test*?" She seemed amused by that. "I guess I passed." She reached for her horse's reins. "I'd like my horse blanket now," she said, tilting her chin skyward.

"Not until you tell me your name."

She shook her head. "It's better you don't know." She swung up into the saddle.

"I can find out. All-around Best Cowgirl. Whitehorse Days."

She held out her hand for her blanket. "My name's Rory." She cocked an eyebrow at him.

"Devlin Barrow." He handed her the horse blanket. "You have a last name?"

They both turned at the sound of riders coming their way.

Rory spurred her horse at the sight of the royal guards riding in their direction and took off, making a beeline for home. All she could think about was getting away from Devlin Barrow.

She was still shaken by her encounter with the groom. All her bravado when she'd been caught by him was long gone. He was even more handsome in the daylight. The kiss had brought back last night and the emotions he'd evoked in her, as well as the desire.

What he must think of her. Worse, what would he think once he knew who she really was? Not that brazen woman from the line shack, that was for sure.

Wouldn't he be surprised to find out she was the woman who refused to sell to his employer.

She glanced back, half afraid he and the royal army were following her. They weren't. She could see his broad back and the way he was standing to face them. If anything he was trying to protect her, she thought with a stab of guilt. She'd run out on him, leaving him to face the consequences.

But Rory assured herself that being caught with her wouldn't have helped his case.

She realized that she believed his story about being drugged and his poor horse shot with a pellet. Maybe there was something to his kiss test after all.

It felt odd, trusting a complete stranger. Except it hadn't felt like that between them. It was as if they had shared more than a night of passion. She'd been joking about saving his life. Kinda. But maybe she had.

Odd as it seemed, she felt as if she knew him.

She could just imagine what Georgia would have to say about that.

Rory just hoped he was all right. Surely those soldiers wouldn't do him harm. And yet even as she thought it, she realized that if she really did believe him, then someone had tried to do him harm just the night before.

She shuddered at the thought. Who would want to hurt a royal groom? Or was it possible that it had something to do with her and her ranch?

Maybe Griff was right. She was seeing conspiracy plots everywhere she looked. But so was her royal groom, then.

Suddenly, all thought of the royal groom or the deputy flew out of her head as she saw where her barbed wire fence had been cut. Not just in one spot but several.

Rory drew up her horse and swung down from the saddle. There were tracks in the soft earth. Boot tracks. Man-sized.

She cursed as she picked up one end of the barbed wire and inspected the clean cut.

Vandals? Or had someone been looking for fresh beef still on the hoof?

The problem was there weren't any cattle being run in this section, so why cut fence? No fool rustler would cut the fence without first seeing cattle on the other side.

Not only that—whoever had cut the fence had apparently walked in from the road—a good half mile away.

Rustlers tended to steal cattle close to the road so they could be quickly loaded into a trailer for a fast getaway. Also, most rustlers worked in pairs. Whoever this was had been alone from what she could tell of the tracks.

This hadn't been a rustler. Nor some drunked-up kid out to destroy property because his girlfriend had dumped him.

No, this person had to have had another reason to vandalize her property.

Rory glanced back the way she'd come. She could see part of the royal family's palatial roofline above the trees.

She shifted her gaze to the two spots where her fence had been cut. This felt more like a warning.

Whatever it was, she was going to have to call the sheriff's department again and that was something she really wasn't looking forward to.

Princess Evangeline watched her husband come into their suite. He hadn't seen her, didn't realize she'd returned.

Broderick went straight to the bedroom. She could hear him in there opening and closing drawers.

Quietly, she got up from where she'd been sitting and moved to the bedroom doorway in time to see him emptying his pockets into one of the drawers. He caught his reflection in the mirror as he closed the drawer. All his attention went to his face.

Hurriedly he wiped at a spot on his cheek, then spun toward the doorway as if sensing her there. She saw the startled, guilty look in his eyes. It was easy to recognize since she'd seen it so many times before.

"Evangeline," he said on whiskey-scented breath. "I didn't realize you were here."

"So I gathered," she said stepping deeper into the room. The scent of whiskey did little to mask the underlying sweet odor of cheap perfume. She blinked back tears, surprised that Broderick could still disappoint her.

Had she really hoped that he would quit his philandering once they were in the States? Then that would make her a bigger fool than even her husband.

"I see you're up to your old tricks, so to speak," she said, furious with herself for thinking he might be capable of change. "You always did stoop to the lowest point possible."

"My dear, my dear," Broderick said with a laugh. "Are we to resort to name calling? I think you might want to reconsider. You know what they say about mudslinging. If you can't take wallowing in it yourself—"

"Aren't you afraid I'll grow tired of your antics and have my father terminate our marriage and throw you back into the gutter where I found you?"

He smiled. "So you admit you knew what I was when you married me. A gambler, a womanizer, a rogue. That, my dear, is what you fell in love with and that's what you get," he finished, throwing his arms wide with dramatic, drunken theatrics.

"You're drunk," she snapped.

"How else could I put up with your tedious lectures?"

She grabbed his arm as he started to turn away. "If I told my father, he'd have you killed."

Broderick laughed. "Not before I told him about you and Alexis and the others." He quirked an eyebrow. "What? You didn't think I knew? While you might be more discreet than I am, you are none the less innocent, my dear. Your exploits, like mine, are legendary. That's why we're made for each other."

"I know you're seeing someone."

"Seeing someone? What a quaint expression."

"You are supposed to be buying up land for my father," she said, growing angrier by the moment. She could just imagine the kind of woman he'd been with. It turned her stomach.

"Haven't I always done your father's and your bidding, my dear?"

"What about the Buchanan property? I assume you closed on it and were celebrating."

He scowled at her. "I'm working on it."

"So you haven't gotten anywhere with the owner."

"Rory Buchanan. Not yet."

"Have you even been over there to talk to the man?" Evangeline demanded.

"I'm taking care of it, trust me."

"I don't trust you and you've already wasted enough time." Evangeline had hoped that buying up land would keep her husband out of trouble. She should have known better.

A laugh floated up to the open window. Lady Monique Gray's flirting laugh.

"Is that who you've been with?" Evangeline demanded,

wondering where the devil Laurencia had been since she had been ordered to keep the two apart at all costs.

"Monique isn't here because of me."

Evangeline didn't believe him for a moment. She rang for Laurencia but got no answer. "Did you happen to see Laurencia on your way in?"

"Laurencia?" There was contempt in his tone. "Sorry, my dear, it appears another of your schemes isn't working so well," Broderick noted with no small amount of scorn.

She shot him a murderous look before pushing past him to storm out of the room.

To Devlin's relief, the royal soldiers were simply riding the property as per orders by the head of security, Jules Armitage.

The lead soldier had recognized Devlin as one of the grooms and apparently the group hadn't seen Rory. Devlin had stepped out of the trees to meet them, hoping to give her a chance to get away.

And she had gotten away.

Again.

But at least now he had a first name. And the information from her horse blanket. Her quick escape had him all the more curious about her. She didn't act like a woman who had nothing to hide.

As soon as everyone cleared out of the stables, Devlin used the phone to call the town of Whitehorse. The small Western town was just down the road.

It took several calls to find out who kept records of winners from the annual Whitehorse Days rodeo. He was directed to one Miss Adele Brown.

After four rings, an elderly woman finally picked up the phone. "Hello?" She sounded ninety if a day.

"Adele Brown?"

Silence, then a weak, "Yes?"

"I recently moved to the area and I'm interested in finding out about Whitehorse Days. In particular, I'm trying to find out about your former All-around Best Cowgirl winners. I was hoping you could help me."

"I suppose so. I could tell you weren't from around here," she said with a chuckle. "If you tell me the year, I'm sure I can tell you who won All-around Best Cowgirl."

He breathed a sigh of relief. This had proved to be easier than he'd thought. "It would have been 1997. I have her first name. Rory."

"Oh." He could almost hear her purse her lips. "I was afraid of that."

"Excuse me?"

"You weren't around so you wouldn't know about our office burning down in 1999," Adele Brown said. "It was one heck of a fire. The fire marshal suspected it was arson, and land sake's, it was. The entire county was shocked when they heard who had started the fire. Misty Justin from up by Stinky Creek. Seems she was mad because she lost. Can you believe that?"

"So what you're saying is…" He'd jumped in at the first opening.

"Everything burned up. Records and all. I can probably give it some thought, ask around and come up with a name if I put my mind to it over the next few days. But the name Rory doesn't ring any bells at the moment. Must not be from Whitehorse, and right now I've got cinnamon rolls cooking in the oven that I have to see to."

Before he could tell her that he might not have a few days, Adele hung up.

7

AS RORY RODE up to her ranch house, she spotted a large dark car waiting for her out front. Was it possible the groom had already found her?

No, she was willing to bet it was about buying her ranch. She thought of her cut fence and reined in her horse, wishing she could rein in her temper as easily.

Sliding out of the saddle, she walked her horse slowly toward the waiting car and the confrontation she knew was coming.

As a man emerged from the backseat of the car she saw from the way he was dressed that he was from the royal family next door. The dark three-piece suit was a dead giveaway. Only undertakers and lawyers wore suits in this part of Montana.

"Is Rory Buchanan available?" the man asked in that now familiar foreign accent. "I would like to speak with him on a matter of shared importance."

She smiled, amused, although it wasn't the first time someone had thought Rory was a male name. "*I'm* Rory Buchanan."

The man's gaze widened only slightly. "I see."

She figured he did as she put her hands on her hips, knowing what was coming next.

"Prince Broderick Windham," he said with a slight bow. "I have come in the name of Her Royal Highness Princess Evangeline Wycliffe Windham to make an offer on your property," he said, pulling out a long white envelope from his breast pocket beneath his coat. He held the envelope out, but she didn't move to take it.

"My ranch isn't for sale," Rory said calmly, not in the least impressed that the prince had come himself to make the offer. "I believe I've made that perfectly clear. So you can stop cutting my fence because it isn't going to make me change my mind. All it's going to do is make me madder."

The man frowned, looking confused. "I wouldn't know anything about your fence."

She almost believed him. "Right." She turned to lead her horse toward the corral.

"You might want to take a look at the offer," he said behind her.

She turned back to him. "I said no. And I mean *no*."

"We both know you'll sell eventually. It would be in your best interest to sell now," he said biting off each word.

Rory's gaze drilled the man. "That almost sounded like a threat." She caught the smell of alcohol and something sweet like perfume.

The prince sighed. "The princess, the only daughter of King Roland Wycliffe, wants your property. We can save ourselves a lot of trouble if we settle this now. Just tell me how much you want." He pulled out a checkbook and pen and looked up at her expectantly.

Jamming her hands on her hips again, she stared at him in disbelief. "How many times am I going to have to say this? My land isn't for sale at *any* price."

"I don't think you understand—"

"Oh, I understand. But I'm not selling. Especially to your princess. I don't like the way you do business. I don't like you buying up Montana. I wouldn't sell to you if I didn't have a dime and was starving to death. And tell your Royal Highness for me that if any more of my fence gets cut I'm not going to call the sheriff. I'm going to come over there personally."

The prince smiled as he knew what a waste of time that would be for her. He slowly put the pen and checkbook away. Clearly, he didn't see her as much of a threat.

"I'm sorry you feel that way," he said smoothly, "but I can assure you Her Royal Highness had nothing to do with the cutting of your fence. Perhaps someone has played a joke on you."

"Some joke. I think you'd better leave now."

He met her gaze. "I do hate to see you make a mistake you will regret."

Her eyes narrowed at the implied threat. The second within minutes. She thought about the shotgun just inside the back door of the house. Probably not a good idea.

"If you come here again," she said not mincing her words, "it will be *your* mistake. I'll call the sheriff on you." Like that would help. Since the sheriff was out of town. With her luck, Griff would come out again.

"Good day, then," the prince said as he turned and climbed back into his big black car with the dark tinted windows. The engine revved and the driver turned the car around.

Rory watched until it left her property and tried to calm down. It took all her self control not to get back on her horse and ride over to her neighbor's and demand to see the princess herself.

But Rory was certain someone would call the sheriff's department before she got near Her Royal Highness. And knowing Griff, she'd be the one to end up behind bars.

Devlin had the strangest feeling that someone was watching him as he hung up the stables phone after calling Adele Brown about Whitehorse Days. He'd unsaddled his horse as soon as he had returned to the stables. By now, he'd hoped to have the full name of the woman.

What he planned to do with it, he had no idea. After meeting her—and kissing her—did he still believe she had something to do with his being lured into the woods last night?

He knew he was in jeopardy the longer he stayed there. As Nicholas had said, clearly someone there knew who he was and why he'd come to Montana.

The stables seemed eerily quiet. It was late enough that no one was around. Or at least he'd thought that was true. Dust hung in the air along with the scent of horseflesh and oats.

He turned at a scurrying sound in time to see one of the house servants slipping past. Had she been eavesdropping on his conversation? Gossip was a pastime among the servants and grooms, he knew only too well. But if this information got back to the wrong person…

Devlin took off after her. The woman appeared headed for the grooms' cottages. Servants were forbidden to fraternize with the grooms and trainers, which would explain why she appeared to be sneaking along the side of the stables.

As she reached the end of the building, Devlin came around the corner, making her jump back in surprise at the sight of him.

She was much older than he'd first thought. As she raised her head, he saw her face. "Anna?" His mother's friend and housemaid.

She glanced around as if afraid of who might be lurking in

the dark. "I shouldn't have come." She took a step back, her face a mask of terror.

Nicholas had sent her, just as he'd said he would.

"I must speak with you. No one will know," Devlin assured her as he took her arm and drew her into the shadows.

"I can't be seen with you," she whispered, sounding close to tears.

"You found my mother the night she was murdered," he said, keeping his voice low and watching the shadows for any sign they weren't alone. "I have heard that the person who killed her wore the colors of the crown. Is this so?"

She gave a quick, frightened nod. Tears welled in her eyes. "Your mother was kind and good."

"Yes," Devlin agreed. That's why her murder was such a mystery. Clare Barrow had worked with nobles all her life, teaching them and their children and grandchildren to ride horses, boarding their horses, training their horses, pampering both.

She wasn't the kind of woman who made enemies. Everyone loved her. She was beautiful in so many ways.

Devlin had always wished he'd been more like her instead of like the father he'd never known. His mother had raised him alone from birth. His father, Leonard Barrow, had been killed in an accident shortly after he'd married Clare. Leonard had never even known about his wife's pregnancy.

Devlin could only assume he'd gotten his impatience, his intolerance for most of the rich and privileged and his temper from his father. All these years he'd tried to be more like his mother, but he'd failed miserably.

Maybe that was one reason he refused to take the royal government's word that his mother had been killed by a stranger, a beggar who'd been passing through town even though Devlin's mother's stolen brooch had been found on the poor man.

If a beggar had come to the door, his mother would have offered him food and shelter. But not the brooch his father had given her on their wedding night.

Devlin suspected that the brooch had been put on the poor beggar so that Clare Barrow's murder would appear solved. Add to that Anna Pickering's disappearance shortly after she discovered the body—and the rumor that a man dressed in the colors of the crown had been seen running from the house.

"I have heard that she was still alive when you found her. Did she tell you who killed her? Is that why you're so frightened? Why you left and came to the States?"

Anna shook her head.

"But you must know something. Please help me. I have to know the truth." He saw compassion fill her lined face.

"The princess," she answered in a sob-choked whisper. "She has the papers. She knows your mother's secret."

"What papers?" His mother had never kept anything from him. Or had she?

"You are not safe here and if I am seen with you…" Anna pulled away to leave.

"Where are these papers?"

Anna hesitated. He could see that she wanted to help him but she was afraid for them both. "In the locked bottom drawer of her desk in her suite. But if you try to get them, you will be killed. Please, I must go."

Devlin felt her shudder just before she broke free of him to escape and head back toward the palace.

It was all he could do not to go after her. But he knew she was right. They must not be seen together. He had already jeopardized the woman's life by coming to Montana. If anyone had seen them talking…

Devlin leaned back against the wall of the stables, heart in his throat, and tried to make sense of what Anna had told him.

Princess Evangeline had papers that exposed some secret of his mother's? A secret that got his mother murdered.

Devlin glanced toward the palace and considered how he was going to get into a locked drawer in the princess's suite in a palace full of guards.

Jules Armitage drove to the small western town of Whitehorse, Montana, to talk to Adele Brown that evening. For all the good it did. A fire had destroyed all the records?

"You didn't back up the results on a computer disk?" Jules demanded. He had thought his home country was backward. But then he'd never been to Montana before. "Someone else must have kept records."

Adele shook her head. "What would be the point?" She was a tiny gray-haired woman with sparkling blue eyes and dimples and the habit of smiling a lot. If her cheerfulness wasn't bad enough, the woman was completely disorganized. Her desk was covered in papers stacked so high, he could barely see her over the top.

"The point would be… Never mind." He had to bite his tongue since obviously the point would be that she would still have the records, she would be able to give him a name and he would be out of there.

"Funny, though," Adele said with a chuckle. "Wonder what it was about that year and that title."

He had to ask. "I beg your pardon?"

"You're the second person to ask about that particular winner," she said. "I can't remember the last time anyone asked. Around here, people only care about the year they or someone in their family won and they aren't likely to forget it, so…"

"I get the picture," Jules said irritably. "About this other person who was inquiring—"

"Like I told him, I'll remember who won that year. Sooner or later," Adele said optimistically.

"Did this other person give you his name?"

"Nope. I just assumed you knew each other since you both have the same accent."

Jules blinked. "Did the person leave a number for when you did remember?"

"Caller ID. I got it right here." She dug through the piles on her desk and came up with the number surprisingly fast, all things considered.

"Recognize it?" Adele asked as she copied it down for him on a scrap of paper.

"No, but apparently we're on the same mission." Jules waited until he got outside before he used his cell phone to dial the number she'd given him.

The line rang four times before a young male voice answered.

"Who is this?" Jules demanded.

Silence, then a timid, "Dunhaven."

Dunhaven? One of the grooms?

"Where have I reached?"

"Uh, the stables at Stanwood."

The stables. Jules clicked his cell phone shut and frowned. Devlin Barrow could have made the call. But why would he be searching for the owner of the horse blanket?

After what Jules had discovered in that horrible shack, wouldn't it seem likely that Devlin had known the woman in question?

Rory was mentally kicking herself for calling the sheriff's department. She'd already mended the darned fence and after her talk with Prince Broderick Windham, she had her doubts anything would dissuade the princess. So what was the point except to have the vandalism on record?

She dialed Georgia as she waited for a deputy to come out, wanting her friend to assure her she'd done the right thing.

"A man came into the shop a little while ago asking about you," Georgia told her. "He had a European accent and he wanted to know all about you and your family."

"You didn't tell him anything?"

"Of course not. But after he left he went across the street to Janis Ames's beauty shop and you know he got an earful. He knows you're out there alone."

Rory asked what the man looked like and the car he was in. "Prince Broderick Windham."

"He was a *prince*?" Georgia cried, sounding impressed.

"Georgia!"

"It's just that I've never seen a real live prince before. Especially one that good-looking."

Rory groaned. "Hello? The man is only a prince because he married the princess and he's trying to force me off my ranch. He made it clear that the princess gets whatever she wants."

"If it makes you feel any better, I heard around town that the princess's husband is a rake." Georgia read too many Regency novels. "His noble blood is very watered down. Anyway, they can't *make* you sell. Have you told the sheriff that the man threatened you?"

"Actually, the sheriff's out of town and one of the deputies is coming up the road now. I'll talk to you later."

The minute Deputy Griffin Crowley got out of the car and Rory saw who it was, she knew this had been a mistake.

"What's this about some cut barbed wire?" he demanded.

Rory gritted her teeth. "This morning I found where my fence had been cut in two places and I just had a visit from a prince who threatened me if I don't sell."

Griff gave her a skeptical look. "Threatened what?"

"Said I was making a mistake I would regret and that the princess always gets what she wants." She saw at once that Griff wasn't going to take the threats seriously. She had to admit that they didn't sound as threatening when repeated.

"Yeah. Okay, let's go take a look at your cut fence," Griff said with little enthusiasm.

"I already fixed the fence. There were boot tracks, man-sized, in the dirt that led to that old mining road."

Griff had stopped and turned to look back at her, his gaze pinning her to the spot. "You already fixed the fence?"

"Yes, did you hear what I said about where the fence was cut? It's next to the princess's property."

The sheriff took off his Western hat and raked a hand through his hair before putting it back on his head again. "You aren't trying to tell me that this princess cut your barbed-wire fence."

"I doubt she did it herself," Rory snapped. "She has lots of people to do her dirty work. Georgia said the princess's husband, the prince, was in her shop asking about me and my ranch."

"There isn't any law against—"

"They're trying to run me off my ranch." Angry tears burned her eyes. She willed herself not to cry, but when she spoke, her voice broke. "You know this ranch has been in my family for more than a hundred years. I was born and raised here, my parents and sister are buried on the hill over there with the rest of my ancestors. This is my *home*, my *life*." She swallowed, dangerously close to crying.

She would not be run off this ranch.

"You have any idea when the fence was cut?" he asked.

"The tracks looked fresh."

Griff kicked at a dirt clod with the toe of his boot as if avoiding her gaze.

"What?" she demanded. She and Griff went way back. And while it had been years since he'd put a frog down her shirt and rolled her in a snowdrift, she still knew him and knew this look.

He had the good grace to look uncomfortable. "Are you sure this isn't just a ruse, you know, a cry for help?"

"What?" He'd better not be saying what she thought he was saying.

"I mean is there any chance all this is just a ploy to get me to come out here?" He actually looked hopeful. "I did ask you to marry me and I thought maybe—"

"Stop!" She let out the breath she'd had trapped in her lungs, her blood pressure soaring. "If you're saying that you think I made up the story about the cut fence to get you out here—"

"I know how stubborn you are. If you changed your mind about my proposal, you might be embarrassed to tell me."

She really could not believe this. "Griff, I called the sheriff's department because someone cut my damned fence, snooped around my place and threatened me." She had to bite her tongue to keep from telling him she'd been hoping it would be any deputy but him who responded.

"Okay." He raised both hands as if in surrender. "I'll take another look around."

She knew how much good that would do. Turning on her boot heel, she stalked to the house, slamming the front door behind her for good measure, too furious to deal with Deputy Griffin Crowley right then.

Through the window, she watched him look around the yard half-heartedly until she couldn't stand it anymore and went back outside.

He didn't seem to hear her as she approached. He was moving along the side of the house, his head down. He suddenly stopped next to her bedroom window to bend down to pick up something.

As he started to pocket whatever it was, she demanded, startling him, "What did you find?"

Princess Evangeline had set her plan into motion and now she felt trepidation that this whole thing might blow up in her face.

She was taking a terrible risk. At worst, she could lose everything if her father found out what she'd been up to. At best, she could finally have the life she'd always dreamed of living.

As she stood at the window, surveying her domain, she realized, it wasn't enough. She'd built a replica of the palace back in her homeland, furnished it with the best that money could buy, indulged her every whim.

And still it wasn't enough.

Nothing seemed to satisfy this ache in her. Not food. Nor men. Nor possessions.

She told herself that once she gave birth to an heir to the throne, then she would have everything she wanted. Her father would finally see her value. And once Broderick was gone from her life, she could return home to take her place in society instead of being hidden away in this godforsaken place.

Scowling, she turned at the tentative knock on her door. "Come in," she said irritably, not surprised when Laurencia entered.

"I hope I'm not bothering you."

Sometimes Evangeline wanted to shake Laurencia until her teeth rattled in her head. The woman had no gumption, no backbone, no pride. What had ever made Evangeline think Broderick might be interested in the pathetic woman?

"Where have you been?" the princess asked impatiently. "Never mind." It was too late to do anything about Broderick and she wasn't in the mood for Laurencia's simpering.

"I just thought you'd like to know that Lady Monique sent me away, saying she needed to be alone, complaining of a headache."

Evangeline raised an eyebrow. So her husband hadn't been with Lady Monique after all. It must have been one of the servants. That would explain the cheap perfume.

"Prince Broderick left, saying he was going to buy that last piece of property as per your request."

Maybe Laurencia wasn't as big a fool as Evangeline thought. She was keeping an eye on both the prince and Lady Monique.

"It won't be easy to keep the two apart until the ball," Evangeline said more to herself than her companion.

"It might be easier than you think. I believe that Lord Alexis's being here has dampened the fires of her lady's desire for anyone else." Laurencia smiled.

Monique and Alexis. "I thought he had cast her off?"

"Possibly it was the other way around," Laurencia said with a sly smile. "There seems to be some embers still burning there."

Evangeline couldn't help but smile. Still, though, she knew her husband. And the Black Widow. "You shall continue to keep a close eye on Lady Monique."

"Of course," Laurencia replied with a small, amused curtsey. "And Prince Broderick, as well."

Deputy Griffin Crowley looked startled as he rose and turned around to face Rory. She'd seen him slip something into his pocket and now she saw his guilty expression and felt her heart take off at a gallop.

"What did you just find on the ground?" she demanded.

"Take it easy," Griff said as he slowly pulled a pair of wire cutters from his pocket.

Her pounding heart stuck in her throat. "You weren't going to tell me about finding those." It was an accusation, not a question.

"I was going to ask you if they were yours."

"You know they aren't mine. They belong to the person who cut my fence and now you've destroyed any chance of getting a clear fingerprint off them."

"This is why I wasn't going to show them to you," he said calmly. "In the first place, because of the type of handle on these there is little chance of getting a fingerprint from them. Also they're a common type of wire cutter sold at the local hardware store. Third, even if they were the ones used to cut your fence, there is no proof of that. And what would be the point since you apparently already know who cut your fence."

Rory didn't like his tone any more than she liked his attitude. "What were you going to do with them? Get rid of them so I wouldn't know you found them?"

"I didn't want to upset you any more than you obviously are since they don't prove anything."

"Except that someone has been snooping around my house!" Flushed with anger, suddenly she felt herself turn to ice as she saw where he'd found the wire cutters. Right under her bedroom window. One of the limbs on the bushes had been snapped off where someone had stood next to the building.

Rory hugged herself as a shudder went through her. Her bedroom curtains were gapped open. Just enough that whoever had stood there could have looked through the window…

When had the person dropped the wire cutters? When had they been within yards of her house? Within yards of her?

Anger warred with the cold tentacles of fear that had wrapped around her heart.

"This is why I don't like you living out here alone," Griff said, pocketing the wire cutters again. "Rory, if you would just let me—"

"What I need from you, Griff," she said biting off each word, "is for you to stop my so-called royal neighbor from harassing me. Can you do that, Griff?" She was scared and crying and that made her all the more angry.

"Rory, for just once, can you stop being so strong and let someone take care of you?" He took a step toward her as if he meant to comfort her.

She stepped back. "I don't need anyone to take care of me." She wiped hastily at her tears.

"We all need someone, Rory."

"Not me." She swallowed and looked away, wishing it was true. The other night in the line shack had only made her more aware of the need deep inside her. Seeing Devlin again today, kissing him, had only made it worse.

She had missed the warmth of another person. Missed human touch. Missed the connection that went beyond mere sex. For that time in the shack during the storm, she'd been close to another person. And now she found herself aching for it again.

But those thoughts always involved dark blue eyes and a royal groom with a European accent.

Not Griff Crowley.

He stepped back, a pained look on his face.

She hadn't meant to hurt him. She pulled herself together. For weeks she'd told herself that if she could ride this out, her new royal neighbors would stop once they realized she really wasn't going to sell.

But that was before someone had taken an interest in more

than her ranch. That was before Griff had found the wire cutters lying in the bushes under her bedroom window.

"You're a damned deputy sheriff. Can't you at least talk to the princess, warn her to leave me alone?"

"Rory—"

"You know who's doing this." Her voice broke. "If I'm right, this is just the beginning. When are you going to do something? When they burn down my house? Or worse?"

"Oh, for cryin' out loud, Rory," Griff snapped. "You're making too much of a couple snipped barbed wires. It was probably just kids messing around your place."

She stared at him, hearing the coldness in his voice, the anger.

"Maybe if you took all the offers on your place to the judge, he might think they constitute harassment. Without proof these people are threatening you, Rory, my hands are tied."

But hers weren't, she thought as she looked into the distance, where she could make out a portion of a royal roofline gleaming in the sun.

And it sure as the devil beat sitting around waiting for someone to save her since her life was visibly short of heroes.

Devlin was in the stables when Lord Nicholas Ashford found him.

"Let's take a ride," Nicholas suggested. "I need help on my cantering."

Devlin quickly saddled both horses, knowing that something must have happened and that was why Nicholas was providing them with an opportunity to be alone and talk.

It was dangerous, though. As head of security, Jules Armitage would find out. He was already suspicious of Devlin.

But nothing could have stopped Devlin from taking the

ride with his friend. Whatever was wrong, Nicholas thought he needed to know about it—and at once.

They rode out across the wide pasture, the tall golden grasses swaying in the breeze in contrast to the fringe of deep dark pines in the distance. Overhead the sky arched from horizon to horizon, a blinding blue dotted with white cumulus clouds.

But it was the air that Devlin had come to appreciate in this strange country. So clear and crisp. He understood why Montana had been called God's country. It was as close to Eden as a man could get.

Unless, of course, the man was there for deceitful purposes and living in a viper's den.

"I saw Anna," Nicholas said as soon as they were out of earshot. "She told me she talked to you. The woman is petrified that she'll be found out. If she's caught, she'll break down. I thought I'd better warn you."

"I can understand her fear," Devlin said, drawing up his horse the moment they couldn't be seen from Stanwood. "I wish there was some way to get her out of Stanwood."

"Believe me, that would only draw attention to you," Nicholas said. "Someone already knows who you are and why you're here. Or at least suspects why you're here."

"Did Anna tell you what she told me?" Devlin asked.

Nicholas shot him a look. "Nobility such as myself? Not likely. She doesn't trust anyone. I'm surprised she came down to the stables. She wanted nothing to do with me. Which just shows she has good taste."

"I need to get into Stanwood proper."

"Of course. I could probably get you in for drinks again, if you're willing to get drugged again."

"Thanks, but I'll pass. No, what I need is the run of the second floor royal wing."

Nicholas looked at him as if he'd lost his mind. "Well, hell, I'll just ask Evangeline to give you your own key."

Aspen leaves rustled gently over their heads. "I have a plan."

"I was afraid you were going to say that."

"But I'll need your help."

His friend smiled. "You're determined to get us both killed, aren't you? So what do you need me to do?"

"It will be risky."

Nicholas laughed. "I would have been disappointed if it was otherwise."

"I need to get into Lady Evangeline's quarters."

Nicholas looked skeptical. "I can't even get you up on the second floor, let alone into the princess's quarters."

"Are there guards?"

"Two posted at the entrance to the royal wing. But even if there weren't guards, you'd be spotted immediately unless…"

"Unless I was wearing the same costume as someone who actually lived on the royal wing," Devlin suggested.

Nicholas smiled. "You *are* the same size as Broderick…"

"I'll just need a costume exactly like his."

His friend was nodding. "I think I can see to that since the princess has hired an in-house seamstress to make our costumes and asked for two of each in case anyone has a spill. There is nothing like royalty." He grinned.

"I assumed she would have the costumes made in-house so there was no chance of seeing anyone else in a costume like her own."

Nicholas nodded. "Ah, vanity. Anything else?"

"I might need a distraction to get upstairs."

"Now that is something I can definitely handle," he said with a laugh. "Leave it to me." He sobered. "You do realize that if you're caught up there…"

"Don't worry. I'll wing it."

"That is what worries me."

"Griff is such a jackass," Georgia cried when Rory called her and told her what he'd said about her alleged cut fence being nothing more than an excuse to see him.

"Tell me you didn't do anything that got you arrested," her friend said. "You aren't calling for bail, are you?"

"No, but it was all I could do not to deck him." Rory walked around the ranch house with the phone to her ear, still angry and frustrated. "I might have threatened to get my shotgun and shoot him."

Georgia groaned. "You told him who you suspected?"

Rory heard the misgiving in her friend's voice. "*I* know it sounds crazy. But who else has anything to gain by cutting my fence?"

"You can't think of anyone else you've ticked off lately?" Georgia asked only half joking. "Bryce isn't back in town, is he?"

Her former fiancé? She certainly hoped not. "You know I thought Griff couldn't shock me any more after he asked me to marry him. But suggesting I cut my fence to give me an excuse to see him? Did I tell you he found a pair of wire cutters under my bedroom window?"

"Rory, that's frightening. That means whoever cut your fence—"

"Came up to my house, possibly looking in my window. Griff says it was probably just kids messing around."

"You're kidding? Well, I hope he plans to do something about it."

Rory sighed. "He says his hands are tied without evidence."

"What about the wire cutters?"

"Apparently they're a common variety that anyone could have purchased at the local hardware store."

"What about fingerprints?" Georgia asked.

Rory loved her for asking. They were both big fans of mystery novels and movies. "Griff says the handles wouldn't hold prints. He said he'd check, when I insisted. But as he pointed out, even if he found the prince's fingerprints on the wire cutters, it doesn't prove he cut my fence or that he was trying to force me to sell my ranch to him."

"But it would prove that he was on your property," Georgia said. "Oh, honey, I'm so sorry. Griff still doesn't think the answer is for you to marry him, does he?"

"He did. But, no, I think he's finally gotten the message," she said, remembering the ice she'd heard in his voice as well as the anger.

"So what are you going to do now?"

"I don't know." Rory feared the vandalism would escalate if she didn't sell to the prince and she wasn't about to call the sheriff's department again.

She would have to take care of it herself and said as much to her friend.

"Ah, I'm not sure that's a good idea, kiddo," Georgia said. "If you're right, messing with this bunch would be dangerous. Have you seen this princess who wants your property so badly?"

"Are you kidding? That place is an armed fortress."

"You aren't thinking about going over there again, are you? I mean after what happened the first time… Maybe you should come stay with me for a while," Georgia suggested.

"I will not be run off my own ranch."

"How did I know you were going to say that?" Georgia laughed. "Promise me you won't do anything…"

"Stupid?"

"I was going to say crazy."

"You know me so well."

"Actually... Have you checked your mail yet today?"

"Why?" Rory asked.

"I've heard some people are getting invitations to a masked ball at Stanwood on Saturday night," Georgia said.

"Believe me, I'm not invited."

"I guess not. But if you could get your hands on one of the invitations, maybe you could meet this princess and explain why you're not willing to sell your ranch. On second thought—"

"No, this is good. A masked ball? It's perfect. Meeting this princess wouldn't do any good, trust me. But Griff said if I had copies of all the offers, I might be able to prove harassment."

"Let me guess, you threw all of yours away?"

"If I could find copies, I could take them to Judge Randall..."

"Why do I not like the sound of this?" Georgia joked.

"Any ideas how I could get my hands on an invitation?" Rory asked.

She heard her friend hesitate. "If the royal couple had the invitations printed down at Harper's Print Shop here in town... Even with an invitation, you'll need a costume and I've heard that there are none to be had in the entire county at this late date, but I might be able to scare up something. As for finding your way around Stanwood, I would imagine the plans for the place are on file at Whitehorse Construction."

"The company where your sister Sara works?" Rory asked with a laugh. "I knew you'd help me," she said, feeling close to tears again. "I owe you."

She'd just have to make sure she didn't run into her groom, Devlin Barrow, on the grounds the night of the ball. Fortunately, a groom wouldn't be invited to the ball so she didn't have to worry once she got inside Stanwood.

Meanwhile, she thought, as she studied the darkening sky outside the window, she intended to lock her doors and keep the shotgun by the back door handy—just in case anyone came snooping around again.

8

THE NIGHT OF the Stanwood ball a huge harvest moon hung over the tops of the pines, spilling shimmering silver rays over the palace.

Millions of tiny lights glittered throughout the grounds. White carriages and the finest horses had been sent down to the parking area on the county road to collect the guests.

Princess Evangeline had sent out several hundred invitations to what she hoped would constitute Montana royalty.

"I want to share Stanwood with them for a night," she'd told Broderick when she'd announced she was hosting a masquerade ball.

He'd laughed pitifully at her. "You are so transparent, Evangeline. You know that few of them have ever seen a princess. You just want to show off."

She'd been instantly angered at his response. Probably because it was partly true. She knew rumors had been running wild about what a bitch she was because of the way she handled people during the building of Stanwood. She planned to squelch those rumors tonight. Everyone would see her at her best.

Broderick, meanwhile, would try to see Lady Monique before the ball when everyone was busy—especially his wife. But Evangeline had foreseen this. Just as she had kept her husband busy since Monique's arrival.

For her plan to work, Broderick had to be desperate for his precious Black Widow. The drug Evangeline would put in his drink later would make this ball the success she was determined it would be.

As she watched her husband dress for the event she told herself that before this night was over, he would regret everything he'd ever said or done to her. She would make sure of that.

"This ball was the best idea I've ever had," she said.

Broderick lifted an eyebrow. "Or your worse mistake yet. Worse than coming to this godforsaken place."

"We are only here because you are a contemptible, lying bastard," she said glaring at him. She couldn't have hated him more than at that moment.

"That is why you and I are so perfectly matched," he said as he slid his mask into place, brushing a kiss across her cheek as he passed her on his way to the door.

"Before you leave, would you mind helping me with this zipper?" she asked as she reached for her costume. Not the one she would don later. That costume was hidden until the appropriate time.

"Where is your precious Laurencia?" Broderick asked, sounding annoyed. "I thought she saw to these matters."

"Lady Monique asked for her help dressing," Evangeline said, turning her back to her husband so he couldn't see her face. Or her his. She wasn't sure she could constrain herself if she saw the disappointment in her husband's face that Monique was otherwise involved.

"I thought that's why we had servants," he snapped. "It's bad enough you treat Lady Laurencia like your handmaid…"

"Since when do you care how I treat Laurencia?" she demanded as she waited for him to zip her.

"Evangeline," he said softly behind her, making her heart quiver. She hadn't heard him use that tone with her since before they'd married, back when he was trying to win her over. "When will you learn?"

He zipped the costume, his fingers brushing the tender flesh at the nape of her neck. She felt herself trembling. Worse, she felt herself weaken toward him, yearning for that tender tone, that tender touch.

"I need a drink," Broderick said, pulling away again as if he feared letting himself be drawn to her. He left, slamming the door behind him.

Evangeline brushed at her tears, straightened and thought of Broderick's funeral, the condolences and sympathy she would receive after the horrendous death of her beloved husband. That day couldn't come soon enough.

It would be all the more touching since she would be carrying the heir to the throne.

Rory Buchanan shivered as she slid from her horse. She could see Stanwood through the pines and catch snatches of melody on the light breeze.

It took her only a few minutes to change into the costume Georgia had found for her—the last costume to be had in the county.

"It's not ideal, but it will hide your hair and, hey, how often do you get to wear a dress?" Georgia said, obviously seeing more humor in this than Rory.

"You don't really think I can ride a horse in that, do you?" Rory had exclaimed.

"So you ride over, change in the woods. Trust me, no one

will recognize you in this costume. That's what you wanted, right?"

Rory pulled on the black wig. She'd braided her chestnut locks so they would be easy to push up under the wig. Taking a deep breath, she straightened her dress and slipped on the mask. Now that she was there, she couldn't help being a little anxious.

She tied her horse, promising to return soon, and headed toward the back of the palace. She'd anticipated that there might be guards, but she didn't see any. To her relief she saw that costumed guests swarmed over an outside terrace. Music spilled out from the open French doors.

Rory studied the crowd milling on the terrace, half afraid she would see Devlin. But after the last time… She hated to think what the soldiers had wanted with him.

She wished she could forget him, but how could she forget the feel of his mouth on hers or the warmth of his body pressed to hers or the way he looked at her with those oh-so-blue eyes?

Her temperature rose a few degrees at just the memory. She fanned herself as she slipped up the stairs to the terrace and was instantly swallowed up in the crowd and the excitement in the air.

Rory moved cautiously toward the doors of Stanwood, expecting someone would stop her and demand to see her invitation. She'd hoped that by coming later as she had that she could go unnoticed.

As she slipped through the door, eyes wide at just the sight of the lavish costumes, decorations, furnishings, her heart pounded. As impossible as it seemed, the place appeared larger inside than it had even from the outside. She couldn't help but feel that she'd just stepped into a fairyland, where anything could happen.

The jewels alone were blinding, not to mention the extraordinary costumes. She felt like Cinderella *before* the ball in the understated costume and ballet slippers. She'd known better than to even consider high heels.

Griffin's description of her bit into her conscience as she watched women dressed in gorgeous costumes dance with handsomely attired men in a huge ballroom.

It made her think of being in the groom's arms, that feeling she'd had of being safe, being cared for, being a woman.

She swatted the thought away, annoyed with herself.

"Excuse me."

Rory froze at the sound of the voice beside her. Slowly she turned to find a waiter holding a silver tray filled with champagne glasses.

He thrust the tray toward her. "Champagne?"

She took one of the fragile stemmed glasses, concentrating on not spilling the bubbly liquid since her hands were trembling with nerves.

The stiff costume made her squirm beneath the starched fabric and the black wig was hot. She should have gone with her first instinct and come as Calamity Jane, the infamous woman outlaw.

But then, as Georgia had pointed out, everyone who knew her would have recognized her.

The ballroom was full, spilling over onto terraces from French doors that circled the massive room. She recognized people she knew drinking champagne and visiting with what had to be some of the royalty given the costumes and the weighty jewels that glittered under the crystal chandeliers.

Across the room, she spotted a wide staircase that wound up to the second floor. Near the top, she saw two guards standing at the entrance to a hallway that led to the south wing. Rory noted that the other hallway entrance had no guards.

She took a sip of the champagne, the bubbles tickling her nose, and she slipped deeper into the crowd as she debated how to get on that wing, which, according to the information Georgia had gotten for her, held not only the princess's suite, but some huge antique desk that had taken six men to carry up the stairs.

It was in that desk that Rory hoped she'd find what she was looking for.

Devlin Barrow moved along the edge of the ballroom that now swam in a sea of brightly colored masks and costumes. There was an air of anticipation mixed in with the orchestra music, the oceanlike roar of voices and the rattle of champagne glasses and silver trays as servants moved among the masses.

All of it turned Devlin's stomach as he watched the opulent extravagance in the name of royalty. He spotted Prince Broderick across the room, talking with Lady Monique and Lord Nicholas. None of the three looked in his direction but he saw Nicholas glance at his watch.

Devlin moved toward the bottom of the staircase and checked his own watch. Only three more minutes before—

He plowed into one of the guests, felt the slosh of icy champagne spill over his arm as he clutched the guest's arm to steady them both as they passed.

Devlin was only vaguely aware that the person he'd collided with was female. His fingers slid over the silken fabric of her sleeve as she slipped past him, both of them moving in opposite directions, neither apparently watching where they were going.

"Sorry," they both said at the same time. At the sound of her voice, his gaze leaped to hers and locked as she slid past, her head turning to look back at him.

Her green eyes wide with surprise.

Devlin felt as if he'd been jabbed with a cattle prod. He stumbled to a stop as the crowd filled in behind her. He would know those eyes anywhere.

In that instant, he'd seen something else in those green eyes. Not only had *he* known *her*, she had recognized him!

Rory! But what was she doing there? His heart began to pound at just the sight of her. It brought to mind the flickering light of the storm, those beautiful unusual green eyes and their lovemaking.

Not to mention the fact that now this woman was here and had recognized him. If he was wrong about her...

Devlin changed directions, fighting the swarm of party-goers, as he started after her. Rory was moving fast, winding her way through the crowd, heading for one of the terrace doors. Once she was through it and out in the night, she would be gone.

He couldn't let her get away. Not again.

Heart pounding, Rory bound through the open terrace doors, pausing to look back, afraid Devlin would come after her.

She told herself she'd overreacted. That couldn't have been the groom from the night of the storm. The man with the dark blue eyes she'd just collided with had been wearing the colors of royalty. Rory was certain no mere groom would have been invited to this ball.

But then she hadn't been invited either, and she was here. And there was no denying the way those blue eyes had looked at her. Had recognized her.

Her heart drummed, her skin rippling with memory of the man's touch, his voice.

"My fair forest sprite. You have bewitched me."

Words whispered into the hollow of her throat as his warm mouth moved over her skin.

She looked back and felt a shiver as she caught sight of him in the throng. Their gazes locked across the crowded room. His expression alone sent another shiver through her. There was both challenge and promise in his eyes. It left no doubt. He had recognized her.

And he was more than wondering what she was doing here. She could have asked him the same question, given the way he was dressed.

He gave her a slight nod of his head, his eyes never leaving hers. She felt confusion and fear. What was he doing at the ball dressed as if he were royalty?

She couldn't move, couldn't breathe. Music, voices and laughter rode as one on the night air. Closer, there came a high-pitched *clink* as someone tapped a piece of silverware on one of the champagne glasses, trying to get the crowd's attention.

As the crowd all turned, Rory spotted Deputy Griffin Crowley. He wore his uniform and a thin black mask. He was looking around, frowning, almost as if he'd glimpsed her in the crowd.

Rory found her feet and fled.

Devlin had gone after her but after a few steps had been impeded by the crowd. He saw that he would never be able to catch her without drawing attention to them both.

He swore under his breath, furious that he'd actually had her in his grasp, only to lose her again. He could only watch with frustration as Snow White disappeared through the French doors and into the night.

It took all his control not to say to hell with everything and chase after her.

A sound drew him back to the ballroom.

"May I have your attention please," Lord Nicholas Ashford called out over the crowd as he tapped a piece of fine silverware to his champagne crystal. "Your attention, please."

The crowd began to quiet, heads turning to see why the music had stopped, why one of the royal guests was standing on the bandstand at the end of the great hall and addressing them.

Forcing away thoughts of the green-eyed woman, Devlin quickly turned toward the stairs at the opposite end of the great hall. He should have been closer, but he'd lost valuable time going after Rory even as far as he had.

Now he might miss his chance to get on the royal wing, miss the chance to find the papers Anna had told him about that somehow involved the murder of his mother.

And yet the memory of those green eyes followed him like a sweet, seductive perfume. How he wanted to chase after her. The fact that she was here made him suspicious of her again. After the kiss he'd been so sure she'd been telling him the truth…

He forced her from his thoughts. Tonight was his only chance of getting upstairs. He had only a limited amount of time to get onto the royal wing, get into Evangeline's suite and find the papers.

He continued to move toward the stairs, weaving his way through the guests as everyone's eyes were on the bandstand and the handsome man before them. Someone handed Lord Ashford a microphone.

"If I may have your attention," he said into it. Expectation fell over the crowd as Devlin slipped to the bottom of the stairs.

"If Lady Gray would please join me," Nicholas said. There

was a murmur of surprise, then a stirring as the Black Widow made her way to him.

Devlin caught sight of Lady Monique's intrigued expression as she joined Lord Ashford. Devlin started up the stairs, moving as if he knew where he was going, belonged there, had maybe forgotten something from his room.

"Lady Gray and I are going to sing a duet in honor of Princess Evangeline and Prince Broderick on this wonderful occasion," Nicholas announced as he took Monique's hand and smiled at her.

At the top of the stairs, Devlin glanced back. All eyes were on the two on stage as the orchestra struck up a tune and Nicholas moved closer to share his microphone with Lady Monique. Devlin could see Prince Broderick at the edge of the stage. The lord prince didn't look happy. Nor did he look as if he would be going anywhere until the two were off the stage.

Devlin walked with his head down as if his mind were on something else as he headed for the royal wing. Nicholas had given him directions to Lady Evangeline's suite and taken the dangerous risk of getting him a pass key from the laundry servant's quarters.

From out of the corner of his eye, Devlin saw both guards look in his direction. He muttered under his breath, staggered a little as if already drunk and walked past them without a look or a word.

His heart was pounding in his ears so loudly that he feared he wouldn't hear them if they called after him. He didn't dare look back.

At the door to the princess's suite, he stopped. Out of the corner of his eye, he could see both guards at their stations down the hall. Neither was looking in this direction.

With shaking fingers he pulled out the key and opened the door to the suite and hurriedly stepped inside.

★ ★ ★

Rory was still shaken after seeing the groom at the ball—dressed as a royal—and Griff. Unlike her, the deputy had probably been invited.

Devlin had seen her and started to come after her, but seemed to change his mind. She'd seen the anger and frustration in his expression. He'd wanted to chase after her but something had held him back. The same thing that had kept him from calling to a guard to stop her?

Which made her think that, as she'd suspected, he didn't belong at the ball any more than she did.

Interesting, she thought as she circled around the palace and tried to decide what to do next. She stopped under some shrubbery, chastising herself for being so foolish as to come here tonight in the first place.

Getting into the ball had been easier than she'd hoped. So had mingling among the many guests. But getting upstairs to this massive desk was a much bigger problem than she'd thought it would be. She'd seen herself having a run of the palace simply because she was in costume.

Discouraged, she glanced upward. According to the plans Georgia had gotten her, the princess's suite should be directly—

Rory started at the sight of a strange light flickering in what was one of the rooms in the royal suite.

She moved to get a better look. The drapes were drawn, but through a space between them, she could see movement. It appeared someone dressed identically to her groom was in the room above her just beyond the parted curtains.

What was he doing in the princess's rooms? Or was that Prince Broderick dressed in the same costume? But if it was the prince, why was the man sneaking around with a small flashlight?

It had to be her groom. But what was Devlin doing in the same room Rory herself had hoped to get into? Apparently they had more in common than she'd first thought.

She watched him. He seemed to be looking for something.

Her gaze took in a second set of French doors that led to the wide balcony, the drapes on its doors drawn. She let her gaze fall from the balcony down the lattice trellis to a small stone wall a few yards in front of her.

As a tomboy, she'd climbed her share of trees. It had been awhile, but she hoped now that it was a lot like riding a bike.

Cursing her costume under her breath, she considered taking the time to go back to her horse and change clothes since she had no reason to return to the ball—especially after seeing Griff in there.

Deciding it would take too long, she crossed to the stone wall, hiked up her dress and swung up to grab hold of the trellis, praying it would hold her weight as she began to climb.

Devlin couldn't have missed the desk—even in the dark. It was huge and took up most of the room just off the balcony.

Using the penlight, he moved to it, noticing a second set of French doors that he assumed also exited to the balcony.

He knew he had to move fast. He was counting on both the prince and princess to remain downstairs at least until Nicholas and Monique finished their songs since Nicholas planned to make the most of it.

The bottom drawer was locked—just as Anna had told him it would be. Taking out the small tool he'd brought, he carefully pried the lock until it broke. Quietly, he opened the drawer.

He had no idea what these so-called papers looked like, not to mention the underlying fear that Anna might have been mistaken. Or that the princess had moved them.

Devlin tried not to think about any of that as he hurriedly went through the drawer. He worried about making too much noise even though the guards were stationed at the other end of the hall and the noise from the party should mask any sounds he made.

Still, he felt exposed being in the princess's quarters. He might be in America, but he was a foreigner. If caught, he would be sent back to his home country. His punishment could be worse than death if he was seen as a traitor, or worse, a terrorist.

He knew that Princess Evangeline could be excessively cruel and, as the only child of the king, was given anything she wanted. She'd want his head if she caught him breaking into what was obviously an antique.

The manila envelope was at the very bottom of the drawer, tucked under some writing stationery. As he pulled it out he saw the government stamp. There was no address. His fingers trembled as he flipped the flap and pulled out the sheets inside.

The papers crinkled in his tense fingers as he saw the royal crest on the familiar document—and his name.

His birth certificate? Why would Princess Evangeline have his birth certificate?

His hands began to shake and he had to put the paper down on the desk to read it, fighting to focus the slight beam of the penlight on the words.

Confusion made the words blur. He'd come up here expecting to find something about his mother's murder.

As the words on the document came into focus, he felt his pulse jump. *What?* That wasn't right. He dropped the penlight.

His heart drummed in his ears and he felt his blood rush from his head. He slumped into the chair, as he snatched up the penlight to read the document again. It had to be a lie. These documents had to have been forged. But why?

Otherwise… Otherwise, he realized with a shock, he held the reason for his mother's death in his hands.

His mother. If this was true, then she had lied to him. His father hadn't died before Devlin was born. His father was *alive*.

He heard a sound behind him and instinctively turned off the penlight. The chair under him creaked as he turned his head to look toward the French doors from the balcony, half expecting to find a royal guard with a weapon coming through them.

For the first time, he saw that the thick dark drapes weren't closed all the way. Through the narrow strip between them, he could make out the balcony and past that the twinkling lights of the grounds in the distance.

Nothing moved. For a moment he thought he'd only imagined the sound as he quietly tucked the documents back into the envelope as he rose from the chair.

The second set of French doors slowly opened, the breeze catching the drapes and billowing them out into the dark room.

9

A GUST OF cold night air stirred the papers on the desk. Even if he could reach the French doors behind him, Devlin knew he wouldn't be able to get out them without being caught. Hurriedly he stuffed the manila envelope beneath his costume jacket.

With no time to spare, he leaped behind the long thick velvet drapes as someone entered the room. He heard the doors close, felt the night breeze still.

Devlin held his breath, afraid to move a muscle for fear he would be discovered. He heard someone move to the desk, brush some of the papers on the edge. A moment later, a drawer opened, then another. Whoever it was seemed to be searching for something. His birth certificate?

He took a shallow breath, still shaken and confused by what he'd found as he listened to the intruder searching the drawers much as he had done.

He wished he had a weapon. He'd become an expert marksman thanks to Nicholas, who'd taught him to shoot. He could also fence. Neither helped at the moment, though.

Carefully, he inched to an opening between the drapes as

his curiosity got the better of him. Who was searching the desk—and why? He feared what they would do when they didn't find the documents he'd taken.

In the glow of the lamp light, he saw the figure bent over one of the drawers, her black wig askew, her Snow White costume torn at the hem and a piece of what appeared to be a twig caught in the fabric.

Rory? What was *she* searching for? He willed himself to stay hidden until she found whatever she was searching for. Unless she couldn't find it because he'd already taken it.

The room was eerily quiet, putting Rory's nerves on edge. Unfortunately, it appeared that her groom had left before she got there. She'd been forced to turn on the desk lamp since she hadn't had the foresight to bring along a flashlight as he had.

What had he been looking for? The same thing she was? But why would he care about offers made on her ranch? Clearly, he wasn't royalty as his costume suggested or why did he need to be sneaking around the princess's suite?

Heart sinking, Rory realized she had no idea what kind of man Devlin Barrow was. Just as he had no idea what kind of woman she was, she thought as she finally found what she was looking for in the last drawer she searched.

The file was marked Buchanan Ranch.

Hurriedly, she pulled it out and leafed through the contents under the glow of the lamp light. Someone had written notations on each copy of the offer that had been sent to her. She tried to read them, but she was too nervous. Especially since she thought she'd just heard a sound out in the hallway.

Just take the file and run!

She realized she should have brought something to carry the contents in. The file was too thick. There was no chance she could hide it under her costume and she had that climb back down—

She jumped at a key snick in the hall door lock.

Rory froze as she watched the doorknob turn, the door begin to open.

A scream caught in her throat as she was grabbed from behind forcing her to drop the file. A hand clamped over her mouth as a strong arm circled her waist tightly and she was dragged back through the dark velvet drapery to slam against the rock-hard body of a man who whispered, "Make a sound and we're both dead."

Devlin held the woman tightly in his grasp as the door from the hallway opened. Light spilled across the floor and under the thin space between the floor and the hem of the drapes.

The door closed.

He could see part of the room through the crack in the drapes and feared that he and Rory could be seen, as well.

But he didn't dare move to the side for fear that the person who'd entered would hear him.

He caught a glimpse of the princess as she headed to the bed and bathroom area of the suite. Fear made him freeze at just the sight of Evangeline. If the two of them were caught here now…

He breathed a little easier as he heard Evangeline moving around in the adjacent room. This had been one hell of night, all things considered. Not only had he found out that his mother had lied to him his entire life, he'd discovered that his father was alive. And now here he was with this woman; their paths just seemed to continue to cross.

Now why was that?

He hoped to hell the woman wasn't a cat burglar. Or worse.

Devlin could feel Rory getting restless and knew she was

thinking the same thing he was—that maybe this was their chance to get out of there before the princess came out.

But before he could make a decision, Princess Evangeline appeared again, only this time in a different costume.

It took him a moment to place the new costume. Wasn't it exactly like the one Lady Monique Gray had been wearing when she'd climbed up on the stage next to Nicholas? Odd that the princess would change into a costume like that of the Black Widow.

Royalty. He didn't even want to speculate as the princess left again.

Breathing a sigh of relief, he waited a few moments before he loosened his grip on the woman in his arms.

"Wait," he whispered next to her ear. He caught the clean scent of her and was transported back to that damned shack where they'd first met. He wished he didn't know this woman—know her intimately. Being this close to her made him feel things he didn't want to feel. Especially now.

What he'd found in Evangeline's desk drawer made him feel as vulnerable as the information made him. This woman, on top of that, knocked him off kilter.

He was more than confused. He was running scared and that made him all the more anxious to get Rory away from there so he could find out who the hell she really was and how she fit in to all this.

The problem was, how the devil were they going to get out of there *together*? Because there was no way he was letting this woman get away again.

Princess Evangeline took the back way to Stanwood's guest wing. In one hand, she gripped the master key that would open Lady Monique Gray's suite. In the other she carried the bag she'd retrieved from the pantry.

Her heart was pounding hard, expectation making her limbs weak. Everything had to be just perfect for this to work. If Broderick suspected for a moment…

She pushed the negative thoughts away as she stopped partway down the hall, looked around and, seeing no one, slipped the master key into the lock of Monique's room and stepped in, feeling like a thief in her own home.

Evangeline stood for a moment, hit with the scent of Monique's perfume. The smell made her nauseous. She tried not to think about her husband and Monique together or recall other times she'd caught this particular scent on her husband.

The silence assured her that Laurencia had been successful in detaining Lady Monique. Evangeline flipped the light switch and blinked at the cluttered suite. Clothes were strewn everywhere. If the woman was planning to seduce the prince tonight, her seduction clearly didn't include a romantic atmosphere.

After quickly cleaning up the room, lighting the candles she'd brought, setting out the drugged bottle of bourbon—Broderick's favorite—and putting the note next to it in a Monique-like scrawl, Evangeline waited.

She was suddenly very calm as she looked around the dim room. She'd seen to everything, including unplugging the lamps, leaving the area around the bed purposely dark.

She was ready. Slowly, she began to take off the costume a piece at a time, dropping each to leave a trail to the bedroom that any fool could follow.

Even Broderick.

By the time she reached the bed, she was naked.

Except for the mask.

Rory couldn't have made a sound or taken a breath if she'd wanted to. Even if she hadn't recognized the man's voice, there was no mistaking the scent of him or the solid feel of his body. The sound of footfalls had long ago died off, and yet Devlin still held her tightly against him.

His breath tickled her ear. His body, so close she could feel way too much of him. She shivered and he drew her even tighter against him as if to keep her warm. The gesture touched her. Until she reminded herself that the man was holding her captive behind the drapes of the princess's quarters—and like her, he apparently had no business here.

So what *was* he doing here? Robbing the place? The thought turned her blood to sludge. If caught, the princess would think they were both burglars, Rory thought indignantly. Not that she hadn't planned to take the contents of her file. But it was a file on *her*...

"We have to get out of here," her groom whispered finally.

She couldn't have agreed more. She just wondered where he thought they were going.

Devlin waited until he believed the coast to be clear before he moved aside the heavy drape and drew the woman out the French doors to the balcony.

The balcony was large with huge planters. He pulled her into a shadowed dark corner. From here all he could see was darkness and pine trees. Nor did he think she could be heard should she decide to start screaming.

Grabbing her arm, he spun her around to face him. "What are *you* doing here?" he whispered hoarsely.

"What are *you* doing here?"

He tightened his grip on her arm. "You first."

"I'm here because your boss is trying to force me to sell my ranch. I'd thrown the offers away. I needed copies but because of you, I had to leave them in there."

"Wouldn't it have been easier just to ask for copies?"

"You really think the princess would have given them to me?" she demanded, pulling away.

She had a point. But breaking into the princess's suite... Was the woman crazy? No crazier than he was, he realized.

Just being this close to her and not being able to touch her was pure torture. The memory of their night together haunted him. He would gladly have thrown caution to the wind and taken her in his arms again had she let him.

But there was little chance of that as she leaned against the balcony railing, glaring at him. "Your turn," she said, her hands going to her slim hips. She looked adorable as Snow White. And a little ridiculous, under the circumstances.

"If I told you, I'd have to kill you," he joked.

"Funny."

"You have no idea."

She started to step past him.

"Where do you think you're going?"

"Back inside. I have to get those copies. I'm not leaving here without them."

"You go back in there and you're risking more than your neck. You're risking *mine*."

She slipped past him so quickly Devlin didn't catch her until they were inside the suite door.

Two loud pops reverberated through the room.

"What was that?" Rory whispered.

Devlin shook his head. "Either someone is opening champagne out in the hall," he whispered, "or there were gunshots in the room next door. Either way, we're out of here."

This time she didn't argue as they hightailed it out of the suite and back to their spot on the balcony. The moon had risen higher in the night sky, filling even the shadows of the balcony, exposing their hiding place.

Devlin saw something move below them in the darkness. A

man watching them. He grabbed Rory and pulled her into a kiss, turning her so the man below them could only see someone dressed in the same costume as Prince Broderick kissing some strange woman. Nothing new there.

At first Rory struggled against the kiss, but after a moment gave into it, her arms coming up to circle around his neck. He loosened his grip on her as she deepened the kiss.

His mistake. She slipped from his arms and dropped over the side of the balcony railing. All he got was a handful of fake hair as the black wig came off in his hand.

Devlin lurched to the edge of the balcony, fearful that she'd fallen to her death. In the darkness, he caught sight of his green-eyed forest sprite clambering down the trellis.

His first instinct was to leap over the edge after her, but she was almost to the ground and heading for the trees. He thought about her damned copies, which she'd risked her neck for.

"Damned woman," he muttered under his breath.

But as he started to turn to go back into the suite, he remembered the man he'd seen watching them along the edge of the building. The man was looking after Rory.

The figure bled back into the shadows and a moment later rounded the edge of the building, heading back as if toward the ball.

With relief, Devlin saw that it was a sheriff's deputy, dressed in uniform and wearing a thin black mask.

Devlin waited until the deputy disappeared back inside. He could hear music and laughter floating up from the ballroom. Devlin had to finish what he started and yet he couldn't help but worry about Rory as he rushed back inside the suite and turned on his penlight.

The Buchanan Ranch file was on top of the desk. He

scooped it up, stuffing it along with his own papers under his costume jacket.

Now how the hell was he going to get out of there?

From the darkness another man watched the deputy go back into the ball as what appeared to be Prince Broderick slipped back into the royal suite from the balcony.

It wasn't the first time Jules Armitage had seen the two in the same vicinity.

As he saw a strange light come on in the princess's suite, Jules debated what to do. Prince Broderick had left the ballroom earlier—not long after the princess. As far as Jules knew, neither had returned.

So if that was Prince Broderick in the royal suite, then why was he using a small flashlight?

Just as Jules's curiosity was peaked and he started to step from the shadows to alert the guards to check the suite, the light went out. The French doors opened and the man slipped out, closing the doors behind him.

To Jules's amazement, the man came to the edge of the railing, looked down for a moment, then swung over the rail and began to climb down the lattice.

The head of security reached for his weapon as the man reached the ground. He'd lost his mask on the climb down. As he turned, Jules saw that it wasn't Prince Broderick.

It was Devlin Barrow.

Jules stayed in the dark shadows as the groom passed by him. Finally, he would have the royal groom right where he wanted him.

10

EVANGELINE HEARD THE snick of a key in the lock. Her heart was pounding, each breath a labor. So much was riding on her being able to pull this off tonight.

The door swung open on a soft *whoosh*. She waited, lay on the big bed, only dim candlelight flickering around her. She'd made sure he wouldn't be able to turn on a lamp. Around her, Monique's perfume scented the air, making Evangeline nauseous.

She could do this. She had no choice.

She heard the door close softly. She held her breath. If it was Broderick, he would do as the note in the hallway had instructed. When it came to other women, Broderick was accommodating.

The soft clink of crystal assured her he was now having the drink she'd left for him. The pills would take only a matter of minutes to work.

If he did as instructed... She heard the sound of him shedding his costume, and she tried to relax. He was following her orders. Only because he thought they'd come from Monique.

Evangeline tamped down her anger. She could be angry

later. If the pills worked their wonder, he would be so out of it by the time he reached the bedroom, he wouldn't know she wasn't Monique until it was too late—if ever.

From behind her mask, Evangeline watched the doorway. She'd never had any interest in sex. Just as she'd never liked alcohol except for an occasional glass of wine.

For her, losing control was her greatest fear. Sex with the right man, she'd heard, could make a woman lose all control. The thought of a man having that kind of power over her terrified her—although she'd had nothing to fear with Broderick.

While Broderick's good looks had appealed to her for propagation reasons, his suave man-about-town charm had always left her cold.

But tonight she must be Monique, a tramp in heat. It would be her best acting role yet.

The doorway filled with the dark shadow of a naked man, relieving her mind that her plan was working as he stumbled and had to lean against the door jamb.

His face, like the room, was in shadow but she could imagine his smile, anticipation and excitement in his eyes. She would have liked to have seen it since she'd never had that opportunity as his wife.

Broderick had never even pretended to be madly in love with her. They both had known why he'd married her. She just hadn't realized he had never meant to impregnate her with an heir.

But after tonight, if the Fates were with her...

He staggered toward the bed, the drug giving him the appearance of being drunk. With luck he wouldn't remember anything.

As he neared the bed, she couldn't see *him* any more than he could see *her* clearly in the near darkness—just as she'd planned it. Now, if he just followed the rest of her directions and didn't speak.

He chuckled, though, as he slipped into bed wearing nothing but his mask.

Rory had looked back only once, afraid Devlin was in hot pursuit. Nothing moved in the darkness. Stanwood cast a long black shadow over the landscape. Along the edge of the building, she spotted a figure.

Not Devlin. But someone else. And she had the distinct impression the person was watching her.

She ran deeper into the woods, disoriented in the darkness and the dense pine forest. Her chest ached from running and she couldn't wait to get out of her ridiculous costume. As she stopped and caught her breath, she heard movement nearby. The soft rustle of dried pine needles, the blow of her horse as the mare snuffled some grass.

With relief, she moved toward the welcoming sound, anxious to end this horrible night. It hadn't all been horrible, she had to admit, remembering being behind the curtain with Devlin and kissing him.

But she hadn't gotten the copies of the offers she'd gone to all this trouble to get. And Devlin had proved to be less than a hero. She had no idea what he'd been doing breaking into the princess's desk. Not only that, he seemed to think she was again part of some conspiracy against him.

Men. No wonder she'd never found her Prince Charming.

Through the trees, she spotted her horse and rushed to the mare, grabbing the reins and swinging up into the saddle. From the time she was young, she'd preferred to be in the saddle more than anywhere else. Not much about that had changed. She felt safe, finally in her comfort zone, as she reined the mare around and headed for home, praying she wouldn't run into any of the royal guards.

Rory thought that once she left the princess's property, she would put this night and Devlin Barrow behind her. But even when she reached home, had stabled the mare for the night and gone inside, locking the doors behind her, all Rory could think about was the groom.

He was probably a thief. Or worse.

And yet she couldn't believe that a man who could kiss with genuine conviction—could be a criminal.

As much as she hated it, Rory found herself charmed by her mysterious groom as she shed her Snow White costume.

Devlin had prayed the trellis would hold his weight. It had. He knew he wasn't thinking clearly as he headed for his cottage to change. After that, he planned to go to the stables, saddle a horse and take the copies to Rory. Something told him there was a lot more to this woman.

It concerned him that the deputy had been watching them from the shadows. Devlin could only assume the law officer had been part of ball security. He couldn't have known whom he was watching. At least Devlin hoped not. Otherwise, wouldn't the deputy have stopped Rory as she'd left? And called the guard to arrest Devlin?

Devlin felt fear snake up his spine at the thought that Rory might have been seen with him. After what Devlin had learned tonight, that information could put her in danger. It was why he had to sneak over to her ranch tonight, drop off the papers and then keep his distance until he had this mess sorted out.

His mother had been murdered. Devlin had every reason to believe he would be next—especially when Princess

Evangeline found her antique desk broken into and the documents gone.

At his cottage, he changed quickly into riding clothes. From the Buchanan Ranch file, he found the location of her ranch. No surprise, her property wasn't far from the line shack where they'd met. With the full moon, he should be able to find her.

He opened the manila folder and took out what appeared to be copies and the original documents. He knew a place he could hide the copies in the stables where they wouldn't be discovered.

The originals he would take with him. He had to get them off the Stanwood estate. It was his insurance policy—if he lived long enough to use it.

Just the thought that he was the reason his mother had been murdered filled him with fury.

At a soft tap at the door, he jumped. *Rory?* Crazy as it was, he hoped to find her when he opened the door. The woman hadn't just stolen his dreams. She'd captured his every waking thought as well as his desires.

He tried to hide his disappointment as he saw that the person huddled on his doorstep looking terrified wasn't Rory. "Anna?"

He quickly ushered her into his cottage, checking to see if she'd been followed. He saw no one in the darkness, but he knew that didn't necessarily mean anything.

"What's wrong?" he asked, seeing that she'd been crying and was now wringing her hands. She'd aged in the months since his mother's death, and he knew how it weighed on her.

"The guards are looking for me," Anna whispered. "I saw them waiting by my door and came right here."

"Guards? Why—"

She clutched his forearm. "I saw who killed your mother. I

thought if I kept quiet…" She began to cry softly. "He came to your mother's house himself, dressed as a royal guard, but I recognized him. It was Prince Broderick. He took the papers and killed your mother. I thought he didn't know I was there, that I saw. I knew no one would believe me."

"I believe you." Prince Broderick had killed his mother. But on whose orders? "You can't stay on the grounds."

But where could he take her where she would be safe? He didn't know Montana and had little resources. But there was one person. His heart told him he could trust Rory. So had her kisses.

"You will come with me. I know a place you will be safe," he told Anna. "Stay here. I will return with horses. You must trust me." For his mother's memory, he couldn't let anything happen to Anna.

When the deed was over, Evangeline freed herself of the weight of Broderick's body, shoving him aside to climb out of the bed.

She sat for a moment on the side of the bed, praying she now carried the heir she so desperately needed. The timing had been perfect, just as she'd planned it.

Now all she could do was wait. She rose, feeling exhausted, disgusted and furious with Broderick.

For a moment she considered taking the lamp base beside the table and crushing his skull with it.

Instead, she quickly dressed in the extra clothing she'd brought herself, stuffing the Monique costume under the bed for the maid to dispense with in the morning.

As she started out of the room, she made the mistake of looking back at Broderick passed out on the bed, the sheet thrown over his head, where she'd tossed it.

She took a couple of steps toward the bed, afraid of what

she would do if she didn't leave at once. If she didn't get out of there now…

Quickly, she turned and headed for the door, surprised how late it was. The last thing she wanted to do was get caught by Monique. This had been humiliating enough as it was.

But as she neared the door, she saw something that made her stagger to stop. The floor was littered with each piece of his costume. Evangeline stared down at it, her blood thundering in her ears.

Nooooooo.

She spun and stumbled back to the bedroom doorway, all her fears hitting her in a rush. This couldn't be happening.

She charged the bed, jerking back the sheet. Too dark. Dropping to the floor, she found the cord for the lamp beside the bed. The lamp flashed on, blinding her.

Getting to her feet, she finally looked at the man lying passed out on the soiled sheets.

She had to cover her mouth to keep from screaming. The man on the bed wasn't Broderick. The man she'd just possibly conceived an heir with was Lord Charles Langston, the family attorney.

Had she been the kind of woman to faint, Evangeline would have. She stumbled back under the weight of what she'd just done, trying to make sense of what had happened. How could her plan have gone so awry?

Where the hell was Broderick?

Rory was dressed for bed even though she knew she wouldn't be able to sleep, when she heard the sound of horses approaching. She jumped up and pulled on her robe and, taking the shotgun from by the back door, moved swiftly through the dark house. Since finding out about the Peeping Tom at her bedroom window, she'd taken to locking her doors and keeping the shotgun loaded and ready.

Moonlight bathed the yard in silver. From out of the pines, two horses emerged. She recognized the horses first. The beautiful Knabstrups. She expected to see two royal soldiers astride the horses and shifted the shotgun, ready to defend herself and her property.

To her shock, Devlin Barrow swung down from the first horse, then went to help the other rider down. An older woman. He led her toward the darkened house cautiously.

Rory snapped on the porch light. Wondering what he was doing here and who the woman was, she opened the front door, still holding the shotgun.

"We need your help," Devlin said, the desperation she heard in his tone cutting straight to her heart. Maybe it was foolish to believe anyone could tell the truth from a few kisses, but she trusted him. Whatever he was hiding, he would tell her when he was ready.

At least that's what she assured herself as she put down the shotgun. "Please, come in." The woman appeared to be shivering, her face taut with fear. "Come back to the kitchen. I'll make some coffee. Or do you prefer tea?"

"Tea, please," the woman said as Rory led them to the back of the house and offered them seats at the table.

She set water to boil on the stove before turning to face the two.

"Thank you," Devlin said, his gaze locking with hers.

Rory felt the full impact of that gaze. She'd run out on him back at Stanwood. And yet he'd brought this woman here because he believed Rory would help.

"This is Anna Pickering. She was a friend of my mother's," Devlin said. "She has reason to fear for her safety at Stanwood. I didn't know where else to bring her."

Rory could see that Anna had been crying and still looked terrified. "You are safe here," Rory said, taking the older woman's hand. Anna's fear seemed to subside a little.

Devlin gave her a grateful smile. "Anna witnessed my mother's murder back in our homeland. She fears the killer knows she saw him—and can identify him."

Rory felt the jolt at heart level. She'd lost her baby sister and both of her parents so she knew the pain he must be feeling. What must it be like to have your mother murdered—and know who had done it?

"You must go to the authorities," Rory said.

"That's not possible." Devlin seemed to hesitate. "The person who Anna saw is Prince Broderick Windham, the princess's husband. Anna would never live long enough to testify against him."

Rory dropped into a chair at the table, too shocked to speak for a moment. "What can you do?"

Devlin shook his head and she saw the fury just below the surface. "While Broderick killed her, we don't know who ordered the murder. That order could have come from the king himself. Until we know..."

Rory feared what he planned to do even before he said it.

"I must go back to Stanwood," Devlin said. "Are you sure about Anna staying here? I promise I will resolve this quickly and come back. But first I have something for you."

He reached inside his jacket and withdrew a thick file. As he handed it to her, she saw the neat lettering on the tab: Buchanan File.

Her gaze flashed to his. "You went back for this for me?" She could not have been more touched if he'd fought a dragon. "Thank you."

"I hope you won't have to use it. I will do my best to keep the prince from bothering you again, but I didn't want you coming away from the ball tonight without what you'd come there for."

She'd gotten more than she'd hoped out of the ball, as it had turned out. Her only regret was that she hadn't gotten to dance with Devlin, she realized.

"I'll put these away," Rory said, needing a minute. Getting up, she walked down the hallway to her bedroom. She was still touched that he'd done this for her, but concerned how he planned to keep the prince from bothering her again.

She laid the papers on the top of her bureau and turned, surprised to find he'd followed her. The next thing she knew, she was in his arms. It seemed so natural she couldn't have said whose idea it had been.

The kiss, though, had been his. Of all his kisses, she thought she liked this one the best. She found herself melting into his arms, never wanting this to end or his arms to let her go. Who said there were no heroes anymore?

She wanted to cry out when the kiss ended. "You're in danger, aren't you?"

"I have managed to put us all at risk," he said with remorse. "I should never have brought Anna here, but I had nowhere else to go."

"You did right. I will make sure she is safe."

His gaze caressed her face. "You are an amazing woman. I feel as if…"

"You don't know how you've lived this long without me."

He laughed. "I do feel like I know you."

She felt her face heat. He knew her *intimately*.

His gaze held hers for the longest time. "I have to go. Are you sure—"

"Anna will be fine."

He smiled at that. "It's you I was concerned about. I saw someone watching you from the shadows as you left Stanwood tonight. While I don't think he recognized us, he saw the two of us together. He saw me kiss you."

Rory thought of the tracks around her house, the wire cutters in the shrubs outside her bedroom window and shuddered. "Did you get a look at him?"

"It was a sheriff's deputy."

Rory swallowed a curse. "Don't worry about Deputy Griffin Crowley," she said calmly, although she was furious. How dare Griff spy on her and Devlin. "The deputy and I are old friends. I'm sure he was just concerned about my safety. I saw him in the ballroom. I think he saw me, too." He must have followed her outside.

Devlin didn't look reassured. "If you need me, call Stanwood and ask for Lord Nicholas. He is a friend. He will see that I get the message. In the meantime, I think it best if no one knows Anna is here."

Rory couldn't have agreed more. Devlin said goodbye to Anna, and Rory walked him to the door. She was still fuming about Griff's spying on her—and she was worried about Devlin.

"Are you sure it's safe for you to return to Stanwood?" she asked, once they were outside on the porch.

"I have no choice." He cupped her cheek and kissed her softly on the mouth, making her ache for more. "Be careful. I will come back as soon as I can."

She watched him swing up into the saddle. He seemed to hesitate, as if there was something more he wanted to say. But he didn't. He reined his horse around and, leading the other horse behind him, rode off toward Stanwood.

Rory had the strongest feeling that she should warn him not to go. She started to call after him, but felt Anna's hand on her arm.

"We will pray for his safety," Anna said, joining her.

"He *is* in danger, isn't he?"

"Devlin is like his mother, strong, determined."

"I shouldn't have let him go."

Anna chuckled. "Nothing could have stopped him. Not even you." As they stepped back into the house, the woman seemed to study her openly. "You should rest. When was the last time you ate something?"

Rory couldn't recall. She felt as if she was fighting the flu. "I'm really not hungry and I don't want you waiting on me. Please, you are my guest."

Anna patted her arm. "You must eat and I must keep busy."

Jules Armitage felt his cell phone vibrate and checked the display. Adele Brown. For a moment, the name didn't register. He'd gone back to the ballroom, hoping to see Princess Evangeline and have a word with her.

The phone vibrated again. Stepping out of the ballroom, away from the music and noise, he snapped open his phone. "Hello?"

"I know it's late, but I'm a night owl and you said to call the moment I remembered. Rory Buchanan."

"What?"

"Rory Buchanan. That's the woman who won All-around Best Cowgirl that year, the one you asked me about. I knew I'd remember."

Jules couldn't help being surprised since he'd heard that name mentioned before. Wasn't that the person who was refusing to sell to the princess? But he'd just assumed Rory was a man's name.

As he disconnected, Jules wondered what the groom had been doing with the ranch owner. Was it possible the two of them were conspiring against the princess, the landowner holding out for more money and the groom cutting himself in for some of the money?

The evidence was stacking up against Devlin Barrow, Jules thought with satisfaction. He suspected the princess would appreciate knowing all about this. At the very least, she would send the groom back to the homeland. It would serve him right. Jules didn't like how Devlin acted as if he were a noble.

As the head of security stepped back into the ballroom, he noticed that it was almost midnight. Time for the unmasking and the ball would wind down.

He just had to make sure no one got away with any of the royal silver. No small chore.

Jules looked around for the princess. At the stroke of midnight, Princess Evangeline planned to lead the unmasking. So where was she?

The blare of trumpets announced the approaching midnight hour. Still no sign of the princess. Or the prince.

The crowd stilled as the band began the countdown.

Ten.

Nine.

Eight.

The *pop, pop* could have been champagne bottles opening. No one else seemed to notice it.

Seven.

Six.

Jules moved toward the stairs, toward the direction the sound had come from, worried that something had happened to the princess.

Five.

Four.

The princess suddenly appeared at the top of the stairs. A rush of expectation filled the huge room. Jules stopped, relieved. As long as she was all right...

Three.

Two.

One.

Confetti fell from overhead like falling snow. Champagne corks popped around the room as masks came off and the music started up again for the last dance of the night.

The princess descended the stairs looking elegant, her mask in her hand. As she passed him, Jules noted that she looked paler than usual.

He wondered where the prince was and could only imagine what had kept him from the unmasking. Not just some woman, he thought as he glanced around the room and noticed who else seemed to be missing.

When the princess found out who'd been sleeping with her husband, there would be more than hell to pay.

Evangeline had been to enough masked balls that she could have sleepwalked through this part of the night. She smiled and shook hands with guests and moved through the crowd as if she just hadn't made love with the royal family's barrister instead of her cheating, lying husband.

Trying not to be too obvious, she searched the crowd for Laurencia. Not that her companion could be held completely accountable for this fiasco, since Evangeline had orchestrated it. But something had gone wrong and Evangeline planned to know why.

She spotted Lord Nicholas. No sign of Lord Alexis. Or Lady Monique. Laurencia had been ordered to release the Black Widow from the steam room before the midnight hour. No sign of either woman. Evangeline hoped nothing had gone wrong.

What would happen when Lady Monique returned to her room to find Lord Charles passed out in her bed? Evangeline couldn't bother herself with that. The fool would no doubt think he'd slept with Monique. Clearly, that had been his intent—and Monique's—was Monique trying to make Alexis jealous? Or the prince? And where was Broderick?

Evangeline wasn't fool enough to think that her husband had disappeared from the ball without a woman being involved. But what woman?

She was shaking inside, furious and scared, a deadly mix, as she made her departure and the ball wound down. She couldn't wait to get to her suite. The guards bowed as she passed. Fumbling her key from her pocket, she managed to get the suite door open, desperately needing peace and solitude for a few moments.

The night was far from over. She had to get herself composed or—

A cool breeze skittered across the floor of the suite as the door swung open. Evangeline frowned as she stepped in, closing the door behind her. Montana was too cold this time of year for her. She missed lying on a white sand beach in some sunny clime with the rest of the aristocrats.

But her suite was never *this* cold. She glanced toward the French doors and saw that one of them was open although she was positive she'd closed it when she'd left. Just as she was sure Broderick hadn't been back up to the suite since he'd left earlier.

Slowly, she moved toward the balcony, debating if she should call for a guard. To her relief she saw in the blinding moonlight that the balcony was empty.

Stars sparkled in the clear, cold sky. Below, guests were leaving, horses clip-clopping away as they drew carriages to where the guests could pick up their vehicles. The bright colors of the costumes and the sprinkling of lights around the grounds reminded her of all her hopes for tonight.

Evangeline turned in disgust, closing the balcony doors behind her as she stood just inside, studying the room. Someone had been here. A burglar?

The expensive artwork was where it had been when she'd left the room earlier. Her husband's expensive watch was where he'd dropped it on the side table.

Her gaze went to her desk. She'd had the antique desk brought over from the palace at home at no small expense. It was her favorite since it had belonged to more generations of Wycliffe women than she could count.

She let out a cry of horror as she saw that the bottom drawer had been pried open, the lock broken. Rage washed over her as she grabbed the drawer handle and pulled it open, already knowing what had been taken.

Her anger and horror over the marred desk turned to fear. Those papers in the wrong hands...

She slumped into her desk chair and tried to calm herself. Who had taken the documents? And what was she going to do now?

This deadly game she'd been playing was about to end. And badly, she feared.

The knock at the door startled her. "Yes?"

Jules stuck his head in. "Your Royal Highness."

"What is it, Jules?" she demanded irritably.

The head of security seemed to hesitate.

"What?" she demanded.

"It's the prince," he said, stepping in with a bow. "He's been shot. He's...dead. The deputy is demanding to see everyone downstairs."

11

THE VOICES IN the dining room carried along the hallway to where Princess Evangeline had stopped.

"I was locked in the steam room!" Evangeline would recognize that whine anywhere. Lady Monique. "I could have been *killed*."

"Don't look at me," Lord Alexis said, clearly disgruntled. "I spent the night looking for you."

Evangeline heard the suspicion in Alexis's voice. While he didn't mind betraying his mistresses, he apparently didn't like it happening to him, she thought with a smile as she continued on down the hallway.

Everyone turned as the princess entered the room and rose to curtsy or bow. Evangeline motioned them back into their seats with a dismissive wave.

"Someone locked me in the steam room tonight," Monique complained, clearly suspicious of everyone at the table.

Evangeline raised an eyebrow. "I'm so sorry. I'm sure the door must have just stuck. I'll see that it's checked at once."

"Is everyone who had access to the second floor here now?" asked a man in uniform. Evangeline vaguely remembered meeting him during the ball. She'd made a point of inviting the local law, Deputy Griffin Crowley, who was apparently filling in for the Sheriff.

She glanced around the room but before she could speak, Monique said, "Where's Charles?"

"*Charles?*" the deputy echoed.

"Lord Charles Langston, the royal family solicitor," Evangeline said.

"Someone find him, please, and get him down here," the deputy said. "You're sure he hasn't left the property?"

"No one has come in or out the front gate since you instructed us to close it," Jules said.

"And you are?" the deputy asked.

"Jules Armitage, head of security."

The deputy nodded, then quickly dismissed Jules. "Your Royal Highness, I assume you've been told about your husband?"

"That he's dead." Evangeline didn't have to fake the trembling in her fingers as she dabbed at her eyes. "There must be some mistake."

"I'm afraid not. Your husband was found shot to death."

Evangeline raised her gaze to the deputy. "Who found him?"

"I did," Lord Alexis said. "When I was looking for Lady Gray, I stumbled across his body in the extra suite across from yours."

Evangeline couldn't hide her surprise.

"Any idea what he was doing there?" Deputy Crowley asked, no doubt seeing her surprise.

"Apparently, he had planned to meet someone there," Alexis said and shot a look at Lady Monique Gray.

"You know anything about this?" the deputy asked Monique.

"No, I told you. I was locked in the steam room the entire time. If Lady Laurencia hadn't found me and let me out..." She wiped at her own tears as she gave a trembling smile to Laurencia, who sat across from her. "Why don't you find out who locked me in there," she demanded, glaring at the people around the table.

A few moments later, Lord Charles Langston stumbled into the room. He looked hung over and appeared still half-drunk. He dropped into a chair and said, "What's this about Broderick being murdered?"

"*Now* is everyone here?" the deputy asked.

Evangeline glanced around the room. "Not quite." She'd never thought there would be an ideal time to say this, but she'd been wrong, she realized.

"Yes?" the deputy prompted.

"Prince Devlin Barrow Wycliffe isn't here."

A murmur circled the table. Evangeline gauged the surprised faces. No one looked more shocked than Lord Nicholas, the man who'd sponsored Devlin as a groom for Stanwood. Was it possible he hadn't known? That no one had known except her father and Clare Barrow? Until recently, that was.

The deputy was frowning at her. "There's another *prince* here?"

Evangeline nodded gravely. "Indeed there is. Only this one is a *royal* prince by birth."

Devlin had time to think on the way back from Rory Buchanan's ranch. He saw everything much clearer now that he knew about his lineage.

It was no coincidence that he'd been allowed to come to the States to work as a groom on the princess's Montana estate.

Evangeline had known who he was. Which meant that when Lord Nicholas had come to her on Devlin's behalf, she had seen through the ruse at once. How she must have enjoyed letting the two men think they were deceiving her when all the time Devlin had played right into her hands.

It was Evangeline who had secreted Anna Pickering away to Montana. Devlin saw now that Anna had been the bait to get him to the States. To get him to Montana.

Her purpose, though, was still a mystery. Had she planned to get rid of him as she had his mother? While Broderick may have been the one to perform the deed, Devlin was sure the order to kill his mother had come from Princess Evangeline. Or the king, his own father.

So why was he still alive? Or had Evangeline tried to kill him that night in the meadow when Rory Buchanan had saved him?

Once Evangeline discovered the drawer broken on her desk and the papers missing, she would have to move forward whatever plan she'd concocted.

Devlin knew returning to Stanwood could be suicide. But it was the only way he could protect Anna—and now Rory. The deputy had seen both him and Rory on the second floor. Devlin was certain now that it was him Evangeline wanted. He would face her and end this.

With all his heart, he wished it a lie. If only he could convince himself that the birth certificate was a forgery. But had it been, his mother would still be alive. All these years she had protected him from the truth. So what had changed to bring this to light?

There'd been a rumor that the king wasn't well. Devlin had heard talk that Prince Broderick, while he couldn't take the throne, was next in line to rule the country.

That was reason enough for the prince and princess to want all evidence of a true prince in line for the throne to be destroyed.

And yet Devlin had found both a copy and the original of his birth certificate. The copy was now hidden in the stables. The original at Rory's ranch. What had Evangeline planned to do with them?

What hurt the most was that none of this had been necessary—his mother's murder, the deception to get him to Montana. He had no aspirations to be prince, let alone king of his country. His love was of horses, the outdoors, not politics.

He had to find a way out of this.

But first he had to know who had ordered his mother killed. Princess Evangeline? Or her father, the king?

Lost in his thoughts, at first he didn't see the soldiers. They came out of the pines, the moonlight making them ghostlike as they rode toward him.

It wasn't until they surrounded him that he saw they had their weapons drawn.

Evangeline studied Devlin's face as he came through the door and into the dining hall. He expected the worst, she thought with amusement. But even so, he looked determined to face it, reminding her of her father. *Their* father.

Devlin Barrow had their father's blue eyes and handsome features, but he'd gotten his dark hair from his mother. The combination was very pleasing. An acid drip of jealousy made her stomach queasy. How she would have liked it if Devlin Barrow had never been born.

Or that, like his mother, he was dead and buried.

But her father already suspected her of having something to do with Clare Barrow's death. If anything happened to Devlin…

She motioned the soldiers away, then rose to her feet and curtsied to her brother. Half brother. Hating that he'd gotten the better half in both looks and gender.

"I present His Royal Highness Prince Devlin Barrow Wycliffe, son of our king," Evangeline announced.

Devlin's shocked expression alone was worth this moment, she thought. Not to mention the shocked expressions of the others around the table, including the deputy.

"Are you saying…" the deputy began.

"Devlin is my half brother. I brought him here for his protection." Evangeline held out her hand, inviting Devlin to join them. "As you might have heard, there is unrest in our homeland. Devlin's mother was murdered. My father felt it best that his only son come to live in the States, where I could make sure he was safe."

The deputy looked skeptical, but nothing like Devlin himself.

"I'm afraid this is all news to me," Devlin said. "A word, Your Royal Highness?"

"Could you give me a few moments with my…brother?" Evangeline asked. "I feared this news would come as a shock to him. I'm sure he has questions."

"*I* have questions," the deputy snapped. Just then the state police and coroner came through the door. "I want each of these people questioned separately," he said to the officers. The deputy shot a look at Evangeline. "Both of you are next. You have five minutes."

Evangeline gave Devlin a nod, then turned and headed for a private room down the hall. She knew he would follow.

Devlin closed the door behind them. "What the hell is going on?"

The princess seemed taken aback. "How quickly you become the royal prince of the manor."

If what she'd said was true and the papers authentic, then

he didn't need to be careful around her any longer and she knew it.

"Why don't we sit down," she suggested.

"Why don't you tell me what's going on?"

She waited a moment for him to sit as ordered. He didn't.

"I thought I made myself perfectly clear out there," Evangeline said finally. "But I suspect it didn't come as a complete surprise. You were the one who broke into my desk tonight, weren't you?"

All of this was coming at him too fast. "What is this about Prince Broderick being murdered?"

The princess shrugged. "I'm told he was shot and killed." She seemed to be taking her husband's death very well.

Devlin knew how the princess operated. For her to announce his lineage, she would have a very good reason. But right now, he was more interested in his mother's killer. "I want to know who killed my mother."

"Don't you already know that, as well? I understand one of our housemaids is missing. Anna Pickering? Didn't she tell you that Prince Broderick killed your mother?" Evangeline smiled. "I see that she did."

Now it was finally starting to make sense. Devlin let out a humorless laugh. "You're hoping to pin Prince Broderick's murder on *me*?"

She raised an eyebrow. "You have to admit, you do have the most to gain. Everyone knows Broderick hoped to one day take the throne in my stead. He was ambitious to a fault and clearly acted on his own. It would be understandable that you would want to revenge your mother's death once Anna Pickering told you Broderick killed your mother. And with him gone, you have paved the way straight to the throne on my father's death."

Devlin shook his head. This was just as he'd feared. Just as

Evangeline had feared, as well. If the king recognized him as his son, then Devlin would be in direct line for throne. His mother had some noble blood. At least as much as Prince Broderick. That meant Devlin was nobility. His father hadn't been a commoner as he'd always believed.

But Evangeline would never allow him to take the throne and they both knew it. "A murderer could never take the throne."

The princess smiled. "That is true. If you killed Broderick—"

"You know I didn't kill anyone, but that's not going to stop you from trying to frame me for his murder."

"You give me more credit than I deserve," Evangeline said.

Heart sinking, Devlin remembered that he hadn't had time to get rid of the copy of the prince's costume he'd hidden in his cottage. He'd played right into the princess's hands.

"I'll swear the documents are forgeries. My mother wouldn't lie to me. What about my other birth certificate that has me the son of a commoner?"

"Destroyed, unfortunately," Evangeline said.

"My mother wouldn't have lied to me. I will swear to that."

"As if your word would carry any weight," she said, disgusted. "Your mother had no choice. She did it to protect you."

"And the king? Did he also keep it a secret to protect *me*?"

Evangeline frowned at his sarcasm. "You would have to ask him." Her gaze seemed to soften. "I am told your mother was the love of my father's life. His father, King Roland the First, forbade it. I do believe allowing his father to force him into marrying my mother was our father's greatest regret."

Was what she was saying possible? When he'd seen his mother with that sad, faraway look in her eyes, he'd always thought it was because she missed the man she'd married and lost. Now he knew no such man had existed. And since there had been no one else in his mother's life, that could only mean that the pain he'd seen in her had been for Devlin's father, the man who had spurned her for another—and forced her to lie about her own son.

"It does not matter what happened in the past," Evangeline was saying. "You have now been acknowledged as the son of a king, a prince."

"Sorry, but I'll pass."

She laughed at that. "I would think you would be pleased to learn that you are of royal blood. The title comes with both wealth and privilege, which you have had little of in your past."

He could argue that. He'd loved growing up at the stables with freedom, the love of his mother and security—even if false. "The timing of this title you have bestowed on me is a little questionable, don't you think? Trying to kill me failed so you decided to kill two birds with one stone—so to speak—and frame me for Prince Broderick's death."

The princess looked puzzled. "Did you say someone tried to kill you?"

"As if you didn't order it."

"When was this?"

"The first night I arrived. Remember the drink I had in your main parlor? It was drugged and I was lured into the woods where someone took a potshot at my horse."

The princess rose from her chair and rang for a drink, her expression one of fury. "This drug? It made you feel as if you were hungover? Lack of memory? Confusion? And yet full of desire?"

"So you're familiar with it," Devlin said, not bothering to hide his sarcasm.

"You remind me so much of our father."

He doubted she meant that as a compliment. A servant arrived with her drink and quickly left.

Evangeline turned with glass in hand to look at him.

"I'm familiar with the drug because of my husband," she said. "I believe he used it on women."

Devlin stared at her, hating that he felt sympathy for a woman he knew had done much worse than Broderick in her life.

"What happens now?" he asked.

"I guess that will be up to the deputy." She took a sip of the drink. He noted that her hand shook. "Unless you can produce an alibi for the time of the murder…"

Devlin had two alibis—Anna and Rory. But he could use neither. If he did, he would be risking both of their lives.

Rory waited for word from Devlin. News of Prince Broderick's murder swept across the county like a range fire.

"You don't think Devlin…"

Anna shook her head, but Rory wasn't convinced. She recalled how upset he'd been when he'd left. She'd waited anxiously for word. All Georgia knew was that the state police had been called in and that Deputy Crowley was busy with the investigation.

"There are lots of rumors circulating," Georgia told her. "I was scared to death you'd done the prince in."

"I never saw the man," Rory told her, but then remembered she *had* seen him in the ballroom. Worse, she'd been seen herself on the second floor balcony with a man wearing the same costume as Lord Broderick.

As the days passed and still no word from Devlin—or a visit from the deputy—Rory thought maybe Griff hadn't recognized her the night of the ball.

Apparently, from what she'd heard, he was restricting his

questioning to the guests and princess since no one else had been allowed on that floor the night of the ball. Not even servants.

But the biggest news by far was that a *second* prince had been on the grounds the night of the ball. The prince was being questioned in Prince Broderick's death.

Rory waited for word from Devlin as to what was happening next door. She grew more antsy as the weather turned as it so often did this time of year. It began with rain, long dark dreary days.

As the temperature dropped, the rain turned to sleet, leaving the yard and Rory's pickup coated in ice. Finally, it began to snow with a vengeance, blanketing the ranch with a foot of the cold white stuff.

Rory had always liked snow. It signaled the end of one season and the beginning of a new one. She didn't even mind the cold mornings, taking the wagon out to feed the cattle.

But she'd sold off the cattle, and between the flu bug she couldn't get rid of, making sure Anna was safe and worrying about Devlin and what was happening with the murder investigation, she didn't have the energy to leave the house anyway. Fortunately, there wasn't much to running the ranch this time of year other than keeping the horses fed and watered.

With Prince Broderick's murder, the offers on her ranch had stopped as abruptly as they'd started. She knew she should feel relieved since Devlin had said he would take care of it. No wonder she found herself waiting for the other shoe to drop.

Had she felt better, she might have at least checked to see if any more of her fence had been cut. But she really wasn't up to that, either.

She wondered if this was delayed grief over her parents' deaths. She'd been so busy trying to save the ranch, she hadn't had time to grieve.

The weather and worry left her with a strange melancholy. If it wasn't for Anna, Rory feared she would have fallen into a deep depression. Anna had insisted on doing all the cooking. Probably after having one of Rory's meals. Now Rory was eating too much and still didn't feel all that well. Although she ached to see Devlin.

A few times over those dark and depressing weeks, she noticed tracks in her yard again. She kept the doors locked now and the curtains drawn even in daylight with Anna there. But some nights, Rory swore she could sense someone just outside. If she let her imagination run away with her, she could hear him breathing against her window pane.

Sometimes she pretended it was Devlin. That he stood out there wanting to knock, but wouldn't allow himself to.

Rory had no knowledge of the strange world he lived in. For all she knew his visa had come due and he'd been forced to return to his birth country.

And yet she sensed that he was still just miles from her. Within reach if only she could reach out to him.

"I'm worried about you," Georgia said the last time she was out to the ranch house. "Are you sure you're feeling better?" Georgia was the only person who knew about Anna. And Devlin.

"I'm fine. It's just this time of year." Winter, once it started, lasted for months in this part of Montana. This year, Rory didn't feel up to it.

"You should come in for my knitted stocking class next month," Georgia suggested. "It's a really easy pattern."

In the past, Rory would have laughed at the suggestion. It was odd. The thought of knitting suddenly had a strange appeal.

That was when Rory knew she probably needed help. Maybe she'd schedule an appointment with her doctor. Her stomach roiled. When was this flu ever going to run its course? Maybe she had an ulcer. She blamed it on nerves.

Rory only half listened as Georgia filled her in on all the Whitehorse gossip. A Texas family named Corbett had bought the old Trails West Ranch, Arlene Evans was now a grandmother—and was dating of all things, and their mutual friends Maddie Cavanaugh and Faith Bailey might both be coming back to town, possibly to stay.

"Are you sure you're all right?" Georgia asked.

She pushed away her coffee, the smell making her ill. "I'm fine."

"Maybe you should see a doctor," Georgia said before she left.

"I'm *fine*," she'd protested and walked her friend to the door. She barely made it back inside to the bathroom before she threw up—and finally admitted that she didn't have the flu.

The next day, Rory called Georgia and asked her to come out. "Would you mind staying here with Anna while I go into town?"

Her friend had been happy to agree. Rory knew she could have asked Georgia to pick up what she needed as Georgia had done over the past few weeks.

But this was something Rory wanted to handle on her own. Also, she hadn't been out of the house in days and thought it might make her feel better to get out.

She knew she was being paranoid, but she had the strangest feeling she was being followed even though every time she looked back, she didn't see anyone.

At the drugstore, she purchased several pregnancy tests, again feeling as if someone was watching her. It was embarrassing enough checking out, especially in a small town where everyone knew everyone's business.

It was also the reason Rory hadn't asked Georgia to buy the tests for her.

Back at the ranch house, Anna was doing what she was always doing, cooking or cleaning, keeping busy.

Rory showed the tests to Georgia, then quickly went into the bathroom to confirm what she already had accepted.

"Oh, Rory," Georgia said as she saw Rory's face when she came out of the bathroom. "It's definite?" she whispered even though Anna was in the kitchen with the radio on and couldn't hear them.

Rory could only nod.

"I suppose I don't need to ask—"

"It's the groom's." Devlin Barrow's baby.

Georgia hugged her friend. "Oh, sweetie. You've fallen in love with your groom?"

All Rory could do was nod numbly.

"You have to tell him," she said as they sat down in the living room.

Anna had built a fire earlier when she'd gotten up. The woman seemed to feel the need to be busy, rising early each morning. The flames licked at the logs, a soft popping sound filling the room.

Rory had thought about nothing else since she'd realized she was pregnant. She hadn't needed the test. She'd known, the way women had always known.

"You have time to decide what to do," Georgia said.

Rory smiled at her friend. The decision had been made the moment she'd finally admitted she was pregnant. "I'm having this baby."

"Shouldn't you discuss this with the father first?"

"He isn't a factor in my decision," Rory said. "He can't

be. He's not even a US citizen. For all I know he's been sent back to his country."

"Rory—"

"I know what you're going to say."

Her friend had tears in her eyes. "It's just that I know you. I've seen you struggle the past four years trying to hold on to the ranch. Once you make your mind up about something…"

"I know it's been a losing battle," Rory said, hating that everyone had been right. Especially Griff. "It's been impossible to let go, though."

"And now with a baby…"

Her hand went to her stomach. She thought of the life growing inside her. "I'm going to sell the ranch." As hard as the words were to say, Rory knew it was the only thing she could do now.

"Are you sure?"

Rory couldn't help but laugh at her friend's expression. "All this time, you've encouraged me to consider selling and now you're worried that I'm making a mistake?"

"Not a mistake. It's just that I know what this place means to you. Won't you resent that you had to sell?"

"I want this baby," Rory said with a rueful smile. "Part of the reason I clung to the ranch was that it was all I had left of my family."

"You are going to tell him, aren't you?"

Rory nodded. "But only because he has the right to know."

"Good." Georgia sounded relieved.

"There isn't going to be a happy ending here, you know."

Georgia shrugged with a wry grin. "I can hope, can't I?" Her expression changed to one of horror. "Oh, God, what happens when Griff finds out about this?"

"Griff is the least of my problems." Rory was worried about what would happen when Devlin found out about the baby.

Anna came in with warm peanut butter cookies from the oven and a pitcher of milk.

"At least Anna will see that you eat like you're supposed to," Georgia said after Anna had left the room. "You don't think she knows, do you?"

Devlin had become a prisoner at Stanwood. He was never without guards.

"It's for your own protection," the princess had told him.

He was also not allowed to leave the country because of the murder investigation. He had little doubt that he would be arrested soon. Unless he produced an alibi for the night of the ball. He had to make sure both Rory and Anna were safe from any repercussions before he could do that.

So far the deputy had told him not to leave Montana.

So he waited for the chance to escape and return to Rory's ranch. He'd dreamed about her every night and worried about her safety and Anna's. To keep himself sane, he'd thought about Rory's ranch house with its rock fireplace, its warm rugs on the hardwood floors, its history.

When Rory had talked about her ranch, he'd heard her love for her home. He missed his home although he'd known he'd never return to Barrow Stables, but he'd thought he would return to his country. Now he knew that wouldn't be possible.

Even *with* alibis, Devlin worried the evidence was stacked against him—and his alibis were both questionable anyway, since one had been his lover—and the other was now his mother's friend, a woman presumed missing.

He no longer wanted to return to his homeland. That had become the past, one of cherished memories of his mother and nothing more. He wasn't fool enough not to realize the danger he would be in the rest of his life as the royal prince in line for the throne in his country.

Devlin had hoped to talk to Lord Nicholas. They'd had only a few words together without being interrupted. He suspected that was the princess's doing. But yesterday Nicholas had managed to get him a quick message.

"Be ready in case there is a fire on the estate," Nicholas had said.

Devlin hadn't understood his friend's meaning. But tonight as he heard the commotion, he saw the blaze in one of the cottages closest to the palace and knew. As the alarm went out, Devlin saw that his guards seemed confused as to what to do. When they finally realized they had no choice but to leave their posts and fight the fire, Devlin slipped out.

When he reached the stables he was none too surprised to find a horse already saddled, waiting for him. He swung up onto the mount, thoughts of Rory driving him forward.

He rode hard, snow blowing up as his horse's hooves churned across the frozen expanse. He breathed in the fresh air, feeling free for the first time in weeks.

As he glanced back to make sure he hadn't been followed, Stanwood rose out of the pines, illuminated by the blaze of the groom's cottage. He half hoped the whole place would go up in flames and put an end to Stanwood.

But he knew the princess would rebuild something even more ostentatious, cold and impersonal.

By the time Devlin reached the Buchanan Ranch it was late. No lights burned from behind the curtains.

He hid his horse in the barn and started toward the house, willing himself not to run although his heart urged him to. He couldn't wait to see Rory and now he was so close...

Through the pines, he could see the snowcapped Bear Paw Mountains and Little Rockies rising from the prairie floor to pierce the huge dark sky.

He suddenly missed his homeland, missed the familiar smells and foods and people. Missed his mother. They'd worked together for years, been best friends.

Devlin had hoped to one day give her a daughter-in-law to love as a daughter. Had hoped to give her grandchildren. That made him clench his jaw as he recalled one of his last discussions with his mother. Had she been trying to warn him?

She had encouraged him to wait for the right woman. "There is no hurry. The right one is out there. Wait for her."

Now, knowing what he did about his birth father, he knew she feared he would marry and produce an heir to the throne. She had protected him for more than thirty years. He'd been safe. As long as he didn't produce an heir before Princess Evangeline did.

He closed his eyes and cursed the king under his breath. His father. The king would have been only a prince when Devlin had been born. Was it possible his mother had been in love with Prince Roland Wycliffe? Or had the man forced himself on her?

Devlin blew out a breath, thinking of his own one-night stand with Rory. He wanted her just as desperately tonight. More so.

He warned himself that the timing was all wrong. Would always be all wrong. Now that he knew who he was.

As he neared the house, he ached at the thought of what he must do. He had to tell her the truth.

Devlin started as the door flew open. Rory ran out, barefoot, the ends of her robe flapping in the breeze. He caught her, picking her up, laughing in spite of himself, their breaths coming out in icy white puffs.

"I knew you would come," she whispered against his ear as he carried her inside and set her down.

"I would have come sooner if I could have." He touched her flushed cheek, warning himself not to kiss her. This was hard enough. "So much has happened. There's so much I need to tell you."

She pressed a finger to his lips and shook her head, then kissed him softly before she took his hand and led him through the dark house.

Rory had awakened to a sound. Instantly, she'd been afraid it was her Peeping Tom outside. But her heart had begun to pound, and she'd found herself flying out of the bed, grabbing her robe as she'd hurried to the door, knowing even before she'd opened it that it was Devlin.

They moved quietly past Anna's bedroom, the older woman snoring loudly enough to be heard even through the closed door.

Rory led him to her bedroom at the back, closing the door behind him.

"We have to talk, Rory," he said. "There is something I must tell you."

Something she must tell him, too. But not now.

Just the sight of him standing there after these many days of worrying, all she wanted was to be held in his arms.

"Please," she whispered, her gaze locking with his. She saw his eyes fill with something akin to love. Or lust. Right now it didn't matter.

He swept her up, kissing her, burying his hands in her hair as he drew her against him as if she was the first breath he'd taken in days.

He peppered her with kisses as his hands moved along her curves, a soft groan escaping his lips before he found her mouth again.

In a flurry, they kissed, tugging at clothing as if in silent assent that they wanted nothing between them tonight.

Naked, they stood clutching each other, movements slow-

ing as their gazes touched. Rory looked into his eyes and saw
the emotional war raging there. The one thing she knew for
certain is that she didn't want to hear what he had to tell her.
Any more than she wanted to tell him her news.

Tonight, she just wanted him. Nothing more. She kissed
him, brushing her lips across his. He caught her up in his
arms again and gently laid her on the bed, lowering himself
beside her.

"Rory." He breathed her name like a promise. Or a curse.

She raised up on an elbow to brush his dark hair back from
his forehead, just as she had done that first night.

His dark blue eyes flashed with a need as strong as breathing. He cupped her head with his hands and drew her down,
his mouth capturing hers, their bodies melding in the heat of
passion and this all-consuming need for each other.

12

AS THE SKY began to lighten, Devlin lay spent; Rory snuggled into the curve of his shoulder. He knew she wasn't asleep and hadn't been for some time.

Devlin didn't want to be the one to break the sated silence between them. He wanted to stay right there, in the big old iron bed, photos of cowboys and favorite horses on the rough walls of the old ranch house.

For weeks he'd been living in the palace, been treated like a prince. He'd hated every moment of it.

He knew what he wanted. But because of the blood that coursed through his veins, he thought it would always be denied him.

He had to tell Rory the truth. The sun would be rising soon. He had to return before he was missed. If he hadn't already been missed.

"There's something I need to tell you," she said.

"Please, let me go first." Whatever she had to say to him, he couldn't hear it. Not until she knew the truth about him.

He drew away from her, getting out of bed and pulling on his britches.

Rory sat up in the bed, looking worried. At a sound at the window, she turned quickly. He saw her expression.

"What is it?"

She shook her head. "Nothing. It's just that I had a Peeping Tom. I'm sure it's just the wind."

He glanced toward the window, thinking if anyone was out there, it would more than likely be royal soldiers come for him. But he didn't like the idea that someone had been hanging around the ranch. At least Anna was here with Rory now, although that didn't relieve his worries about either woman's safety.

"I'm sorry," Rory said. "There was something you needed to tell me."

Devlin nodded solemnly. "The night of the ball, you asked me what I was doing in the princess's desk…"

"And you said you'd have to kill me if you told me."

"What I should have said was that telling you would put your life in danger," he said. "Now your life is in danger because of me anyway and I have no choice but to tell you for your own safety." He hurried on before she could stop him. "I found a document in the bottom drawer of that desk. It was my birth certificate. My *real* birth certificate—and the reason my mother was murdered."

He expelled a breath. "I'm the son of the king, a prince, the prince in line for the throne of my country."

It took a moment for the words to register. "You're a *prince*?" Hadn't Georgia told her that there had been a *second* prince at the ball that night? Someone who was being questioned for the murder of Prince Broderick?

"I had no idea," Devlin was saying. "Even when I saw the birth certificate…" He sat down on the edge of the bed beside her. "You have to understand. I hate this."

"You're saying you have to go back and rule your country?"

"No. It's not that simple," Devlin said.

No, it wasn't simple at all. Rory thought about what she had to tell him. The words froze in her throat. If Devlin was a prince, heir to the throne, then what did that make the baby she was carrying?

The light tap on the door made them both start.

"Yes?" Rory's voice broke as she swung out of bed and away from Devlin. She'd thought she was getting a groom, but he'd turned out to be a prince—and she was devastated by the news. Something was definitely wrong with this fairy tale.

"I have made breakfast," Anna said. "It is almost light. Devlin must return as soon as he has eaten. I have made his favorite."

Rory reached for her clothes, not surprised Anna had also heard Devlin's arrival last night. Apparently Anna also knew more about Devlin Barrow than Rory did.

"Wait, I can't leave you like this," he pleaded.

"There isn't anything else to say. You're a prince and you will be returning to your country." The irony was that she'd fallen in love with a groom and been completely content with that.

The sky was lightening. Shafts of silver filtered through the curtains. Rory dressed quickly and hurried out to the kitchen, avoiding Devlin's gaze as well as his grasp.

Anna glanced back at her; her gaze shifted to something over Rory's shoulder as Devlin followed her into the room. The older woman seemed to study the two of them. She didn't look happy.

"I need to talk to Devlin," Anna said as she slid a plate onto the table.

"I'll go check his horse," Rory said and grabbed her coat

from the hook, disappearing out the back door before Devlin could stop her. Before she let the painful tears reach her eyes.

But not before she'd smelled the sausage Anna had cooked Devlin for breakfast. She hadn't gone two feet out the back door before she was sick to her stomach.

The third test was also negative. Evangeline dropped the testing equipment into the trash can with a curse and gripped the sink, her fingers aching from the pressure. She had failed miserably. Her dreams of returning to her homeland with the next king were shattered.

She was alone, childless, banished to this alien country. For the first time, she let herself break down. It was early, the servants wouldn't be coming up for another hour. And she was alone, able to finally let it all come out.

Huge shuddering sobs racked her body. The pain poured out of her, years of it, until the sobs slowed and she realized she was crying for Broderick. For what could have been between a husband and wife.

Evangeline wiped her tears, pulling herself together. Broderick was a bastard. Now a dead bastard. All she had to concern herself with at present was the arrest of Devlin Barrow Wycliffe for Broderick's murder. Two birds, one stone, she thought.

She had taken care of the threat, but she had failed to produce an heir. Without an heir, all was lost. Her father would never let her return home.

The thought paralyzed her. She'd never taken her fate lying down. She'd always fought back, going after all she wanted. How could she give up now?

At thirty-six, there was little chance of remarrying now that word of Broderick's murder was out. Even with Devlin convicted of the crime, there would be those who would never believe she hadn't done it. She would be seen as a woman as despicable as Lady Monique. A Black Widow.

No noble worthy of producing an heir to the throne would want anything to do with her. Few ever had. At her age there was little chance she could produce an heir even if there had been a man willing to chance suffering the same fate as Broderick.

The husband of a princess was little more than window dressing. Evangeline suspected Broderick hadn't realized that—until he'd married her. He'd wanted more. Most men would.

The princess ignored the knock at her door. She didn't want to see anyone. Especially Laurencia. She'd made a point of avoiding the woman since she'd heard Laurencia had taken to her bed as soon as the deputy had questioned her. Apparently she felt some guilt for the prince's demise. Probably because she hadn't gotten Broderick to the right bedroom the night of the ball.

Had Broderick come to Lady Monique's room, been tricked into bedding Evangeline…

The princess pushed the thought away. Broderick was dead and she wasn't pregnant. Evangeline no longer had any interest in how she'd ended up in bed with the wrong man.

The knocking became more insistent.

Evangeline checked herself in the mirror and went to the door, looking forward to the tongue-lashing she intended to give whoever was standing there.

"Your Royal Highness." Jules Armitage quickly bowed. "I must speak with you. It is a matter of utmost urgency."

"Whatever it is—"

"You will want to hear this, Your Highness." He lowered his voice so the guards at the end of the hall didn't hear. "It concerns Devlin—*Prince* Devlin."

"You wouldn't dare speak evil of the son of the king, would you?" she demanded.

Jules met her gaze. "I serve you, Your Highness. The true heir to the throne."

Evangeline studied the little man for a moment before she stepped back and motioned him into the suite, closing the door firmly behind him.

Devlin started after Rory, but Anna stopped him. "I have to go to her. Can't you see? She's ill."

"Do you not see what is wrong with her?" Anna demanded in a hushed tone as she drew him away from the door.

"I told her about the birth certificate I found in the princess's bottom desk drawer. She is sick because of who she thinks I will become."

Anna frowned impatiently at him. "Rory carries a child. It is morning sickness that makes her ill. Trust me, I know such things."

Devlin looked toward the back door, feeling as if she'd stuck a fork in his throat. "Who is the father?" When Anna didn't answer, he glanced back at her and saw her expression. *"Me?"*

"Can you not tell by how angry she is with you?" Anna demanded.

His mind raced. Was this the news she had meant to tell him? And had changed her mind when he'd told her his news. The impact of that revelation finally hit him.

Rory was carrying his child. He thought *he'd* be sick. "Anna, she can't be pregnant. Not with *my* child. If Evangeline should find out..."

Anna shuddered, wrapping her dimpled arms around herself as if to chase off the chill. "She wants this baby."

"She can't have this baby," Devlin said and heard his pain registered in his voice. *His* child. His child with a woman he'd fallen in love with. And yet, this baby couldn't be born. Not now that he knew whose blood ran through his veins.

"She thinks because I am the bastard prince I must return to our homeland to take the throne. She will change her mind about keeping the baby."

Anna shook her head. "She is strong and determined and in love with you. She will not give up this baby—not at any cost."

Devlin cursed under his breath. "Princess Evangeline is trying to frame me for her husband's murder." The older woman didn't seem surprised. "You and Rory are my alibi, but I can't tell the deputy about either of you—especially now. You must make her understand. If Evangeline finds out Rory is pregnant with a possible heir…"

The back door opened on a gust of cold snowy air. Rory stood silhouetted against the dawn. "Your horse is ready and I just saw the deputy's patrol car headed this way. Also I found fresh footprints outside my bedroom window."

"Have you told the deputy about this?" Evangeline asked when Jules Armitage had finished.

"No, Your Highness. I wanted to speak with you first."

"And you are sure you saw both Prince Devlin and this Rory Buchanan on the second floor outside my suite?"

"Yes. I will swear to that."

She thought about the trouble Broderick had had purchasing the Buchanan Ranch. "You say they met before that night?"

"In an old line shack on your property. They were intimate, Your Highness," he said, clearly reading that was what she most wanted to know.

"Lovers?"

He nodded.

She remained still even though her insides were in turmoil. If Devlin and this ranchwoman were lovers on his first night in Montana… "Is there more?"

Jules nodded. "I believe Rory Buchanan is harboring your missing servant, Anna Pickering." He took a breath, no doubt knowing how the next news would affect the princess. "I also have reason to believe that Rory Buchanan is with child. Prince Devlin's child."

Rory waited back in the kitchen, fighting not to breathe in the sickening smell of sausage. Anna was now hidden upstairs in the attic.

"You must trust Devlin," Anna had said before going up. "He is a good man. He will make the right decision about the future."

"He's a real prince."

"Yes," Anna agreed, missing Rory's sarcasm.

Now Rory heard the slamming of a car door in front of the house. She braced herself for the worst. Footfalls on the porch, then pounding on her front door.

Let this not be about Devlin.

She stood and went to open the door to the deputy.

"You're up early," Griff said the moment he saw her dressed and wide-awake at the door.

"Griff." She glanced at her watch. "Is something—"

"Are you alone?"

She blinked as his question sunk in. "What?"

He pushed past her. "I asked if you're alone."

"Yes," she snapped. "Why would you ask?"

He was standing in the middle of her living room. The county deputy sheriff. And yet she felt an odd sense of unease.

He turned to look at her, anger in his expression. "The last time I saw you, you *weren't* alone."

She frowned. Had he seen her with Devlin earlier?

"The night of the ball," he supplied. "I saw you on the second floor balcony with a man."

"You were *spying* on me?" she demanded, going on the offense.

He wasn't fazed. "I checked. You didn't have an invitation to the party."

The smell of fried sausage unfortunately still wafted in the air. Rory tried to hold down the nausea as she faced the deputy. "Why would you care whether or not—"

"Surely you've heard. Prince Broderick Windham was murdered the night of the ball."

"What does that have to do with me?"

Griff was looking toward the kitchen. "You've already had breakfast?"

"Why? Are you hungry? I think there's some sausage left."

"I didn't come out here for breakfast," he snapped.

"Well, then, I don't understand what you're doing here." She feared she understood only too well. Devlin had gone back to Stanwood after learning that Prince Broderick Windham had killed his mother. Devlin would have told the deputy where he'd been at the time of the murder when he gave his statement, wouldn't he have? So why was Griff asking her about this?

"What were you doing at the ball?"

She stared at him. "You don't think I killed the prince, do you?"

"You said you were going to take care of your problem with your neighbors yourself."

"Not by killing some stupid prince."

"You were *there*."

Rory couldn't believe this. She didn't feel well and had

to sit down. "I went to get copies of the offers made on my ranch so I could prove harassment just like you suggested."

Griff took off his Western hat to rake his fingers through his hair in obvious agitation. "I didn't think you would *break* in to get them."

"I didn't break in. I crashed a masked ball. I don't believe that's a criminal offense."

He slapped his hat back on his head. "I know what a hothead you are. You threatened me with that shotgun you keep by your back door just the other day."

"I said I was going to get my shotgun. That's not the same as threatening you with it."

"You were on the second floor where the prince was killed," Griff shouted at her.

She cringed and he lowered his voice.

"What were you doing with that man? How is it you even know him?"

So he had seen her and Devlin together. Or Devlin had told him. "I'm sure Devlin told you how it happened. As I said, I was there for the offers on my property."

"I asked how it is you knew him?"

"I don't really know him." It was her first lie. "We just crossed paths." That at least was true. And if you were a person who believed in fate...

"And the night of the ball was the first time you'd met him?"

"What does this have to do with the murder?"

"Prince Devlin Wycliffe Barrow is the number one suspect in my murder case."

Rory took the news badly. "He didn't kill anyone."

"And you know this how, since you barely know the man?"

She shook her head. All this was coming at her too fast

and the smell of sausage was making her sick. "I was with him. I'm his alibi."

The moment she said it, she saw Griff's expression and knew Devlin hadn't told him. Why wouldn't Devlin have told him that he was with her and couldn't have killed Broderick?

"Why wouldn't he have mentioned that he was with you?"

"I don't know. Maybe to protect me."

"A woman he barely knows?" the deputy asked sarcastically.

"I'm telling you the truth."

"All I have is your word that you were with Prince Devlin at the time of the murder."

"My word has always been good enough before," Rory said, her anger growing. Griff had been spying on her at the ball. He knew damned well she hadn't killed anyone. He also knew she hadn't been alone on that balcony.

"You have any other guns in the house besides the shotgun?" he asked, all business now.

"You know I have my father's guns, but I keep them locked up."

"Let's see 'em."

She couldn't believe this was happening. Getting to her feet, she led him to her father's den. His gun cabinet was against the wall. She reached on top of it to take down the key. Opening the old-fashioned pine gun cabinet, she stepped back so Griff could get to the contents.

The deputy had pulled on latex gloves, she saw. Fear made her weak as she watched him rummage in the cabinet, pulling out several of her father's pistols.

He sniffed the barrel end of the .45. "When was the last time this was fired?"

She shook her head.

"I'm going to have to take this to the lab."

Rory could only stare at him. He didn't really believe she

would shoot someone. This was about her turning down his marriage proposal. That and Devlin. He'd seen her with Devlin. Had he also witnessed the kiss?

She thought of Anna in the attic and prayed Griff wouldn't do something crazy like insist on searching the house. Rory was all set to demand a search warrant.

"I'm going to need you to make a statement as to your whereabouts the night of the murder."

"I can come down to the station as soon as I change."

His gaze took her in.

She was feeling a little green around the gills.

"No need. We can do it here."

She would have much preferred meeting him at the station away from the house—and Anna. But she also didn't want to make him suspicious by insisting on going into town to the sheriff's department.

She watched him bag her father's .45, then had her sign that she'd allowed him to take it. The whole thing seemed ridiculous, but she said nothing as he pulled a small tape recorder from his pocket and set it on the coffee table in front of her.

"You look pale."

"I'm fine," she said noticing the way he was looking at her. "I don't think my early breakfast agreed with me."

He looked at her as if he knew she was lying.

But there was nothing he could do about it. And she wasn't about to tell him what was really going on with her.

"Tell me everything," Griff ordered, officious again and clearly angry as he snapped on the tape recorder. His gaze locked with hers. "And I mean *everything*."

Rory had the horrible feeling that Griff knew everything already. Or at least a lot of it. Devlin had told her that the deputy appeared to have been following her the night of the ball. Did he just want to hear it from her? Then what?

Griff's cell phone rang. He cursed, checked the screen, then cursed again. "I have to take this." He shut off the tape recorder, rose and stepped out onto the porch.

Rory watched him from the window. Whatever news he was getting, Griff seemed to be upset by it. When he finished the call, he placed one.

She'd expected him to come back in when he finished. Instead, he walked to the porch railing. She saw that he was gripping the top rail, his knuckles white from the pressure.

Rory glanced toward the stairs, all her instincts telling her to get Anna out of there, and fast. But the older woman wouldn't be able to go far in the snow on foot even if she knew which way to go.

Maybe if she hid in the barn—

The front door opened and Griff came back in. She noted his face was flushed, his eyes appearing red-rimmed.

"I have backup on the way," he said in a calm voice that belied the look in his eyes. "I know you have been harboring a criminal." He glanced toward the stairs. "Anna Pickering is wanted as an accomplice in the murder of Prince Broderick Windham. Along with providing Devlin Barrow with inflammatory information about his mother's death, she also gave him detailed information about the palace."

"Anna had nothing to do with Broderick's death and neither did Devlin," Rory snapped. "Someone is trying to frame her."

"Frame her?" The deputy snorted. "Just like someone is trying to frame Devlin Barrow? Excuse me. *Prince* Devlin Barrow Wycliffe." He must have seen her expression. "Proof has been found that implicates him as well as Anna Pickering."

Griff stepped toward the stairs and Rory instinctively moved in front of him to block his way.

He glared at her, his eyes as hard and cold as obsidian. "Either get her down here or I'll go up and drag her down and arrest you for aiding and abetting. Your choice, Ms. Buchanan."

13

AT THE SOUND of sirens, Rory went upstairs to get Anna. She knew Griff would make good his threat although Rory wasn't worried about herself, but Anna. She'd seen something in the deputy's eyes that had warned her he could be cruel to Anna to get back at Rory.

Anna and Rory waited downstairs with one of the state investigators as Griff and the others searched the house and the grounds. Rory couldn't imagine what they were looking for. Devlin? Or proof that he'd been there?

When they returned to the living room, though, Rory could tell from the deputy's displeased expression that he hadn't found what he'd hoped for.

"We're taking Anna Pickering in now," Griff said and ordered the investigators to cuff her.

"Is that really necessary?" Rory demanded. "I doubt she is capable of overpowering you since she isn't half your size."

Griff shot her a warning look, but told the man to forget the handcuffs. "I'm not through with you," he said when the others had gone out to the patrol cars. "Don't leave. I'll be back. I still need a statement from you."

Rory said nothing as she watched him go. All she could think about was that, according to Griff, Devlin would be arrested for the murder of Prince Broderick Windham. She remembered what Devlin had told her about who to call if she was in trouble.

She hurried to the phone and dialed Lord Nicholas Ashford's cell number. It rang only twice before he picked up.

"Nicholas," he answered.

Rory could hear a racket in the background. "It's Rory Buchanan. I'm—"

"I know who you are."

"They've arrested Anna Pickering as an accomplice to the prince's murder," she said quickly. "The deputy sheriff said they were going to arrest Devlin—"

"They already have," he said. "The royal guards are holding him until the deputy sheriff gets here."

She choked back a sob. "He didn't kill anyone. He was with me the whole time or Anna when Prince Broderick was killed. Surely once he tells—"

"I'm afraid that information would only put both you and Anna in more danger," Nicholas said. "You must trust me. I'm doing everything I can to help Dev. Right now he is only worried about you."

"I'm fine." She didn't take Griff's threat seriously. Even if he did arrest her for aiding and abetting alleged criminals, Rory knew once she told Judge Randall her side, he would throw the case out.

Unfortunately, the judge couldn't help Anna or Devlin, not with them both facing murder charges.

"I have to go," Nicholas said. "I'll tell Devlin you called and that you're safe."

"Tell him I..." Fortunately, Nicholas had already hung up before she had the chance to make a fool of herself.

★ ★ ★

"Your sister sent me," Charles Langston said as he glanced into Devlin's small cell block, nose wrinkled.

"The last person I need help from is my...sister or her father's barrister," Devlin said, not bothering to get up from the cot where he sat. He was more worried about Rory and Anna than himself even though Nicholas had assured him that Anna had been taken into custody and Rory had said to tell him she was fine.

"Princess Evangeline insists," Charles said as he looked around for a place to put down his briefcase. "I'm sure you'll want to know about the evidence against you at this point."

The barrister found a stool and dragged it to the front of Devlin's cell. "Now, let's see. Motive. According to the princess's statement to the deputy sheriff, Anna Pickering had informed you before the ball that Prince Broderick had murdered your mother and had made an attempt on your life, as well."

The royal attorney took a breath and continued. "Opportunity. You were seen on the second floor wearing a costume like the one Prince Broderick had worn the night of the ball. The head of security has testified as much and the costume you wore was found in your cottage. Apparently the seamstress had made copies of the original design as per the princess's request in case of any accident prior to or during the ball."

Evangeline had thought of everything, Devlin realized.

Charles looked up at him. "All that seems to be missing is the weapon. Deputies are searching the grounds as we speak. The princess is sure the gun will be found."

"I'm sure she is." Devlin got up from the cot to move to the bars, wishing he could reach through them and get his hands around the attorney's neck. "I'm sorry, other than to let me know that the princess has me right where she wants me, what is your purpose for coming here? I know it isn't to help me."

"You're wrong," Charles said indignantly. "The princess says she will ask for leniency for you to keep you from the death penalty. She also," he rushed on before Devlin could comment on that, "asked me to tell you that the head of security is in possession of evidence that you met one—" he checked his notes "—Rory Buchanan at a small cabin on your first night at Stanwood and again the night of the ball, if not on several other occasions, for the purpose of driving up the selling price of her ranch and thwarting Prince Broderick's attempts to buy said ranch."

Devlin gripped the bars. "That's a damned lie."

Charles didn't even blink. "The princess wanted me to inform you that she would be willing not to take action against said Rory Buchanan. She also would consider helping clear Anna Pickering so that she might be sent back to her homeland to be with her family."

Devlin stared at the man. "In exchange for what?"

Rory called Georgia crying. "He's a prince," she blurted out the moment she heard her friend's voice.

"*Rory?*"

"Devlin. He's the prince. The other one. The one who's not dead."

"Sweetie, what are you talking about?"

"Devlin told me. He's going to be king. He's..." She couldn't stop crying.

"I'm coming out to the ranch. Don't move. I'll be right there."

True to her word, Georgia arrived only minutes later. By then Rory had gotten control of herself.

"Hormones," she said as she opened the door and felt herself tear up again at just the sight of her friend.

Georgia hugged her and led her over to the couch. "Now what is this about Devlin?"

"He's a prince. He found his real birth certificate. He's the son of the king and in line to the throne."

"He's that *other* prince we heard about?"

Rory nodded.

Georgia's eyes lit up. "You're in love with a prince? You're having a baby with a prince? Why are you crying?"

"I don't want to be in love with a prince. I don't want to have a prince's baby. I wanted a groom who would stay here on the ranch with me and our baby."

She'd said it. Her fairy-tale fantasy. And Devlin had gone and ruined it all by being a prince who would be a king. "He has to go back to his own country to become the king. I really don't want to be married to a king." She teared up again. "Why couldn't he just be a groom?"

Georgia laughed and took her hand. "Do you realize how many women would love to find out the man they love is a prince? I'm sure the two of you can work something out. You told him about the baby, right? Oh, Rory, you didn't. Why not?"

"I couldn't and now he's been arrested for Prince Broderick's murder. Griff saw the two of us together. I told him that Devlin couldn't have done it. That he was with me at the time of the shooting."

"He thinks you're covering for Devlin."

Rory nodded. "Anna's been taken into custody as well and charged with aiding and abetting Devlin."

"Oh, no." Georgia seemed to hesitate. "Griff doesn't know that you're pregnant yet, right?"

Rory shook her head.

"I think that's good. Sweetie, Griff seems a little too obsessed with you."

"He'll just have to accept it."

Georgia didn't look convinced. "I hope so."

"He's just jealous, but I'm afraid he'll use it against Devlin and Anna."

Georgia nodded. "I'm more afraid he'll use it against you."

"I can handle Griff."

"I hope so. Rory, you have to tell Devlin. He needs to know everything if he hopes to defend himself against these charges."

"What did Prince Devlin say?" Evangeline asked when Lord Charles arrived at Stanwood after coming straight from the local jail.

"He denied everything."

She smiled. "I'm not surprised."

"He asked what assurance you could give that you wouldn't go back on your word."

Evangeline laughed. Her bastard brother was no fool. He clearly had taken after their father.

"I believe he suspects you plan to use Broderick's murder as a way to get the Buchanan ranch and get rid of him and Rory Buchanan," Charles said. "He says he wants no title nor does he aspire to the throne."

"Everyone wants to be king and have all that that entails," she snapped angrily. "He will change his mind when my father dies."

Charles shrugged. "How shall I proceed?"

"Hire him a lawyer. A good one, but not too good." She waved her hand through the air. "That's all."

Evangeline waited until Charles left before she rose to pour herself a drink. She needed to take the edge off, but she never drank to excess. Control was as essential as breathing for her.

For the first time in weeks, she felt as if she finally had the situation in hand.

Turning at a sound behind her, she was shocked to find Lady Laurencia standing in the middle of the room. Had she not heard the knock? Or had the woman simply walked in without being acknowledged?

"What are you—"

"I came in as Charles left," Laurencia said.

Evangeline was taken aback by the impatience she heard in her friend and companion's tone. Nor had Lady Laurencia curtsied or greeted her as was custom.

The woman looked awful, her face puffy, eyes red.

The princess said as much, assuming this explained her friend's rude behavior.

"I just came from the doctor."

"You're ill?" This, Evangeline thought, would give her the perfect excuse to send Lady Laurencia back to their homeland—and out of her sight.

Laurencia straightened, her gaze locking with the princess's. Evangeline had only an instant to realize that something had changed in her companion.

"I'm pregnant."

Evangeline stared at her, wondering why she hadn't seen it. The weight gain, the times Laurencia had seemed weak and ill. Evangeline had thought her a malingerer.

"Pregnant?" This silly nit was having a baby out of wedlock when Evangeline had to go to extraordinary levels to attempt to get pregnant? And when had Laurencia found time to propagate as busy as the princess had kept her?

"Yes, pregnant," her companion said, her look almost challenging.

"Who is the father?" Evangeline couldn't imagine. Someone back in their homeland because, on closer observation, Laurencia appeared to be fairly far along.

"Don't you know?"

Evangeline was tired of whatever game Laurencia was playing. "Just tell me," she said with an irritated, bored sigh. "Or don't. I suppose this means you'll want to return home."

Laurencia didn't answer but walked to the window, her back to the princess. "That's up to you."

"I'll make the necessary arrangements for you to return," Evangeline said, glad to have it settled. She didn't like this Laurencia and thought it must be hormones. Otherwise the woman would have known better than to disrespect the princess, let alone to flaunt her pregnancy.

Laurencia would be useless pregnant anyway. Evangeline would find herself taking care of her companion instead of the other way around.

"You might want to reconsider," Laurencia said, smiling as she turned to face her again. "I'm carrying the next heir to the throne."

For a moment, Evangeline thought she had to have heard wrong. "You're carrying Devlin's child?"

Laurencia laughed. "Devlin? The bastard prince?" She shook her head. "No, I'm pregnant with Broderick's baby."

The floor seemed to collapse under Evangeline. She grabbed the back of a nearby chair. "You're lying."

"This from the woman who threw me at her husband?"

Evangeline would have gone for Laurencia's throat had she not felt so ill herself. "How dare you speak to me—"

"Why don't you call a guard? Or shoot me like you did Broderick. Or...we can make a deal."

Evangeline stared at her. She'd rather rip the woman's head off than make a deal with her. How long had she been playing her? Obviously for months and all the while sleeping with Evangeline's husband.

"A deal?" the princess repeated.

"You need this baby I'm carrying. The doctor confirmed it today. I'm carrying a boy."

A male heir. Isn't this what Evangeline had prayed for—for herself? And most feared that her husband would conceive some bastard with one of his whores? She just hadn't thought it would hit so close to home.

"My blood isn't quite as royal as yours, but it's noble enough on both sides of the family and Broderick's. You should be able to pass the baby off as yours."

Evangeline battled through her confusion and anger. "Are you telling me you're willing to sell me an heir to the throne?"

"You can afford it and you really can't afford to pass on my offer," Laurencia said with a chuckle. "I know too well, and just in case you're thinking what I know you are, I took out an insurance policy. If anything should happen to me or this baby… Well, I don't have to tell you how this works. You wrote the book on deception."

"Whatever made me think you were stupid? Or meek? Or loyal?"

"I *am* loyal. I'm the best friend you've ever had although you always treated me more like a servant," Lady Laurencia said as she placed her hand over her bulging belly. "I'm giving you what you always wanted. An heir to the throne."

"And what am I giving you, Lady Laurencia?"

"I want to see the prisoner," Rory demanded of the dispatcher when she reached the sheriff's department.

"Neither prisoner is allowed visitors," she said. "Deputy Sheriff Griffin Crowley's orders."

"You tell Griff that I'm going to see what Judge Randall has to say about this if he doesn't—"

"Rory." Griff stuck his head out the doorway from the back of the department. "Send Ms. Buchanan back."

Rory pushed through the swinging gate and down the hallway to where Griff stood waiting for her. His glare didn't faze her. Nor did his threats. She was running on high-grade fury.

"Step into my office," he ordered, opening the door and practically shoving her inside. "I could have you arrested for coming down here, causing a disturbance and threatening me."

"Who's threatening who? If you were going to put me in jail, you would have already done it. You know the princess is behind this. Just like she was behind trying to buy me off my ranch. If you'd let me see Devlin—"

"His lawyer's in with him."

"I'll wait," Rory said, hugging her purse to her as she took a chair across the desk from Griff. "Devlin didn't kill anyone and Anna certainly had nothing at all to do with this."

"So you've said," Griff said, leaning back in his chair, his gaze intent on her.

"Had you let me give my statement, I would have told you about Devlin's alibi." No matter how she felt about Griff at the moment, she'd known him her entire life. He would do the right thing once he understood what was going on. "I was with Devlin at the time Prince Broderick was murdered."

Griff raised an eyebrow. "You'd better tell me everything. How again do you even know Devlin Barrow?"

She told him about the night of the thunderstorm and being trapped in the line shack with Devlin.

"That was the morning I asked you to marry me," Griff said. "I thought you said you were alone?"

Rory couldn't help but look shamefaced. "It wasn't some-thing I was proud of. I—"

"You slept with him?" Griff was on his feet, his voice raised. "You..slept…with…him?"

Rory felt all the air rush from her. "I—"

"Get out."

She stumbled to her feet. "Griff—"

"Get out."

"Let me see Devlin. Let me talk to him."

"Go home, Rory. Haven't you heard? There's a winter storm warning out. You'll be lucky to get home before the blizzard hits."

She'd heard about the storm on the radio coming into town. "Please, Griff. This isn't about you and me. Let me see him."

"No visitors are allowed."

"Don't you mean just me?" Rory demanded.

Griff looked her in the eye. "Especially *you*. At his request. He doesn't want to see you, Rory. Now go home. I'll call later to make sure you made it."

"Don't bother." She turned and left, fighting tears as she stepped out of the sheriff's department into a blizzard. The winter storm had already begun.

14

DEVLIN HEARD THE *whoosh* of the cell block door opening, followed by footfalls as the door clanged shut. If it was that royal attorney coming back with another deal...

Deputy Sheriff Griffin Crowley came to a stop in front of Devlin's cell. "I hope your accommodations are satisfactory. I know you've grown accustomed to living in a palace now that you're a prince."

Devlin ignored the man's sarcasm.

"I just spoke with Rory Buchanan," the deputy said after a moment. "She tells me she was with you at the time of the shooting."

Devlin recalled what Rory had said about Deputy Griffin Crowley being her friend, the two of them having grown up together. "It's true. We were together. We heard what I believe were two shots being fired. The sound seemed to be coming from the next room."

The deputy looked surprised. "Why didn't you tell me that when I took your statement right after the ball?"

"I was fearful for Rory's safety."

The deputy pushed back his hat. "Why is that?"

"I didn't want her involved."

"In Prince Broderick's murder?"

Devlin swore. "I told you. I didn't kill him. Deputy, I have to make bail and get out of here."

"That's not likely since you're a flight risk."

"You don't understand. I can't protect Rory if I'm locked up in here."

"That's real noble. Still, you're facing murder charges. I would think if you had an alibi…"

"I didn't mention that I was with Rory because I was afraid Princess Evangeline would find out."

"What makes it your job to protect Rory from your sister?" the deputy inquired.

Devlin hesitated for only a moment. The deputy was Rory's friend. The man obviously cared about her or he wouldn't have been keeping an eye on her the night of the ball. "Rory's pregnant with my baby."

"What?" The deputy scoffed. "I thought you said the first time you were together was on that balcony at the ball—"

"We were together before that. The night of the big thunderstorm back in September."

The deputy's eyes narrowed. "At that old line shack."

How had he known about that? Rory must have told him.

"You can understand now why I'm worried about Rory and why I need your help. Please, you're Rory's friend."

"Friend? Is that what she told you? That we're just friends? We're a lot more than that." The deputy smiled and Devlin felt his stomach lurch. "I knew something was wrong with her. Pregnant. With your baby?" The deputy let out a curse as he slammed his fist into the cell door.

Blood spewed across the concrete floor as the man cursed and drew his injured hand into his mouth.

"Rory is mine," the deputy spat. "She has always been

mine. Even when she was engaged to that dumb jackass Bryce. I knew it wouldn't last. All I did was make sure it ended sooner rather than later. Bryce was a fool. He would believe anything you told him."

The deputy had a faraway look in his eye now that frightened Devlin more than his earlier rage. "I waited it out, telling myself that my day would come. Just give her time. Do you know how many years I've waited? Did she tell you I asked her to marry me? Bet the two of you had a good laugh about that."

Devlin had stepped back, fearing that the deputy would open the cell door.

"And now she's pregnant with some foreigner's baby?" The deputy shook his head as if it was all too much for him. "Friends? I couldn't be friends with a woman like that. No," he said. "Rory isn't having some murdering foreigner's baby. I can tell you right now that isn't going to happen."

"I need to talk to my lawyer," Devlin said as the deputy backed away from the cell door.

If the deputy heard him, he gave no indication as he turned and stalked toward the cell block door.

The door *whooshed* open, clanging shut behind the deputy. Devlin stood, too stunned to move for a few minutes, all his fears paralyzing him to the spot.

From behind his small barred cell window, he heard the rev of an engine. In two strides, he was on the cot and looking out the window as the deputy in his patrol car sped down the street in the direction of Rory Buchanan's ranch.

Devlin jumped back over to the cell door, grabbed the bars and screamed for a guard.

"You keep that up and—"

"I will give you a million dollars if you bring me a phone." The guard blinked. "Like you have—"

"I am Prince Devlin Barrow Wycliffe, the son of a king. Bring me a phone and I will see that you never have to work another day of your life."

The guard licked his lips and looked around the empty cell block. "I suppose it would be all right for you to make a call."

Devlin called Rory at once, but the connection was terrible. He couldn't be sure she'd heard him before the line went dead.

Panicked, he had no choice but to make the second call. Surprisingly, he had less trouble than calling Rory, who was only a few miles out of town.

"Tell him my name is Devlin Barrow Wycliffe, son of Clare Barrow. It is urgent he take my call. A matter of life and death."

King Roland Wycliffe's voice wavered only slightly as he took the phone. "Who is this?"

For a moment, Devlin was at a loss for words. "Devlin Barrow Wycliffe, son of Clare Barrow and King Roland Wycliffe the Second. I'm calling from jail in Montana. I need your help."

Over the wind, Rory had barely heard the sound of the phone ringing. She'd hurried to the phone before she remembered that Griff had said he would call to make sure she'd made it home safely.

Her hand wavered over the receiver as it rang a second time and a third. Finally, she picked it up. "Hello."

"Rory, get out of there now! He's on his way—" The line popped and crackled too loudly for her to make out the rest of his words.

"Devlin?"

No answer, the interference on the line growing louder and then nothing.

"Devlin? *Devlin?*" He was gone. Worse, she feared the line

had gone dead. The blizzard outside. Often the phone went out, snow taking down the lines. The power often failed as well in a storm of this magnitude.

It had been Devlin. But where had he been calling from? The jail? Or had he gotten released?

She hung up, picked up again, planning to call the jail. No dial tone. The line was dead.

She tried to remember his exact words before they'd been disconnected. *Get out of there now.*

Out of the house?

He couldn't have meant that. Not in the middle of the worst blizzard of the year. What kind of sense did that make?

He's on his way...

The urgency she remembered in Devlin's tone more than the words had her glancing toward the front of the house.

He's on his way...

A chill rippled over her skin. She reached for her coat and truck keys, going on nothing more than faith. It had been Devlin. He'd been trying to warn her. But warn her about whom?

The wind whirled snow around her in a blinding funnel of cold white as she stepped out onto the porch. She could barely see her pickup parked only yards away. A snowdrift had formed around it. She'd pay hell getting out her road and when she reached the county road, the drifts could be even worse.

For a moment, she hesitated, the warmth of the house calling her back along with her common sense.

The urgency and fear she'd heard in the voice on the phone forced her down the steps. The snow was deep and getting deeper by the moment. She plowed through it to the pickup and jerked open the door, slipping a little on the running board as she climbed in.

Once behind the wheel, she dug her keys from her coat pocket. Her fingers trembled from the cold inside the pickup as she found the right key and stuck it into the ignition. The temperature had dropped drastically.

She thought of her parents. They'd gone off the road in a blizzard only four years before. Because of the lack of traffic on roads in this part of Montana, they'd been trapped in their car until a snowplow had discovered them.

Even with extra clothing, some food and water her mother had always carried in the winter, they'd died. Frozen to death when the temperature had plummeted, their car running out of gas after hours trapped in a snowdrift.

Going out in this weather could be suicide. But staying...

Rory turned the key in the ignition. Over the howling wind she heard a click. She tried again. The pickup had always started, even in the dead of winter. Had to be one of the battery cables again. She tried once more, then picking up the wrench she used for this particular problem, she popped the hood release and climbed out into the storm again.

Breaking through the drifts to the front of the pickup, she raised the hood, her breath coming out in white puffs, her fingers and toes already cold and aching. She couldn't wait to get the pickup going, turn on the heater and—

As she reached in with the wrench to tap the battery cable connection, she froze. The battery was gone.

Devlin couldn't believe it when the guard came back into the cell block, this time carrying the keys.

"You have some mighty powerful friends," the guard said. "The governor himself called to say we had to let you go. I told him the deputy sheriff in charge wasn't here right now and he said I was to get my ass down here and let you out right away. So..."

Devlin waited anxiously as the guard put the key in the lock. There was a clank and the door groaned open. Devlin was out in an instant.

"I'm going to need a car. Any car. I'll pay," he said to the guard.

"Pay how much?" the guard asked warily.

"Give me the keys to whatever you've got. I'll pay you twice what it's worth. Three times as much. Just give me the damned keys and your gun."

"My gun?"

"Come on."

The guard dug out his keys and handed over his weapon, looking dazed. "The governor didn't say anything about giving you my keys or my gun."

"Where's your car parked?" Devlin asked as he tucked the pistol into his jail-issue pants and covered it with his shirttail.

"It's that old blue pickup outside the front door. It ain't worth much, but it's got four-wheel-drive and you're going to need it if you're planning to go anywhere in this storm."

The last of the guard's words were lost to Devlin as he borrowed a coat and ran out of the sheriff's department and into the storm.

The pickup was right where the guard had said it would be. The engine turned over on the first try. Devlin shifted the truck into Reverse and backed out.

He knew which way to go since he'd seen the sign to the Buchanan Ranch when he was taken from Stanwood in the patrol car.

The deputy had a head start. Worse, Devlin couldn't be sure that Rory had gotten his message. If she hadn't, she would open the door to the deputy, still believing she had nothing to fear from him.

Devlin drove through the blowing and drifting snow toward the ranch, praying he'd get there in time to save Rory. And their baby.

Rory slammed the hood and glanced down. The snow had drifted, obliterating all tracks. Was whoever had taken her battery still here on the property?

She had to assume so. Someone didn't want her leaving.

She moved around the side of the pickup, gauging the distance between her and the house. Her tracks had already filled in from where she'd tromped through the snow to reach the truck.

The wind swirled the snow around her in a cold, blinding whiteout. She could barely see the house let alone tell if someone was waiting for her on the porch.

Her shotgun was hanging by the back door. Her only hope was reaching the house, getting the gun—

She took an exhausting step toward the house, then another, plowing through the blowing snow. The cold seeped into her bones. Fear already had her chilled. She sought anger, hoping to fuel her for what she had to face.

She was almost to the house when she was struck by a feeling so intense she stopped to spin around, knowing she was about to come face-to-face with—

There was no one there. Just snow and cold and wind howling eerily off the eaves of the house. But the feeling that she wasn't alone was still with her, so strong it made her skin dimple with goose flesh. She stumbled as she turned and practically ran the rest of the way to the house.

The porch appeared empty as she darted up the steps, across the worn wood and grabbed open the door. The wind caught the storm door, ripped it out of her hand and slammed it against the house.

The glass shattered, tinkling into a million pieces onto the cold porch floor.

Rory had her hand on the knob of the large wooden door behind it and was shoving the front door open, stumbling in as she hurried to get the door closed and locked behind her.

She knew he was probably in the house waiting for her but she had to try to get to her shotgun. Even with the gun, she didn't have great odds since she had no idea what she was up against.

The shotgun held two shells. That meant she would have two chances. But without the weapon, she'd have no chance.

Running on adrenaline and fright, she looked down the dark hallway toward the kitchen and the back door. Even as she reached for the light switch, she knew her power line was out. Either down because of the storm or cut like her phone line.

The suffused white light from the storm bled in through the windows, ghostlike.

Rory could see the kitchen wall and the shape of the shotgun on its rack by the back door. Between her and the shotgun were the doors along the hallway.

If he was in the house, he was probably hiding in one of the rooms off the hall. Waiting to grab her as she passed. She couldn't shake the feeling that he'd been watching her for weeks. Maybe even longer. Waiting for this day.

Every fiber in her wanted to run down that hallway to the shotgun, but the wood floor was slick under the snow-coated soles of her boots, forcing her to walk.

She kept her gaze on the shotgun, all her hopes pinned on it as she walked. The only sound was the squeak of the snow beneath her boots and the blood rushing to her head. Just a few more feet.

Rory passed the first door, then the next, her nerves on

edge. At the sound of a gust of wind blowing snow against the kitchen window, she jumped and had to get control of herself again.

She couldn't panic. Not yet, anyway. As she stepped into the large ranch kitchen, she couldn't hold herself in check any longer. She sprinted to the back wall, grabbed the shotgun and spun around, knowing he was there. Had been there all along.

He was.

15

DEPUTY GRIFFIN CROWLEY stood in the kitchen doorway, silhouetted against the light of the storm. "Easy, it's just me."

Rory swallowed back a scream, relief making her weak, the shotgun in her hands suddenly too heavy. She let it slump down against her thighs as she took a shaky breath.

"You scared me. I thought…" She shook her head. What had she thought? She was just so relieved that it was only Griff.

"Someone took my battery out of my pickup," she said. "My phone went dead and the power is out. I think the lines have been cut."

"Who would do that?" Griff asked.

"The Peeping Tom."

"I thought you were so sure it was one of your royal neighbors?"

Griff hadn't moved and while she couldn't see his features in the dim light of the storm, she felt a pang of disquiet. His body language seemed all wrong. So did his tone of voice.

She'd just told him that someone had taken the battery from her truck, possibly cut her phone and power lines, and it was as if he hadn't heard her. The same lack of real concern he'd shown when she'd told him about someone sneaking around her place, cutting her barbed-wire fence.

"What are you doing here, Griff?" Her voice broke.

"Don't you need me, Rory?"

"Yes, but..."

"You only need me on *your* terms, isn't that right? But I've always been here for you, Rory. When Bryce left town, I was here. I tried to help you then, but you weren't having any of it, were you, Rory?"

Her fingers tightened on the shotgun, but she tried not to make any quick movements. Devlin's urgent words on the phone. "Get out of there now. He's on his way—"

Griff? Is that who Devlin had tried to warn her about?

"I did everything I could," Griff was saying. "I thought once you realized that you couldn't run this place without me... I figured once you knew someone had been around the place, cutting your fence—"

"You cut my fence?" Her heart slammed against her chest. She swallowed back the bile rising in her throat and tried to breathe.

Griff took a step toward her. "I just wanted you to see that you needed me."

All this time it had been Griff. The wire cutters in the shrubs outside her bedroom window—they'd been his? She had a flash of a memory of his pocketing the tool. He'd said he hadn't wanted her to see it, to protect her, but he'd been protecting himself.

A mixture of fear and revulsion threatened to drown her. She took a step back, remembering the broken shrubbery where someone had stood and looked in her bedroom window. Deputy Griffin Crowley.

She was going to be sick. Why hadn't she seen it before?

Rory willed back the wave of nausea and lifted the shotgun, pointing it at him.

"What are you going to do? Shoot me?" Griffin asked. He sounded more hurt than worried.

"You've been stalking me?" Her voice cracked.

"You had to have known how I felt about you."

She shook her head.

"I asked you out after you and Bryce split up. I thought you just needed time. But it turns out you just needed a prince instead of a deputy."

"I want you to leave," she said motioning with the shotgun. "I mean it, Griff. I don't want to shoot you, but I will."

He took a step toward her. "I'm not going *anywhere*. I've waited for you and waited for you. Now I'm going to take what I should have had a long time ago."

She felt her blood turn to ice as she flipped off the safety on the shotgun and pulled the trigger.

A loud click filled the kitchen. Alarm rocketed through her. Griff had removed the shells.

He snatched the shotgun from her hands and threw it across the kitchen. The gun crashed into the cabinet, wood splintering. His palm smacked the side of her face with a stinging blow, the sound of the slap filling the silence.

She ducked as he tried to hit her again and he knocked her to her knees. His hand threaded through her long hair. She let out a scream as he dragged her across the kitchen floor and down the hallway toward her bedroom.

"Griff, no! Please!"

He stopped and spun on her. She cowered on the floor, afraid he would hit her again. Instead, he knelt next to her, jerking her head up by her hair so that their faces were only inches apart.

"I told myself you couldn't shoot me," he said, spittle and

stinking breath hitting her in the face. "Rory couldn't kill me. Not the man who has loved her all these years, the man who has been here for her whenever she needed help. But I thought just to be safe, I'd take the shells out anyway. You disappointed me, Rory. And now you're going to make it up to me."

He tightened his hold on her hair and jerked her off balance. She was sliding on her back now as he dragged her down the hall to her bedroom doorway.

Rory fought to get her feet under her. Her hands clutched at the walls, the edge of the bedroom door frame, anything to keep this from happening. She had no illusions about what he planned to do to her.

Hurt her. Hurt her in the worst possible way.

"Griff, for God's sake, please. Don't do this. I'm sorry if I hurt you. I had no idea how you felt."

They had reached her bedroom. He let go of her hair to kick the door closed. The only light in the room was that coming in through the curtains from the storm.

Rory scrambled to her feet, frantically looking for something in the room that she could use as a weapon.

But Griff was on her before she could take a step. He closed one large hand around her neck and forced her down on the bed. She dug her fingers into his forearms, fighting to take the pressure off her throat as he held her down.

"Your life is in my hands," he said. "I could kill you right now."

She said nothing. Couldn't have gotten a word out with his fingers digging into her throat. She clamped her hands around his wrist and pushed as hard as she could, relieving a little of the pressure.

Her gaze locked with his. Tears filled her eyes from the

pain, the horror and the realization that she'd never known this man. Or what he was capable of.

His expression changed. He loosened his hold. "Rory," he said, his voice thick with emotion. "I didn't want it to be like this. Why couldn't I have been the one you loved?"

His head jerked up as if he'd heard something. She could see him listening. She did the same, praying someone was coming. But all she heard was the wind and the sound of ice crystals pelting her bedroom window. No one would be out in this weather. By now the road was probably closed.

Griff let her go, stepping back to her closet, all the time keeping her in view as he reached in and dug around.

She glanced behind her, desperate for something she could use as a weapon. Her letter opener was on the desk on the other side of the bed.

She knew she'd never be able to get to it before Griff caught her. Even as he dug around in the closet, he was watching her, expecting her to do something. Maybe even hoping she would so he could hurt her some more.

He moved away from the closet with one of the large, worn T-shirts that she slept in. "Here, put this on. Nothing else."

She noticed his other hand was behind him as he tossed her the T-shirt. She was shaking so hard, the T-shirt slipped from her fingers.

"If you can't do it…" He took a threatening step toward her. Oh, God, what was he holding behind him?

"I can do it," she said quickly. She hadn't realized she was crying until then.

Griff reached toward her with the hand that she could see. She flinched. He swore under his breath. "Stop acting like you're afraid of me," he said as he tenderly brushed a tear from her cheek.

Rory swallowed and tried to stem the tears, but the heaving sobs boiled up from deep within her.

"Don't cry," Griff said softly. "I'm here to help you now. I'll take care of you. I can make this all go away."

His tone was so gentle, she looked up at him. Was there a chance he wasn't going to rape her? She told herself she would agree to whatever he wanted, anything, just to buy time and delay whatever he had planned for her.

She stripped out of her clothing, feeling his eyes greedily on her. Her stomach roiled with fear and repulsion as she slipped the T-shirt over her head, tucking it around her.

Griff smiled at her modesty. "Well, Rory?" he asked as he wiped at her tears, his thumb pad rough against her cheek. But it was the other hand, the one he still held behind him, that sent her terror spiraling. "What's it going to be?"

Rory tried to breathe, the weight against her heart making it next to impossible. She thought of the baby she carried and knew she would do anything to protect it.

"What do I have to do?" she asked meekly, thinking of the letter opener on her desk behind her.

"All you have to do is get rid of that foreign bastard's baby," he said, to her horror. "Don't worry. I'm going to help you."

He pulled his hand from behind him and she saw that he held one of the wire hangers from her closet.

Devlin almost missed the turnoff to the Buchanan Ranch. Visibility in the blizzard was only a few feet in front of the pickup and the ranch road had blown in.

He'd been busting through drifts all the way down the county road. Now he touched his brakes as he realized he'd missed the turn. The pavement had been warmer than the air when the storm had begun.

Now it was black ice, shiny in the old pickup's headlights. He felt the tires lose traction and begin to slide.

Fighting the wheel, he pulled it out of the slide only to crash into a drift. The pickup spun like a top, careening off the road and into the ditch. Snow flew up over the windshield as the pickup kept going.

When it finally came to a stop, Devlin tried to drive it out, but the snow was too deep, the pickup bogged down, the drift so deep the pickup would probably be there until spring.

He had to put all his weight against the driver's side door to push it open and then fight the snow to reach the road.

Not much time had passed and yet he felt as if he was moving in slow motion as he started down the road at a run.

The deputy had a head start. He would already be at the house. Already be with Rory. *God, don't let me be too late.*

The wind blew the snow horizontally across the road. If it hadn't been for the tops of the fence posts sticking out of the drifts, Devlin wouldn't have known he was even on a road.

He hadn't gone far when he saw the patrol car in the ditch. Only faint indentations could be seen in the snow where the deputy had climbed out and made his way down the drifted-in road.

Through the pelting snow, Devlin caught sight of the ranch house ahead. No lights burned behind the curtains. Maybe Rory had understood his phone call before they'd been cut off. Maybe she'd gotten out in time.

All hope of that died, though, when he saw her pickup nearly buried by a drift in her front yard.

"Rory." Her name blew out in a puff of frosty air. A cry of pain and prayer.

He pulled the weapon he'd taken from the guard and slowed his pace as he neared the house. The front stairs had disappeared in the snow. He stumbled and almost fell as he stepped into the deep snow only to hit his boot toe on one of the stairs beneath the snow.

Grabbing the railing, he climbed up to the porch, trying to be as quiet as possible even though the wind howled around him like a wounded animal.

No sound came from within the house as he tried the front door. Locked.

Backtracking, he made his way around to the rear, telling himself if it was locked as well, he would break in through a window, do whatever it took to get inside that house.

The back door was unlocked. He let it swing into the kitchen, his pistol ready.

An eerie silence filled the kitchen as he stepped in and closed the door behind him. He was breathing hard. He steadied his breath and his hand holding the gun as he listened.

Voices. He took a step toward the sound of Rory crying, with murder in his heart.

"Griff. No." Rory scrambled back on the bed. "You'll kill me." The desk was behind her. Just a few more inches and she would be able to reach the letter opener.

But she knew the letter opener would be useless unless Griff was within striking range. She would get only one chance. She had to make the blow count or she was dead. Griff was too close to the edge of sanity, wavering like a tightrope walker on that thin line.

Once she went for the letter opener, it would push him over, she had no doubt of that. She could only imagine what he would do to her. If she failed, she prayed he would kill her quickly.

Just the thought of the baby she carried almost killed her courage. Maybe she could talk Griff out of this. There had to be another way that she could save her baby. Firing the shotgun at him was different from stabbing the man with a letter opener. What if she froze?

Griff began to unwind the coat hanger, straightened it to a horrible point, all the time watching her. She didn't dare move, barely breathed.

His hand grabbed her ankle to pull her toward him.

Rory flung herself backward. Her hand came down on the surface of the desk. She'd underestimated where the letter opener had been. Her fingers brushed it. The cold metal skittered away.

She reared back farther, her fingers closing around the blade as Griff's fingers locked on her ankle and jerked her toward him and the edge of the bed.

He was so much stronger than she was. She slid across the bed, banging her head on the edge of the desk as she was jerked toward him.

He laughed as if he'd thought she'd been clutching at the desk, reaching for something to hold on to. His attention was on her naked thighs as he parted her legs, the coat hanger scraping her inner thigh.

She sat up, letting the momentum as he dragged her toward him carry her forward. With the letter opener clutched in her fist, she barely noticed the bedroom door open.

Her arm shot out in a roundhouse swing, the blade of the letter opener catching the light from the storm, as she drove the point into the side of Deputy Griffin Crowley's neck.

Griff looked up. His fingers dug into her thigh. "You ungrateful bitch!"

A scream broke from her throat, filling the air with a high-pitched terrified cry as she felt the clothes hanger pierce her skin.

Even the sight of Devlin coming through the door seemed surreal as if she'd conjured him up out of nothing but air. She watched as if no longer part of the scene as Griff was dragged backward, the tip of the clothes hanger scraping the length of her leg as she screamed in pain and horror.

At the sound of a struggle, she scrambled wildly back on the bed, landing on the floor on the other side, pressing herself against the wall, unable to stop as if the scream had a life of its own.

The boom of the gunshot finally silenced it.

Rory clung to the wall. She could feel blood running down her legs. *The baby. Oh, God, not the baby.*

When a large, dark figure came around the end of the bed, Rory recoiled.

Not until Devlin spoke her name and knelt next to her, taking her trembling body to him, did she finally let the tears come.

16

DEVLIN RODE IN the front of the snowplow, holding Rory wrapped in a quilt. She'd stopped crying but still trembled, her eyes glazed over as if she'd seen something so terrifying it had blinded her.

He could only imagine what had happened before he'd gotten to the ranch house. Her face was bruised, her lip cut, one eye swollen shut.

As he'd wrapped her in the quilt, he'd seen the blood that had run down her leg and the bright red cut that trailed from her inner thigh to her ankle.

It had been all he could do not to put another bullet into that crazy son of a bitch lying dead on the floor.

As the hospital came into view, Devlin saw the state patrol cars waiting for them, light bars flashing.

The moment the snowplow came to a stop, one of the state troopers opened the passenger side door. From inside the emergency room, medical personnel rolled out a gurney. Within minutes, Rory was taken inside.

"I don't want to leave her," Devlin said to the state investigator.

"I'm sorry, but you have a lot of explaining to do," the trooper said.

"Just let me make sure she's going to be all right first, then I'll tell you everything."

Several of the troopers exchanged looks. "We'll go in with you."

It wasn't until Devlin was assured by the emergency room doctor that Rory's injuries were superficial that he finally let himself take a real breath.

"What about the baby?" he asked.

"She didn't lose it. But after what she's been through…"

Devlin knew it was too early to know what the emotional damage would be. Or if she still might not miscarry.

"We're going to keep her here for a few days," the doctor said.

"Can I see her?"

The doctor shook his head. "We have her lightly sedated."

"Would you tell her when she wakes up that I'll be back as soon as I can?"

The doctor nodded and glanced toward the waiting troopers. "I know Rory Buchanan. She's a strong woman. Little can keep her down."

Devlin hoped the doctor was right about that as he left the hospital with the state troopers.

It was several days before Devlin was released and cleared of the two killings—one he had actually committed but only to save Rory's life and that of his child's.

His statement about Deputy Griffin Crowley was supported by what Rory had told the state investigator—and what they found in Crowley's house.

In one room, a large bulletin board was covered with surveillance-type shots of Rory. The photos had been taken from various vantage points around her ranch with a tele-photo lens. All of the shots had been candid ones taken with-out her knowledge.

In a drawer at the deputy's house, they'd found evidence that he had spied on other residents—just not to the extent he had Rory Buchanan.

During that time, the murder investigation of Prince Brod-erick had also taken an unexpected turn. Lady Monique Gray had been arrested.

She had been apprehended trying to leave the country. Trace evidence of gunpowder residue had been discovered on one sleeve of her masquerade ball costume. She swore that she hadn't killed Prince Broderick, that there was a second costume like hers, but no such costume was found.

In the Black Widow's luggage, a .45 pistol had been discov-ered, the same one used to kill Prince Broderick. Apparently she'd shot him with his own gun. Lady Monique continued to argue her innocence, saying she'd never fired a weapon in her life and that she'd been framed.

But upon her arrest, investigations were underway in the deaths of not only her former husbands, but also some of her now-deceased lovers. Further charges were expected to be filed in other countries.

Anna Pickering had been released and allowed to return home to her country. Princess Evangeline Wycliffe Windham had no comment on Lady Monique's arrest or Anna Picker-ing's release. The princess was reportedly holed up in the pal-ace, sending everyone except her best friend and companion Lady Laurencia back to their homeland. Word spread that the princess was with child.

The day Devlin was released, a free man, all he could think about was getting to Rory. That's why he hardly noticed the large black car waiting for him outside the sheriff's department until the back door opened and he saw King Roland Wycliffe waiting for him.

"A moment of your time," the king said and Devlin climbed into the back of the car next to his father.

Rory had been home two days when she heard a vehicle coming up the road. She was still jumpy, every little sound making her nervous. She hated feeling afraid. She kept the doors locked all the time and found herself always looking outside as if she feared she'd see Griffin Crowley peering in through the frosted window at her.

She no longer felt safe in her home. She feared she'd be putting bars on the window and doors just like homes in big cities and cursed Griffin Crowley to hell for making her feel this way.

At the sound of a vehicle coming up the drive, she looked out. The snowplow had been in earlier to clear the road again since the snow had continued for days now. The driver had told her that the deputy's patrol car had been removed from the ditch back up her road, that reminder at least now gone.

He'd said he just wanted to make sure she was all right and see if she needed anything. Rory thanked him and sent him on his way before going back into the house. She no longer trusted anyone who said they wanted to make sure she was all right out here alone.

The door to her bedroom was closed. She wasn't sure she could ever go in there again even though Georgia had come in with Faith Bailey and some friends and cleaned the room after the state investigators had finished.

Rory thought it might be Georgia who'd pulled up in the yard. Her friend had practically moved in over the past few days she was there so much.

But it wasn't Georgia. Rory saw Devlin climb out of the

back of a large black car. She caught sight of an older man in the rear and what appeared to be armed guards in the front.

As Devlin got out and closed the door, the car pulled away, leaving him standing out front.

Rory stepped to the front door, unlocked it and, opening the door, walked out onto the porch, hugging herself against the cold and the inevitability of Devlin's visit.

She'd been expecting him to come by and tell her he would be returning to his country. That's what princes who were destined to one day be kings did. She'd warned herself of this day, dreading it and aching to see him one more time.

At just the sight of him her heart took wing. She felt tears blur her eyes and quickly brushed them away. This was the man who'd stolen her heart, given her something so precious and saved her life. If he hadn't braved the storm to get to her...

He smiled as he climbed up the steps to the porch where she stood. She was a sucker for that smile. "You look so good."

She laughed. She knew she looked pretty bad, her bruised face discolored, her black eye still swollen.

His touch had the exact effect she'd sworn she wouldn't let it have. When he reached for her, she stepped into his arms as if she was coming home instead of saying goodbye. When he kissed her, Rory told herself she was only making things worse by kissing him back.

"You're freezing," he said and led her into the house.

Once inside, they stood facing each other in the living room, suddenly both seemingly shy and tongue-tied.

"You can't stay here," he said. "At least not for a while."

"I'm not staying." Her throat tightened around the words in a stranglehold. "I'm selling the ranch."

His look brought fresh tears to her eyes. "You can't sell this place. You can't let what happened erase everything that came before it. I know how much you love this ranch, what staying on it means to you."

Rory said nothing. Even if she could have spoken without crying, she wasn't sure what she would have said.

"I want to take care of you," he said quietly. "I want to marry you and give our child a name."

"What name would that be? Barrow? Or Wycliffe?" She shook her head. "You're a prince. I'm just a cowgirl. You belong in your country. I belong in mine."

He smiled ruefully. "I'm no prince. You can attest to the fact that I'm not even a gentleman." His hand dropped to her stomach, his palm warm.

She returned his smile. "You saved my life."

"You saved mine. If I hadn't met you…" She watched as Devlin stepped to the fireplace, reached behind one of the stones and pulled out some folded light green papers.

"What are those?" she asked, stepping over to join him in front of the blazing fire. She'd built the fire hoping it would scare off her chill. It hadn't.

"It's my original birth certificate. Evangeline had it stolen from my country's archives office."

Rory gasped as he tossed the papers into the fire. The flames licked over them an instant before the paper burst into flame and disintegrated before their eyes.

"Devlin, what have you done?"

"I've burned up any proof that I am the son of King Roland Wycliffe the Second."

"But you're the *prince*. You're to be the next king of your country."

Devlin chuckled as he pulled her to him. "I never wanted to be a prince, let alone a king. I'm a groom. All I know is horses."

"But your father—"

"He and I have spoken. We are in agreement about the future. It turns out that my father is a romantic at heart. He once loved a woman with a mind of her own—"

"Your mother."

Devlin nodded. "She was pregnant with his child, but unlike me, he made the mistake of letting that woman get away from him. He's regretted it to this day. I refuse to have that kind of regret."

She shook her head. "You would give up all of that—"

"To stay here and raise our child together? I already have, Rory. The only question is whether you will have me."

Devlin took Rory in his arms. "I love you. I love our baby. Rory Buchanan, marry me."

He looked into Rory's eyes. The most beautiful green eyes he had ever seen. Like priceless jewels. Rare as the woman.

He wished his mother was still alive so she could have known Rory. He knew she would understand the power of love. All she'd ever wanted for him was to be happy.

"You would give up being a prince? Give up your homeland?"

"My home is where you are," he said as he kissed her until she finally gave him what he wanted—a breathless yes.

EPILOGUE

MOST THINGS IN that wintry part of Montana got back to normal after that.

Rory Buchanan and Devlin Barrow were married by the Justice of the Peace in Whitehorse. They honeymooned in Hawaii, where Devlin studied to become a US citizen.

Back in Montana, there were only a few reminders of what had happened. A former sheriff's department guard was now driving a brand new four-wheel-drive pickup and throwing money around like he had it.

Just before winter really set in, a son was born to the princess in a home birth at Stanwood. Lady Laurencia was in attendance for the birth of Prince Roland Wycliffe the Third and received a king's ransom for it.

Within weeks, Evangeline and her son had returned to their homeland. Stanwood estate was put up for sale. The horses had already been purchased, and were being boarded at the Buchanan Ranch.

The palace sold much faster than anyone in town had expected. There was speculation on who'd bought the place and what he planned to do with it.

A huge garage sale was held that brought people from all over the world. The furnishings were sold at pennies on the dollar.

The biggest shock came that spring when one day the guard house was gone—and so was the palace as if it had been carried off stone by stone.

Wasn't long after that that the rumors were proven true. The whole place, horses, acreage and all, had been given to Devlin and Rory as a wedding present by King Roland Stanwood Wycliffe the Second.

"Do you think Lady Monique really killed Prince Broderick?" Rory asked her husband one winter night when they were curled up in bed together.

"Maybe. She was capable. But I think more than likely it was Princess Evangeline."

"She got away with murder?"

Devlin pulled Rory close. "No, I'm sure the king is familiar with the way Evangeline operates. She won't be beheaded or thrown in prison. After all, she is the princess."

"But surely she won't be allowed to get away with murdering your mother or her husband."

He shook his head. "She will be a prisoner at the palace, not allowed out of her chambers except to make the appearance of being a mother to her son, the next heir to the throne." Devlin kissed the top of her head. "Don't worry. Our child is safe."

He'd known from the moment his mother had been murdered and he'd sworn he'd get justice for her that he'd never be able to return to his homeland. His heart had ached at the thought.

But that was before he'd met Rory Buchanan. Her love for this land—and him—had healed that ache. He belonged there, with Rory and their unborn child. There was no place on this earth he wanted to be other than right here in Rory's arms.

"Any regrets? You could have been married to a prince," he whispered against her hair.

She laughed softly. "I am."

★ ★ ★ ★ ★

We hope you enjoyed reading

INNOCENT BY ASSOCIATION
by *New York Times* bestselling author
LISA JACKSON
and
MONTANA ROYALTY
by *New York Times* bestselling author
B.J. DANIELS.

Both were originally Harlequin series stories.

INTRIGUE

Look for six *new* romances every month from
Harlequin Intrigue!

Available wherever books are sold.

**EDGE-OF-YOUR SEAT INTRIGUE,
FEARLESS ROMANCE.**

HIHALO01385TR

SPECIAL EXCERPT FROM

HARLEQUIN®

INTRIGUE

*Police officer Gina Galvan refuses to be pulled from the line of duty from a
gunshot, but physical therapist Mike Cutler isn't about to back down from
her challenge—or from the emerging threat of a persistent killer.*

Read on for a sneak preview of
KANSAS CITY COP
from USA TODAY *bestselling author Julie Miller*
in her bestselling series **THE PRECINCT**.

"Captain Cutler?" That wasn't right. The blue eyes and chiseled features
were the same, but she'd never seen the SWAT captain with that scruffy
catnip on his face.

She wasn't any closer to understanding what she was seeing when he knelt
beside her again, opening the kit and pulling out a compress. She winced as
he slipped the pad beneath her vest and pressed his hand against her wound to
stanch the bleeding. The deep, sure tone of voice was a little like catnip to her
groggy senses, too. "I'm Mike Cutler. I've had paramedic training. Lie still."

Why were her hormones involved in this conversation? She squeezed her
eyes shut to concentrate. She was a KCPD police officer. She'd been shot.
The perp had gotten away. There was protocol to follow. She had a job to do.
Gina opened her eyes, gritting her teeth against the pressure on her chest and
the fog inside her head. "Check my partner. He's hit."

"You're losing blood too fast. I'm not going anywhere until I slow the
bleeding." The brief burst of clarity quickly waned. The Good Samaritan
trying to save her life tugged on her vest the moment her eyes closed. "Officer
Galvan? No, no, keep your eyes open. What's your first name?"

"Gina."

"Gina?" He was smiling when she blinked her eyes open. "That's better.
Pretty brown eyes. Like a good cup of coffee. I want to keep seeing them,
okay?" She nodded. His eyes were such a pretty color. No, not pretty.
There wasn't anything *pretty* about the angles of his cheekbones and jaw.
He certainly wasn't from this part of town. She'd have remembered a face
like that. A face that was still talking. "Trust me. I'm on your side. If I look
familiar, it's because you're a cop, and you probably know my dad."

Mike Cutler. My dad. Gina's foggy brain cleared with a moment of
recognition. "Captain Cutler? Oh, God. I'm interviewing with him… Don't

tell him I got shot, okay?" But he'd left her. Gina called out in a panic. "Cutler?"

"I'm here." Her instinct to exhale with relief ended up in a painful fit of coughing. "Easy. I was just checking your partner."

"How is he?"

"Unconscious. As far as I can tell he has a gunshot wound to the arm. But he may have hit his head on the door frame or pavement. His nose is bruised."

"That was…before." She tried to point to the house.

"Before what?"

The words to explain the incident with Gordon Bismarck were lost in the fog of her thoughts. But her training was clear. Derek was shot. And she had a job to do.

"The prisoner?" Gina tried to roll over and push herself up, but she couldn't seem to get her arm beneath her. The snow and clouds and black running shoes all swirled together inside her head.

"Easy, Gina. I need you to lie still. An ambulance is on its way. You've injured your shoulder, and I don't see an exit wound. If that bullet is still inside you, I don't want it traveling anywhere." He unzipped his jacket and shrugged out of it. He draped the thin, insulated material over her body, gently but securely tucking her in, surrounding her with the residual warmth from his body and the faint, musky scent of his workout. "The guy in the backseat is loud, but unharmed. The lady at the front door looks scared, but she isn't shot. Lie down. You're going into shock." He pulled her radio from beneath the jacket and pressed the call button. "Get that bus to…" Gina's vision blurred as he rattled off the address. "Stay with me. Gina?" His warm hand cupped her face, and she realized just how cold she was. She wished she could wrap her whole body up in that kind of heat. She looked up into his stern expression. "Stay with me."

"Catnip."

"What?" Her eyelids drifted shut. "Gina!"

The last thing she saw was her blood seeping into the snow. The last thing she felt was the man's strong hands pressing against her breast and shoulder. The last thing she heard was his voice on her radio.

"Officer down! I repeat—officer down!"

INTRIGUE

EDGE-OF-YOUR-SEAT INTRIGUE, FEARLESS ROMANCE.

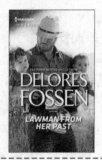

Save **$1.00**

on the purchase of ANY Harlequin® Intrigue book.

Redeemable at participating Walmart
outlets in the U.S. and Canada only.

Save $1.00

on the purchase of any Harlequin® Intrigue book.

Coupon valid until April 30, 2018.
Redeemable at participating Walmart outlets in the U.S. and Canada only.
Limit one coupon per customer.

52615463

Canadian Retailers: Harlequin Enterprises Limited will pay the face value of this coupon plus 10.25¢ if submitted by customer for this product only. Any other use constitutes fraud. Coupon is nonassignable. Void if taxed, prohibited or restricted by law. Consumer must pay any government taxes. Void if copied. Inmar Promotional Services ("IPS") customers submit coupons and proof of sales to Harlequin Enterprises Limited, P.O. Box 31000, Scarborough, ON M1R 0E7,Canada. Non-IPS retailer—for reimbursement submit coupons and proof of sales directly to Harlequin Enterprises Limited, Retail Marketing Department, 225 Duncan Mill Rd., Don Mills, ON M3B 3K9, Canada.

U.S. Retailers: Harlequin Enterprises Limited will pay the face value of this coupon plus 8¢ if submitted by customer for this product only. Any other use constitutes fraud. Coupon is nonassignable. Void if taxed, prohibited or restricted by law. Consumer must pay any government taxes. Void if copied. For reimbursement submit coupons and proof of sales directly to Harlequin Enterprises, Ltd 482, NCH Marketing Services, P.O. Box 880001, El Paso, TX 88588-0001, U.S.A. Cash value 1/100 cents.

5 65373 00076 2   (8100)0 12339

® and ™ are trademarks owned and used by the trademark owner and/or its licensee.

© 2018 Harlequin Enterprises Limited

HICOUP01385TR